Praise for the Lieutenant Bak mysteries by LAUREN HANEY

"In a sea of romanticized visions of Egypt's ancient past, Haney's work stands out among them all with a gritty realism that rings true to life. ... The heat, dust, and sweat of Hatshepsut's Egypt rolls off each page in a sensory barrage which is pure delight."
Ray Johnson, Field Director, Epigraphic Survey, Chicago House, Luxor

"[Haney's] ancient Egyptian police lieutenant is appealing, sympathetic, and totally convincing in a setting drawn with expert skill. I could almost feel the sand between my teeth."
Dr. Barbara Mertz

"Rewarding ... as much for Haney's faithful, loving attention to [the] details as for her easy prose style, skillfully constructed plot, and fully realized characters."
KMT: A Modern Journal of Ancient Egypt

"What might seem an alien culture is drawn in human terms, and Haney limns her characters in loving detail as she weaves an intriguing tale of murder and human frailty."
Publishers Weekly

LAUREN HANEY

A PLACE OF DARKNESS
A MYSTERY OF ANCIENT EGYPT

AVON BOOKS
An Imprint of HarperCollinsPublishers

This is a work of fiction. Names, characters, places, and incidents are products of the author's imagination or are used fictitiously and are not to be construed as real. Any resemblance to actual events, locales, organizations, or persons, living or dead, is entirely coincidental.

AVON BOOKS
An Imprint of HarperCollins*Publishers*
195 Broadway
New York, NY, 10007

Copyright © 2001 by Betty J. Winkelman
ISBN: 0-380-81286-X
www.avonbooks.com

First Avon Books paperback printing: October 2001

Avon Trademark Reg. U.S. Pat Off. and in Other Countries, Marca Registrada, Hecho en U.S.A.
HarperCollins ® is a trademark of HarperCollins Publishers Inc.

Printed in the U.S.A.

10 9 8 7 6 5 4 3

Acknowledgments

I wish to thank Dennis Forbes, editor of *KMT: A Modern Journal of Ancient Egypt*, for his generosity with both his time and his books. Without his loan of H. E. Winlock's *Excavations at Deir el Bahri*, this novel could not have been written. I also wish to thank Tavo Serina for taking the time to critique the manuscript in its rough form.

I owe a special thanks to all those Egyptologists and other specialists who have published information about the small objects and details necessary to bring a novel to life. Because of them, I can place ancient Egyptian furniture in my characters' homes, I can put the proper food in their mouths, animals and plants in their fields, tools and weapons in their hands.

CAST OF CHARACTERS

At the Fortress of Buhen

Lieutenant Bak	Egyptian officer in charge of a company of Medjay police
Sergeant Imsiba	Bak's second-in-command, a Medjay
Commandant Thuty	Officer in charge of the garrison of Buhen
Troop Captain Nebwa	Thuty's second-in-command
Kasaya	Young Medjay policeman
Hori	Youthful police scribe
Nofery	Proprietress of a house of pleasure in Buhen, serves as Bak's spy
Captain Amonemhet	The shady captain of a cargo ship
Nenwaf	A shadier trader

At the city of Waset, western Waset, and the queen's new memorial temple of Djeser Djeseru

Ptahhotep	Bak's father
Amonked	Storekeeper of Amon, the queen's cousin, a friend from the past
Lieutenant Menna	Guard officer, responsible for guarding the cemeteries of western Waset

vii

Pashed	Senior architect at Djeser Djeseru
Montu	Another senior architect at the memorial temple
Perenefer	Foreman of ordinary workmen
Seked	Perenefer's twin brother, also a foreman
Ramose	Chief scribe at Djeser Djeseru
Amonemhab	Ramose's father-in-law, another scribe
Ani	Ramose's son and apprentice
Heribsen	Chief artist at Djeser Djeseru
Useramon	Chief sculptor at the temple
Kames	Chief stonemason at the temple
Kaemwaset	A priest of the god Amon, responsible for religious duties at Djeser Djeseru
Mutnofret	Montu's wife
Sitre	Mutnofret's daughter
Teti	Montu's scribe and estate manager
Commander Maiherperi	Head of the guards of the royal house
Mai	Harbormaster at Waset
Huy	Guard assigned to watch over Ptahhotep
Imen and Ineni	Guards at Djeser Djeseru
Pairi and Humay	Fishermen who dwell in western Waset
Dedu and Huni	Two of the many victims of unfortunate accidents

Plus various and sundry scribes, guards, craftsmen, workmen, fishermen, servants, and townspeople

Those who walk the corridors of power in Kemet

Maatkare Hatshepsut	Sovereign of the land of Kemet
Menkheperre Thutmose	The queen's nephew and stepson; ostensibly shares the throne with his aunt
Senenmut	Chief architect, Overseer of Overseers of All the Works of the King

The Gods and Goddesses

Amon	The primary god during much of ancient Egyptian history, especially the early 18th Dynasty, the time of this story; takes the form of a human being
Maat	Goddess of truth and order; represented by a feather
Hathor	A goddess with many attributes, such as motherhood, happiness, dancing and music, war; often depicted as a cow
Re	The sun god
Khepre	The rising sun
Set	An ambivalent god generally representing violence and chaos; a mythical creature usually shown with the body of a man and a dog-like head
Thoth	Patron god of scribes; usually shown with the head of an ibis

The three temples in the valley

- Memorial temple of Maatkare Hatshepsut, called Djeser Djeseru, which is under construction

- Memorial temple of Nebhepetre Montuhotep, a large ruined structure many centuries old that lies beside Djeser Djeseru

- Ruined mudbrick temple of Djeserkare Amonhotep and Ahmose Nefertari, ancestors of Maatkare Hatshepsut, which is gradually disappearing beneath Djeser Djeseru

A PLACE OF DARKNESS

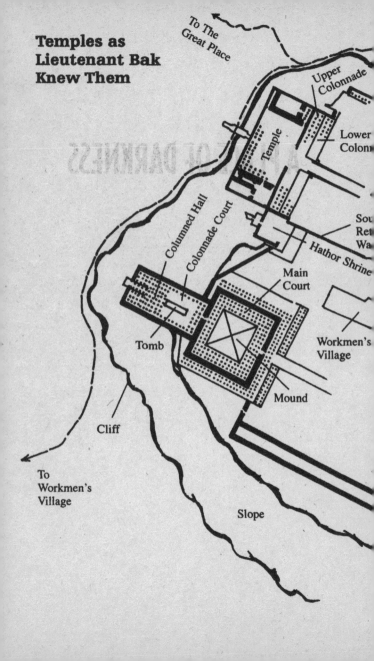

Temples as Lieutenant Bak Knew Them

To The Great Place

Upper Colonnade

Lower Colonn

Temple

Columned Hall

Colonnade Court

Sou
Ret
Wa

Hathor Shrine

Main Court

Tomb

Workmen's Village

Mound

Cliff

To Workmen's Village

Slope

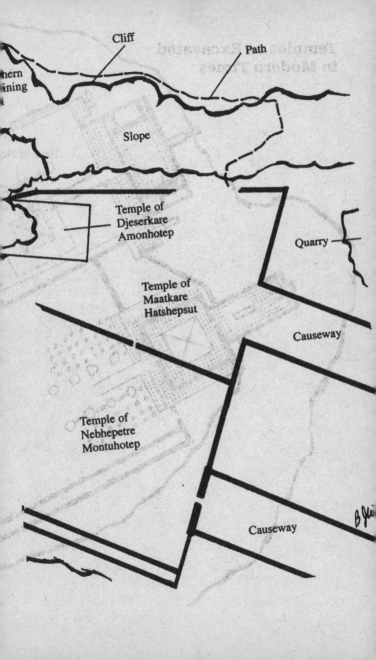

Cliff

Path

hern
ining

Slope

Temple of
Djeserkare
Amonhotep

Quarry

Temple of
Maatkare
Hatshepsut

Causeway

Temple of
Nebhepetre
Montuhotep

Causeway

B Gra

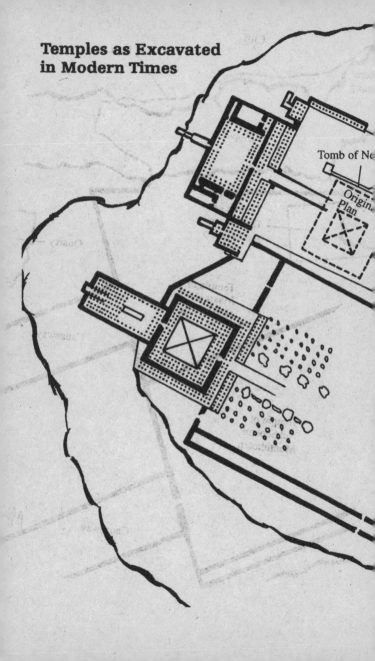

Temples as Excavated in Modern Times

Tomb of Ne

Origin
Plan

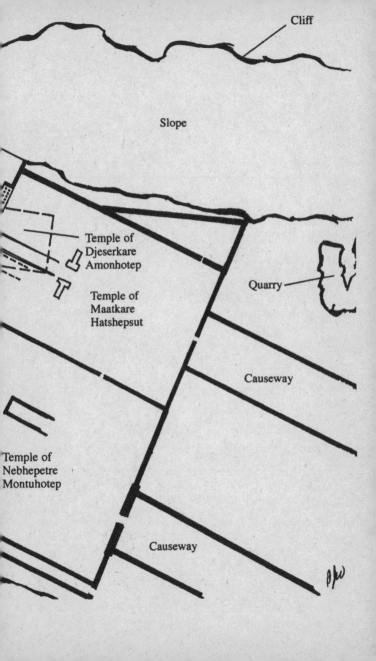

Chapter One

"You've no need to inspect my vessel, Lieutenant." The short, stout ship's captain scratched the thick black hair on his chest in a show of indifference. "You know how careful I am with what I take on board."

Lieutenant Bak, officer in charge of the Medjay police at the fortress of Buhen, laid an arm across the man's sweat-damp shoulders. His voice was a bit too genial, as was his smile. "It's not you I worry about, Amonemhet. It's the traders you bring south and the goods they bring with them."

"I provide nothing but transportation," the captain said, trying with meager success to conceal his worry beneath a veneer of self-righteousness. "I'm not responsible for the kind of products my passengers choose to export from Kemet, or for the quality of their merchandise."

"Then you've no reason to object to an inspection."

Bak glanced at his Medjay sergeant, Imsiba, who stood a few paces away with a half-dozen Medjay policemen and the elderly scribe who would document their findings. The swells from a passing ship lapped at the long stone quay beneath their feet and rocked the squat, broad-beamed cargo vessel moored alongside.

Captain Amonemhet slipped out of Bak's embrace as if unable to tolerate such an intimate display of friendship. His manner turned hostile. "If you wish to waste your time, Lieutenant, feel free to do so. When my passengers com-

1

plain of damaged goods, I'll refer them to your commandant."

Grinning to show how unconcerned he was, Bak stretched
out his arm, his open hand inviting the captain to precede
him and the Medjays up the gangplank. The ship had been
moored less than an hour earlier beside the central of three
quays that formed the harbor of Buhen. The vessel was unpainted, its deck darkened by time and dirt and spilled oils.
It smelled of stagnant water, probably seepage through the
hull. The sail, furled against the lower yard in a slipshod
manner, was yellowed with age and dappled with lighter
patches. Mounds of cargo were lashed down the length of
the deck, allowing barely enough space for the ragtag crew
to use the oars and work the sail.

Bak fell back to talk with Imsiba, who had allowed their
men to go on ahead. Where the officer was slightly above
medium height, broad in chest and shoulders, the sergeant
was tall and muscular, a sleek dark leopard in human form.
Both had short-cropped dark hair. Both wore thigh-length
white kilts damp from perspiration and a minimum of jewelry, a single bronze chain around each man's neck from
which hung a half-dozen colorful stone amulets. Both
looked at the world with sharp, intelligent eyes.

"Amonemhet takes care to keep his fingers clean, my
friend, as you well know. He fears losing his ship by confis-
cation." Imsiba gave Bak a sharp look. "What are you really
after?"

Bak laughed at the Medjay's acumen. "The trader Nenwaf."

"Nenwaf? The wisp of a man standing in front of the
deckhouse?"

"Each time he passes through Buhen, I feel he's laughing
at us. As if he's gotten away with something. Let's find out
this time what it is."

Bak stood on the prow of the ship, watching his men
move slowly down the deck from one trader's merchandise

to the next, inspecting the mounds of goods destined for the land of Kush. Sweat poured from his body; his thirst was unquenchable. He wished he had planned a shorter, quicker inspection.

The day was hot, the air still. The sky was colorless, bleached by a sun that offered no mercy. The river was a leaden sheet, reflecting birds of passage and the golden orb of Re. A smell of decaying fish wafted up from a muddy backwater. Sails hung limp on a scattered fleet of fishing boats. The words of an age-old river song drifted across the water from an approaching traveling ship, sung by oarsmen forced to take up their long paddles when the prevailing northerly breeze failed. Blue and white banners drooping from masthead and yards were those of the garrison commandant, who was returning from Ma'am, where he had responded to a summons from the viceroy. Bak wondered fleetingly how the journey had gone.

The Medjays had begun at the stern and worked their way forward to the deckhouse. Thus far their inspection had revealed few transgressions and no surprises. A large basket of trade quality beads brought south from Mennufer had been found to contain four military issue bronze daggers, special gifts for special friends, the portly trader had said, never mind that trade in army equipment was forbidden. Over a hundred brilliant blue faience amulets pilfered from the workshop of the mansion of the lord Ptah near Mennufer had been found among several rolls of heavy export linen. A randomly chosen wine vat had revealed that a bearded trader from the land of Retenu had brought mediocre wine from his homeland at the eastern end of the Great Green Sea and labeled it as a prime vintage from a northern vineyard in Kemet.

Imsiba and his men rounded the deckhouse. Nenwaf greeted them effusively and invited them with open arms to inspect his merchandise. Bak sauntered back to join them, getting a broad smile and the same smug look that had initially attracted his notice a year or more ago. The trader had something to hide, he was convinced.

In less than a half hour the Medjays had examined all
Nenwaf possessed. They had found every object listed on
his travel pass—and nothing more. Absolutely nothing. The
trader's smile grew more expansive, his demeanor much like
a cat licking the taste of sparrow from its whiskers. Bak's
conviction strengthened. The man was smuggling. But
what? And how?

Standing beside Imsiba, gently tapping his baton of office
against his leg, Bak studied the objects spread out on the
deck before them: rolls of linen; jars of wine, beer, honey,
and oil; baskets of beads and cheap jewelry; coarse pottery
ware; crudely made faience cosmetic pots; and toilet articles
such as combs, mirrors, tweezers, and razors. Much the
same merchandise as the other traders were taking to Kush.

No, he erred. There was a difference.

Few traders dealt in beer or honey, and none aboard this
vessel but Nenwaf. Beer was as easy to make in the land of
Kush as in Kemet, and the large pottery jars in which it was
stored were ungainly to handle and easily broken during
transit. Bees were raised in far greater numbers in Kemet
than Kush, but honey could sometimes kill, the reason unknown. Since an unfortunate incident a few months earlier
where several small children had died, many traders feared
deadly retribution in a remote and alien land.

Kneeling beside a basket filled with reddish jars of honey,
he lifted two from among the rest. Each was ovoid in shape,
fairly wide-mouthed, and as tall as his hand was long. Each
was plugged with dried mud and carried the seal of . . . He
did not recognize the seal but guessed it had been impressed
by the beekeeper. He glanced at Nenwaf, saw an odd closed
expression on his face.

"Why do you take beer to Kush?" he asked. "Is that not
like taking horses to the land of Hatti?" All the world knew
that the strongest and finest horses came from the distant
northerly kingdom.

"The beer I trade is lighter and finer than most, with fewer
solids in the bottom of the vat." Nenwaf came forward, hov-

ered. "I trade with a minor king who demands the best."

Raising a skeptical eyebrow, Bak replaced the two jars and picked up two others. Nenwaf's hasty smile, no longer so smug, told him the man was worried, but whatever was amiss evaded him. "Is the honey unusual as well?"

"The bees drink the nectar of fine clover and thyme. The king—the one who enjoys a good brew—prefers their bounty over that of other bees."

Bak examined the two jars, found the same plugs and seals as before, put them back in the basket. "You've no fear the honey will make him and his loved ones ail and die?" he asked, reaching for two more jars.

Receiving no answer, he glanced at Nenwaf. Noticing Bak's probing look, the trader formed another smile a shade too unconcerned, shrugged. "If he wants the best, he must take the risk."

An argument as thin and wispy as the man who had mouthed it. Doubly alert, Bak studied the pair of jars. Both were plugged and sealed like those he had seen before. One, unlike the rest, had a rough drawing around its neck of a necklace with a pendant bee. A sketch on a jar was not unknown, neither was it common.

He looked closer at the image. His eye was drawn to a flattened streak of mud down the side of the container. Mud deposited by chance when the jar was plugged and partially wiped away? he wondered. Or mud deliberately plastered on the jar to cover a crack? A device to gain full value when full value might not be warranted. He slipped his dagger from its sheath and scratched the streak. Dried mud flaked away, revealing a long and very fine irregular crack.

Nenwaf's face looked skeletal, his smile stretched tight.

Bak tamped down his elation and, with a grave look at Imsiba, stood up. "We'd best keep this jar, Sergeant, and examine the rest more thoroughly. Honey, beer, the lot. Only the lord Amon knows what Nenwaf thinks to pass off to his customers."

One of the Medjays, a hulking young man named Kasaya,

stepped forward to loom over Nenwaf. His countenance was dark and threatening. "Perhaps the evil demon that carries death has entered the honey through that crack."

Nenwaf took a quick step back, bumping against the deckhouse. "The jar is mine, Lieutenant. One I mean to keep for my own use. You can't take it from me."

"Oh?"

"I'll give you its value and more."

"More?" Bak asked, curious as to exactly how valuable the jar was to the trader.

"Five times more. Enough to share with all these Medjays."

Bak exchanged an enigmatic look with Imsiba, a look that could have meant anything.

The trader noticed. "All right. Ten times more. Twenty!"

Kasaya looked startled. Another Medjay whistled.

Bak eyed Nenwaf, his expression speculative. "Kasaya, go forward to the crew's hearth and bring back a bowl. I wish to see for myself honey of such immense value."

Nenwaf leaped forward, reaching for the jar. Bak jerked it away. Imsiba grabbed the trader by the upper arm and flung him at two Medjays, who caught him between them and held him tight. As Kasaya walked away, the trader pleaded for release, swore his offer had been misunderstood. The more he babbled, the more convinced Bak was that whatever the jar contained would be well worth the long, painstaking inspection.

Kasaya returned, silencing Nenwaf. The Medjays and scribe came close so they, too, could see what was worth so large a bribe.

Bak broke away the plug, drawing a moan from deep within the trader's breast, and tipped the jar over the grayish bowl Kasaya held out to him. Imsiba and the men stood silent, rapt. A large glob of thick golden honey dropped from the jar's mouth. For a long moment the viscous liquid ceased to flow. Then the honey again burst free and a solid object dripping with liquid gold dropped into the puddle at the bottom of the bowl. Immediately another fell and another and another, solid drops of gold and color falling with the slowly pouring liquid. After the sixth object dropped from the jar, the flow continued unabated, revealing nothing further entombed within.

Bak held out the bowl so all could get a better look. Soft murmurs of awe and wonder burst forth. Two bracelets and four rings lay in the small golden pool. Jewelry of an elaborate design made of gold, lapis lazuli, carnelian, and turquoise. He drew his dagger, fished a bracelet from the thick, sticky substance, and held it, dripping, above the bowl. A circlet of gold and precious stones hung from the pointed tip of the blade.

Nenwaf whimpered. And no wonder.

Bak, the sole man among them who could read, pointed to an oval symbol of protection, which traditionally surrounded the names of the kings of Kemet, on back of the pieces. " 'Nebhepetre Montuhotep,' " he read aloud.

"I didn't know what the jar held!" Nenwaf sobbed. "I was told only that it was valuable. That I'd lose my life if I didn't deliver it unopened and intact."

His words were lost among the indignant and angry growls of the group. Nebhepetre Montuhotep had ruled the land of Kemet many generations ago, long before Buhen was built. He was one of the first rulers to come from Waset, one of the first to be buried there. The jewelry was that of a woman. The name within the oval indicated that she had been close to the king. A royal consort or a princess.

The jewelry had to have been taken from an ancient tomb. The tomb of a woman of royal blood rifled and desecrated.

"You're to be commended, my friend." Imsiba clapped Bak hard on the back. "If you hadn't recognized Nenwaf for what he is, he'd have carried on his smuggling for many years to come."

"The infantry sergeant in Waset who stole the weapons we found in the beer jars has much to account for. As for the

jewelry . . ." Bak glanced at the bowl he carried. "We've
snared Nenwaf, but he's a mere tool. I fear the one who
robbed the tomb will seek a new way of exchanging its
riches for a wealth he can use without raising the suspicion
of others."

"Did you believe Nenwaf when he said he didn't know
what was in the jar? That a man he barely knew asked him to
pass it on to another man in Kerma?"

Bak looked up the quay at the prisoner, shackled between
two Medjays who were hustling him into the deeply shadowed passage through the massive twin-towered gate of the
fortress. Stark white towered walls framed the centrally located portal and a similar opening to the north, while a grand
pylon gate rose to the south behind which stood the mansion
of the lord Horus of Buhen, the local manifestation of the
falcon god. From these gates the three quays reached into
the river. At the base of the fortified wall, two terraces
formed broad steps along the water's edge. Other than a sentry standing in a sliver of shade near each gate, not a creature
stirred. Even the various ships' crews had sought shelter
from the heat. As had the sentry atop the wall, Bak suspected, for he could see no pacing figure on the battlements,
as he should have.

"He certainly knew the jar contained something of value."
Imsiba shook his head regretfully. "I fear we must apply
the stick."

"We've no choice." Bak had slight faith in any truth
gained by a beating, but for a deed so vile, not merely an af-
front to the lady Maat, goddess of right and order, but the
desecration of an ancient tomb, the cudgel must be used.
The commandant, the viceroy of Wawat, and the vizier himself would all demand firm questioning.

"Lieutenant Bak!" Hori, the chubby young police scribe,
burst through the gate and raced down the quay. A large,
floppy-eared white dog sped after him, nipping playfully at
his heels and yapping.

"What now, I wonder?" Imsiba murmured.

Bak bestowed upon his friend a disgruntled frown. "We'll have no swim this afternoon, I'll wager."

"Sir!" Skidding to a halt, the youth wiped the sweat from brow and upper lip. "Commandant Thuty wishes to see you, sir. Right away. In his private reception room. You and Imsiba."

"Both of us?" To request the sergeant's presence was highly unusual. "Do you know what he wants?"

"No, sir." Hori grabbed the dog, an animal he had adopted as a puppy, by the scruff of the neck to quiet it. "It must be important, though. He stopped by the guardhouse soon after his ship came in from Ma'am. Before he went on to the residence."

The commandant's residence was the heart of the garrison, serving both as military headquarters and as a dwelling for Thuty and his family.

Hori gave the bowl Bak held a brief, distracted glance. "You're to stop by the garrison for Troop Captain Nebwa. He wants to see all three of you at once."

Bak and Imsiba exchanged worried looks. Whatever the commandant had to say, it must be serious indeed.

Bak, Imsiba, and Nebwa found Commandant Thuty seated in his armchair in his private reception room, reading a scroll Bak recognized as the garrison daybook for the current week. Thuty raised his eyes from the document and beckoned them inside. Taking care where they walked lest they step on a toy or a discarded scroll or one of twenty or more arrows littering the floor, they crossed the room to stand before him. He had to have noticed the bowl in Bak's hand, but he made no comment. Instead, he turned around and snapped out an order to a boy of five or so years who was trying to stuff arrows into a quiver. If any of the missiles survived the child's rough treatment, the gods would surely have performed a miracle.

Watching the boy scurry away, Thuty shook his head in dismay. "Why did the lord Amon bless me with so many children?"

The question, oft-repeated, required no answer.

The commandant laid the scroll on a low table beside his chair and wove his fingers together across his stomach. "Clean the playthings off those stools and sit down." He nodded toward several low seats scattered around the room, providing transitory surfaces for dolls, pull toys, balls, and a child's board game. "I've a most important item to discuss."

Bak sat between Nebwa and the big Medjay. Feeling somewhat ridiculous with a bowl on his lap, he placed the honey and its precious cargo on the floor by his feet. The room was hot; a slight breeze drifting through the courtyard door had not the power to dry the thin film of sweat coating his face and body. A strong scent of braised catfish and onions wafted through the air, reminding him that he and Imsiba had missed their midday meal.

Thuty stared at the bowl, obviously curious, but before Bak could explain, his eyes darted away, his thoughts leaping to the purpose of his summons. "I've been asked to take command of the garrison at Mennufer. I like Buhen better than any other place I've been, but I feel I must move on to the more prestigious post. I've accepted the task."

Bak was stunned, the news too difficult to grasp. Imsiba gaped, unable to believe. Nebwa, the commandant's second-in-command, muttered an oath beneath his breath, his usual response to so startling a pronouncement.

"When will you leave, sir?" Bak managed.

Thuty's eyes settled on Nebwa, as if he had asked the question. "I'll remain in Buhen until my replacement arrives. The officer selected, Commander Neferperet from the garrison at Waset, should report here in about a month."

The troop captain, an untidy, coarse-featured man in his early thirties, looked stricken. "A man new to this land of Wawat?"

Bak's heart leaped out to the officer, one of his closest friends. All who dwelt in Buhen knew of Nebwa's long posting in the garrison and his high level of competence. Few had doubted he would be given command should Thuty leave.

Thuty looked exceedingly uncomfortable. "I know you hoped to replace me as commandant of Buhen, but Viceroy Inebny thought to make you commander of Semna instead. Later, he said, you'll have the additional experience needed to occupy my chair."

"I understand, sir." Skipping a rank was unusual and they all knew it, but Nebwa's disappointment was plain. He was as well-schooled in the commandant's many duties as Thuty himself.

"I countered with a suggestion I believe far more advantageous—to you and me both." Thuty leaned back in his chair and crossed his arms over his chest. His brows were heavy, his chin firm, and the normally hard set of his mouth was relieved by what looked suspiciously like self-satisfaction. The same look he displayed when proclaiming a positive outcome to an impossible assignment not yet begun. "I wish you to go north with me, Troop Captain, north to Mennufer."

Bak sucked in his breath, startled by the idea, dismayed at the thought of losing so close a friend.

"Sir?" Nebwa asked, as if not sure he had heard right.

"Mennufer is a large and important training garrison directly under the eye of Menkheperre Thutmose." Thuty spoke of their sovereign's nephew and stepson, co-ruler in name only, a youth who had taken upon himself the task of rebuilding an army that had languished from years of neglect. "If I'm to do my task well—and I'm determined to do so—I must have as my right hand a man I can trust, one of unusual competence and ability, one uninvolved in political intrigue. I see you as that man."

Nebwa looked doubtful. The son of a common soldier, born and reared in Wawat, he had always been posted on the southern frontier. Of equal importance, his wife was a local woman. A move to Kemet would not be easy for either of them. "Is that an order, sir?"

"I'd make you my second-in-command, Nebwa, as you are here, and head of all training. I believe the rank of troop captain too low for such a responsible task."

"I'll be leaving everything I know, sir." Nebwa glanced at Bak and Imsiba. "Including men I hold closer in my heart than I would a brother."

Thuty waved off the objection. "I suggested to Inebny that Lieutenant Bak also accompany me to Mennufer."

Bak felt as if he had been hit hard in the stomach: a bit sick and his breath torn away. "What of my men, sir? How can I leave them?" Immediately after the words were spoken, shame washed through him. Imsiba, his logical successor, was as competent a leader of men as he was. Maybe more so. To leave behind a friend so close would be abominable, but if the big Medjay gained by the loss, the breach should be easier to accept.

"The Medjays in Mennufer are civil police." Thuty's eyes drifted toward the bowl on the floor. He paused as if losing his thought, then looked back at the man to whom he was speaking. "I need a dependable force to maintain order in the garrison, a force part of and yet separate from the army, as you and your men are here. And so I told Inebny. He's agreed that you may go with me as a unit, should you desire. If so, he'll request a fresh company of Medjays to replace the men."

"Am I to go with them, sir?" Imsiba asked. The very fact that he had been summoned with Bak portended change.

"I recognize how invaluable you are to Bak's company, but I hesitated to recommend that you move north with us. You're fully capable of standing at the head of the new unit of Medjays, and you're worthy of promotion to an officer's rank. In addition, I know your wife's cargo ship sails out of Buhen and her business thrives."

"Yes, sir."

"You've a choice to make, Sergeant. To step into Bak's sandals and move up in rank, or to go with your friends to Mennufer." He looked back at Nebwa, who clung to his doubtful expression as if it were molded of gold, and added, "If they decide to go."

Bak thought of how fond he had become of this desolate fortress to which he had initially been exiled. Buhen was his home, a place he loved above all others. How could he leave? How could any of them leave? "Can you give us a few days to think on the matter, sir?"

"A day or two at most. Should you choose to go, Inebny will need time to summon replacements." A scowl flitted across Thuty's face, an afterthought that must be aired. "One thing more you must know, Lieutenant, Sergeant. If you choose to go with me, I can promise no increase in rank. You'd both have to prove yourselves once again—not to me, but to the many men in lofty positions who've nothing better to do than sit on their plump backsides and criticize their betters."

"Yes, sir," they said as one.

Nebwa joined in the chorus, as aware as Bak and Imsiba that he also would have to impress the bureaucrats who dwelt and toiled in the northern capital.

Thuty's glance dropped to the bowl at Bak's feet. "Now what have you brought, Lieutenant?"

"I can just about understand a man, one whose family is starving, breaking into a tomb in a time of need." Thuty dropped heavily onto his chair, rubbed his eyes. "But today? No. We live in a time of prosperity, where every man has a task and none face want."

Bak let the bracelet fall from the tip of his dagger and sink back into its viscous gold bath. "Greed is seldom related to need, sir."

Ignoring the banality, Thuty motioned him to sit. As soon as Bak had told his tale, Imsiba and Nebwa had hurried away, both to talk to their wives about the prospect of leaving Buhen for a new and different life in the faraway city of Mennufer. Bak was grateful he had no one close to tell, no one to whom he must break such startling news. Except Hori. And the Medjays. Men he must speak with right away, before they heard from some other source.

"Other than getting the truth from Nenwaf and seeing that he's punished, the theft isn't our problem," Thuty said. "We must send these objects to Waset, where men closer to the burial places can seek out the vile criminal who's robbing the dead."

"After we learn all Nenwaf knows—if anything—I'll prepare a report and send it north by courier." Another thought struck. "Your wife could take it, sir, along with the jewelry. Does she not have family in Waset? Will she not pack your household goods and go on ahead of you, stopping there to see them on her way to Mennufer?"

"She will, but . . ."

"To lessen the chance of discovery, a man must dispose of a few objects at a time over a long period. I doubt a speedy delivery is necessary."

Thuty hesitated a moment, reached a decision. "You must take them, Lieutenant." He glanced quickly at Bak and, with a smile that may or may not have been sheepish, amended the order. "If you decide to move with me to Mennufer, you'll want to stop in Waset to visit your father. You could leave Buhen right away and deliver the jewelry. That would give you a month or two with your parent before I reach the capital. You could sail from there to Mennufer with me."

Bak smiled at the so-called error. He knew Thuty well, knew he was already assuming the men he wished to take with him would ultimately decide to go. "If I choose to remain in Buhen, I'll send my report by courier. To whom shall it go, sir? The mayor of western Waset?" He was referring to the small city across the river from the capital, an urban area whose residents supported the growing number of cemeteries, memorial temples, and small mansions of the gods that overlooked the vast cultivable plain along the river.

Smiling at the not-so-subtle reminder that he might not get his way, the commandant rose from his chair and strode across the room to open the door leading to a long stairwell that rose from ground level to the battlements. Cooler air escaped from the dark, enclosed passage. "We don't know the mayor. We do know Amonked. We know we can trust him to do what has to be done. The report should go to him and so should the jewelry."

Bak nodded agreement. The decision was a good one. Amonked was cousin to their sovereign, Maatkare Hatshepsut. They had come to know him several months earlier when he had journeyed south up the river, inspecting the fortresses that guarded the southern frontier. He had made many difficult-to-keep promises and had successfully followed through on them all.

"So I'll be free of you at last." Nofery leaned back in her chair, one of the few in Buhen and an object she valued highly, and smiled. "The lord Amon never ceases to bestow abundance on those who praise him."

In the wavering light of the torch mounted beside the courtyard door, Bak studied the obese old woman, searching for any sign of regret. He could find none. He knew how adept she was at hiding her feelings, but he was hurt nonetheless. "I spoke with Hori and my Medjays for over an hour. Buhen is our home, its people our family, but in the end we had no choice. How could we refuse such an unlikely offer, where all of us will remain together?"

"Even the three who've taken local women as wives?" Her attention was focused on the open doorway leading to the large room at the front of the building, where her customers reveled. Her voice was cool, indifferent. Troublesome to one who thought of her as a friend.

"I've given them leave to stay, should they desire."

Nofery's eyes slid toward Nebwa. "Well? What have you decided?" She stared hard at him, offering no more warmth or regret than she had given Bak.

He queried Bak with a glance, the questions plain on his face: Could the woman care so little about them? Could she have been feigning friendship throughout the years they had known her? "Faced with a choice of imminent promotion to commander in an important garrison like Mennufer or spending several years in a like position in a backwater like Semna, what would you do?"

"What of your wife? Will she not object?"

Nebwa laughed ruefully. "She wants to go. Can you believe it? A woman who's never been farther away from Buhen than a day's walk, and she wants to see the world."

Voices rose in the next room, men wagering. Knucklebones clattered across the floor, followed by a triumphant laugh and the exaggerated moans of loss. A scantily clad young woman came through the door, leading a soldier who offered a halfhearted salute to the two officers and the proprietress of the house of pleasure. A low growl drew the man's eyes to a half-grown lion lying on a mat in the corner, sending him rushing through a rear door. Flashing a dazzling smile at Nebwa and Bak, the girl followed.

"What of Imsiba and Sitamon?" Nofery demanded. "Will they, at least, remain behind to keep an old woman company?"

Bak noted a faint tremor in her lips. She *was* upset about their leaving. He spread his hands wide, shrugged. "We've heard no word."

"Could we not go, too?" A sleek youth of a dozen or so years stepped out of the shadows of an adjoining room. His dark, oiled skin glowed in the uncertain light. He knelt beside the lion and rubbed its head, making it purr. "Hori has told me of the wonders of Kemet, and I'd like to see them for myself."

Nofery scowled at the boy who, along with the lion, had been given to her by a Kushite king. "How would we live, Amonaya? My place of business is here."

"After Hori leaves, I'll have no one to teach me to read and write."

"How many times have you told me you hate those lessons he gives you? How many times have you vanished when you know he's coming?"

He stared down at the lion, his face sullen. "It's a game we play, that's all."

"A game. Ha!"

Bak leaned forward and patted a plump knee hidden beneath the long white sheath Nofery wore. "There are many houses of pleasure in Kemet, old woman. You could trade this one off to a man of Buhen and get another in Mennufer."

"Start over again? A woman old and alone, as I am?" Blinking hard, she turned her face away.

Bak had an idea she was crying. He sorrowed for her, but was at the same time pleased that her indifference had been a sham. "You'd not be alone. You'd have me and my men, Nebwa and his wife, and if the gods smile upon us, Imsiba and Sitamon as well." He glanced at Nebwa, a silent plea for help, but the troop captain, who could never cope with tears, looked more at a loss than Bak as to how to convince her. "Anyway, I can't let you walk free and clear, with no further obligation. I'll still need your services as my spy."

Rather than pacify her, as he had hoped, the gentle teasing further upset her. Sobs burst forth, her shoulders shook with misery. "Spy! How could I be your spy in a city as large as Mennufer? Where I'd lose my way at every turn of a lane? Where I'd know no one? Where I'd hear no secrets to pass on?"

"You'll learn, as I will, and Nebwa, and Imsiba—if he chooses to come with us."

"Imsiba has so chosen." A small, delicate woman with shoulder length dark hair, stepped through the door, brightening the courtyard with a radiant smile.

The big Medjay, following close behind, slipped an arm around his wife's shoulders. "Sitamon is not as fond of Buhen as we are. After dancing around the truth, unwilling to hurt my feelings, she admitted as much." He gave her a fond smile. "As for her business, she hopes to trade her ship in Abu for a bigger, newer vessel to ply the waters of Kemet."

Bak let out a secret sigh of relief, but had second thoughts. "I for one would miss you greatly if we had to part," he admitted, "but are you sure this is what you want?"

Nebwa looked as doubtful as Bak felt. "You'd give up the chance to reach a higher rank and become a leader of men?"

"Commandant Thuty will see that we get our due— sooner or later." Imsiba grinned suddenly at the two officers. "Your friendship, the needs of the woman I love, and the men who look to us for leadership are more important to me by far than standing at the head of a group of strangers."

Bak caught his friend by the shoulders and he swallowed hard to clear the emotion from his throat. "If you're sure this is what you want, I'll bend a knee before the lord Amon for months to come. I feared I'd bid you good-bye and never see you again."

As he stepped back, making way for Nebwa, sobs shook Nofery's heavy body.

Sitamon, quick to understand, knelt before the old woman and clasped her hands. "You must come with us, Nofery. You must trade away your place of business and move to Mennufer, as I intend to do."

"I've the boy, the lion, the women who toil for me. I've furniture, dishes, jars of wine I'd hate to leave behind. This chair. So many objects, so many people to move. How can I?"

"Lest you haven't noticed, Nofery, my ship has a large deck. Plenty of room for all of us and all we hold dear."

Nofery leaned forward and encircled the younger woman with her arms. Her tears continued to flow, trickling around a tremulous but broad smile that told them how much she had come to love them, how touched she was that they cared for her.

Chapter Two

"You've heard nothing from Amonked?" Hori asked.

Laughing, Bak ran his fingers under his belt, wet through with sweat although the day was young. While dwelling in Buhen, he had imagined Kemet to be cooler, and he supposed it was. But he had found his homeland during this, the hottest time of the year, to be no less uncomfortable than the southern frontier. "I didn't send off my message until late yesterday, after we moored at the harbor in Waset."

The young scribe hoisted himself onto the mudbrick wall that surrounded the paddock where Bak's chariot horses were kept. The animals, two fine black steeds named Defender and Victory, were grazing at the edge of an irrigation ditch. Bits of greenery peeked up through dry and brittle grass and weeds badly in need of the floodwaters soon to swell over the thirsty land. Brown geese waded in a muddy puddle beside the mudbrick watering trough, while several ducks nibbled grain strewn before the door of a shed at the far end of the paddock. Outside the wall, several goats and two donkeys nibbled a mound of hay on the floor of a lean-to. Beyond, a small herd of cattle, sheep, and goats grazed on the dry stubble of a neighbor's field. The young girl who watched the animals was playing with her dog, making it bark.

"What did your mother and father think when you ran off so early this morning?" Bak asked.

19

Hori shrugged. "I told them I was to meet Kasaya here, which was the truth."

"You're both free to go your own way until we travel north to Mennufer. How many times have I told you so?" Bak gave the youth a stern look. "You've been gone for many months. Your parents surely want to spend time with you."

Unable or unwilling to meet Bak's eyes, the youth stared at his right foot, which he was bouncing against the wall. "I've reached my sixteenth year, yet they treat me as a child. You don't."

Recalling his first time home from the army and the way he had been treated by his father's housekeeper, the only mother he had ever known, Bak could not help but sympathize. How would she behave now, he wondered, if she were here? After so long an absence, would she revert to the past and baby him as she had before, or would she recognize his maturity? He must wait to find out. She had traveled to Ipu to tend to her daughter during childbirth.

"What's Kasaya's reason for escape?" he asked. "Or have you lured him from his home so you'll have a partner in truancy?"

"He's worse off than I am—if that's possible. His mother started in on him the instant he set foot in their house." A sudden laugh burst from Hori's lips. "She's found a suitable young woman, and she insists he take her as his wife."

Bak could not help but laugh with him. Kasaya was a good-natured individual of fine appearance, but was not overly endowed with intelligence. Women of all ages adored him, and he responded to their needs until they—or their parents—mistook his friendship for more serious intent. He had barely evaded permanent entanglement more than once while they had dwelt in Buhen.

A new thought silenced Bak's laughter. He would be the man Kasaya turned to if he needed a voice of authority to escape the fate his mother had planned for him. Shuddering at the very idea, he crossed a patch of drying grass to the horses he had, against all sound reason, refused to part with when exiled to Buhen.

He did not know if the animals recognized him or not. After all, he had been away more than two years. But, when first he had gone to them the previous evening, both had accepted him without hesitation. When he had come out to groom them at daybreak, they had seemed to glory in the touch of his hand as he caressed their muzzles, brushed their sleek coats, combed their long manes and tails. He had not hitched them to the chariot—he had first to make sure time had not damaged its various parts—but he doubted they would accept the lightweight two-wheeled vehicle as quickly as they had him. His father, Ptahhotep, a physician, had no use for a chariot, preferring to walk, so the animals had rarely left the paddock in which they spent their days or the shed where they were kept at night.

"Do you think Amonked will ask you to seek out the man who stole the jewelry from the old tomb?" Hori asked.

Bak eyed the youth across the horses' backs. He had thought Hori had outgrown the urge to play an active role in tracking down men who offended the lady Maat. Apparently not, thus this early morning visit. "He's the Storekeeper of Amon, Hori, not a police officer."

"He could go to the man who's responsible and suggest you investigate."

"If moved to do so, I suppose he could."

"Would you accept?"

Bak grinned—at himself as much as the boy. "What do you think?"

"Why don't you ask him?" Hori's wide-eyed eagerness left no doubt as to how he felt. "You'd need my help, wouldn't you? Mine and Kasaya's?"

"Bak!" Ptahhotep called.

The physician came around the modest white house that stood twenty or so paces from the paddock. He had gone off on an early morning call and was returning by way of a raised path between fields. Close on his heels walked a slight young man a year or two younger than Hori wearing a calf-length kilt down which ink had been spilled. An apprentice scribe, Bak guessed.

The pair crossed an open plot of scrubby grass in front of the portico that ran the length of the house, which was shaded by date palms and a tall sycamore. Bak had been given the house and the small section of land as a reward for solving a crime when first he had gone to Buhen. He looked upon the property with mixed emotions. It was a reward he had earned but not the gold of valor he longed for.

Praying the scribe had brought a message from Amonked, doubting a summons would come so early, Bak crossed to the wall to greet them.

"This is Huy," Ptahhotep said. "He's come to take you to Amonked." Anyone who saw the physician and Bak together could not help but know they were father and son. The older man was slimmer, to be sure, his hair faded to white, his forehead and the corners of his eyes and mouth wrinkled. But in spite of the toll the passing years had taken, the resemblance was there for the world to see.

Bak offered a silent prayer of thanks to the lord Amon. Deep down inside, he had feared Amonked might ignore his message, thinking he had come to the capital in search of patronage. He vaulted over the wall, paused, exchanged a quick glance with Hori, a promise of sorts. Like the youth, he had no desire to spend a quiet month in Waset.

Amonked clasped Bak by the shoulders like an old and valued friend. "Welcome to Waset, Lieutenant. I felt sure you'd stop to see your father on the way to Mennufer—and I dared hope you'd come to see me."

"You knew of our new posting?" Released by the older man, Bak stepped back, laughing. "Of course you did. You may've left behind the land of Wawat, never to return again, but if I've learned nothing else about you, I've learned that your interest, once attracted, never wanes."

Smiling his pleasure at what he rightly took as a compli-

ment, Amonked laid an arm across Bak's shoulders and ushered him into the shade of a portico built across the front of
a storehouse of the lord Amon. "It's true. I never fail to read
the abbreviated daybooks Thuty sends north to Waset."

Huy followed at a respectful distance, awaiting fresh orders. The building, which consisted of ten long, vaulted
magazines, stood near a quay that allowed cargo to be off-
loaded from ships moored reasonably close to the many
warehouses of the god. Eight of the structure's doors were
closed and sealed, while two stood open, releasing the odors
of grain and cooking oils. Five scribes sat on reed mats at the
far end of the portico, scribbling on papyrus scrolls.

Basking in the warmth of Amonked's welcome, Bak
dropped onto a low stool and studied the man he had come
to see. He was rather plump and of medium height, and sat
on a chair befitting his status as Storekeeper of Amon, with
plenty of colorful pillows for comfort. He wore the simple
calf-length kilt of a scribe and a minimum of colorful
beaded jewelry. Unashamed of his thinning hair, he wore no
wig. He had not changed, Bak was glad to see, since washing away the sand and sweat of Wawat to return to this easier, more comfortable life.

"First things first," Amonked said, and ordered Huy to
bring close a low table on which sat two stemmed bowls, a
jar of wine, and bowls of fruit. "Tell me of Buhen and all
that's happened since last I saw it."

Sipping a rich, flower-scented wine, Bak first thanked him
on behalf of Commandant Thuty and himself for the promises he had kept. He went on to speak of the many individuals Amonked had come to know during his long journey
south. The Storekeeper of Amon, in turn, invited Bak to his
home to renew acquaintance with those who had accompanied him to Wawat. A gentle breeze and the soft cooing of
doves blessed their reunion.

When finally they had caught up with the news, Amonked
set his drinking bowl on the table and his face grew serious.
"You wish to report an offense against the lady Maat, so said

your message. A vile deed that must be resolved here in Waset."

Bak pulled loose from his belt the square of linen in which he had carried the ancient jewelry. Untying the knot, he spread wide the fabric and held out the open package. He had a brief moment of regret that the bracelets and rings no longer lay in the honey. The presentation would have been more dramatic, a jest he felt sure Amonked would have appreciated.

"I found these while inspecting southbound trade goods passing through Buhen," he said.

Amonked took the package and lifted out a golden bracelet encrusted with turquoise and carnelian. After reading the royal oval and the symbols inside, he studied the other five objects.

Grave of face, he said, "The jewelry of a royal consort or princess, without doubt. A woman close to Nebhepetre Montuhotep, the first of a long line of kings to make Waset their seat of power." He laid the square of cloth and its precious contents on the table by his side. "Tell me how you found the jewelry and who had it."

Bak explained in detail and spoke of the subsequent interrogation. He summed up the result in one brief sentence: "I'm convinced Nenwaf knows no more than he told us."

Eyeing the jewelry, Amonked's expression grew dark and unhappy. "This isn't the first time such items have been found on board a ship bound for some distant land. Of the eighteen objects the inspectors at the harbor have retrieved, some, like these, were taken from a royal tomb, while others came from the burial places of individuals whose names we don't know. They're all quite beautiful and valuable, objects once worn by the long-dead nobility."

Bak whistled. The jewelry discovered would be a small fraction of the total amount stolen. The situation was more serious than he had imagined. "Were all the pieces taken from the same burial ground?"

"That we don't know. The four smugglers apprehended

knew no more than your Nenwaf did." Amonked picked up his drinking bowl. "Even if the jewelry taken from a non-royal tomb contained the owner's name, we probably wouldn't know its location. Some objects are of a style common to the reign of Nebhepetre Montuhotep and his immediate successors; the rest are of a less refined workmanship, somewhat later in origin, possibly made at a provincial capital."

Bak understood the problem. Records so old were hard to find—if they existed at all. A portion of the intervening time had been plagued by famine and war, turning the land of Kemet upside down and the archives into places of chaos. "Nebhepetre Montuhotep's memorial temple and tomb are in western Waset. Would not the women close within his heart be buried nearby?"

"Other men's thoughts have followed the same path, Lieutenant." Amonked plucked a cluster of grapes from a bowl on the table and plopped one into his mouth. "Lieutenant Menna, the officer who stands at the head of the men who guard the cemeteries of western Waset, has been given the task of laying hands on the thief. Thus far he's had no luck. Oh, he finds an open tomb now and then, small and poor, certainly not one in which jewelry of this quality would be found." He spat a seed into his hand. "If anyone can resolve the problem, he can. He's held his position for more than three years, and he knows the area well." Beckoning Huy, he added, "I'll summon him. You must get to know him."

While he issued orders to the apprentice, the beat of drums and the rhythmic song of oarsmen announced the departure of a cargo ship. As it pulled away from the quay, another similar vessel approached the dock to moor in its place. The quay seldom stood empty at this time of year, Bak knew. The harvest was over and the time had come to share a portion of the year's bounty with the royal house and the lord Amon. The men who toiled day after day, carrying the offering from the laden ships to the god's storehouses, sat on the ground beneath a cluster of palms, awaiting the next cargo. One man was whistling, a few played a game of chance, the rest were chatting and laughing, men who saw each other daily but never ran out of words.

Amonked's extensive knowledge of the thefts roused Bak's curiosity. After the youth hurried away, he said, "You aren't the man responsible for the investigation, are you?"

"Not at all. My task, one given to me recently by Maatkare Hatshepsut, is to watch over the construction of Djeser Djeseru, her memorial temple." Amonked eyed the grapes again, but refused to be tempted. "My sole interest in the robberies is that they could be taking place right under the noses of the men who are building the temple."

"I'm to remain in Waset a month or more, until Commandant Thuty comes north from Buhen." Not wanting to appear too eager, Bak took a date from a bowl, pretended to study it. "I'd be glad to help."

Amonked looked amused, as if he had seen through the casual facade. "No doubt you would, and you'd do the task well, but I've another I feel more urgent."

Bak's heart sagged within his breast. Hori would be disappointed. By the breath of Amon! So was he.

"It's a task you may not find as much to your liking," Amonked admitted, "but one that must be resolved before other lives are lost."

Lost lives? Bak tamped down a surge of hope. To feel joy at other men's misfortunes was not seemly. "Yes, sir?"

"Djeser Djeseru has been plagued by a series of accidents, beginning shortly after construction began a little over five years ago. A few at first, but the numbers have escalated. Several men have died. A much larger number have suffered injury, some more serious than others. I suspect deliberate intent, and I want you to investigate."

Bak did not know what to say. Construction sites were inherently dangerous places. Accidents happened all the time, some caused by careless men, others by the whims of the gods. How could he be expected to learn the reason behind each and every mishap that had occurred over five long years?

More important, the temple was Maatkare Hatshepsut's proudest creation, a place she held close within her heart. How would she react if she learned a man she had exiled to the southern frontier was treading its paving stones? Would she send him back to Buhen, a place he had come to love? Or, far more likely, to some far-off and remote post where he would be lost to the world forever? He wanted nothing to do with the task.

Amonked must have read his thoughts. "You need not fear my cousin, Lieutenant. You'll report to me alone and to no one else."

"If she questions my presence?"

"I've but to remind her of your skills as a hunter of men. Can she turn you away? I think not."

Bak took a sip of wine, one of the best vintages he had tasted in a long time. He was not entirely satisfied with the promise. He trusted Amonked, but he doubted even the Storekeeper of Amon, as close a relative as he was, could stand up to the most powerful sovereign in the world when she sent her heart down a specific path, as she had when she had exiled Bak. Yet how could he refuse? "Exactly how many men have been hurt or slain?" Maybe the number of accidents was no greater at Djeser Djeseru than anywhere else.

"Thirteen have died: two foremen, nine ordinary workmen, a scribe, and a guard. Seven have been seriously injured, never to return to their tasks at the temple. That number includes my scribe Thaneny, whom you knew in Wawat."

"I remember him well, sir." A good man, Bak recalled, one whose mutilated and stiffened leg had testified to the seriousness of the accident that had nearly taken his life.

"Several more men have been badly hurt," Amonked said, "but none so disabled they couldn't go on to other, less demanding tasks. Of course, there've been innumerable lesser accidents, three or four a month, I'd guess."

Bak had to admit the numbers seemed excessive. He had nothing to compare them to, but if he were responsible for a task with so many dead and injured, he, too, would be concerned. "What do the workmen say about the mishaps?"

Amonked screwed up his face in distaste. "They blame a malign spirit."

No surprise there, Bak thought. Men of no learning were superstitious, finding it easier to blame misfortune on the mysterious rather than other men or the gods. "Have tools turned up missing? Have the men been paid in short measure? Has the quality of workmanship been wanting?"

"Is corruption a concern, you mean?" Amonked shook his head. "I've scribes who go through the scrolls each time I receive a report. They check every inventory that pertains to the project, searching for theft of property or equipment, and they conduct their own random inventories. They look into tales of bad morale, quarrels between men, reports of personal theft, and all the other minor crimes that befall a project so large. They've found nothing out of the ordinary."

"You trust them."

"I'd place my life and my honor in their hands."

Bak did not doubt Amonked's judgment of his scribes, but honest men ofttimes missed the rotten core hidden within the fruits of men's labors. "I'll walk the same path for a short distance lest they've missed something. Other than that, you've not left me much to work with." His smile was wry, containing a minimum of humor. "Nothing but a malign spirit."

A rotund man with a black mole on his chin walked under the portico. He spoke briefly with the chief scribe, who ushered him to Amonked and introduced him as the captain of the ship that had just arrived. They spoke of the cargo, mostly wheat and barley, and of other matters related to the shipment. Listening with half an ear, Bak watched the crew of the vessel prepare to unload and the foot traffic on the busy street, which gave access to the numerous warehouses within Amonked's domain. A flock of chattering sparrows darted among the passing feet, snatching grain that had spilled from a bag earlier in the day.

He spotted Huy coming toward the warehouse at a fast pace and with him a tall, well-formed man who carried a baton of office. The guard officer investigating the tomb robberies, Bak assumed.

Amonked bade good-bye to the ship's captain, waited for the pair to draw near, and introduced Bak to the newly arrived officer, Lieutenant Menna, as he had guessed.

"You two should get on well together," Amonked told Menna. "Lieutenant Bak has stood at the head of a company of Medjays at the fortress of Buhen for over two years. He's a most talented investigator." Pointing to a portable stool Huy drew close, he added, "I've told him of your own knowledge."

While Menna sampled the wine and fruit, Bak studied him surreptitiously. He was a man of thirty or so years, freshly oiled and smelling of a scent he had used after bathing. His kilt was the whitest of whites, his broad beaded collar and bracelets gleamed. His belt buckle, the grip of his dagger, and his baton of office glistened. Bak doubted he had ever met a man so careful of his person. He wondered how he looked after tramping through the sandswept cemeteries of western Waset for hours on end.

Amonked handed Menna the precious objects lying in the square of cloth. "Lieutenant Bak found this jewelry on a cargo ship moored at Buhen. If not for him, these pieces would now be adorning the wife of some minor Kushite king."

After looking closely at each object, Menna tapped with a finger the name within the ring of protection. "I'll wager these came from the same tomb as the cowrie necklace and girdle the inspector found on a ship moored in Mennufer two months ago."

"I'd not be surprised." Amonked's voice hardened. "This abomination must stop, Lieutenant. You must find that tomb.

That and the others being rifled. Of greater import, you must snare the man responsible."

Menna flung a quick glance at Bak, obviously unhappy at having a witness to what amounted to a reprimand, and looked back at Amonked. "As you well know, sir, my men and I have thoroughly examined the cemeteries in western Waset. More than once. We've found nothing amiss. I'm beginning to think the tombs that have been robbed are elsewhere. Near Mennufer possibly, where the majority of the jewelry has been found."

Amonked scowled. "Next you'll be telling me Nebhepetre Montuhotep buried his loved ones at Buhen."

Menna flushed. "No, sir."

"That worthy king was entombed here, as were his successors. You can't seriously believe his consort or daughter would be set to rest far away from the man who lifted the one above all others and gave the other her life."

"If a princess, she may have wed a man who took her . . ." Menna must have realized how useless it was to press against an immovable wall. His argument foundered. None too eagerly, he said, "All right, sir. We'll go over the same ground again. And again and again if we must."

"So be it." Amonked turned to Bak. "I wish you to repeat to Lieutenant Menna all you've told me about finding these precious objects."

"Yes, sir," Bak said, and went on to do so.

When he admitted he had gotten nothing of value from Nenwaf, Menna said, "So you know no more than I do."

Having made no claim to superior knowledge, Bak was irritated. "Far less, I'd wager. I've not known of the rifled tombs as long as you have, Lieutenant, nor have I been in a position to walk through the cemeteries day after day."

"Would you like to assist me in my task? There are hundreds of tombs in western Waset, and we could use another man."

The officer's voice was level, carrying no hint of rancor, but Bak was left with a feeling that the suggestion was barbed. Either Menna was still nettled because he had witnessed his censure or, in spite of Amonked's warm introduction, Menna saw this newcomer from the southern frontier as unworldly and unaccomplished. One who knew nothing of locating and snaring those who offended the lady Maat, one who could walk by the open mouth of a sunken tomb and fail to notice. Bak resented the notion, not uncommon among officers who had never been posted outside the capital.

Amonked eyed Menna, his face revealing none of his thoughts, a mask Bak had come to know well in Wawat. "Lieutenant Bak will be spending a great deal of time in western Waset, but he'll have no time to aid you. I've asked him to seek out the source of the many accidents at Djeser Djeseru."

Menna gave Bak a surprised look, smiled. "I wish you luck. From what I hear, you'll be tracking most elusive game."

"I'm not a superstitious man, Lieutenant."

"I'm not implying you are. I'm merely saying that superstition breeds accidents."

"Perhaps," Bak said, refusing to give Menna the satisfaction of argument or agreement. "You made no comment when I mentioned the drawing around the neck of the jar in which the jewelry was hidden, a necklace with a pendant bee. Did it mean nothing to you?"

"Not a thing."

The response was not one that welcomed a suggestion, but Bak went on anyway. "Do you know of a beekeeper who labels his honey in that manner? He could've slipped the jewelry into the jar or, if the jar was reused later, he might know who used it after he did."

Menna shrugged. "I've never seen such a drawing, nor do I know of any man who uses a like symbol."

"According to the man I snared in Buhen, the sketch was placed on the jar so both he and the recipient would know exactly which container was of special value. Some such method of identification would be needed if he and his fellows were simple couriers, as he claimed, with no knowledge of what was hidden inside. Have any inspectors noticed such a drawing?"

He had Menna's full attention now. "Not to my knowledge, but it's worthy of discussing with the harbormaster. I'll do so today." He stood up, preparing to leave. "In fact, I'll speak with him this morning, before I cross the river to western Waset. I appreciate the suggestion, Lieutenant, and I commend you for being so astute."

Bak watched him hurry away, suspecting that condescension lurked within that final bit of praise. At least Menna had been sufficiently impressed to follow a new course that might bear fruit.

If only their roles were reversed. If only he, Bak, could investigate the tomb robberies and Menna look into the construction accidents. Like the guard officer had said, superstition gave birth to mishaps, and Bak very much feared such was the case at Djeser Djeseru.

Then again, an inordinately large number of accidents had occurred.

Chapter Three

"Two senior architects are responsible for the project: Pashed and Montu." Amonked hastened up the wide causeway, setting a pace few men could maintain for long.

The four porters bearing the carrying chair he had spurned hurried along behind. Bak had spotted them more than once wiping their brows in an exaggerated manner and exchanging glances of mock exhaustion, and not because of the midday heat. They were registering a good-natured acceptance of their master's refusal to ride. An idiosyncrasy among those who walked the corridors of power.

"Two very different men," Amonked went on. "Pashed is sensible and reliable, as firm as a rock. Montu is as slippery as the snake you'd find under that rock. Both are equally competent in their tasks, and both should be credited for all you'll see before you today."

Surprised, Bak asked, "Is not Senenmut, our sovereign's favorite, the architect responsible for Djeser Djeseru?" The instant Bak uttered the word "favorite," he regretted the slip. It was common usage among ordinary people when speaking of Senenmut, but he doubted it was aired above a whisper by denizens of the royal house. Too disrespectful by far.

Looking amused, Amonked said, "He has overall charge, yes, but the project is large and he has a multitude of other important and time-consuming duties."

"Thus you've been given the task of relieving his burden."

33

"So it would seem."

"I see." Bak knew he should let the matter drop, but a twinkle in his companion's eye prompted him to go on. "I've heard many times that he alone created the unique design of Djeser Djeseru. Is that not true?"

Amonked's laugh hinted at cynicism. "The ruined memorial temple of Nebhepetre Montuhotep lies beside that of Maatkare Hatshepsut. You can look down upon it from my cousin's new structure. After you've seen it, I'll tell you of Senenmut's initial plan for Djeser Djeseru."

Bak looked up the long, sloping causeway toward the distant construction site. The broad smooth path allowed materials and equipment to be hauled from a canal at its lower end to the upper reaches of the valley floor, an undulating landscape of golden sand nestled within a natural bay, a curving sweep of high cliffs with tower-like projections of varying height cut from the face by erosion. When building the causeway, sandy mounds and rock protuberances had been leveled and the low ground filled to make the ascent smooth and straight, the grade easy. Later, a small temple would be built at the lower end and the path would be paved and walled. Stone lions with the faces of Maatkare Hatshepsut would line either side of the walkway.

From so low a perspective, he could see only a portion of the temple at the far end of the valley, where the cliff reached its highest point. A lower terrace, divided at the center by a ramp, was partially lined with pale limestone columns. A second, higher terrace had about half the columns in place at either end. The structure was being built along the base of a steep slope of rock fallen from the soaring cliffs that formed a golden brown backdrop. Bak was impressed. The setting could not have been more spectacular—or more befitting a mighty sovereign of the land of Kemet.

To the south and on lower ground, broken columns and a tumbled mound of stone stood atop a sandswept terrace, the ancient ruined temple of Nebhepetre Montuhotep. Bak had played among those columns as a child, brought into the valley by his father's housekeeper, who had come sometimes to bend a knee at a shrine to the lady Hathor. The valley had been quiet during that long ago time, a place of adoration. If the rising dust ahead told a true tale, he would find no peace and tranquillity now.

"Does Senenmut come here often?"

"As I said before, my young friend, he's a busy man." Amonked's mouth twitched. "A very busy man."

Bak, letting out a long, slow breath of relief, barely noticed the humor. Senenmut was no more a friend of his than was Maatkare Hatshepsut.

"As you can see, the sanctuary is nearly complete."

The senior architect, Pashed, stood aside so Bak could look the length of the long, narrow chamber that had been dug into the hillside. The enclosed space smelled of the four men inside, sweating in the heat, toiling in sunlight reflected from outside by means of a mirror. They barely glanced at the newcomer. They were too preoccupied with adding color to the shallow reliefs that adorned the walls, images of Maatkare Hatshepsut making offerings to various deities. Bak did not tarry. He would have plenty of time to see details later.

"The same may be said of the memorial chapels to our sovereign and her father," Pashed said, hurrying on with his admittedly perfunctory tour of the construction site. He was a short, slight man of forty or so years whose brow was stamped by the deep wrinkles of an individual perpetually harried by life.

"Where's Montu?" Amonked asked. "I want Lieutenant Bak to meet him."

The architect slipped around a ramp of rubble at the end of an unfinished segment of portico, which when finished would surround the open court at the heart of the temple. Several architraves and roofing slabs lay at the foot of the ramp, waiting to be positioned atop twin rows of sixteen-sided columns. About half the portico was complete. Large limestone drums that would be stacked to form additional columns were scattered around the open floor in the center. Wall niches to either side of the sanctuary door stood empty, awaiting the placement of statues of Maatkare Hatshepsut. The work lay dormant, with not a man in sight. Bak could not understand the lack of activity.

Pashed's voice grew taut, censorious. "I haven't seen him today."

"I spoke to him last week." Amonked made no attempt to hide his irritation. "Apparently my warning did no good."

Bak glanced at the two men. Anger and discontent were far more likely causes of accidents than malign spirits, and Amonked wanted him to meet Montu. Did he suspect the missing architect of disrupting the work, not with intent, but out of neglect?

Mouth clamped tight, Pashed stalked through an open portal on the south side of the courtyard. Bak found himself in an as yet unadorned anteroom off which two doorways opened. A pair of carefully placed mirrors caught the sunlight reflected from a mirror outside and sent it into two inner rooms.

"Maatkare Hatshepsut's memorial chapel and that of her father," the architect told Bak, his tone waspish.

Ignoring the anger, aware it was not directed at him, Bak dutifully peeked into the two chambers. Inside the smaller room, three men were painstakingly carving delicate reliefs of food offerings on the walls, while five painters were toiling in the larger, applying bright colors to carved processions of servants bearing offerings of fruits and vegetables, beef and fowl. Though Bak appeared indifferent to the discussion in the anteroom, he missed not a word.

"Montu claimed his country estate takes up much of his time," Amonked said.

"The property isn't his. It belongs to his wife, inherited from a previous husband." Pashed sniffed. "The sole task that occupies him is ordering her around. Her and her daughter and the scribe who's managed the estate since long before they were wed. They're the ones who toil alongside the servants, not him."

"His duty is here, and here he must come each day. And so I told him."

Noticing Bak standing at the chapel door, waiting to move on, Pashed beckoned. "Come. I'll take you to the shrine of the lord Re."

He led them outside and along the incomplete wall at the front of the court. A break in the center wide enough to admit the large sledges on which stones were hauled would someday be made into a portal. A granite lintel and jambs lay nearby, waiting to be installed. Bak eyed the broken wall and half-finished portico, astounded that the court was not a beehive of activity. Why was the task not proceeding?

"I'm tempted to have Montu sent north to toil on the shrine of the lady Pakhet," Amonked said. Pakhet was a fierce lion-headed provincial goddess, and the new building was located in the desert west of the province's very rural capital. Not a place a man accustomed to life in sophisticated Waset would wish to go.

Pashed's laugh carried an edge of meanness. "I can think of no task more fitting."

Passing through a doorway at the north side of the court, the architect hurried them through an anteroom whose roof was supported by four sixteen-sided columns and into a large chamber in which ten steps rose up the side of a high altar dedicated to the lord Re. The room was open to the sky, allowing the priests to commune freely with the deity. Here again Maatkare Hatshepsut, depicted in fine, brightly colored reliefs, was shown making offerings.

"This shrine is complete except for statues of our sovereign that will be placed here and in the anteroom," Pashed said.

The trio returned to the courtyard, where Bak stopped to look around. "Djeser Djeseru has been under construction for five long years, Pashed, and still this upper level is in-

complete. Why do you not have men here, finishing the portico?" Bak spoke more sharply than he intended, but
Amonked's nod of agreement told him he had not stepped
beyond the bounds expected of him.

"The workmen..." Pashed hesitated, glanced at
Amonked, said, "All right, you've come to learn the reason
for our many unfortunate accidents, so you may as well hear
the truth." He paused, screwed up his face to show distaste.
"The men fear a malign spirit. They spend more time looking over their shoulders and listening to whispered tales of
lights in the dark and shadows where none should fall than
in performing the tasks for which they receive their daily
bread."

"They believe this part of the temple more fearful than the
rest?"

Pashed flung his head up in a superior manner. "If that
were the case, neither artists nor sculptors would toil here,
would they?"

"There's some truth in what Pashed says," Amonked told
Bak, "but he's failed to mention another obstacle in the way
of progress. Senenmut has several times changed the plan.
He's thinking now of making this open court a columned
hall. Thus the work has stopped, awaiting his decision."

Looking distinctly uncomfortable, Pashed clamped his
mouth tight, refusing to admit he had skirted around a part
of the truth rather than lay blame on the man to whom he
owed his well-being.

Amonked, his thoughts masked, eyed the architect briefly,
then turned away, led his companions out of the building,
and stopped at the top of the mudbrick and debris ramp up
which materials and equipment were hauled to this upper,
most sacred part of the temple.

The view was glorious: the hot, sunny bay nestled at the
foot of the cliffs and, in the distance, a patchwork of brown
and golden fields, of green garden plots and palm groves,
marking the broad strip of farmland along the river, made indistinct by the heat haze.

They were standing on the upper terrace Bak had seen
from afar, in reality a portico which, when completed,
would span the front of the temple. The twin rows of
columns, square in front, sixteen-sided behind, covered by
roof slabs, were split into two segments by the wide gap in
the center, yet to be completed. Two oversized painted
statues of Maatkare Hatshepsut in the form of the lord
Osiris had been erected against the two northernmost ex-
terior columns. Similar images would be placed all along
the portico, looking out across the valley for all the world
to see.

Bak looked down upon the unfinished, lower colonnade
he had glimpsed from the causeway. To either side of the
ramp, which he assumed would ultimately be finished as a
stairway, two rows of columns were being erected to form a
portico. Just a few at each end had been built to their full
height, with roof slabs in place. The roof of this lower portico, when completed, would form a broad, open terrace in
front of the upper colonnade, which stood above and slightly
behind the retaining wall that contained the earth on which
the temple was being built.

In front of the lower colonnade, the sloping terrain had
been leveled to form a flattish surface, a terrace of sorts. To
the north, the high side of the valley floor and a part of the
fairly steep slope at the base of the cliff were being cut away
and a retaining wall built to hold back the hillside. Another
retaining wall was being built to the south to hold in place
the dirt and debris shifted from north to south to build up the
low side of the terrace.

Raw stone newly taken from the quarry, and roughly
shaped blocks whose purpose was impossible to guess,
shared the terrace with stone cubes to be made into square
columns, drums to become sixteen-sided columns, rectangular slabs for lintels and jambs, architraves and roof slabs.
Scattered here and there, sometimes singly and sometimes
in groups, were dozens of statues of Maatkare Hatshepsut in
various stages of sculpting, from roughed-out blocks of

stone to nearly complete sitting or standing figures or images of reclining human-headed lions. To the east, where the
terrace fell away to merge into the landscape, the remains of
an old mudbrick temple, neglected and crumbling, was gradually being consumed as the terrace was extended.

Scattered among the stones were the craftsmen who
were shaping and polishing parts of columns and statuary,
and the workmen who provided unskilled labor. The
skilled artisans dwelt in villages outside the valley along
the edge of the floodplain, while the other men lived in
huts built in a shallow hollow between Djeser Djeseru and
the ancient temple of Nebhepetre Montuhotep. These men
had come from throughout the land of Kemet, men whose
crops had been gathered, leaving them free to serve their
sovereign. They had been pressed into duty to haul stones,
dig ditches, build walls, whatever they had to do to pay off
their debts or those of the noblemen on whose lands they
lived, or to repay with labor offenses against the lady
Maat.

To either side of the terrace, men toiled at the retaining
walls, those to the north cutting away the slope, those to the
south shaping and placing the stone blocks. A ragged line of
youths carried dirt and debris by the basketful from the high
side of the terrace to the low. Other boys walked among the
men with donkeys, carrying skins of water. Well over a hundred men and boys whistling, laughing, calling out to each
other, or talking among themselves. None afraid of malign
spirits, at least in the light of day.

A nearly naked man, a workman if the dust and sweat
covering his body told true, raced up the rubble ramp down
which materials were moved from the terrace to the men
building the southern retaining wall. He sped through the
clutter of stones, drawing every eye, silencing the laughter
and talk. Clearly agitated, he stopped among the columns
below. "Pashed! Sir! I must speak with you, sir. Right
away!"

The architect looked at the workman and at Amonked, his

face a picture of indecision. Amonked was an important man, while the workman's message might well be as urgent as he appeared to believe it was.

"Go to him," Amonked said. "We'll await you here."

Pashed hurried away with the workman, both soon to vanish behind the southern retaining wall.

"Another accident?" Bak asked.

"I pray not."

They strode to the southern end of the unfinished colonnade and tried to see where Pashed had gone. Thanks to the vagaries of construction, they could look down upon a new shrine to the lady Hathor and the four men laying foundation stones, but the incomplete segment of wall that would close off the end of the colonnade blocked their view of the area along the base of the retaining wall. They saw a dozen or so workmen standing about, looking toward the wall and talking among themselves, but Pashed was nowhere to be seen. With Amonked unwilling to intrude unless summoned, Bak resigned himself to waiting.

Standing on the edge of the terrace, he looked across the workmen's huts to the ruined memorial temple of Nebhepetre Montuhotep. It was as he remembered it, yet vastly different. The mound of rubble in the center was lower, the remaining columns had decreased in number and fewer were standing, none to their original height. Two men scrambled among the ruins, and even from a distance he could see they were searching for stone that could be recut and reused. A small crew of workmen levered the blocks the pair selected onto wooden rockers, which they used to raise the stones onto sledges. These were towed by another team of men from the old temple to the new.

Amonked pointed toward the center of the ruin. "You see the mound of stones that might once have been a pyramid—or whatever it was? The three rows of fallen and broken columns that once formed a covered walkway around the mound? The wall enclosing those columns?"

"Yes, sir."

"That, my young friend, is exactly the plan Senenmut started with. Same size, same shape, but set well forward of the older temple. Clearly his inspiration was not unique."

Bak had the distinct impression that Amonked did not share his cousin's affection for Senenmut.

"Was the building ever started?"

"Over a hundred men toiled here for several months. When they went home to harvest their crops, he altered his plan. I'm not sure why. My cousin came out here, and perhaps she suggested something more worthy, more unique."

"Sir!" The same workman who had come for Pashed stood among the columns below. "Pashed wishes you to come right away, sir. You and Lieutenant Bak. The matter is urgent, he said, most urgent."

"Bata found a body in an ancient tomb." Pashed flung a hasty look at a reed-thin workman who was shaking so badly another man had to hold a beer jar to his lips. The architect was standing in front of a rough hole in the sand that opened near the end of the incomplete retaining wall. He looked gray around the mouth, beleaguered. "A man struck down from behind."

Bak knew no man long dead and buried would rouse such strong reactions. "The body is fresh?"

"So it looked to me."

"Who is he?" Amonked demanded.

"I don't know. I didn't draw close. Nor did Bata, so he says."

Bak thanked the lord Amon. With luck he might find some sign of the slayer. Or maybe he should thank the so-called malign spirit for holding back all who would otherwise have trampled over the scene.

"I'll need a good, strong light," he said, eyeing the dark opening.

The short, stout foreman responsible for building the wall, Seked by name, sent a workman off to get a fresh torch. The foreman's grim expression and a tendency to rub the ugly scar running across his forehead betrayed his outward calm as a sham.

Bak glanced at the onlookers standing well back in a loose half circle: Bata's fellow workmen, a dozen or more sweat-stained men, whose faces registered equal measures of excitement and alarm. Coming at a fast pace across the sand were the men he had seen removing stones from the ancient temple. Others were gathering along the top of the retaining wall. By end of day, every man at Djeser Djeseru would have told the tale over and over again, each time embellishing it. Bak took care to conceal his annoyance; if he was to resolve the problem of the malign spirit, he would need their goodwill.

He walked close to the hole into which he must go and looked into the black void. Located at the edge of the mound of dirt and debris that formed the terrace, it was directly in the path of the retaining wall. The sand around it was hard-packed. He guessed the tomb had been open for some time and the men had concluded they had nothing to fear from whatever was inside.

"Why did Bata enter the tomb?" he asked.

Seked stepped forward. "We needed to go on with the retaining wall, sir. We thought to fill the shaft today so we could build over it."

"I gave them permission," Pashed said. "The tomb was never completed or used, so we had no need to summon a priest to offer prayers."

The foreman flung a bleak look at the dark opening. "I thought it best that we send a man down before we filled it. I feared some lazy workman might've slipped inside to take a nap."

Bak nodded. He, too, would have wanted to be sure no man was trapped below. "Someone must go down with me," he said, giving Pashed a pointed look, "one who knows by sight most of the men who toil within this valley."

Pashed nodded slowly, reluctantly.

The workman hurried back with a flaming torch. Bak took the light and strode to the tomb. No hesitation for him. No time to let grow within his heart the tiny grain of apprehension he felt. No time to give the onlookers the satisfaction of thinking he might share their superstitious fears.

Holding the light before him, he picked his way down a steep flight of irregular steps, keeping his head low so he would not bump the rough-cut ceiling. He could hear Pashed's heavy breathing behind him. The tunnel at the bottom, its roof so low he had to hunch down, leveled out and turned gradually to the right. It was less than two paces wide, the air close and hot. He held the flame near the floor, looking at the footprints in the thin layer of fine sand that covered the stone. Two sets of prints coming and going, one shod, the other bare, those of Pashed and Bata, he felt sure. If any other prints had been left, they had unwittingly destroyed them. At times, he glimpsed short straight indentations near the walls. At first they puzzled him but then he realized they were the remains of tracks left by the wooden runners of a sledge.

At least two dozen paces beyond the steps, he saw the body, a man lying on his side, facing the rough wall that marked the far end of the shaft. The back of the head was matted and bloody, dark and glistening in the torchlight. The smell of death, though not strong, was pervasive. Bata's prints and those of Pashed ended where Bak stood, where they had glimpsed the dead man and fled.

He walked slowly forward, examining the floor. Except for one indentation no longer than his hand left by the sledge, the sand was smooth and unmarked. The slayer had brushed away his tracks. Kneeling beside the body, he looked back. Pashed hovered several paces away, sweat streaming down his face. The shaft was hot, but not that hot. The architect was afraid.

Turning back to the dead man, Bak's eyes fell on the head, the crown crushed and broken, a mass of dried blood and flesh crawling with flies. The body was limp, the pallid flesh beginning to swell. The man had been dead for some time, or had he? In the warmth of the tomb the process of decay would be faster. He could have been slain as recently as the night before.

"Who is he?" Pashed whispered.

Sucking in his breath, Bak laid his hands on the lifeless form and rolled the dead man onto his back. Flies rose in a cloud. Bak swallowed hard and forced himself to concentrate on the man's appearance. He was of medium height and of middle years, with fading good looks and muscles going to fat. He wore the long kilt of a scribe and elaborate, probably costly, multicolored bead jewelry.

"Come forward, Pashed. You must tell me his name." After a long silence, he heard the whisper of sandals approaching across the sand.

The architect bent over, stared. "May the gods be blessed. It's Montu."

What a strange thing to say, Bak thought. "Are you sure?"

"We've toiled together here at Djeser Djeseru for over five years. I'd know him anywhere."

"Montu." Amonked sighed. "I can't say I liked the man, but to die like that . . . An abomination."

Bak eyed the half circle of men standing well back from the mouth of the tomb. From the size of the crowd, he guessed every man at Djeser Djeseru had abandoned his task to come and see for himself what had happened. Most men spoke together in hushed voices, speculating about the dead man and his manner of death. A few at the front of the circle were silent, trying to hear what the police officer and the Storekeeper of Amon were saying.

"Are you certain he didn't fall and strike his head on a projecting stone?" Amonked asked, not for the first time.

"He was murdered, sir, struck down from behind."

Amonked glanced at the onlookers. "I fear the men will see this as another in the series of accidents we've had. More serious, of course, but one among many. Are you sure . . . ?"

"There was nothing in the tomb against which he could've fallen, sir. The floor was smooth, and the walls, though rough, had no protrusions so large they'd damage his head in such a way." Bak could see that Amonked was unconvinced or, more likely, did not want to believe. "I found almost no blood under him and I saw the tracks of a sledge. Seked assured me he's sent no sledge into that tomb. I'm convinced Montu was slain somewhere else and his body hauled from that place to here. Everyone watching the progress of the retaining wall knew the tomb would soon be closed forever. What better place to hide a murdered man?"

The guard who had been summoned to escort the dead man to the house of death came halfway out of the mouth of the tomb. A hush fell over the crowd. He spoke a few words to Pashed, waiting at the top, then turned around and said something to the men in the shaft behind him. Message relayed, he climbed to the surface. Two workmen Pashed had pressed into service stumbled out of the tomb. They carried between them the litter on which they had tied Montu's body. At Bak's suggestion, they had taken a length of linen with them to cover the dead man, but still the flies swarmed around. Both bearers looked a bit green, and Bak knew exactly how they felt.

Murmurs rose among the men looking on, prayers taking the place of speculation. Nodding at Bak and Amonked, the guard led the bearers toward the ring of onlookers and the ramp that would take them up to the terrace. Men scurried out of the way, breaking the circle apart. As the two workmen carried their grim burden past, the rest craned their heads, trying to see all there was to see, hoping to glean a bit more gossip.

Amonked took Bak's upper arm as if he needed support and they walked together through the break in the circle. Not until they reached the top of the ramp and were standing among several partially finished statues of Maatkare Hatshepsut did the shorter, stouter man release the younger, more fit of the pair.

Amonked slumped down onto the twice-size, almost finished face of Maatkare Hatshepsut wrapped for eternity as the lord Osiris, which was lying on its back in the sand. "I thank the lord Amon, Lieutenant, that I had the good sense to enlist your help this morning. I can honestly report to my cousin and Senenmut that I have the matter well in hand."

"I pray I can live up to your expectations, sir."

"You will. I'm sure you will. I've every confidence in you. You'll not only lay hands on the slayer, but you'll find the source of the many accidents that have plagued Djeser Djeseru and set to rest these tales of a malign spirit."

The responsibility was a heavy one, and Bak offered a silent prayer to the lord Amon that his shoulders were strong enough to bear it. Noting the carved features beneath Amonked's buttocks, he added another, equally fervent prayer that the Storekeeper of Amon would keep his vow to stand between him and Maatkare Hatshepsut.

Chapter Four

"A murder!" Hori was not actually dancing up the causeway, but his step was almost as light and quick. "Much better than jewelry stolen from an old tomb. A far more serious matter." The plump scribe glanced at the large, muscular Medjay walking by his side. "The gods have indeed blessed us, Kasaya."

The young Medjay's eyes darted toward Bak. "It's a good excuse to get away from my mother," he said, apparently thinking the admission more prudent than Hori's open enthusiasm.

"I doubt Montu's wife is taking his death so lightly," Bak said.

Hori flushed. "Oh, no, sir. I didn't mean . . ." His voice tailed off, the lightness vanished from his stride.

Kasaya had the good sense to let the matter rest.

The trio strode up the causeway, keeping pace with their long shadows cast by the early morning sun. Each had brought along his tools of office: Bak carried his baton, Hori his scribal pallet and water pot, and Kasaya his spear and shield.

The sun had tinted the cliff ahead a reddish brown, the colonnades of Djeser Djeseru a pale red-orange. The air was warm, barely stirred by a light breeze; the day might well grow unbearable. A smell of fish, onions, and burned oil lingered, drifting from the rough workmen's huts built between

48

Djeser Djeseru and the ancient temple. Several crows hopped around a garbage heap behind the interconnected buildings, squawking, picking clean discarded bones, squabbling over the other meager offerings they found.

"You're no longer boys," Bak said. "You must learn to guard your tongues."

"Yes, sir," Hori and Kasaya chorused.

Shouts drew their attention to the quarry north of the causeway, a foreman yelling at men pulling a sledge laden with a single massive block of stone up a steep ramp from its depths. Bak eyed the huge, irregular hole. The thuds of mallets on chisels carried on the air, but he could not see the men toiling below. The bottom was too deep. Was this the quarry from which stone was taken for the temple? he wondered. Or was it of too poor a quality? Had it been used instead to level the causeway, filling the low spots, making the ascent smooth and gradual?

"Most of the men who toil at our sovereign's new temple are simple souls from the countryside. Whatever you say, they'll take as fact. You must give them no reason for misunderstanding."

"What questions shall we ask?" Kasaya had accompanied Bak more than once on a quest for a slayer. Reality mitigated his enthusiasm, but not entirely. He was too glad to be released from his parents' dwelling.

"Start first by showing interest in the men's tasks," he said. "No matter how high or low, they're sure to enjoy speaking of their accomplishments. When you're certain they're well satisfied with themselves and with you, direct the conversation toward the many accidents, the malign spirit, the chief architect and craftsmen and foremen. After you've led them along the path of your choice, let their talk go where it will. You never know what they might reveal."

The trio walked across the sunny terrace, weaving a path through the rough and not so rough blocks of stone and the men who were completing the various architectural ele-

ments so they could be positioned within the temple. The
sand felt hot beneath their feet and the men they passed
reeked of sweat. Hori and Kasaya looked upon the scene
wide-eyed and enthralled. The workmen looked furtively
upon them, very much aware of who they were. Bak could
almost feel their apprehension, their mistrust of the authority
he and his men represented.

He wished Imsiba were with him, or another, equally ex-
perienced man. He knew well Kasaya's response to adversity, knew his faults and strengths, the way he thought, the
way he fought. He had no doubt the Medjay would give his
life for him if need be. Hori was another matter. He knew the
youth only in the safety of the garrison, a young man wed to
his scribal pallet, ever willing to do what had to be done, one
whose heart was generous and whose good humor was
neverending. A young man with no training in the arts of
war, one whose physical courage was untried and unknown.

With luck and the help of the gods, Hori's bravery and
stamina would not be tested while they set about snaring
Montu's slayer and discovering the reason for the many accidents.

A workman told them they would find Pashed at the base
of the southern retaining wall, and so they did. He stood
with the foreman Seked near the mouth of the tomb in which
Montu's body had been found, watching a line of boys carrying baskets of sand and rubble to the hole, where a second
chain of youths relayed them inside and sent out the emptied
baskets for another load. Men were laying foundation stones
to within a pace or so of the hole, anticipating the moment
when the tomb shaft would be packed with earth and they
could build over it. As Bak and his men approached, every
eye turned their way. One boy stumbled, the youth behind
him paused, the next in line bumped into him. Dirt rained
from his basket.

Seked shouted a curse to focus their attention on their
task, nodded a greeting to the newcomers, and moved a
dozen or so paces away to stand at the base of a rubble ramp

built along a segment of wall raised almost to its completed height. Shading his eyes with a hand, he looked up at two men at the top, who shoved a heavy block of stone off a sledge and into position. The front and upper surfaces of the stone, like those of its neighbors, had not yet been smoothed so facing stones could be laid in front of them. Other small crews were scattered along the top of the ramp, the nearest chipping away the rough surfaces, the next installing facing stones, the third dressing them. The ramp would be raised as each new course was completed.

Farther west, near the point where the wall joined the retaining wall that supported the mound on which the new shrine of the lady Hathor would be built, the rubble ramps had been removed and scaffolds built for the men who were doing the fine detail work. One crew added the finishing touches to plinths with recessed paneling, while others were carving and polishing deep reliefs of the royal falcon and cobra located at regular intervals high upon the wall.

Pashed's greeting was unenthusiastic but resigned. The wrinkles in his brow looked deeper than before, his general air more long-suffering and harried.

He gestured toward the line of youths. "We need to go on with the retaining wall. I trust you have no objection to our filling the shaft?"

"None."

Turning his back so no one but Bak would hear, Pashed murmured, "I feared if we allowed too much time to pass, the men would convince themselves that Montu's shade might in anger come back to the tomb and do them harm."

Bak spoke as softly as the architect. "I understand. Djeser Djeseru doesn't need another malign spirit." Raising his voice to a normal level, he introduced Hori and Kasaya. "They'll serve as my right hand and my left. I wish them to go where they want unimpeded, to ask what they will and be answered with the truth."

Pashed eyed the pair critically. "I'll not tolerate a disruption of the work."

."They'll not intrude. If they do, they'll answer to me."

Not entirely satisfied, or so he looked, Pashed beckoned to a stoop-shouldered, white-haired scribe squatting in a narrow slice of shade beside the wall. The elderly man, his eyes sharp and curious, dropped a limestone chip as big as his hand into a basket filled with bronze tools, laid his scribal pallet on top, and came forward. On any construction site, Bak knew, one of the first tasks of each day was that of the scribe, who had to distribute tools where needed and take back in return those in need of repair or sharpening, recording each transaction as he did so.

"You must take these men to the foremen and chief craftsmen, Amonemhab. Tell them . . ." Pashed repeated Bak's every word even though the scribe, like all who toiled nearby, had certainly heard.

With the good humor of a man accustomed to going about his business unseen by the mighty, the scribe led Hori and Kasaya away, taking his basket with him and the tools for which he would be held accountable. After a few paces he realized Bak was not with them. He paused and looked back, waiting.

Bak waved them away. "I must speak with you, Pashed."

"Me? Why me?" The architect tried to appear surprised, but as the sole remaining man of authority who toiled daily at Djeser Djeseru, he had to have known he would be the first to be questioned.

Taking him by the upper arm, Bak ushered him to an open stretch of sand well out of hearing distance of the many curious individuals toiling near the wall. Pashed's stride was quick and jerky, agitated.

Bak hid a smile. The architect was clearly upset, but he was also a man of purpose, and that purpose was to complete the construction of Djeser Djeseru. "You made it clear when you were speaking with Amonked yesterday that you didn't like Montu, that you thought him a man who shirked his duty."

"I didn't slay him, if that's what you think," Pashed said, indignant.

"I'm not saying you did. But if I'm to lay hands on the man who took his life, I must speak with everyone who knew him, you included." Bak could not remember how many times he had given the same assurance since walking at the head of the Medjay police at Buhen.

Pashed pursed his mouth; the wrinkles in his brow deepened. "I can tell you nothing of significance, I assure you."

"You resented him—understandably so—for letting you carry his load as well as your own."

"I did."

"A man so thoughtless must've had other, equally intolerable traits."

Pashed opened his mouth to speak, then closed it tight and shook his head.

"What thought did you swallow?" Bak asked.

The architect released a long, unhappy sigh. "Can you not go to the foremen? The chief craftsmen? They've as much knowledge of Montu as I. More."

"Pashed . . ." Bak frowned at the architect. "Though Senenmut holds the ultimate responsibility, you and you alone now carry the burden of building our sovereign's memorial temple. Do you wish to see the project falter while my men time and time again question one workman after another? You can be sure that endless questioning will plant turmoil in their hearts, no matter how much care we take to calm them."

The architect toyed with the hem of his kilt, shook grit from a sandal. When at last he spoke, the words came out with as much difficulty as a sound tooth being pulled from a healthy jaw. "He never failed to throw his weight around, ordering everyone to do what he thought beneath him. And let me assure you, he felt every task beneath him except issuing orders." His chin shot into the air, his tone grew resentful. "He treated all of us—including me—as men placed on this earth to do his bidding. As servants. In spite of the fact that without me to see that the project went on, with or without him, Senenmut might long ago have seen through him."

Had Senenmut truly failed to see, Bak wondered, or had he simply ignored the dead man's faults? "How long did Amonked take to notice his many absences?"

"Two weeks at most," Pashed admitted with grim satisfaction. "Montu underestimated him and failed to alter his indolent ways. He never once noticed that Amonked came day after day, without a break, and that he never failed to see an error in any man's ways."

"Senenmut, on the other hand, is a busy man, one who seldom comes to Djeser Djeseru."

Pashed glanced quickly at Bak, as if suspecting him of being facetious. "Montu's most disagreeable trait, one we all despised, was that he never failed to take credit for other men's ideas. The more creative the thought, the quicker he was to make it his own."

"For example . . . ?"

Once begun, the architect would not be turned onto a lesser path. "He fawned over Senenmut, gaining his ear, telling tales, making himself look good and everyone else mediocre at best. To hear him talk, he alone created this magnificent building."

Having heard many tales in the garrison of Senenmut's penchant for self-aggrandizement, Bak had an idea the bragging fell on deaf ears. Or on the tolerant ears of one who knew he could squash Montu like an insect any time he chose to do so. "Was Montu a competent architect?" he asked, recalling Amonked's statement that he and Pashed were equally skilled.

"He was," Pashed admitted reluctantly, "when he shouldered his load."

"Pashed! Sir!"

A workman came racing down the ramp from the terrace and sped across the sand to where they stood. Every boy out-

side the tomb, every man toiling on the wall, stopped to look
and listen.

"Sir!" The workman halted before Pashed, gasping for
breath. Sweat ran down his face and chest. "Another old
tomb has been found. Perenefer wishes you to come."

Pashed stared, distraught, at the messenger and then at
Bak. "Not another murdered man. No, just an old tomb. I
pray!"

"The donkey stepped in a hole." The foreman, Perenefer,
ran his hand up and down the brush-like mane of a gray donkey laden with large reddish water jars. He was short and
stout, and looked so much like Seked, the foreman in charge
of the south retaining wall, that they had to be brothers.
Twins. The sole difference as far as Bak could see was that
this man had no scar on his forehead. "As he struggled to
free himself, the sand fell away. For a time, we feared he,
too, would drop out of sight."

"How'd you save him?" Bak asked the small boy who
held the rope halter.

"I yelled, sir, and Perenefer came, and so did they."

The boy pointed at five men standing nearby, ready to
help should help be needed. Or, more likely, unwilling to
leave, fearing they would miss something. They were covered with the fine white dust risen from nearby limestone
drums, which they had been shaping into sixteen-sided column segments.

"They caught his front hooves and pulled him free." The
boy stared wide-eyed at the black hole, as big as two men's
hands placed one beside the other, down which sand was
still trickling. "I thank the lord Amon they were close by.
Only the greatest of gods knows how deep the tomb is."

"Shall we open it, sir?" Perenefer asked.

Pashed glanced at the lord Khepre, the morning sun
climbing the vault of heaven toward midday. "We've most of
the day ahead of us. Do so." He turned to Bak. "We've been

warned of robbers in the local burial places. We dare not leave these old tombs open for long."

"Have you unearthed many?"

"A dozen or so since first we began to level the land. More than I expected. The surrounding hillsides are riddled with tombs. I thought most of the ancient nobility to be buried there, not here."

Perenefer glared at the stonemasons, who had begun to edge away. "Why're you standing there gaping? Come on. You surely can brush away a little sand."

The men came forward with scant enthusiasm, but once they set about the task, they toiled with a will. Beneath the windblown sand they found three rectangular stone slabs lying side by side. The corner of one had broken away. A fault had allowed the stone to collapse beneath the donkey's weight.

At another command from Perenefer, the men took up levers and began to shift the broken stone sideways. The boy led his donkey to a safer spot a few paces away. So he could see better, Bak climbed onto the back of a large red granite statue of a reclining lion with the face of Maatkare Hatshepsut. Only luck and the will of the gods had placed the statue, heavier by far than the donkey, so close yet so far from the weakened stone and the hole into which it might well have toppled. If it had fallen into the tomb, it would have appeared to the workmen as the most dire of omens.

"Unless appearances deceive, the tomb has never been opened," Pashed said with obvious relief. "We shouldn't find a new death here."

With Perenefer urging the masons on, the slabs were quickly shifted and the mouth of the shaft gaped open, a hole as wide as a man's arm was long and too deep to see to the end.

"Bring a pole and place it across the shaft," the architect ordered, "and bring a rope and torch. I must go down, and someone must go with me." He bestowed upon Bak the same pointed look Bak had given him before they entered the tomb in which Montu had been found. "I want no man to accuse me of robbing the dead."

Bak clung with one hand to the rope and, with the other, held the torch low, trying to glimpse the bottom of the shaft before he reached it. The light danced against the rough-cut walls, forming shifting patterns of dark and glitter. The air, sealed inside for many years, was still and close and hot. He spotted the bottom and glimpsed the black mouth of either a chamber or a transverse tunnel. His feet touched stone and he released the rope. Calling to the men above to raise the line for Pashed, he turned to peer down what proved to be a horizontal shaft. More than a dozen paces long and lined with crumpled baskets, it opened into a room; the burial chamber, he assumed. How large it was he could not tell. The light from his torch did not reach inside.

He longed to go on, to see all this tomb contained and return to the surface. He did not like enclosed dark spaces. But his task was to lay hands on a slayer and learn the cause of so many accidents, while Pashed was the man responsible for Djeser Djeseru. He had to respect the architect's authority.

The men above shouted a warning and the rope creaked as Pashed swung out over the open shaft. Bak held the torch high, letting him see where he was going. The short, slight man proved surprisingly agile, dropping from the rope before his feet touched the floor. Hands on hips, he looked upward, gauging the depth of the shaft down which they had come. Turning, peering into the horizontal tunnel, he held out his hand for the torch. This was not the first old tomb he had entered, and with no expectation of finding a fresh body, he showed no fear.

Careful not to bump baskets whose age had made them fragile, Bak followed the architect to the burial chamber. It was small, three or four paces to a side, and the ceiling low. What had once been a magnificent rectangular wooden coffin filled more than half the space. Water had come in, probably more than once, and a vague smell of decay lingered, blending with the faint scent of flowers or aromatic oils. Pottery jars lay scattered about, a few broken but most whole and sealed. Jumbled together in a corner were three small wooden boats and their tiny wooden crews. Beside them sat several wooden boxes containing tiny wooden men and women and animals, tools, jars, furniture. Miniature necessities of a nobleman's life thrown into disorder.

The coffin had broken apart and much of it rotted away, revealing an inner coffin in an equally poor state. The wrappings on the body were stained and decayed, exposing a portion of the painted plaster mask, one foot whose flesh was gone, leaving behind a broken pile of bones, and a wrinkled and blackened arm wearing two bracelets. Tiny inlaid butterflies adorned one; the second was a wide gold band with three miniature golden cats lying in a row along the top. Both were exquisite.

As expected, no fresh body shared the chamber with the ancient body.

Bak bent to look closer at the bracelets. The five pieces he had found in Buhen were similar in workmanship to these. They had been taken from a tomb much like this one, he felt sure. A richer tomb, most likely, but the noble man or woman who had been laid to rest here had gone to the netherworld at about the same time. If he walked in Lieutenant Menna's sandals . . . He did not. He could only suggest that Menna look closer at the ancient burial places in the vicinity of Djeser Djeseru. And he could keep his own eyes open, wide open.

"I must notify Lieutenant Menna of this tomb," Pashed said, "and I must summon Kaemwaset. They can come together."

"I've met the guard officer, but who is Kaemwaset?"

"A priest in the mansion of the lord Amon in Waset. The first prophet has given him the responsibility for all the routine rituals performed while Djeser Djeseru is being built. Each time a man is injured, he comes with the physician to offer the necessary incantations that will aid in healing. Each time we find an old tomb, he utters the necessary prayers before we seal the burial chamber and cover it over. If the lord Amon smiles upon us, he'll come long before nightfall."

Bak thought of the lord Khepre, making his slow progress toward midday. He had seen for himself how quickly Pashed could and would close a tomb, but if a man wished to rob the dead, leaving this one open for even an hour would tempt fate.

"You must assign a guard to stand watch until this sepulcher is closed. The bracelets we see are of great beauty and value. Can you imagine what treasure lies hidden beneath the bandages?"

Bak found the chief scribe Ramose sitting cross-legged on a tightly woven reed mat beneath a lean-to built against the mudbrick wall of a workmen's hut. His task was to keep track of equipment and supplies, of labor performed and food and objects given in return. Two other scribes shared the burden and the square of shade cast by the palm frond roof. The older one was the large, stooped man who had taken Hori and Kasaya off to meet the chief craftsmen and foremen. The other was a child of twelve or so years, an apprentice who, if appearances did not deceive, was Ramose's son. Bak had seen the three of them together, standing among the onlookers when Montu's body had been carried away.

Ramose rose to his feet to greet him. "Welcome to my place of business, Lieutenant. I've been expecting you."

"Because you're now next in line in importance to Pashed?" Bak smiled to lighten the weight of his words. "Or because when trouble arises on a construction site, the first man to be suspected of wrongdoing is the one who keeps the accounts and minds the store?"

The chief scribe laughed. The pair behind him exchanged an uneasy look.

"Will you take a seat, sir?" Ramose pointed to a low stool he evidently reserved for worthy guests and returned to his mat. "I'm afraid the beer we have is of poor quality, but on a hot day such as this, a bitter brew is better than none."

He offered a jar, which Bak accepted. The beer on the southern frontier, usually strong and sometimes appalling, had toughened Bak's palate to a point where he could drink almost anything. He found the warm, thick, acrid liquid a close match to the worst he had ever tasted.

"As you must know," he said, "Amonked has asked me to look into Montu's death and find a cause for the many accidents here at Djeser Djeseru."

"Yes, sir." The chief scribe was in his middle years and of medium height, neither slim nor heavy. He had short, straight dark hair and the ordinary features of a man easily lost in a crowd.

"Montu's life was taken by another man," Bak said.

"So we've heard."

Bak saw not a speck of sadness or regret. Nor did he see sorrow on the faces of the other two scribes. He was reminded of Pashed's words upon seeing the body: "May the gods be blessed," he had said. "Do you think his death related to the series of accidents?"

"If he was slain by another man . . ." Ramose's eyes leaped to Bak's face, sudden concern clouding his features. "Is there some question about the accidents? Does Amonked believe they were brought about not by carelessness and the whims of the gods, but were deliberate attempts to disrupt construction with injury and death?"

The older scribe looked up from a scroll onto which he was transferring notes from a pile of hand-size limestone flakes. "The workmen talk of a malign spirit."

Bak gave him a sharp look. Could he, an educated man, truly believe such superstitious nonsense? Or was he jesting? "I seek Montu's slayer in the company of men, not among the demons of darkness. And if I find the accidents to be something other than what they've all along appeared to be, I'll look for a man, not a spirit."

Ramose scowled at the old man. "This, sir, is Amonemhab, father to my first wife, long deceased. He's a good man, but ofttimes the bane of my existence."

Looking disdainful, Amonemhab tossed the shard onto a pile of discarded flakes. "Could a man cause so many accidents? I think not. Too many occurred in the light of day with other men looking on."

"Not all were so straightforward," Ramose said.

A short burst of metallic clangs drew Bak's eyes toward a patch of shade beneath a lean-to a dozen or so paces away. Two metalsmiths, dripping sweat, toiled in the heat of a small pottery furnace, sharpening and repairing tools collected from the workmen. Ramose believed in keeping a close eye on the equipment for which he was responsible.

"With rumors of a malign spirit planting fear in men's hearts, they might well stumble or fumble or tumble, bringing about any number of accidents." Bak drank from his beer jar, taking care not to stir up the sediment that lay in the bottom. "I know for a fact that a malign spirit did not slay Montu."

"He was not well liked," Ramose admitted.

"I see no sadness among the three of you."

"Montu was a swine!" the old man said with venom.

Ramose shot a warning look his way. "You must listen to Amonemhab with half an ear, Lieutenant. He's become outspoken in his dotage and not always rational."

"Humph!" the old man said, glaring.

"Grandfather knows of what he speaks," the apprentice said. "No one liked Montu."

"Ani . . ." Ramose scowled disapproval.

With a fond smile, Amonemhab ruffled his grandson's hair. "If you seek his slayer among the men who toil at Djeser Djeseru, Lieutenant, you must look at every man here."

Thinking of corruption, of stolen equipment and false

records, Bak's eyes settled on Ramose. "Was he a man who found fault with the work of others and threatened to lay bare their mistakes?"

The chief scribe was not a stupid man. He realized what Bak was getting at and his voice grew hard, taut. "He tried to find fault, yes, but when he sniffed around here, he found nothing wrong. We allow no man to get away with what isn't his, nor do we take more than our share. We allow no theft of supplies and equipment, nor do we condone the distribution of too much or too little in return for the effort a man makes each day. The records we keep are as accurate as men can make them, the quantities checked and rechecked."

"Then you won't object if my scribe Hori looks over your accounts."

"I do object." Ramose's attempt at civility came close to failing. "I object wholeheartedly, but can I prevent it? No. Nor will I make the attempt."

"Amonked's scribes have found no fault." The old man gave Bak a sour look. "Do you think that boy of yours has a sharper eye?"

"Montu was a disgusting man!" Ani's hatred burned bright on his face. "If you're to find his slayer, look at the man himself, not us."

Ramose hissed like a snake, trying to silence him. Which alerted Bak that another truth lay close to the surface of their hearts. He set his beer jar on the sand by his feet, crossed his arms over his breast, and stared hard at the boy. "Why do you feel so strongly about him?"

Ani looked down at the scroll in his lap, mumbled, "Everyone hated him. Not me alone. Everyone."

"You know as well as I that no secrets remain hidden for long, especially in a place of work such as this." Bak spoke to the father and not the son. "I don't know what you're hiding, but you can be sure I'll soon learn. If not from you, from someone else. A tale built upon by the teller's imagination, which may or may not be in your favor."

The boy looked one way and another, refusing to meet his

father's blame-filled eyes. Rather like a beetle caught in a deep bowl, scrabbling here and there and everywhere for a means of escape.

"All right," Ramose said, his voice harsh, angry. "Montu made advances to my new wife. She's young and I like to think her beautiful. That imbecile . . ." He glared at his son, who looked mortified. ". . . was born of my first wife, who died bearing me a daughter some years ago."

"Montu went to our house while we toiled here." The old man spat out the words; that he shared Ramose's anger was plain. "He wanted the woman, said if she didn't comply he'd send the three of us to the distant frontier. With no one in Waset to protect her, she'd have to submit."

The boy's gloom vanished in an unexpected grin. "He didn't know her very well, did he, grandfather?"

A hint of a smile flickered through the old man's anger. "He grabbed her, tried to force her. She screamed for a servant, who came running. A mere child, but one of infinite courage. She hit him on the head with a stool, forcing him to release Ramose's wife."

"Paralyzed with fear at what she'd done, the servant backed off." Ramose's chin came up and his breast swelled with pride. "Fearing he'd not give up, my wife threw a hot brazier, which shattered on his back, throwing forth the smoldering fuel and burning him."

"A well-deserved reward," Bak said, "but I'm surprised he didn't retaliate by sending you away."

"Blackmail can go both ways." Ramose bared his teeth in a mockery of a smile. "He thought because he was of exalted status, he could do as he wished. That same pride in his lofty position made him loath to be made to look the fool."

Chapter Five

"We talked with twelve men and not one among them doubts that a malign spirit walks within this valley." Hori laid his writing implements on the lap of a rough-finished white limestone seated statue of Maatkare Hatshepsut and bent to scratch an ankle. "They speak with certainty, but when pressed for details, they say, 'Oh, Ahmose told me . . . ' or 'Montu said . . . ' or 'Sobekhotep swears he saw . . . ' "

"You spoke with whom?" Bak asked.

"The craftsmen toiling in the sanctuary and memorial chapels. We had no time to speak with anyone else."

Rubbing the sweat from his face, Bak dropped onto a large irregular block of sandstone lying on the terrace between the completed portion of the southern retaining wall and the ramp that led downward. He could hear the men below singing an age-old workmen's song, its words repetitive, as monotonous as their task of relaying the final baskets of fill into the tomb where Montu had been slain.

"Interesting," he said. "I saw no fear among them yesterday, yet the sanctuary and chapels are places of relative solitude. Places where a malign spirit might seek them out."

Kasaya sat down on the base of the white statue and leaned back against his sovereign's stone legs. "Perhaps they feel the lord Amon's presence."

"It's the heart of the temple, yes," Hori scoffed, "but it's not been sanctified."

The Medjay's expression remained earnest, untroubled by the scribe's teasing. "The spirit's only been seen at night, and seldom up there."

"Most of the accidents have taken place in the light of day," Bak pointed out, "while the men were toiling at their various tasks."

"No artists have been slain, sir." Hori rested a hip against a limestone thigh. "One man was hurt some months ago. A scaffold collapsed when he was outlining the images high on the face of a wall. He was thrown to the floor and his arm was broken. If the malign spirit loosened the rope that bound the poles, it did so at night."

"They now look more closely at their scaffolds," Kasaya said.

"And each morning," Hori added, "they bend a knee in what's left of the temple of our sovereign's worthy ancestors, Djeserkare Amonhotep and his revered mother Ahmose Nefertari."

The youth pointed east toward the remains of mudbrick walls that were gradually being consumed as the terrace was extended. One outer wall rose to shoulder height, but the remaining walls were lower, their bricks carried away to be used elsewhere in construction ramps and as fill. What little remained of the lower courses and foundation was covered over as the terrace was lengthened.

Silently cursing the superstitions that made men so illogical, Bak eyed the workmen's huts clumped together like a small, impoverished village on the broad strip of sand between Djeser Djeseru and the ancient temple of Nebhepetre Montuhotep. The chief scribe Ramose dwelt there much of the time, though he had talked of a more comfortable home in a village at the edge of the river valley.

"Where's this malign spirit most often seen?" he asked.

"Sometimes over there." Hori pointed toward the ruined temple beyond the huts. "Sometimes in the old tombs on the slopes overlooking this valley." He waved his hand in the general direction of distant colonnades visible on the hill-

sides. "Sometimes on this terrace among the unfinished statues and architectural elements."

Kasaya's eyes darted around the immediate vicinity. He
tried to appear casual, tried hard not to betray his fear that
the malign spirit might be hidden among the surrounding
blocks of stone.

"Almost everywhere, you're saying."

"It's never gone near the workmen's huts, so they say."

"Amazing," Bak said, not at all amazed.

He looked upward, but could see nothing of the heart of
the temple. The upper colonnade that would serve as its facade was a long way from being finished, as was the wall behind it, but the terrace on which he stood was too low to
allow him to see inside. The workmen's huts in the hollow
between the two temples were considerably lower. "Where
are the night guards when the malign spirit shows itself?
Have they ever seen it?"

"We'll talk with them next, sir," the scribe said.

"Ask them." Bak scowled. "Also, you must find out what
they do when they see it. Do they run away? Or have they
tried to catch it?" He suspected they turned their backs, preferring to have seen nothing rather than risk the gods alone
knew what in a vain attempt to catch a wraith.

"Catch it, sir?" Kasaya asked, looking incredulous.

"If they reported to me, they'd at least try. They'd better."
Bak left no doubt how he felt about men who failed to do
their duty. To Hori, he asked, "What appearance does this
spirit take?"

"It's never seen in the daylight, as you said yourself, sir.
At night it's either a dark and distant shadow in the moonlight or a spot of light flitting among the stones."

Bak looked thoughtfully at the cluster of workmen's huts.
Unpainted mudbrick. Light roofs of reed, palm frond, and
mud construction. A lean-to added here and there. "The
craftsmen dwell in villages outside this valley, do they not?"

"Most dwell in a village near the end of the ridge to the
north." Lieutenant Menna, who had approached so silently

none of the three had heard him, came the rest of the way up
the ramp and crossed to them. "It's within easy walking distance so they can go home each night and return the next
morning."

"That's why none have seen the malign spirit," Bak said
to Hori and Kasaya. "They're never here during the hours of
darkness when it shows itself."

"Then that's why they know nothing of Montu's death,"
the scribe said. "They weren't here the night he was slain."

"If he was slain in the night," Bak said.

Grimacing, Menna brushed a faint trace of dust off his
kilt. "Your morning, it seems, has been as unproductive as
mine."

Bak studied the guard officer, who was almost as neat and
clean as when they had first met. Dusty feet and a rivulet of
sweat trickling down his breast betrayed no greater effort
than walking from the river to Djeser Djeseru. He could not
resist asking, "You've been looking for rifled tombs?"

Menna looked sincerely rueful. "Unfortunately not. I had
reports to dictate. I'd barely finished when I received
Pashed's message that another tomb had been found."

Rising to his feet, Bak looked across the blocks of stone
toward Ineni, the man Pashed had assigned to watch the
open shaft. The guard, a lean man of medium height with a
reddish birthmark on his neck, was leaning against the reclining lion statue, talking to a dozen or so men. Telling tales
of a treasure, he felt sure. Irritated, he asked, "Did you bring
the priest Kaemwaset?"

"I couldn't find him, so I thought it best I come without
him. As soon as I return to Waset, I'll look further. With luck
and the favor of the lord Amon, we'll return before nightfall."

Bak cursed beneath his breath. "I hope the tomb is made
safe before dark. I'll sleep better tonight if it's closed and
sealed for eternity."

"You saw jewelry on the body, Pashed said."

"We did."

Menna stared at the cluster of men near the reclining lion.
"Ineni is a good man, but I think it best I assign Imen to the
task. He's more responsible by far—and not nearly so talka-
tive." Looking none too enthusiastic, the officer added, "After I've dealt with that, I must see the tomb."

Bak glanced around in search of Pashed, but the chief architect was nowhere to be seen. Rather than take the time to
search for him, he said, "I'll go with you."

He did not mistrust Menna, but he was firmly convinced
that no man should enter a tomb alone. Especially a sepulcher in which jewelry had been seen. At least not until the
men who were robbing the dead were snared and taken
away.

"You see the bracelets," Bak said, bending over the
wrapped body, his eyes on the jewelry glittering in the torchlight. "They're of similar workmanship to those I found in
Buhen. I'd not be surprised to find that they all were made in
a royal workshop."

Menna knelt for a closer look. "If the shaft hadn't been so
securely closed, the stones too heavy for a few wretched
robbers to move without discovery, I'd suspect the objects
you found came from this very tomb."

Bak could understand how tempting the thought was. To
conclude that one tomb was being rifled was far more palat-
able than the thought that several had been robbed. Which
he was certain was the case. The jewelry he had found in the
honey jar had been that of royalty. The individual in this
small tomb had been important, but not so exalted.

"This makes me more certain than ever that the looted
sepulchers are to be found in this area." He had no authority
to tell the guard officer how best to perform his task, but he
had every right to ask a few questions. "Have you begun to
look again at the cemeteries in western Waset? Especially
those near here, where Nebhepetre Montuhotep, his successors, and their noble followers were entombed?"

Menna's voice grew stiff, defensive. "I wanted first to finish the reports I spoke of earlier. Now that dreary task is complete, leaving me free to lead my men on a new search." He stood up, added with a stingy smile, "Never fear, Lieutenant. We'll begin at first light tomorrow, retracing our steps once again, examining the burial places with the same diligence as before."

With increased diligence, I hope, Bak thought.

The torch sputtered, emitting a puff of smoke. The odor of burned oil blended with the smell of decay and dry, dusty flowers.

"Don't misunderstand me." Bak turned away from the body and, holding the flickering torch before them, led the way down the horizontal tunnel. "I'm in no way criticizing you. I know from experience how difficult it is to snare a man whose very life depends upon remaining unknown and free."

"I've had no experience in pursuing criminals of so vile a nature," Menna admitted, "but I well know the cemeteries in western Waset, and I know even better the men who dwell here, many of whom look with a covetous eye upon the tombs and the vast wealth they believe they contain."

"Do you have suspects?"

"I suspect them all."

In other words, Bak thought, he has no idea who the thief is. He vowed again to keep his eyes open—wide open. And, at the first opportunity, to explore the burial places around Djeser Djeseru and the neighboring temple.

At the top of the shaft the guard Menna had selected had replaced Ineni. Imen was a man of medium height and years with ruddy weathered skin, strong muscles, and the work-hardened hands of one who had toiled in the fields or on the water for much of his life. He looked to be tough and tenacious, a man not easily frightened. Warned not to gossip, he stood alone. Bak wondered if he would maintain his silence after they left.

"Montu was a pompous ass." The chief artist Heribsen was either totally without guile or did not care what Bak thought. "The less I had to do with him the happier I was. I went out of my way to avoid him."

"This temple site is large, but much of it is open to view," Bak said. "You surely saw him at a distance."

The gnome-like man led him through the gap in the incomplete wall and into the temple and its unfinished courtyard. The lord Re had dropped behind the western mountain, leaving much of the building in the shade of the cliff that rose high above it. "He may've been slain two days ago, you say?"

"We found him yesterday, as you know. He died the night before or the previous day, I'd guess. Common sense says in the night, but . . ." He spread his hands wide, shrugged. "Who knows?"

"I did see him that day," Heribsen admitted. "Near mid-afternoon, it was. I'd come up here to take a look at the sanctuary and I saw him on the terrace below." He laughed—at himself, Bak felt sure. "I slipped inside, hiding from him, plain and simple."

Bak smiled, sharing the jest, but quickly sobered. "Why did you feel so strongly about him?"

"He was critical of anything and everything. He'd strut into the sanctuary or one of the chapels, brush and pallet in hand. He'd look around at the drawings, approach a figure already corrected and ready to carve—never one that needed altering, mind you—and he'd make some nonsensical change."

"Always?" Bak walked into the antechamber of the chapel to the lord Re. He strolled around, looking at the lovely colored reliefs of Maatkare Hatshepsut making offerings, each image creating an ideal of royal piety. The colors were as vivid and bright as if touched by the sun. "These walls look perfect to me, blessed by the gods."

The chief artist was too involved in his complaint to notice the compliment. "At first, I and my men were furious, which added zest to the stew, making Montu all the meaner. He began to demand that the reliefs be changed, a far more harmful and difficult task than altering a drawing." He ran a loving hand over a brightly painted, deftly carved image of the lord Amon. "This was one of the first, I recall. He insisted the face be identical to that of our sovereign, softened to look like a woman. I was furious and so was the man who'd carved it. You see what a marvelous job he did. What dolt would change that?"

Bak frowned, puzzled. "I don't understand. You say Montu made ridiculous changes, yet this relief is nothing less than perfection."

"Your praise is appreciated—and well-founded." Heribsen's sudden smile was like night turning to day. "This is the original figure, which he told us to alter and we failed to do."

Bak eyed the little man with interest, the bright twinkling eyes, the laughter that threatened to bubble forth at any moment. "Explain yourself, Heribsen. Your good spirits tell me you won a battle Montu never realized he lost."

"You're a perceptive man, Lieutenant." The chief artist rubbed his hands together in delight. "We knew Montu wouldn't return for a couple of days, so we went on with the work as originally drawn, praying he'd forget, agreeing we'd all pay the price if he remembered." A chuckle bubbled out. "He did forget! He went instead to another relief, demanding changes there."

"How often did this happen?" Bak asked, smiling.

"Regularly." Heribsen had trouble containing his laughter. "His stupidity became a joke the width and breadth of Djeser Djeseru. I've been told that the other craftsmen, all of whom he plagued as often as he did us, adapted the ploy to their own situations."

"Your good humor does you credit, Heribsen. Pashed does not speak so lightly of Montu."

The chief artist grew serious. "He bore the weight of Montu's indolence and haughty attitude. He could not so easily shrug him off."

"Amonked told me Montu was an accomplished architect, and Pashed agreed."

"He was, yes, but he was not an artist." Heribsen led him

out of the antechamber, into the unfinished court. "He knew where a column should be placed to best advantage and he could tell us to place reliefs of offerings in a chamber where offerings were to be made, but he knew nothing of drawing the human face or figure."

With the sun's bright rays unable to reach the open court, the mirrors could throw no light inside the surrounding rooms. The artists who toiled within the sanctuary, the first chamber to be so deprived, were hurrying down the ramp to the terrace. Other men were filing out of the southern antechamber, preparing to leave.

Bak raised a hand to stop them. "I know how eager you must be to go to your village and your homes, but I'm sorely in need of help."

The eight men bunched together outside the door, querying each other with looks that ranged from fear to curiosity.

"Yes, sir?" a tentative voice piped up from among them.

"We've never seen the malign spirit," a tall, thin man said.

"Never," said a grizzled old man, "and so we told your scribe and the Medjay."

Heribsen glared. "Malign spirit! Bah!"

"I've another, different question," Bak said, giving them a smile he hoped would reassure them. "One my men failed to ask."

Heribsen's glowering countenance brooked no refusal to comply. They nodded in reluctant accord.

"When did you last see the chief architect Montu?"

To a man, the men relaxed, preferring to speak of the dead rather than the unknown.

A short man with paint-stained fingers stepped forward. "He came two days ago, sir, shortly before we lost the sun. He went from one wall to another, examining the painting we'd done and the carving of reliefs. We thought he'd never finish."

"When he finally left, we waited a few moments and then followed him down the ramp," the older man said. "The last we saw of him was down there . . ." He pointed vaguely toward the end of the southern retaining wall. ". . . near the white statue of our sovereign."

"Did he seem happy? Angry? Expectant? He was apparently in no hurry. Did he seem to be awaiting someone?"

Again the men looked at each other, trying to decide. Bak suspected they had all been so eager to go home, they had noticed nothing but the passage of time.

"He criticized, as always, but not with his usual scathing tongue, and he demanded no changes." The bald man who spoke glanced at his fellows, seeking agreement. Several nods drove him on. "We joked later, saying he must be looking forward to a night of pleasure."

Well satisfied, Bak thanked them with a smile and sent them on their way. He had narrowed the time of death considerably. Montu had been slain sometime in the evening or, more likely, early in the night, a time when the malign spirit was said to appear.

Following the men down the ramp, he said, "Tell me of the malign spirit, Heribsen."

"I've never seen it, nor do I expect to."

"You don't believe it exists?"

"I don't."

"What of the many deaths and injuries at Djeser Djeseru? Do you believe them accidents and nothing more?"

A long silence carried them to the base of the ramp. The chief artist stopped and offered a smile, but it was off center, lacking his usual good humor. "How can I speak of accidents when thus far my crew has remained untouched?"

"A scaffold fell, I've been told, and a man injured."

"It fell within the sanctuary while we were painting an upper wall. A binding had come loose, a knot that didn't hold. We inspect them more carefully these days."

"Did the malign spirit make the scaffold unsafe? Or was it done at the hands of a man?"

Heribsen looked pained. "Would a man come up here in the dead of night to loosen a binding when all who toil here know a malign spirit inhabits this valley?"

"But you don't believe in a malign spirit."

"I don't. Nor would I risk my life to come in the dark to do damage to a scaffold."

Bak gave up. Heribsen did not believe, but he feared. The contradiction confounded him.

"They say the tomb contains a treasure." Useramon, the chief sculptor responsible for the army of statues that would one day adorn Djeser Djeseru, stared toward Imen across the many blocks of stone lying on the terrace. The guard stood alone; the priest had not arrived. "Is that true?"

Bak had known the news would spread, but it irritated him nonetheless. "The sepulcher is small," he said, avoiding an outright lie, "and contains a few wooden models and some pottery as well as the wrapped body."

"From what I heard . . ."

"I'm here to speak of Montu, Useramon."

The large, heavily muscled sculptor nodded, unperturbed by the implied reproach. "Heribsen and I spent many an hour complaining about him, I can tell you." He sprinkled a soft piece of leather with water and dabbed it in a bowl of silica powder, collecting a thin layer of the shiny abrasive. "For all the good it did us."

"You spoke to Senenmut?"

"To Pashed, who had problems of his own."

Bak seated himself on the legs of the colossal red granite statue of Maatkare Hatshepsut he had found the sculptor polishing with loving care. The image lay on its back, Useramon on his knees beside it, toiling on its right shoulder. When standing to his full height, Bak guessed the craftsman would be two hands taller than the diminutive chief artist. They must be quite a sight when walking together, he thought. "Heribsen told me of his complaints. What were yours?"

"We're artists, too, and he treated us as such. He never ceased to criticize our work or failed to alter the patterns drawn on the stone. At first he was content with that, but during the past year or so, he waited until the sculpting began, the early stages too far along to reasonably change the image." Useramon placed the gritty leather on the statue's arm and began to rub the surface. "If he'd not been so friendly with Senenmut, so quick to tell tales, I'd have waylaid him in a dark and empty lane and . . ." He looked up, laughed softly. "Well, he'd think the malign spirit gentle in comparison."

"You didn't let him think you'd changed the design when you hadn't, as Heribsen's crew did?"

"We did, but the need to pretend was as vexatious as making the changes." Useramon grinned. "Well, not quite. At least we had the satisfaction of producing a respectable piece of sculpture."

The whisper of the abrasive, the methodical back and forth movement, could easily put a man to sleep, Bak thought. "Didn't you enjoy making him look the fool?"

"I'd have enjoyed it more if he'd had the wit to see what we were doing. My one regret is that he was slain before this temple was finished. I planned to tell him on the day of its dedication how foolish we'd made him look."

Bak glanced toward the tomb where Imen stood. The sun was sinking behind the western peak, casting a bright red afterglow high into the sky. If Kaemwaset did not soon arrive, the tomb would remain open through the night. "Has your crew been involved in any of the many accidents that have occurred on this project?"

"We don't invite trouble, Lieutenant. When a statue must be lowered to the ground or raised, when it must be moved, we summon ordinary workmen to do the task for us."

"The malign spirit has struck no one toiling for you? Neither sculptor nor workman?"

"Malign spirit." Useramon's hand stopped moving, he looked up from his task and barked out a laugh. "A statue did roll off a sledge on which it was being moved, and a workman's ankle was broken. That was sheer bad luck, nothing more. The rope with which it was secured was faulty. I saw for myself the weakened fibers."

"Did Heribsen not tell you of the scaffold that collapsed beneath one of his men?"

"He told me. We both agreed that a malign spirit had nothing to do with either accident. As I said before, it was bad luck. Nothing more, nothing less."

"He failed to discount altogether the idea of a malign spirit."

Useramon returned to his task. "All the world knows such spirits exist. The question is: why would one inhabit this valley? A shrine to the lady Hathor has existed here since the beginning of time. The ancient temple of Nebhepetre Montuhotep has been a place of deep respect for many generations. The temple of our sovereign's illustrious ancestor Djeserkare Amonhotep and his beloved mother Ahmose Nefertari, the remains of which can still be seen at the end of this terrace, has been a place to bend a knee for many years."

"A new shrine has been started for the lady Hathor, making the old one useless," Bak countered. "Stones are being taken from the ancient temple to be used in the new. And the old temple of Djeserkare Amonhotep and his mother will vanish beneath this terrace. Maybe a man and not a spirit is annoyed that Djeser Djeseru is supplanting so much of the past."

The whisper of grit on stone stopped. Useramon looked up. "I've several times asked my village scribe to write a message on the side of a bowl, pleading that such was the case. I've filled the bowl with food offerings and left them at the temple of Nebhepetre Montuhotep, where the spirit most often has been seen."

Unable to think of an appropriate response, Bak rose to his feet, bade good-bye to the sculptor, and headed toward the newly opened tomb and the guard Imen. He marveled again at how quick the men were to deny the existence of the malign spirit, yet how firmly they believed.

"Menna never returned." Bak did not bother to hide his exasperation. The guard officer's sense of urgency was certainly not his own.

"He said he'd be back, sir. With a priest. But they haven't come." Imen stood like a rock, a man untroubled by the broken promises of men more lofty than he. "I doubt they will now. The day's too far gone."

"What'll we do, sir?" Hori asked.

Bak stared at the open mouth of the tomb, an invitation to robbery, and the darkness overtaking the valley. "You must spend the night here, Imen."

"So I assumed." The guard looked at the twin streams of men, some hurrying away from the temple to homes near the river valley, the majority walking at a slower pace toward the workmen's huts. "I'll need something to eat, sir."

"Hori can bring food." Bak looked again at the open shaft. He recalled the thin sliver of moon he had seen in the sky the previous night and guessed how dark this valley would get. He thought of the tale of a treasure the artisans would take with them to their homes, and how fast it would spread throughout the surrounding villages. He envisioned a man bent on theft sneaking up on a man alone.

His eyes darted toward Kasaya, who stood beside the lion-bodied statue of their sovereign. The Medjay's expression was bleak. He had traveled with Bak often enough to guess what lay in his heart.

"I know how eager you are to go home to your mother, Kasaya, but you must remain here with Imen."

"Yes, sir," Kasaya mumbled without a spark of enthusiasm.

"I can stand alone, sir." Imen nodded toward his spear and shield. "I'm well able to take care of myself."

Hori stared wide-eyed. "Don't you fear the malign spirit?"

Bak shot an annoyed glance at the youth. "He has far more to fear from thieves sneaking up in the night than a distant shadow or speck of light."

After parting from Hori at the edge of the floodplain, Bak walked alone along the raised path that would take him to his father's farm. The heat of the day had waned and a thin haze was settling over the river. Faint points of starlight were visible in the darkening sky. The soft evening air smelled of braised fish and onions, of animals and some fragrant blossom he could not see.

Why would anyone slay Montu? he wondered. The man had not been well-liked. He had, in fact, gone out of his way to anger one and all. However, his would-be victims had ignored his senseless demands, making him look the fool, a figure of fun. Who would slay a beast whose fangs and claws had been pulled?

Chapter Six

"You left Imen to guard the tomb alone?" Bak, who had hastened to Djeser Djeseru at daybreak, glared at Kasaya. He prayed the Medjay was making a poor joke, but his too-stiff spine, his guilt-ridden look, spoke of a man who had disobeyed orders. "Explain yourself!"

"I wasn't gone for long." Kasaya stared straight ahead, unable to meet Bak's eyes. "Half an hour at most." With one hand he clung to his spear and shield, in the other he held a packet wrapped in leaves, food Bak had brought for the young man's morning meal.

"What, in the name of the lord Amon, possessed you?"

"The malign spirit."

Bak bestowed upon him the countenance of a man sorely tried. "Spirits possess men who know no better, Kasaya. Men of no learning who know nothing of the world beyond their field of vision. Not men who've traveled to the far horizon, as you have."

The Medjay gave Bak a hurt look. "You misunderstand, sir. I saw the spirit and I gave chase."

Bak recalled their conversation of the previous day, the comments he had made about the guards and his feelings about men who failed to do their duty. Kasaya, though superstitious to the core, had taken his words to heart, it seemed.

Irritation fleeing, he dropped onto a stone drum awaiting

79

placement as part of a sixteen-sided column on the upper
level in front of the temple. "Seat yourself, Kasaya, and
while you eat, tell me what happened."

Not entirely reassured by the milder tone, the young Medjay sat down on a similar drum. Laying spear and shield beside him, he unwrapped the packet and began to eat the
braised fish and green onions he found inside. Imen, at the
mouth of the tomb thirty or so paces away, was also eating.

The lord Khepre, peeking above the eastern horizon,
sent shafts of yellow into an unblemished sky. A thin sil-
ver mist hovered over the floodplain to the east, filtering
into the faint blue morning haze lingering over the river.
The workmen, early to rise and quick to begin their day,
were spread over the building site, as vociferous as men
who had been parted for days rather than the few short
hours of night.

"Two, maybe three hours after nightfall, Imen thought he
saw a light among the columns of the upper colonnade."
Kasaya tore away a bite-sized chunk of fish and popped it
into his mouth. "At first I saw nothing, but then I, too, spotted a light. It looked to be entering the temple. Since every
man who toils here fears the malign spirit . . . Well, I knew
none of them would go into the temple in the dead of night."
He stopped chewing, his voice grew hushed. "My blood
went cold, and the worm of fear crept up my spine."

"Yet you gave chase," Bak said, knowing well the
strength of will it must have taken.

"Not because I wanted to, I tell you." Kasaya broke off
another chunk and paused, holding it in midair halfway to
his mouth. "Giving myself no time to think, I raced across
this terrace, passing innumerable statues and sections of
columns behind which hid I knew not what. Up the ramp I
went, and into the temple. The building was dark, the moon
a sliver so thin and weak the unfinished colonnade cast no
shadow." He glanced at the piece of fish in his hand, returned it to its bed of leaves. "I saw no one, heard nothing. I
felt obliged to search the sanctuary and the chapels to either

side. I crossed the courtyard to the sanctuary, but beyond its portal lay nothing but black. As was the case in the rooms to the south. I feared greatly and longed for a torch."

Bak could almost see the young Medjay, standing in the dark, wide-eyed and quaking with fear, trying to convince himself to step into one of those fearsome chambers.

"I heard a faint noise behind me. I spun around and spotted the light. It was near the entrance to the chapel of the lord Re. A tiny flicker that vanished in an instant." Kasaya took a deep, ragged breath. "Thinking it had gone inside, I followed. All the while I walked around the altar, I thanked the lord Re that the chamber had no roof, that I could see my hand before my face. I found nothing; the light had vanished like the spirit it was."

Or, more likely, a quick and agile man, Bak thought. One with a vile sense of humor. "Did you smell anything? Smoke, for example, from an oil lamp?"

"No, sir." Kasaya lifted the bite of fish to his mouth and ate. "I smelled nothing, heard nothing, saw nothing more."

"The sanctuary and the southern chambers were empty?"

Kasaya flung him a guilty look. "I peeked inside, sir, but in the end I didn't search them. They were too dark, and I could see nothing. Anyone or anything hiding there could've slipped past me and I'd have known no better." Giving Bak no time for comment good or bad, he hurried on, "Instead, thinking you'd say I'd chased a man and not a spirit, I seated myself in the entrance near the top of the ramp, intending to remain until daylight, hoping to catch a man if a man it was." He paused, frowned, offered up another point in his favor, "From there I could see Imen and go to his aid if need be."

"He'd remained at his post?"

"Yes, sir. He told me later that he'd never have chased the malign spirit, as I did. I think he was afraid. He didn't admit he was and spoke instead of disobeying orders, but how long has the malign spirit been seen in this valley with no guards giving chase?"

"How long did you stay at the temple?"

"I'd barely had time to settle myself when I glimpsed a light in the old temple of Nebhepetre Montuhotep. The spirit had flitted from Djeser Djeseru to there in the time it takes to blink an eye. I started down the ramp, but it vanished again. I ran to the southern retaining wall and waited awhile, but it didn't reappear. Certain no man could ever catch it, I finally decided to return to the tomb and Imen."

Bak suspected the so-called malign spirit had lured Kasaya into the chapel of the lord Re, and had slipped out of the temple when he was safely out of the way. He also suspected, because of the light's speedy appearance in the older temple, that more than one man had been roaming the valley floor, each carrying a small oil lamp.

He glanced across the field of partially worked stones toward the burly guard. "As far as you know, did Imen remain at his post all the while you were searching the temple?"

"I can't swear to every moment," Kasaya admitted, "but each time I looked, there he was."

Bak eyed the young Medjay. By rights he should chastise him for abandoning his post at the tomb, but how could he reproach a man who had shown such courage in spite of his strong superstition, his fear of the unknown?

"Go back to the tomb and stay there," he said. "Let me know when Menna arrives with the priest from the mansion of the lord Amon."

Could Imen have entered the tomb during Kasaya's absence? Probably not. Visible from the temple and assuming the Medjay might return at any moment, the guard would have had neither the time nor the freedom to do so. Nonetheless, Bak wanted to know for a fact that the body was intact, to be sure the ancient jewelry was on that bony wrist when the tomb was sealed for eternity.

As Kasaya strode away, Bak walked to the southern retaining wall and looked beyond the workmen's huts to the old temple of Nebhepetre Montuhotep. Had the Medjay been deliberately drawn into the new temple? If so, for what purpose? To allow the malign spirit freedom of movement in the ruined structure? No one could have predicted the young policeman would have the courage to leave Imen's side and give chase, but if the objective was worthy enough, perhaps the risk could not be ignored. Or had the second light, that in the old temple, been meant to draw Kasaya from Djeser Djeseru? Had he interrupted someone intent on setting up another accident?

"There's Kames, sir, the chief stonemason." Hori, arriving at Bak's side unnoticed, pointed toward a crew of workmen toiling at the northern end of the lower colonnade. "You said you wished to speak with him. The white-haired man looking on."

Bak tore his thoughts from Kasaya's adventure and tamped down a sudden, nearly overwhelming desire to explore the ruined temple. He must speak first with the living, saving until later his quest for lights and shadows.

"I found plenty to fault in Montu, but he knew what he had to do and he did it." Kames scratched his head, making his short white hair stand on end. His body was tall and angular, very thin, a living skeleton covered in leather-like skin. "You can't criticize a man for doing his duty, now can you?"

"You're more forgiving than anyone else I've talked to," Bak said. "In fact, I've been told he shirked his duty."

"He was critical, to be sure, and never quite satisfied with where we placed the stones. But he had every right to be. The responsibility for the finished temple rested heavily on his shoulders."

Kames's eyes darted toward a man checking the four sides of a block of stone, making sure they were square to each other and the top surface. Evidently not quite satisfied with what he saw, he moved closer to watch. The stone was one of many that would be stacked to create the square columns of the lower colonnade. The sides of the stone, like that of its mates, were rough, not yet dressed to a smooth surface. The final smoothing would be done after they were installed, before reliefs were carved and painted. Other stonemasons were scattered nearby, forming blocks similar in shape and size. The tapping of mallets on chisels made Bak think of giant birds, pecking away at some equally colossal food source. Two rows of square columns would ultimately stand before the retaining wall that held back the fill beneath the upper colonnade. As Bak had noticed before, the roof over this portico would form an open terrace along the front of the temple.

For the first time, he was struck by the fact that no construction ramps marred the facade to either side of the central ramp. "You surely use a ramp to raise these blocks into position, and also the architraves and roof slabs that will sit on top. Why is none here?"

Several of the men glanced at each other and exchanged surreptitious grins. The chief stonemason's expression turned stormy. Bak saw at once that he had poured natron into an open wound.

"The last time our sovereign visited this temple, we had to take down the ramp we had here and another at the southern colonnade." Kames's nostrils flared with anger. "Senenmut said she wished to see the facade unencumbered by ramps, and so it was. I thought it wise not to replace them for a while, to rough out many of the column parts so we can position them all at one time. Thus saving us extra effort should she soon come again."

A prudent decision, Bak suspected. Much effort was required to build or tear down a ramp. Not as much as building a permanent mudbrick or stone structure, but the number of hours expended could be better used elsewhere. "Did Pashed not shoulder more than his burden of responsibility, while Montu sought the ear of Senenmut, taking much of the credit for building this temple?"

Kames shook his head in mild disgust. "Oh, I know. Pashed complained all the time, saying this, that, and the other. Always critical of Montu, with never a word of praise.

But you have to understand: Montu was an artist while Pashed is a mere artisan. You can't expect an artist to take an interest in the dreary day-to-day tasks of a project as big and important as this one."

An unexpected puff of air lifted the dust from the steep slope to the north and flung it on the men below. Bak snapped his eyes and mouth shut as grit peppered his face and shoulders. Kames's attitude was so different from that of the others to whom he had spoken that he could not help but wonder about the discrepancy. "Were you and Montu related in any way?"

A toothy grin let him know the stonemason understood exactly what he was getting at. "We weren't even friendly."

The smile, the flippant tone, promised a game of words Bak refused to be drawn into. A stream of curses drew his eyes to the northern retaining wall, where a crew of workmen were dragging a sledge laden with stone blocks up a construction ramp. Given time, Kames would explain himself, he felt sure. "You know Amonked has bade me look into the many accidents that have occurred since construction began on this temple."

The stonemason's smile was swept away by an inexplicable bitterness. "I wish you luck, Lieutenant."

Bak eyed him closely. That he had struck a sensitive spot was apparent. "You and your men work with the stone, sometimes placing heavy blocks high above a man's head. Have you lost anyone to an accident?"

Kames glanced at the men scattered in front of what would one day be the colonnade, beckoned Bak to follow, and walked far enough away that none could hear. "A man died. Ahotep. A foreman." He spat out the words, his voice hard, rough with emotion. "Seven months ago, it was. We'd just begun to raise the columns at the northern end of the portico, the end nearest the southern retaining wall."

"How did it happen?"

"A part of the cliff broke away, sending stones plummeting down the slope and onto the temple." Kames stared balefully at the cliff and went on with obvious effort. "Ahotep had gone up the ramp along which we were raising the blocks. We'd reached no higher than the second course, so the ramp was low. He was checking the placement of stones, making sure they were seated properly. An enormous boulder came hurtling down from the face of the cliff, bringing others with it and tearing away lesser rocks and earth. The retaining wall collapsed and he was struck down. Buried. We dug him out, but could do nothing for him. His back was broken. He lived an hour that seemed a day, unable to move, helpless." The stonemason cleared his throat, but could not clear away the grief on his face. "His death was a gift of the gods."

Laying a gentle hand on Kames's shoulder, Bak said, "He was close to you, I see."

"He was my firstborn son."

Bak muttered an oath. No wonder the old man ached. "Were any other men injured?"

Another puff of air, this stronger than the first, blew dirt across the terrace. Bak swung away and raised his hands to his face, protecting eyes and mouth. As the breeze abated, he saw Kames wiping tears from his cheeks, tears of anguish, he felt sure, not moisture caused by the grit.

"Four were hurt," the stonemason said. "Two will never toil again as once they did, their limbs too damaged to regain strength. The others are now raising the walls of a set of chambers our sovereign is having built in the mansion of the lord Amon in Waset."

A bitter blow, Bak thought. Most of the work crews were men who had toiled together for years. To lose so many would not only upset the smooth functioning of the crew, but would rend the survivors' hearts for months to come. "Do you, like most of the men toiling here at Djeser Djeseru, believe a malign spirit responsible for the accident?"

"I'd like to think not. I'd like to believe that one day I'll lay hands on the one who loosed the rocks and break his back as my son's back was broken. A vain hope, I'm forced to admit. How could a man make a cliff face fall?"

Eyeing the cliff looming above the northern retaining wall, Bak made a silent vow to climb up and see if he could find an answer to that question. Unfortunately, four months was a long time. Too long, he suspected, to find telltale signs of a man—if a man had indeed been responsible. The cliff face and the tower-like formations that had formed at the front of it were high and steep, cracked and pitted, scarred where rock had broken away and fallen. The slide might well have been a natural occurrence. "Does the accident have anything to do with your dislike of Pashed, your sympathy with Montu?"

Kames flung Bak a quick, smoldering look. "Pashed allowed us no time to mourn, no time to make peace within ourselves. He sent the crew back to this northern end of the portico. The men feared another rockfall above all things, but what choice did they have? They returned and here they remain. Montu faced Pashed, saying no men should be put to such a test. His words struck deaf ears."

Bak had always heard that if a man came close to drowning, he should immediately go back into the water. If such was the case, and he had no way of knowing the truth of the matter, Pashed had done the right thing. "Was Montu sincere, or did he wish to make himself look good in your eyes and Pashed look bad?"

"Why would he wish me to think well of him? I'm a lowly stonemason, a man of no wealth or influence."

Uneasy about the open tomb, Bak stood at the rim and looked into the darkness below. Would Menna never bring the priest? Did the guard lieutenant have another report he felt more important than seeing that the shaft was filled before nightfall?

He eyed the long palm trunk that had been removed from the opening and laid alongside after he and Menna had returned to the surface the previous day. The urge to go down again, to have another look around, was difficult to resist, but in the end he decided to wait. However, if Menna failed to bring the priest by mid-afternoon . . .

"Here they come, sir." Kasaya pointed eastward toward the causeway. "Lieutenant Menna and the priest."

Relieved, Bak watched the guard officer weave a path among the worked and unworked chunks of stone scattered across the terrace. A slight older man and a boy of ten or so years trailed in his wake. The man's hair was close-cropped and he wore a knee-length kilt. He had to be the priest. The youth carried a basket containing, Bak assumed, a censor, water jar, incense, and everything else required to purify the tomb. The wind gusted, raising the dust around their naked limbs and the stone images among which they walked.

As the trio drew near, Bak smiled. "I thank the lord Amon that you've arrived, Lieutenant. I was making ready to go into the tomb to check its integrity."

"Why?" Menna gave him a sharp look. "I've every confidence that Imen remained on guard through the night."

"As did Kasaya," Imen said. "Lieutenant Bak thought I shouldn't stand watch alone."

Menna's mouth tightened. "Do you not trust my judgment, Lieutenant?"

Bak did not appreciate being placed on the defensive, but he smiled pleasantly anyway. "I do, but a man alone looked to be fair game should a gang of men come to rob the tomb. How would you have felt if we'd found Imen at the bottom of this shaft, his neck broken in the fall, and the tomb desecrated?"

"As I believe I told you earlier," Menna said in a stiff, unyielding voice, "I know well the men who dwell in this area, those who thrive at the expense of the dead. They'd never take a life merely to rifle one small burial place such as this. There are, without doubt, other tombs easier to enter, tombs isolated enough that they could be robbed at will, with small risk of being caught."

If you know them so well, Bak thought, why haven't you laid hands on those who took the baubles I found in Buhen or the jewelry found on ships in the harbor at Mennufer? He was being unfair, he knew, too quick to judge. Menna had admitted he was not a seasoned investigator, and his resentment of a man usurping his authority was understandable.

The priest stepped forward, filling the uncomfortable silence. "I'm Kaemwaset and you must be Lieutenant Bak."

"Yes, sir."

"Amonked told me of your many successes as a hunter of men. He has every confidence that you'll not only bring a halt to the accidents here, but will lay hands on Montu's slayer."

"I pray I won't disappoint him."

"He's an excellent judge of character, young man. I'm sure you'll live up to his expectations and reach beyond them."

Bak was jolted by such supreme confidence. He had thought, when he left Commandant Thuty in Buhen, that he was free for a time of the burden such conviction added.

Another gust forced mouths and eyes closed and added a sense of urgency to the priest's demeanor when finally the dust fell away. "Shall we enter the tomb, Lieutenant Menna? After midday, I must teach this boy . . ." He laid a hand on the youth's shoulder. ". . . and seven more as witless as he to understand the sacred writings of the lord Ptah."

"Move the palm trunk across the shaft," Menna said, including Kasaya as well as Imen in the order. "Bring the rope and light a torch." His eyes darted toward Bak. "We won't be in the tomb for long. You need not wait."

Though annoyed by so curt a dismissal, Bak kept his expression untroubled, his tone amiable. "I've a slayer to lay hands on, Lieutenant. I wish to speak with Kaemwaset after he performs the necessary ablutions."

The guard officer swung around without another word, watched Imen and Kasaya position the palm trunk and light the torch, and prepared to descend. When all was ready, he turned to the apprentice who had come with Kaemwaset. "Go to Pashed and tell him your master has come. He must send men to fill this shaft. The task must be completed before end of day."

"Yes, sir," and the boy hurried away.

Menna glanced at Bak—an apology of sorts, perhaps. Getting an affable nod in return, he turned away, soon to be swallowed by the tomb shaft. The priest promptly followed. Imen sat on his haunches at the rim, awaiting the order to bring them up. Bak knelt for a time beside the guard, watching the faint glow of Menna's torch at the lower end of the shaft. He heard the murmur of voices below and smelled a hint of incense, but his thoughts were on tasks completed and others left to do. He rose to his feet and joined Kasaya, who sat with his back to the human-headed lion statue, out of reach of the wind.

"Go summon Perenefer or Seked," Bak said, "whoever can leave his men untended for an hour or so. I wish to learn what he thinks about the accidents and also look at the cliff that rises above the northern retaining wall. A portion broke away a few months ago, slaying one man and maiming others. I wish to know what made it fall."

The smell of incense was quickly swept away by the sharp, warm breeze. The leaves Kasaya had thrown aside after his morning meal played tag with the dust sporadically racing across the terrace. Not far away, a crew of workmen manhandled a column segment onto a sledge, the amount of effort required measured by how loud their overseer bellowed. Snatches of a workmen's song were carried by the wind, the source impossible to locate.

Kaemwaset's apprentice returned with the men Pashed had sent to see the tomb properly closed: Perenefer, his crew of workmen, and two brickmasons. Three boys wearing yokes across their shoulders carried suspended on flat, square wooden trays the dry mudbricks that would be used to build the wall to seal off the tomb before the shaft was filled. The men huddled against various statues and column parts, keeping out of the wind as best they could while they waited for Kaemwaset to finish the necessary prayers. The long line of youths who had been carrying debris from north to south across the terrace swung eastward to bring the fill to the open shaft.

A call from below sent Imen scrambling to his feet. He brought up the basket containing the priestly implements, and Kaemwaset followed. After shaking out a tangle in the rope, the guard beckoned the first of the two masons who would wall in the tomb and helped him descend into the shaft. The second mason attached the first tray to the rope and began to send the mudbricks down to his partner.

"How did you find the tomb?" Bak asked, drawing the priest away from the many prying eyes and ears.

"Just as it should be. You and Lieutenant Menna are to be applauded for keeping it safe through so many hours."

Bak responded with a wry smile. "Maybe the local tomb robbers fear a malign spirit."

"Malign spirit, Lieutenant?" The priest snorted. "Our sovereign was conceived by the lord Amon himself. Would any vile specter dare approach the memorial temple of one so beloved of the greatest of the gods?"

"The men who toil here are convinced a malign spirit is responsible for the many accidents, and my Medjay saw it last night, walking through her temple and that of Nebhepetre Montuhotep."

"Bah! Such spirits are meant to frighten the poor and uneducated—as they've done here at Djeser Djeseru—but not the man of learning you so obviously are."

Bak relented, smiled. "I seek a man of flesh and blood, Kaemwaset. Probably more than one."

"I thank the lord Amon!" the priest said, openly relieved. "I've been summoned to purify the temple each time a man has died or suffered injury. In each case, I've been told of an accident that might've been brought about by a careless man or by worn or faulty equipment or, in a few cases, by the whims of the gods. I've found no evidence to the contrary, but I believe none of those reasons. Nor is a malign spirit an acceptable explanation."

Bak eyed the old man thoughtfully. "What are you trying to tell me, sir?"

Kaemwaset glanced at the workmen and drew Bak a few steps farther away, as if a single overheard word would be of major import.

"Our sovereign is a woman," he said, speaking softly and intently, "a beautiful and talented woman who rules the land of Kemet with a firm yet beneficent hand. She has many enemies, foremost among them those who believe only a man can rule our land. Those individuals, I believe, are responsible for the many accidents, the rumors of a malign spirit."

"What do they hope to gain? She isn't one who gives up easily. She'd never send the workmen home and let the temple languish, incomplete as it is today."

"Of course not. It will be built—no matter what the obstacles."

"I've heard of no similar problems at other locations where she's set men to toil: the mansion of the lord Amon, the shrine of the lady Pakhet, the quarries at Abu or Khenu or Wawat . . ."

"Djeser Djeseru will have special significance. By causing trouble here, they think to discredit her, to make her look weak in the eyes of the people, to make her look less than what she is: daughter of the lord Amon himself." Kaemwaset paused—for effect, Bak suspected. "You see, young man, upon the walls of this temple will be depicted the tale of her divine conception."

Later, after Menna and the masons returned to the surface, while Kaemwaset was mumbling additional prayers and performing further libations, Bak thought over the theory the old priest had offered. It sounded good, believable, but he suspected it owed more to necessity than reality. A tale created by Maatkare Hatshepsut's followers within the mansion of the lord Amon. A tale designed to take advantage of a series of events for which they had no explanation.

Pashed arrived to make sure the tomb shaft was properly closed. Their duty completed, Kaemwaset and his apprentice returned to Waset. Lieutenant Menna strode away, saying he must inspect the guards who stood watch night and day at other burial places near the valley. He left Imen on duty with instructions to remain until the shaft was filled. Bak waited at the top with Pashed, watching baskets of debris being lowered to Perenefer and the workmen whose duty it was to fill the horizontal shaft.

Kasaya finally returned with Seked, Perenefer's brother. Leaving the Medjay behind with the architect to see the sepulcher fully closed, Bak and the foreman set off across the terrace.

"Kames told me of the cliff that fell above the northern retaining wall and of the havoc it wreaked," Bak explained. "I wish to see for myself the landscape above the wall."

Seked gave him a probing look. "You think the fall not a natural one, sir?"

"I don't know—and we may never learn the cause. The accident happened some months ago and the site may've changed."

"It's not rained since," Seked said thoughtfully, "but rocks fall all the time. You can see for yourself how they've formed the slope at the base of the cliff. The bigger the fall, as that one was, the more rocks come down over a longer period of time."

"You've no hope we'll find signs of man or beast? Or malign spirit?"

The foreman smiled. "Your Medjay told me that's what you seek."

"You look skeptical."

Bak stopped ten or so paces from the partially completed retaining wall to study the incline up which they meant to climb. Their presence silenced the men toiling on the wall, who peered around, curious as to their purpose. Other men, cutting away the slope at the end of the wall, forming a fairly smooth surface against which the builders would lay courses of stone, eyed them with no less interest. As Seked had said, the slope was covered with rocks, some broken into chunks and others pulverized by their fall, and looked treacherous to climb but by no means impossible. The gusting wind sent dust racing across the slope in spurts, pelting the men below.

"Let me put it this way, sir. If I see a light in the dead of night and it comes my way, I step aside lest a man bump into me, and at the same time I mutter an incantation to protect myself from I know not what."

Bak burst into laughter. He had heard few men speak with so gifted a tongue, and certainly none at Djeser Djeseru. The men building the wall and those cutting away the slope smiled tentatively at each other, trying to share a jest they had not heard.

Sobering, Bak strode to the end of the cut and began to climb the untouched slope. A puff of wind drove dirt around him, forcing him to turn his back momentarily. "How long had you known Montu?"

"I'd toiled at his feet since I was a callow youth." Seked, keeping up step for step, expelled a cynical laugh. "I may as well open my heart to you, sir, for I'm a poor liar and will in the end give myself away. I couldn't stand the sight of him in the beginning, and I shed no tears the day his body was found."

"Strong words, Seked."

"He was a man of no principals, fonder of himself than of the lord Amon or of any other god. When younger and less self-satisfied than in his later years, he would without qualm work a man to death if he thought to gain a smile from one loftier than he."

"Did your brother feel as you do?"

"If the truth be told, not a man at Djeser Djeseru felt otherwise. If he'd not been slain openly, as he was, he'd soon have met with a fatal accident."

"Which would've been blamed upon the malign spirit."

Seked's smile was grim. "Cannot a spirit enter a man's heart, sir? Cannot the malignancy fester and grow?"

Bak climbed on in silence, taking care where he placed his feet. The earth and stones that had most recently fallen were loose and unstable, sliding easily down a slope made hard by time and weather. Spurts of dust forced them to close their eyes, hiding the surface from view when every step counted, leaving no choice but to pause until the wind died down.

If Montu had been destined to die in a contrived accident, he wondered, why had the slayer taken his life openly? Why risk an investigation into his death when an accident would go unexamined? Then again, he had been meant to vanish, with no one knowing where he had gone. True, a search would have been made, but how thorough a search and for how long was anyone's guess.

"Do you have a specific reason for disliking Montu so, or has the feeling grown through the years?"

The foreman's mouth tightened to a thin, stubborn line.

"Speak up, Seked. You've told me the worst already, why hold back now?"

Seked stopped to face Bak. The slope was steep and he stood as if sideways on a stairway, one foot higher than the other. "I'll tell you the truth, for I'm an honest man, but you must lay blame on neither my brother nor I. We wanted him dead, but we didn't slay him."

"Come," Bak said, climbing ahead. "The cliff will keep us safe from the wind."

A gust of dirt-laden air spurred Seked on. "Several years ago, while toiling at the mansion of the lord Amon, Montu bumped into a scaffold, causing it to fall. I was struck as it collapsed and knocked senseless, my forehead sliced open." He touched the scar with the tips of his fingers. "When

Perenefer tried to aid me, to take me to a physician, Montu accused him of turning his back on his duty. Perenefer carried me off anyway. Montu sent a guard after him, and he, too, helped carry me to the physician. The two of them together saved my life."

He let out a low, bitter laugh. "Montu pressed the issue, charging them both with desertion. They were sent together far away to the turquoise mines as punishment. The guard died. My brother survived."

Bak climbed the last few paces to the cliff face. As if smiled upon by the gods, the air was still and hot, protected from the wind by the tall vertical columns of rock. "How did Perenefer manage to come back as a foreman? Was his so-called crime forgiven and forgotten?"

"The officer in charge of the mines recognized his competence and ability. He saw to his early release and found the task for him here."

"Did not Montu recognize the two of you? Identical twins are not easy to forget, and the scar on your forehead would be a unique reminder."

Seked's voice grew harsh, angry. "Montu acted as if the accident was of no consequence, as if the guard's death and Perenefer's imprisonment were insignificant, a passing occurrence."

A man asking to be slain, Bak thought.

He walked a couple steps down the slope and turned around to look up the cliff face. A high wall of golden stone, made irregular by tower-like protuberances and the crevices between them, by niches and slabs of rock that looked ready to come tumbling down. Weathered by wind and sun, heat and cold, by the infrequent torrential rainstorms that drowned anything in their path.

A scattering of sand peppered his head and shoulders. He looked upward, thinking a falcon might have a nest above them. Several rasping sounds followed, and stones large and small began to fall. Thoughts of a bird fled and his muscles bunched, ready for flight. A sharp crack rent the air, followed by the quick rumble of tumbling stones. Recognizing the sound, knowing it for what it was, he yelled a warning to the men below. Grabbing Seked's arm, he shoved him across the hill. Stones rained down upon them.

Chapter Seven

The silence brought Bak to his senses.

He hoisted his shoulders off the slope and shook his head to clear it. The rockfall had stopped. The valley was still, all movement arrested, speech hushed. The cloud of dust rising around him and from rock and debris that had fallen to the terrace was torn asunder by a gust of wind. A man below began to curse; another prayed to the lord Re and to the sanctified Djeserkare Amonhotep and his mother Ahmose Nefertari.

"What happened?" Seked mumbled. He touched a thin line of red trickling down the side of his face and stared at his fingers, puzzled. "What happened?"

"Rocks fell from the cliff, causing a slide." Bak rolled half around, sat up, looked at the scene below. No! he wanted to shout. No! But the words caught in his throat.

The end of the northern retaining wall where the men had been working had taken the brunt of the rock slide. Rocks large and small, stone rubble and sand, had flowed over and buried the ramp on which they had been standing. The mound stood taller than the completed, undamaged portion of the wall and ran a third of the way across the terrace. The lower colonnade where Kames and his stonemasons had been toiling was blessedly free of rubble, having been spared a second, devastating blow.

The slide was not directly below, but slightly to the east.

Bak remembered running diagonally across the slope with Seked, dirt and stones falling all around, the foreman below yelling and frantic workmen shouting.

"The lord Amon smiled upon us this day," he said, the fervor of his voice equaling that of his prayer for the men he felt sure had been trapped beneath the rubble.

In the distance, a man yelled. Others took up the call, their shouts horrified, filled with fear, a terrible sense of urgency. Men ran toward the retaining wall from all across Djeser Djeseru, leaving behind small tools and equipment, bringing levers and mallets and sledges, objects they would need to save men they knew. Men they toiled beside day after day, dwelt with every night. Men whose food they shared, whose jokes and gossip they enjoyed. Men they loved or disliked. Friends, acquaintances, close or distant kin. Boys dumped the dirt from their baskets and ran to help fathers, uncles, older brothers.

Bak looked closer at his companion, saw scratches and cuts, but no sign of broken bones. "Are you all right?" he asked, thinking of rocks that had struck his own head, and how addled Seked looked.

A man below moaned, and low sobs somewhere farther away mingled with a cry for help.

Seked registered the sounds. His eyes darted toward the pile of rubble. He shook his upper body like a great patriarchal baboon and scrambled to his feet. "Men are hurt, injured, maybe dying. We must move that mound."

"Let's go!"

They raced together down the slope. Loose rocks and debris slid and rattled beneath their feet, half carrying them to the bottom. Reaching the terrace ahead of everyone else, they quickly found the foreman, lying prone at the edge of the slide, a bleeding gash in his hair. His breast rose and fell, his eyes fluttered, but he remained senseless.

"I'll take his place," Seked said. "His men will need guidance."

Twenty or more workmen scattered around the mound,

men who had run for their lives, slowly, shakily lifted themselves off the terrace, cut, bruised, and trembling but otherwise unharmed. One man approached the slide with
dragging feet, staring upward as if expecting the cliff face to
fall a second time. Another was on his knees, head bent to
the earth and covered by his hands, muttering to himself. Yet
another, trying to rise, cried out in pain when he rested his
weight on an injured wrist. As they all began to comprehend
what had happened, as they realized that many of their fellows had been buried alive or dead, they shrugged off hurt,
fear, and the shame of having run and threw themselves
upon the mound, tearing at it with their bare hands.

Pashed and Kasaya were among the first to reach the
scene from farther afield. Studying the catastrophe with a
pale, shocked face, the architect began to shout orders. He
broke the arriving men into crews, ordered Seked and the
other foremen to take charge, assigned each of them sections
of the mound to keep them from treading on each other's
feet. He sent a boy racing off to summon a physician, and
pointed out a place well out of the way where the injured
should be taken. He organized the effort so those digging
away the mound would not want for water, the injured
would not go untended, the terrace would be cleared by
day's end.

With many anxious hands to help, rocks were moved,
sand and debris carried away, men released from certain
death. No man shirked his duty. Artists, sculptors, stonemasons, ordinary workmen toiled side by side beneath foremen they knew only by sight. Word spread to the
neighboring farms and villages, and their men came to help.
The usual chatter was missing, the good humor and laughter
absent. Finding a man alive with no serious injuries was
cause for a quick drink of water and a grim smile. Finding a
man with a crushed or broken limb brought forth angry
curses and lent a greater urgency to the digging. Finding a
man dead made the survivors sick at heart.

As the lord Re dropped toward the western horizon, the

wind died down, allowing the heat to build and the dust to settle on sweaty bodies. Thirst was ever-present, and the water boys hustled back and forth to the nearest well. Children came from the nearby villages, leading donkeys laden with water.

Bak shared the burden and so did Kasaya, moving stones and debris, carrying the injured to the physician, locating friends or relatives who would see the walking wounded safely home. Hori wanted to help, but Bak sent him back to the tomb to stay with Imen. He felt certain that the cliff face had fallen at the hands of a man. The raspy sounds he had heard might well have been that of a lever being used to pry away rock, the sharp crack had sounded like the breaking away of stone. He was uncertain of the reason. Had he, Bak, been meant to die? Or had the rockfall been intended as a distraction so someone could . . . What? Rifle the tomb? Or was it meant to seem a warning from the malign spirit that any who doubted its existence would bring catastrophe upon Djeser Djeseru?

"This temple is cursed," Bak heard a man say. The voice was loud and angry and every man on the mound could hear. "There've been too many accidents, too many men hurt or slain. We must leave this valley before we all die."

"What're you saying?" another man asked.

"I say it's time we turned our backs on this temple, this valley."

"Our sovereign would never allow it."

A third man broke in, "If we all lay down our tools, what can she do?"

"Yes," a fourth said, as if the idea was new to him. "What can she do? Not a thing."

"She can bring prisoners to toil here in our place," a fifth man said. "She can send us to the desert mines."

No one heard him. No one wanted to hear him.

The first man said, "I say we—all of us together—go to Waset and stand before Senenmut. He's responsible for the building of this temple. Let him tell our sovereign we'll never again risk our lives in this accursed valley."

"She's known of the malign spirit for months, and what's she done about it?"

"She sent her cousin. Amonked."

"What's he done? Nothing!"

"He brought in that Lieutenant Bak."

"Who's he?" Scorn entered the man's voice. "A soldier. An officer from the southern frontier. A man who'll say what he's told to say."

"This is what I think we should do," the first man said. "We should meet here on the terrace at first light tomorrow and . . ."

Bak stood on the slope above the fallen section of retaining wall. The dead and injured had been carried away and the men were clearing the last of the slide. Their words, their anger and fear, ran through his thoughts. Their scorn rankled, but was of no significance compared to their threat to lay down their tools and walk away, a threat that had spread to every man and boy since first he had heard it. They might dismiss Maatkare Hatshepsut as helpless and turn their backs on her temple, but as one who had suffered her wrath, he could not take her so lightly. The men must remain at Djeser Djeseru.

Cursing them for creating so foolhardy a plan, he turned his back on the temple and forced himself to concentrate on the cliff face. A large elongated scar, lighter than the rest, marked the source of the fallen rock. In his heart he was certain someone had pried loose a boulder to start the fall. A man, not a malign spirit. A man responsible for yet another death, another serious injury, and three more broken limbs. Not to mention the cuts and bruises, the heartache, of those who had survived.

Anger boiled within him each time he thought of the slide, the injured and the dead, the many workmen who had been willing to toil until they dropped to save their fellows.

This so-called accident was the most recent of many, perhaps not the last. Unless he could lay hands on the culprit.

He must do so. He must. And as a beginning he must climb that wretched cliff. He and Kasaya.

The husky young Medjay, standing on the terrace below, called, "I think we must grow wings, sir."

"If someone else climbed up there, we can."

"Surely a man would've been seen from below."

"Not if he climbed up farther to the east and crossed along the tops of those tower-like formations."

"The men are convinced a malign spirit . . ." The Medjay bit back the rest. He knew well how Bak felt about that subject.

Giving no sign that he had heard, Bak walked along the slope, studying the cliff looming above him. Its face was far from smooth. For untold generations the soft limestone had been eroded by heating and cooling, by the wind, and by infrequent but pounding rainstorms to form the deeply weathered tower-like formations that protruded from the mass. As far as he could tell, none had actually broken free of the cliff face. Immediately above the slope where he stood, a row of these formations rose about a third of the way up the seemingly endless wall of eroded rock that reached for the sky behind them. They bunched against other tower-like projections, taller and much more irregular, that rose between them and the upper rim. The scar marred the surface of one of the lower formations.

Lower, yes, but a long, hard climb nonetheless.

This late in the day the clefts between the towers were shadowed and not easy to see. He walked back the way he had come, his eyes probing their depths. Some were shallow and very steep. Others had been etched deeply into the cliff, giving them a more gradual rise and what appeared from below to be an easier slope. Rocks had fallen and lodged there. Weathering had formed rough, irregular steps. Sand had blown or trickled from above, filling cracks and crevices, blanketing only the lord Amon knew what.

Could he come down from above? Certainly not before
nightfall. The trail over the high ridge that connected Djeser
Djeseru to the Great Place, the deep dry watercourse in
which Maatkare Hatshepsut's illustrious father Akheperkare
Thutmose had chosen to have dug his eternal resting place,
rose up the slope some distance to the east. Its path was cir-
cuitous, traversing a fairly steep but, to Bak's way of thinking, reasonably easy grade in an easterly direction to a point
where the cliff diminished and merged into the ridge. There
the trail turned back on itself to follow the top of the cliff,
passing above Djeser Djeseru, where a branch path as-
cended to the summit, passed a cluster of workmen's huts,
and dropped down to the Great Place. Given enough time, a
long enough rope, and several men he would trust with his
life, he might be able to climb down from that path, but time
was crucial. He must go without delay, while signs of tres-
pass remained: the tracks of a man or possibly the mark of a
chisel or lever.

Two clefts in the rock face looked less steep than the others and easier to climb. He selected the one closest to the
whitish scar.

"Come, Kasaya. We must be up and back before darkness
falls. We don't want to spend the night on the cliff."

"We could climb up at first light," the Medjay said hopefully.

Bak scowled at him. "I've explained once why we must
go now, and I'll not repeat myself."

With ill-concealed reluctance, Kasaya lifted a coil of rope
onto his shoulder, tied a small bag of tools to his belt, and
picked up a goatskin water bag. Climbing onto the slope, he
scrambled up to Bak's side.

"We must climb with care and patience," Bak said, head-
ing upward. "Should one of us fall and be seriously hurt or
killed, or should we cause another rock slide, the workmen's
conviction that a malign spirit walks this valley will be impossible to dislodge."

"They're already convinced. You heard their threat to lay down their tools—as did I."

"You'd better pray that threat is empty, Kasaya. If they're sent to the desert mines, there to spend the remainder of their days, we may spend the rest of our lives guarding them."

"Will this accursed climb never end?" Kasaya mumbled.

"We're almost to the top," Bak answered, though he was certain the young Medjay had been talking to himself. "Just a few more steps, I think."

"What do you mean by *a few* . . ." Kasaya's foot slipped on the sand-covered edge of rock that was his sole support while he lifted the other foot. He muttered something Bak could not hear, added, "Sir?"

Very much aware that the sun no longer reached the cliff face and of the long distance they would fall if fall they did, Bak stopped to study the boulder that barred their path. This was one of the steps he had referred to. He could barely see over it, but it looked to be the highest—he thanked the lord Amon. It filled the cleft from one side to another. It seemed to be solidly planted, but he had learned early on not to trust appearances. Should he forget, a long patch of chafed skin on his left thigh burned like the very sun itself, reminding him to value caution.

He placed both palms against the boulder and shoved. It did not move. Putting his weight behind the task, he repeated the process several times, studying the edges of the boulder and the sand built up around it. Not a grain trickled into some hidden void. It looked to be safe.

"Give me a hand, Kasaya."

The Medjay gingerly shifted his weight to test the solidity of the rocks beneath him. Satisfied none would move, he wove his fingers together and held out his hands. Bak stepped into them and let Kasaya heave him upward. He scrambled onto the boulder, which held steady.

"How am I to get up there?" the Medjay asked.

Bak scrambled to his feet and studied the irregular rock steps and the steep slope between him and the top of the formation. "The rest of the cleft looks easy enough to climb. I should be able to do it without help." He looked down upon the younger man, who was taller and heavier than he, and not an easy lift. "If you want to stay where you are, you may. If not, cut hand- and footholds for yourself and call me if you need help."

Kasaya looked upward, undecided. Irresolution turned to certainty and, his mouth tight with determination, he dug into the sack of tools tied to his belt and retrieved a chisel and mallet.

"You'd better use the rope for safety," Bak said.

A short time later, with precautions taken to prevent the Medjay from falling to a certain death should he make a misstep, Bak issued a final warning. "Don't do anything to dislodge this boulder, and don't take any unnecessary risks."

"No, sir."

Conscious of the passage of time, Bak climbed from one stone step to another, testing each before he placed his weight on it. At the top lay debris that had fallen from the cliffs towering above. A thin layer of loose sand and stones overlay a firmer base that had been packed through the years to form a steep but fairly stable incline. He climbed slowly, looking for signs of another man's passage, but the rough surface held its secrets. In a short while he stood atop the tower, a rounded patch of weathered stone separated from its mates and the parent cliff by sand-filled crevices.

A faint breeze ruffled his hair and kilt and dried the sweat on his face and chest. Swallows chattered in the nearby cliffs, undisturbed by the sharp tap-tap-tap of Kasaya's mallet. Bak wished he had thought to get a drink before leaving the water bag behind with the Medjay.

The valley spread out below, an open bay enclosed on three sides by the high walls of the cliff, floored with sand faded, so late in the day, to pale gold. Nestled within their own shadow, the tall eroded walls had turned a deep, dark brown cut by crevices black and mysterious. The sun had dropped lower than he expected, the time they had taken to climb the cleft longer. They must soon return to the valley or spend the night cold and hungry.

The two temples, shrunk by distance, spread across the head of the valley, the older a mass of fallen stones, the newer fronted by a field of stones waiting to be raised. Neb-hepetre Montuhotep's temple stood empty and abandoned except for a pack of dogs nosing among its fallen columns. The temple of Maatkare Hatshepsut should have been equally deserted but for the guards assigned to stand watch through the night.

Instead, not a man who toiled there had left. They were standing or kneeling or sitting among the statues and column parts and rough stones strewn across the terrace. Located at what they must have believed to be a safe distance from the northern retaining wall, they were looking up toward the face of the cliff. Watching him and Kasaya, Bak guessed. Waiting to see if the malign spirit would strike them down. He spat out an oath. That's all they needed. Men watching their every action while they slipped and stumbled and slid down the cleft. He thought to wave, but decided not to. Why tempt the gods with too brazen an action?

Erasing the workmen from his thoughts, he looked for the scarred stone. He could not see it from where he stood. He recalled the terrain as he had seen it from below and compared it with the rocks and crevices around him. He was too high, he decided, too far west. Climbing down a narrow defile, he found a ledge about five paces long and less than a pace wide. Careful not to think of the long deadly drop should he fall, he crossed to a shallow slope of sand that filled another, wider crevice, this running along the face of the cliff behind the tower-like formation. The scar that marked the fallen stone was clearly visible beyond the sand, where the crevice narrowed and dropped off into space. He saw at once that the crevice walls would almost completely conceal a man from below.

He knelt at the upper edge of the sand. No footprints marred its surface, and neither was it as smooth as were other nearby patches. It was slightly rippled, as if someone had hurriedly brushed away with his hand any signs left behind, any footprints. He was certain of what he saw, but Kasaya was a better tracker. Thinking to preserve the ripples so the Medjay could see them, he sidled along the wall to the lower end of the crevice.

The whitish scar on the cliff face was much larger than he had expected, a long trail left by large chunks of stone knocked loose by what had probably been a single boulder torn from a spot near where he stood. Wind, heat, cold, and rain, he guessed, had slowly eaten away a vein of more fragile stone, forming an ever-deepening crack. The loosened rock, a large and heavy chunk, would have fallen sooner or later. But someone had been unwilling to wait. Several deep, bright-white gouges told him the boulder had been broken away with the aid of a pointed metal tool, a lever.

"You were right all along, sir." Kasaya stared at the scarred wall of rock, his expression as dark and angry as Bak felt. "A man was here—no question about it—and he broke loose the boulder that started the slide. If ever I lay hands on him . . ."

He said no more, leaving the rest to the imagination.

"He was very careful. I doubt he left anything behind." Bak looked at the deepening shadow in the valley below and tamped down a sense of urgency. He had no desire to spend the night on the cliff. "Nonetheless, we must sift through the sand."

Kasaya, too, looked at the shadowed valley. "Can't we come back tomorrow, sir?"

"If you want to climb down by yourself, do so. But take care. I'd not like to find you battered and bruised partway down the cleft."

Kasaya stood undecided, looking as miserable as a man could look. He knew his officer well enough to know that he would remain through the night if need be.

Bak dropped to his knees near the scarred cliff and began to run his fingers through the soft warm sand. Another long moment passed and Kasaya dropped down beside him. Bak bit back a smile. The Medjay was far from the brightest policeman in his company, but he was among the most loyal and steadfast.

Bak found the amulet within a pace of the scarred cliff face. It was a fish, a Lates, slightly longer than the width of his thumb. It had been carved from a green stone, malachite. From a tiny hole bored through its head, he guessed it had been part of a broad beaded collar. It must have torn free while its wearer was swinging the lever, the intense physical exertion causing the cord to break.

"Others must've fallen, too," Kasaya said, and set to work with renewed enthusiasm.

Bak was not so certain. The tiny fish was beautifully carved. If the collar was of the same quality, each bead and amulet would have been individually tied. If they were to find another, the lord Amon would indeed have smiled upon them.

They searched with care, leaving no grain of sand unturned, but diligent effort proved fruitless. By the time they reached the upper end of the sandy incline, their sole trophy was the single green amulet.

Dusk had settled on Djeser Djeseru when Bak and Kasaya came down the final slope. Hori raced across the terrace to meet them at the retaining wall. Pashed and the chief scribe Ramose hurried after him. The many men waiting among the statues and column parts came to life, rising from their makeshift seats to mingle, to chat, to speculate. Bak heard a jumble of words, felt the relief of men who had feared his action might bring upon them the wrath of the malign spirit.

A tentative relief, he sensed, not everlasting freedom from fear.

He gave the youthful scribe a broad smile and greeted Pashed and Ramose as if nothing of note had occurred since last he had seen them. With luck and the help of the gods, the men would take heart from that smile and casual greeting.

"What did you find up there, sir?" Hori asked.

Bak raised a finger to his lips, warning the men around him to speak softly. He had thought long and hard of how best to slay the rumor of a malign spirit, but to let the workmen overhear would sap the strength of what he planned.

"No malign spirit," Kasaya whispered, as scornful as if he had never believed in so ridiculous a thing. "The signs of a man, as Lieutenant Bak expected."

Pashed, his face gray from fatigue, looked like the weight of a monolithic column had been added to the burden on his shoulders. Ramose muttered a litany of curses.

"Who, sir?" Hori asked.

"I don't know, but one day I will." Bak's voice and his expression were hard, determined. He turned to Pashed. "Send the men to their dwelling places. They must eat and sleep, for tomorrow is another day of toil."

The chief architect's mouth tightened. "They talk of rebellion. Of laying down their tools and never again treading the sands of this valley."

"So they truly mean to act." Bak snorted his disgust.

"You must tell them without delay what you know," Ramose insisted.

"If I speak here and now, they'll convince themselves that I'm saying what I've been told to say, or the malign spirit has blinded me to the truth, or it's inhabited the body of a man. We didn't climb all the way up that cliff to add strength to the tales they're already telling."

"We'd hoped you'd set their thoughts to rest."

Bak could see how tired Ramose and Pashed were, how discouraged. He regretted he had nothing more positive to offer, only a plan that might or might not bear fruit. "You must tell the men that no more work will be done on the northern retaining wall until you know for a fact that it's safe to toil there, then dismiss them. After they've gone, I'll tell you what I plan and what you must do to help. We must convince them to remain at Djeser Djeseru."

While the chief architect, with Ramose at his side, spoke to the men, Bak sat down on a large irregular chunk of rock that had fallen from the cliff. It had been left where it lay in the expectation that it would be useful as a column drum or for some other architectural purpose. He was tired to the bone. The rescue effort and the climb had exhausted him. At least dusk had brought some relief from the heat. "Has the tomb been closed?" he asked Hori.

"Yes, sir. As soon as Perenefer knew that every man who'd been toiling near the wall was accounted for, he brought his men back to fill the shaft."

"I thank the lord Amon," Bak said fervently. At least one task had been completed without mishap.

"The Lates is held sacred in Iunyt," Ramose said, looking at the green amulet in Bak's hand. Its exquisite workmanship was lost in the light of the torch Kasaya had stuck into the sand just outside the lean-to. "Could the man who wore this be from that city?"

Bak, seated on Ramose's stool, eyed the small figure, wishing it could talk. "Possibly. Then again, it may've been one of many different kinds of amulets in the collar."

"A missing element won't be easy to spot." Pashed settled himself beside Ramose, Hori, and Kasaya, seated on mats around Bak's feet. "You've thought of a way to prevent the men from laying down their tools?"

"I thought to take advantage of their never-failing willingness to believe rumor rather than fact." Bak leaned forward, elbows on knees. "I wish you, Ramose, to allow your son Ani to speak with Hori. I wish the two of them to be seen with their heads together, speaking softly, secretly. After

Hori departs, Ani must whisper in several men's ears, telling them he's heard from one who would know that I found signs of a man on the cliff, and I know for a fact that he caused the rocks to fall. That he's all along been deliberately planting fear in their hearts by causing many of the accidents that have befallen Djeser Djeseru."

Ramose threw Bak a sharp look. "Such a tale will bring danger upon your head."

"We must keep the men here, and we must stop the death and injury. I can think of no other way."

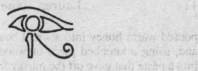

Chapter Eight

"You've become foolhardy, my son." Ptahhotep's scowl left no doubt as to how much he disapproved of his offspring. "A man who brings about one accident after another, one who causes the death and injury of innocent people, won't hesitate to slay you if he feels he must."

"Not all the mishaps were deliberate." Bak thanked the lord Amon that he had long ago outgrown the tendency to wiggle every time his parent reprimanded him. "Accidents happen all the time on construction sites. You know as well as I that many men who work in stone end their years with a disabled limb or a twisted back."

"This is the second time that cliff face has fallen." Ptahhotep, seated in the shade of a lean-to built atop his house, gave his son a stern look across a three-legged pottery brazier blackened and crusty from long use. The mound of charcoal inside, burned down to a reddish glow, was too small to throw off much heat. Nor had the lord Khepre risen high enough in the eastern sky to heat the day or melt the haze hanging over the river. "Tell me again how many men have dropped beneath the weight of its stones."

He knew very well the answer to his question. Bak had told him less than an hour before. "The accidents must stop, Father. Not just those at the northern retaining wall, but all across the construction site."

"And you must also find Montu's slayer." The physician

113

poured warm honey into a small bowl of blue-green leaves and, using a knobbed piece of wood, began to crush them into a paste that gave off the musky fragrance of rue. "Could his death be in some way related to the accidents?"

Bak stood up and walked to the edge of the roof, where he could look down upon his horses. He could breathe easier with his father's attention turned away from what he knew in his heart was a foolhardy plan. "Except for Kames, every tale I've heard thus far leads me to believe he asked to be slain, that he was killed because someone hated him."

"You told me yourself he looked more a fool than a villain."

"His death was no accident, Father. He was struck on the head and dragged into the tomb. If not for the foreman's fear of burying a man alive, he would have vanished forever. As he was meant to."

Ptahhotep sprinkled a few drops of natron into the mixture and added a dollop of animal fat. "Could he have come upon the man who's been causing these accidents?"

"I'd not be surprised. From what I've learned, he was slain after dark, and only then have men seen the malign spirit. But what was he doing at Djeser Djeseru in the dead of night? Was he not afraid, as everyone else is?"

"The workmen still spend each night in the valley."

"After dark they stay close to their huts, where they have lamps and torches and each other's company to give them courage." Bak spotted Hori and Kasaya coming toward his father's small house along a raised path between dessicated fields. "Not surprisingly, the malign spirit stays well clear of those huts."

"Why must you refer to that vile criminal as a malign spirit?" Ptahhotep asked irritably. "He's a man, and so you should describe him."

"I use the words as a name, for I've no other name to call him."

The physician grunted, not happy with the answer but unable or unwilling to come up with anything better. "Did Montu often stay late?"

"He was usually the first to leave, so we've been told, and he always went to his home in Waset or to his estate a half hour's walk upriver. He evidently enjoyed his comfort. Those workmen's huts are simple affairs, and the food is plain and monotonous."

Ptahhotep added a pinch of ground willow branch to the bowl. "If he learned a man was causing the accidents, he'd have no reason to fear a malign spirit."

"Would he not have greater reason to fear that man than a nonexistent being created to take advantage of men's superstitions?"

They both knew that any man who had brought about so much death and destruction, especially at a place as important as their sovereign's memorial temple, would be certain to face a horrible death by impalement. He would kill and kill again to keep his secret.

"Montu might've stumbled upon the men who've been rifling the old tombs," Bak said, giving Ptahhotep no time to return to the subject of his own safety. "I've not explored the hillsides that enclose the valley nor have I searched the valley floor, but where kings are buried, the tombs of the nobility are close by—as the construction of our sovereign's new temple has proven."

"The confusion of a large project would provide good cover," Ptahhotep said thoughtfully.

"Yes, but there'd be many extra eyes to spot an open tomb or furtive act." Bak waved to Kasaya and Hori to let them know he had seen them, ducked beneath the lean-to to pick up his sheathed dagger, and tied it to his belt. "Of course, a malign spirit would discourage prying."

"Do you suppose Lieutenant Menna has considered the possibility?"

"I don't know. He's not very forthcoming. He fears I'll tread on his toes." Bak scooped up his baton of office. "One

thing I do know: a man who creates a malign spirit is not superstitious—which eliminates most of the men who toil at
Djeser Djeseru. And the average tomb robber, too. At least
the local men Menna believes are involved."

"Where do you go today, my son?" The worry returned to
Ptahhotep's face. "Back to that valley of death?"

"I'll go first to Montu's home in Waset. If the lord Amon
smiles upon me, he'll have left behind the reason he remained at Djeser Djeseru the night he was slain."

"Will you not wait until my poultice is warmed? That
abrasion on your thigh looks dreadful."

"Later, Father. Tonight when I've more time." Bak flashed
his parent a teasing smile. "Besides, I don't wish to walk the
streets of Waset wearing a bandage from hip to knee."

Ptahhotep scowled, but did not press the point. "I must go
to Waset after midday, to the house of life. If you remain in
the city until an hour or so before nightfall, you can sail back
with me."

"I'll not forget." Bak walked to the interior stairway,
paused. "Don't expect me, but don't be surprised to see me
there, either. I wish to give the workmen time to hear the rumor I started, to let it seep into their hearts." He walked partway down the stairs, turned back, grinned. "I'll send Hori
and Kasaya in my stead, Hori to follow the rumor's progress
and make sure it travels a true path and Kasaya to guard his
back."

Ptahhotep glowered at his son's flippancy. "A true path?"

"With luck and the help of the gods, and with Ramose's
knowledge of the men and Hori's deft tongue, their fear will
turn to anger that one no different than they has toyed with
their fear of the unknown."

Montu's dwelling—brought to him through marriage,
Bak recalled—was located in a highly respectable neighborhood a short walk from the mansion of the lord Amon, one
among many structures that had been handed down from
parent to child for innumerable generations. Long blocks of

houses lined both sides of a narrow street that seldom saw
sunlight and, as a result, smelled stale and a bit rancid.
Standing side by side, most were three stories high, with a
lower floor that provided shelter and a place of work for the
servants, and two upper floors for family use. On the roofs,
Bak glimpsed cone-shaped granaries, pigeon cotes, and
lean-tos for additional storage and work space.

The entrance to the home he sought was three steps
above the street and set off by a low balustrade lined with
potted poppies. Two young sycamores, also in pots, stood
like sentinels on either side of the door. Bak was impressed.
He had not expected the architect to live in so sumptuous a
house.

"Montu lied to me at times, yes, and he had an eye for a
pretty woman, but he treated us as well as could be expected." Mutnefret, Montu's widow, sat on a low stool in a
rather stiff and formal room used for greeting guests. Her
husband's chair sat empty on the dais behind her. "I'd
brought a daughter to the marriage, as you know, and he
very much wanted a son."

"The property you possessed must've eased his disappointment," Bak said in a wry voice. "This house is most im-
pressive, and I'm told you have a substantial country estate
across the river."

"We lived well, to be sure." She was comfortably plump
and, to Bak's eye, looked every cubit a motherly figure, but
the smile on her face was strangely contented for one whose
husband had so recently been slain.

Seated on a stool similar to hers, he faced her across a low
table, sipping a tangy red wine and nibbling sweet cakes and
honeyed dates. Two columns carved and painted to look like
lilies supported the ceiling, two large pottery water jars
stood on a stone lustration slab, and niches in the wall contained paintings of the divine triad: the lord Amon, his
spouse the lady Mut, and their son the lord Khonsu. Beside
the dais stood a large wide-mouthed bowl of sweet-scented

white lilies floating on water. A hint of a breeze wafted
through high windows, barely stirring the warm air. He
found the formality of the room and even Mutnefret's hospi-
tality distancing, not conducive to easy talk, putting him at a
disadvantage.

"I've been told he shirked his duty, not only at Djeser Djeseru, but at your country estate. That you and your daughter
toil alongside your servants, and his sole task was to issue
orders."

"You've been listening to gossip, Lieutenant." Her eyes
darted toward a side door, drawn by the sudden appearance
of a slender and quite pretty young woman of fourteen or so
years. "He had his faults, I know, and didn't always get
along with his colleagues, but he meant well."

"Mother!" The girl stalked across the room to stand before her parent, hands on hips, fire in her eyes. "Montu was
lazy. His sole preoccupation was to do as little as possible."

Mutnefret looked hurt. "He was a good father to you,
Sitre."

"My father, the man who gave me life, was kind and gentle, one who toiled from dawn to dusk." Sitre pulled a stool
close and plopped onto it. "That wretched Montu could in
no way replace him."

Bak, startled by the young woman's outspoken behavior,
eyed her surreptitiously. The simple white sheath she wore
hardly concealed her shapely figure; rather, it enhanced it.
Her long, glossy black hair, her dark eyes, and her vivid
mouth were most attractive. Why was she not yet wed? he
wondered. Certainly her sincerity, her spirit, would not ap-
peal to every young man.

"Children!" Mutnefret shook her head at the unfairness of
it all. "When first I wed Montu, I prayed to the lady Hathor
that I'd give birth time and time again, but now—"

"All you wanted were sons!" Sitre tossed her head, flinging her hair across her shoulders. "Boys to satisfy his desire
to reproduce himself."

Her mother ignored her. "Now I thank the goddess that I

had just the one and that she's of an age to wed."

"Then what will you do?" the young woman asked, her tone scathing. "Go find another man like Montu who has a worthy position but no wealth to speak of?"

"Sitre!" Mutnefret glared at her daughter. "Have you never heard the ancient maxim: 'Do not give your mother cause to blame you lest she raise her hands to god and he hears her cries'?"

Bak was beginning to feel uncomfortable. It was one thing to listen to people divulge secrets that might lead him to a slayer or thief, quite another to hear them continue an argument that had most likely been going on from the day Mutnefret wed Montu. Of course, the argument might have led to the architect's death, but if so, why was he slain at the memorial temple instead of closer to home? "Did he ever speak of Djeser Djeseru, of the many accidents that have occurred there?"

"He mentioned the accidents, yes," Mutnefret said.

Her daughter snickered. "And the malign spirit that's been causing them."

Bak eyed the young woman with an interest that had nothing to do with her appearance. "He believed in the malign spirit?"

"He didn't," Mutnefret said, giving her daughter an overly generous smile, "but it pleased him to tell Sitre he did. She's of an age where she thinks she knows more than her betters, and he enjoyed tweaking her nose."

Her daughter flushed, whether from embarrassment or anger, Bak could not tell. "Don't you remember what he said, Mother? That he saw with his own eyes the malign spirit, and another man once told him he did, too?"

Bak's head snapped around. "He saw it?"

"He was jesting," Mutnefret said.

The younger woman stared defiance at the older. "So he told us, and I believed him."

"When and where and what did it look like?" he demanded.

"He wasn't serious," Mutnefret insisted. "Sitre is so gullible he couldn't resist teasing her."

The young woman flashed her mother a vicious look. "He saw something." Her eyes, large and intense, darted toward Bak. "He spoke of it last week. He wasn't specific about where he saw it, but somewhere at Djeser Djeseru. As for its appearance . . . Well, from a distance, he said, it looked like light and shadow, but when I asked him how it appeared close up, he laughed and waved a hand, dismissing the question and me."

"My dear child." Mutnefret reached for her daughter's hand. "You want to believe the worst about him. You want to think him a fool. He wasn't. He was a good, kind man. He had faults, to be sure, but so do you."

Sitre jerked her hand away, shot to her feet, and flew from the room. Angry sobs reached them through the door.

"She cries for a lost love, not my husband," Mutnefret said regretfully. "She wished to wed a soldier from the garrison, an infantry officer, a nice young man with no future. Montu forbade it, insisting instead that she accept the petition of an older man, a wealthy landowner whose country estate adjoins ours. She's never forgiven him." She rose to her feet. "I must go to her, Lieutenant."

Bak also stood up. "Do you have any idea why Montu remained at Djeser Djeseru the night he was slain?"

"I, too, have wondered." A puzzled frown creased her forehead. "When he didn't come home for his evening meal, I thought he had gone to our country house. Our scribe, who manages the estate, had been toiling there all day. He returned to Waset, thinking to find him here."

"Did you not begin to worry?"

"He often spent his evenings in a house of pleasure near the mansion of the lord Ptah, and he'd mentioned a new woman there, pretty and young, he'd told me. I assumed he was with her."

Bak had met women who willingly shared their husbands with other women, but few as untroubled by unfaithfulness as Mutnefret appeared to be. "I must see Montu's place of work, mistress."

She bowed her head in acknowledgment. "I'll send a servant, who'll show you the way."

As she hurried out the door, he picked up a date and popped it into his mouth. He wondered who had been using who: Montu, who had gained comfort and wealth through the alliance, or Mutnefret, who had won a man of some status and the pleasures of the bedchamber.

Bak followed a spindly white-haired servant up an enclosed zigzagging stairway. Large wine vats lined the walls of each landing, giving off a heavy musty scent that failed to overpower the yeasty smell of baking bread that wafted through the house. At the top floor, they crossed a small sunny courtyard where three female servants were sitting in the shade of a palm frond lean-to, weaving coarse white household linen on upright looms. Beyond lay Montu's private domain.

The architect's office was spacious and bright, with three sturdy white-plastered mudbrick columns supporting the ceiling and, Bak guessed, heavy granaries on the roof above. Four high windows made secure by wooden grills allowed the smallest of breezes to cool the interior. Not sure where he should start, he walked around the room, looking without touching. Along one wall, a wooden frame supported several dozen pottery storage jars, most plugged and sealed but a few open to reveal scrolls. Fortunately, Montu or, more likely, the scribe who assisted him in handling his affairs was an orderly individual, who had noted the contents on each jar's shoulder. About half of them related to the business of the household, the remainder to Montu's task as an architect.

"Where's your master's scribe?" Bak asked the old man. "I could use his help in going through these scrolls."

"I'm sorry, sir, but our mistress sent him to her country estate. Someone in authority had to be there, and since she has many decisions to make here in Waset, she sent Teti in her place."

Bak nodded, well aware of the many options she would have to choose among when arranging for her husband's embalming and burial. "Does Teti spend much of his time over there?" he asked, recalling that the scribe had been across the river the final day of Montu's life.

"Two days out of three, sir." The old man hesitated, added, "Our master enjoyed the bounties of the estate, but had no talent for farming. Teti managed both land and accounts."

"He appears to be a man of uncommon worth."

"Indeed he is, sir."

Turning away from the files, Bak studied the rest of the room. A thick pallet lay on the floor at the brightest end, marking Montu's place, while a woven reed mat accommodated the scribe. Between the two lay scribal palettes, a water dish, and cakes of red and black ink; a bowl of aromatic leaves and dried flower petals; and a half-empty wine jar and a stemmed bowl with a reddish crust on the bottom. He eyed the bowl with satisfaction. If it told a true tale, no servant had cleaned the room since the architect's death.

Close to Montu's pallet were a basket of tied scrolls and several piles of papyrus scraps held in place beneath smooth, flattish stones. Near the scribe's place were baskets of pottery shards and limestone flakes and three small plaster-coated boards, all used for rough calculations and writings. Well out of the way against a far wall were surveyors' and builders' tools and rock samples. A cast-off tunic lay on a low table, and a pair of fine leather sandals had been kicked off near the doorway.

Bak dismissed the servant, dragged one of three stools close to the files and, with a resigned sigh, set to work. A cursory inspection of the household accounts verified his assumption that Montu had wed a wealthy woman. Mutnefret and Sitre had inherited in equal amounts the house in Waset and the substantial country estate on the west bank of the river. Bak was not a scribe, but he could see that the properties had increased in value slowly but steadily over the years. Whether the scribe Teti had been guided by Montu—and Bak doubted he had if the architect had shirked his duty at home as at Djeser Djeseru—the women's property had not suffered.

Moving on to Montu's professional life, Bak found scrolls that revealed a man of modest talent who, as he moved up from the smaller projects to the large, had always toiled among others of equal rank, and had always stood behind another, more dynamic man. One such as Senenmut, who relied on lesser men to make his projects a success.

Beneath the stone weights, Bak found orderly piles of documents, half-completed drawings, and sketches of architectural elements. The rock samples, limestone one and all, he guessed had been taken from various locations around Djeser Djeseru. The pottery shards and limestone flakes would have been gleaned from a trash dump, their smooth, unblemished sides to be used for rough drawings, notes, and quick calculations of too small importance to be placed on the more valuable papyrus.

Glimpsing sketches and scraps of writing on some of the shards, he drew the loose-woven and rather worn basket close to take a better look. If Montu had already used them, he might have carelessly thrown away some hint of what he had been doing that had led to his death.

Lifting out one shard after another, he quickly realized the sketches were not the work of Montu, nor, he assumed, were the bits of writing. He found many fully realized drawings, most having no color, each created by an artist of exceptional talent. He recognized them as trial copies of the reliefs that adorned the walls of Djeser Djeseru, thrown away after the drawing was transferred to the temple wall. The back sides of the shards were bare, which explained why Montu—or, more likely, someone in his stead—had collected them for future use.

Rougher sketches embellished the remainder of the shards. Almost cartoon-like, they revealed a highly developed, sometimes vulgar sense of humor. Many were general in nature, funny but irreverent commentaries on daily life in the capital, on the surrounding farmland, at Djeser Djeseru and the Great Place. A small percentage represented Senenmut or Maatkare Hatshepsut, a few in an extremely unflattering way. These sketches, like the more accomplished drawings, had come from a trash pile at Djeser Djeseru, he felt certain.

Smiling at an especially humorous erotic sketch of an aging lover with a courtesan, he reached deeper into the basket. The shard he retrieved was the shoulder and neck of a broken jar. Curious, he turned it right side up. His breath caught in his throat. The sketch on its outer surface was incomplete, but enough remained to recognize the wing tips and rear segment of a bee and what might well be two beads in a necklace. It had not been drawn by as accomplished a hand as most of the other sketches in the basket. In fact, it looked very much like the drawing on the jar he had confiscated in Buhen.

Whether Montu had picked up the shard by chance or had deliberately hidden it among the others, Bak had no way of knowing. Could the architect have made the drawing himself? Could he have been the man stealing from the old tombs? Only a mission as serious as that, one that required secret activity, would account for his presence at Djeser Djeseru in the dead of night.

With rising excitement, he searched through the remaining shards. He found nothing more, which forced him to admit the shard could have been thrown away by anyone. Still, Montu could have gone into the valley to rob a tomb and by chance have bumped into the malign spirit. That man, fearing the terrible death he would face for causing the many deadly accidents, would most certainly have slain one who could, and no doubt would, air his identity.

Bak had not once considered Montu a tomb robber, but with the shard in his hand, the possibility filled his heart.

Tamping down his excitement, telling himself he had no real proof, he returned to the main floor and told a comely young female servant he wished to speak again with Mutnefret.

"I'm sorry, sir, but she's gone to a sculptor's studio to purchase a votive statue upon which our master's name will be carved. She plans to have the image placed in the mansion of the lord Amon so it can share in the bounty of offerings presented each day to the greatest of gods."

Is she easing her conscience because she doesn't care that he's dead, Bak wondered, or does she really believe him worthy of offerings? A man who cheated his co-workers out of his fair share of effort, one who may have robbed the dead. "Is mistress Sitre available?"

"You wish to speak with me, Lieutenant?" Sitre asked, stepping through the doorway. She waved her hand to dismiss the servant, dropped onto the stool Bak had occupied earlier, and offered him the other seat. Her eyes were clear, beautifully made up. Her sobs had evidently been of short duration. "Did you find anything of interest in that wretched Montu's place of work?"

"The basket of pottery shards," he said, opting to stand. "Do you know when he brought them home?"

The young woman was too preoccupied with adjusting her broad beaded collar to notice the shard in his hand. "A week or two ago, I suppose."

"Was he in the habit of collecting them personally or did he ask others to do it for him?"

"Are you jesting, Lieutenant?" Her eyes darted toward him and she laughed, a harsh, jarring sound from one so lovely. "He'd never have stooped so low as to go through a trash dump. Especially not at Djeser Djeseru, where dozens of men lesser than he would've see him."

Her dislike of her mother's husband colored everything she said, irritating Bak, making him wonder how much could be at best an exaggeration, at worst untrue. "Do you have any idea who might've gathered them for him?"

"The chief scribe Ramose has an apprentice, his son, I believe." She plucked a lily from the bowl and held it to her nose. The scent was strong, too sweet for Bak's pleasure. "Montu liked to take advantage of the boy. Of Ramose, really, since he could not refuse."

Vowing to speak with the youth as soon as he returned to Djeser Djeseru, Bak rested his shoulder against a column. "Are bees kept at your country estate?" Ordinarily he would not have asked such a question of a young woman of means, but if Pashed had been correct in saying she and her mother toiled beside their servants, she would know.

"Of course. Doesn't every farmer keep them?"

He could see she was puzzled by the new subject. "Do you use all the honey you harvest, or do you have excess to trade?"

"I think we use it all, but you'd have to ask our scribe Teti to be sure. Why do you wish to know?"

He held out the shard so she could see the sketch. "I found this among Montu's possessions. Do you identify your honey containers in this manner?"

"We don't, no, but I think I've seen the symbol somewhere."

"Can you recall where?"

"At the market here in Waset? At someone's estate?" She waved the flower slowly back and forth beneath her nose, trying to recall. "Must've been a long time ago. The answer eludes me."

"A neighbor, perhaps? Or someone with whom Montu was friendly?"

"I've no idea."

Disappointed, he dropped onto the second stool. "Did Montu name the man who told him he also saw the malign spirit?"

"Are you serious?" Her laugh was scathing. "He thought himself the most important man in Kemet, Lieutenant. No others equaled him and none were worthy of mention except in passing."

"He gave no hint, such as the man's occupation?"

"He referred to him merely as 'another man.' "

"With Montu no longer among the living, will you wed the young soldier you wished to wed before he interfered?" He was fishing and he knew it, throwing out a line in the hope of catching almost anything.

"My mother told you of him?" Sitre's voice rang with indignation. "After letting that wretched husband of hers betroth me to another, how dare she speak of him!"

"She was making excuses for you. Offering a reason for your dislike of Montu."

"Montu was vile, plain and simple." She let out a scornful snort. "He couldn't keep his eyes off me, yet he dared not touch me. He dared not risk angering my mother, losing her wealth and property. And he dared not soil me, for he'd promised me to a wealthy nobleman, thinking to raise his own position in life. Thinking to walk side by side with one familiar with the corridors of the royal house. Thinking he'd be considered an equal by men of royal blood."

"Montu sounds to me like a swine," Bak said, welcoming the opening she had unknowingly offered. "Dishonest through and through."

Sitre looked thoughtful. "I don't think he was out-and-out dishonest, Lieutenant. He had what I've always thought of as a convenient honesty. An honesty prompted by whatever he needed or desired at the time."

Her answer seemed sincere, not inspired by her dislike of the man. Which led Bak to wonder exactly what Montu had hoped to attain that had driven him to rifle the ancient tombs, putting at risk a life of relative ease and luxury, a life most men would envy.

Chapter Nine

"You found this in Montu's home?" Lieutenant Menna took the shard from Bak, walked to the door of his office, and looked at it in the better light of the portico that surrounded the spacious courtyard outside.

Bak followed, escaping from the tiny, cramped room with its overabundance of scrolls and pottery jars whose gaping mouths revealed additional documents. "The sketch of the bee looks too much like the one I found in Buhen not to be by the same hand."

"And, like the jar you found there, you think this may've been used to smuggle jewelry."

"I don't know," Bak admitted, "but we can't overlook the possibility."

"We." Menna walked a few paces along the portico, swung around, and walked back. "I know you mean well, Lieutenant, and believe it or not, I do appreciate your offer of help."

Bak clamped his mouth shut tight. He had come to assist, not quarrel.

Menna glanced at three perfectly groomed men—guard officers in the royal house, Bak suspected—standing in the shade of a large sycamore in the center of the court. They were deep in conversation, much too preoccupied to pay attention to what Menna had to say. The breeze had stiffened, carrying the smell of horses from a nearby stable. Dogs barked not far away, animals held in the kennels Bak had come upon while searching the large police compound for Menna's office. Animals used for tracking, guard duty, desert patrol.

"I freely admit I'm an infantry officer with no experience at investigating criminal activity," Menna said, "and I must confess that these thefts have me stymied. But I'll learn best through my own mistakes and successes."

Bak realized the guard officer was trying hard to tread a middle ground, to have his way without offending. He acknowledged his understanding with a nod. "I was a chariotry officer when I was sent to Buhen to stand at the head of the Medjay police. I knew nothing about my new task and had no one to instruct me. I erred more than once, and I'd like to believe I'll never make the same mistakes again."

"I've held this assignment for three years." Menna's tone was light, meant to be cynical, but it carried an edge of bitterness. "The guards who report to me have excelled in laying hands on men of no consequence who steal from burial parties, from people who visit the tombs of their justified dead, even from their fellow workers. I myself have surpassed all others in preparing reports about their many small successes."

Bak smiled at a jest that was obviously too close to the truth to seem funny to Menna. "Amonked says you know very well the cemeteries in and around western Waset and the people who dwell in the area. I'd think that would ease your task considerably."

"The people know me and I believe they like me, but they won't confide in me. Any theft they might mention could lead to the arrest of a brother or cousin."

"Perhaps you're too close to the problem and in need of another, less involved man's thoughts." Bak quickly raised his hand, stifling an objection. "Should you wish to talk, I'll not tread on your toes. That I vow."

Menna stared at him, undecided. After an interminable silence, he found stools for the two of them and ordered a servant to bring beer. He spoke at first haltingly, guarding his words, but the desire to speak out, the need, quickly banished these signs of mistrust. He had thoroughly inspected all the cemeteries in western Waset, he said, and had found no disturbed shafts. He'd considered the ruined memorial temple of Nebhepetre Montuhotep as the key to the rifled tombs, and had searched the desert plain and surrounding cliffs with no luck. He had personally examined each tomb opened by chance by the workmen building Djeser Djeseru and had watched as each had been sealed and covered over.

"You appear to have left no pebble unturned," Bak said.

"I've missed something. What it is, I can't imagine."

"More than one man would be involved. Digging out a tomb shaft is hard labor."

"Not many, I'd think. The more who know, the greater the chance of a loose tongue."

"You've heard no rumors?"

"Only that ancient jewelry was confiscated at the harbor; therefore, an old tomb had to've been broken into. There's been a considerable amount of speculation as to who might've done the deed, but no one can name the thief with any certainty. Each time I question men I suspect, they prove themselves innocent."

The robbers had to be a close-knit group and exceptionally careful not to be seen or found out.

Bak picked up the shard, which he had laid on the ground beside his stool, and looked at the image of the bee. Could Montu have been rifling the old tombs? he wondered again. As before, the query took him back to the other, equally important question: what other reason would he have had for being at Djeser Djeseru in the dark of night? "What can you tell me of Montu?"

"The man was insufferable." Menna nudged away with his toe a gray-striped cat that was sniffing his beer jar. "He'd threaten at the drop of a wig to complain to Senenmut each time I suggested changes to improve security at Djeser Djeseru."

Bak's interest heightened. If Montu had been rifling the old tombs . . . "What kind of suggestions did he spurn?"

"I can't remember one that he accepted. At first, he infuriated me, but when I realized he treated everyone with equal venom, I learned to ignore him."

"He showed no specific interest in precautions that would interfere with tomb robbers?"

"None." Menna's eyes narrowed. "You don't think he was the man I've been seeking?"

Bak shrugged. "I found the shard in his office, which is suggestive, but it was in a basket of similar shards that I feel certain were collected from a trash heap at Djeser Djeseru."

"He was a vile man. I'd not put thievery past him." Menna's brow furrowed in thought. "In fact, now that you've drawn my attention to him, I can't think of a man more likely. As an architect, he'd know better than most where to find the old tombs. I must look into the possibility." His expression turned from satisfaction to consternation and he muttered a curse.

"What problem do you see?" Bak asked, puzzled.

A wry smile touched the guard officer's face. "Montu's wife's daughter. Sitre. She's lovely. I've admired her from afar for some time, but never approached her because I couldn't bear the sight of him. Upon hearing of his death, I hoped . . ." He let out a soft, cynical laugh. "If I prove him guilty of tomb robbery, I'll humiliate her mother, and the woman won't allow me near Sitre."

Bak clapped him on the shoulder. "I must admit I couldn't tell exactly what Mutnefret was feeling, but I sensed no depth to her mourning. I suspect she secretly feels she owes the malign spirit—or whoever slew him—a debt of gratitude."

Menna gave Bak a sharp look. "Was he slain by the malign spirit, do you think?"

"By the man who pretends to be a malign spirit," Bak corrected.

"A man? Are you certain?" Menna's face clouded, doubt

filled his voice. "I, too, have questioned its existence at times, but men who dwell in the workmen's huts have actually seen it."

"Lights and shadows. Nothing more. And those far away." Bak found it difficult to believe that an intelligent man such as Menna could be so naive, but he should know better by this time. Other equally intelligent men clung to the belief as a bird holds fast to a branch in a high wind. "I climbed the cliff yesterday, after the accident at the northern retaining wall, and I saw signs of a man. A two-legged, thinking creature made the boulders fall, not some ethereal being."

"You're certain?"

"I found a fresh scar where a lever was used to pry away a section of rock."

Menna looked thoughtful. "Could Montu have been the malign spirit?"

"He was not among the living yesterday," Bak pointed out.

"The cliff face has fallen before. How do you know the scar was not made several weeks ago?"

"It looked fresh."

"We've had no rain and no wind to speak of, nothing to make it lose its shape and color."

"The wind blew hard yesterday morning," Bak said with a touch of impatience.

"Did it not blow from north to south? Coming over the ridge as it did, would it not have left the cliff free of wind?"

"You could be right," Bak admitted grudgingly, "but I know in my heart that you err. The scar was fresh, as were marks we found of a man who'd brushed out his footprints. Montu may well have been your tomb robber, but he was not the malign spirit. Your task may be eased, but I must continue with mine."

As a small child, Bak had many times visited the house of life with his widowed father, who could spend hours hunting through the ancient documents for an obscure poultice or incantation or the source of some lesser known malady and its treatment. Bored with waiting, he had sometimes ventured into other parts of the vast holdings around the mansion of the lord Amon, the many storehouses, offices, and dwellings, the narrow lanes and unexpected courtyards. Each time, he had lost his way and some kindly priest or scribe had returned him to his worried parent.

Years had passed and, though he found the sacred precinct smaller than he had thought it in the past, the many buildings and crowded lanes were no less confusing. Directed to one place and another by priests and scribes scurrying around like ants, preparing for an upcoming religious festival, it took him over a half hour to find Kaemwaset. As he approached the building, he realized he was no more than one hundred paces from a gate that led directly to the police compound. He could have saved himself much time and effort if he had but known.

The man he sought sat cross-legged on the ground beneath a portico that shaded three sides of a small, open courtyard. Ten boys of eight or so years sat in two rows before him, limestone shards on their laps, writing time-honored maxims their instructor read aloud. Spotting Bak, he assigned a boy to take his place and ushered his visitor across the court to a mudbrick bench shaded by a half-dozen date palms. The breeze had strengthened further, making the fronds rattle and sending dust and dried grasses scurrying across the ground.

The priest, whom Bak guessed was in his late forties, explained that he had just returned from Djeser Djeseru. He had spent an hour or so praying for the dead and injured at the scene of the accident and had gone on to make offerings in the chapel of the lady Hathor, one of the few old structures still intact at Djeser Djeseru. The small but venerable mudbrick building would in a few years be abandoned, its goddess moved to the new and far more elegant chapel that would be an integral part of Maatkare Hatshepsut's memorial temple.

"So the workmen decided after all not to lay down their tools." Bak was pleased. Common sense had won out.

"Thanks to the urging of Pashed and Ramose . . ." Kaemwaset's lips twitched, hinting at a smile. ". . . and a rumor going round—spread it seems by that scribe of yours and Ramose's son."

Bak nodded his satisfaction, but made no comment.

The priest's smile—if smile it had been—vanished, and worry creased his brow. "Word has traveled throughout Djeser Djeseru that you found on the cliff face signs that a man set the rocks to falling. Is it true?"

"Without doubt."

Kaemwaset released a long, unhappy sigh. "How could any man cause so much injury and death in so heartless a fashion?"

"I don't yet know, but I mean to find out."

No man could mistake his determination, and the priest's quick nod, his grim expression, signaled approval. "When we spoke yesterday I aired the official rationalization for the many accidents, the reason most often uttered among our sovereign's allies in the mansion of the lord Amon. I could see you weren't convinced."

Bak eyed the priest with interest. "You use the word *rationalization*. Does that mean you have doubts?"

"Politics are politics, Lieutenant. In order to satisfy those who must be made content, the tales and actions produced out of necessity or zeal seldom conform to reality."

The priest was a realist, a trait Bak liked. "The theory could be true to some extent—I'll not discount it altogether—but it's no better than any other I've thought of and set aside."

Kaemwaset shook his head as if unable to cope with the reality. "What's becoming of this world of ours? Are the gods turning their backs to us?"

The question was unanswerable, as they both knew.

Childish laughter drew the priest's eyes toward the boys. "Why have you come to me, Lieutenant?"

"You often spend time at Djeser Djeseru. I'd value your thoughts, your impressions, any conclusions you may've reached that might help me lay hands on the man who pretends to be the malign spirit, the man who may've slain Montu."

"I fear I can't help you," Kaemwaset said regretfully. "My task there necessarily means I stand apart from the others."

Bak's expression turned skeptical. "How long have you been priest to Djeser Djeseru?"

"Since construction began."

"Five years. That's a long time to close your eyes and ears to your surroundings."

The priest glanced again at his charges and scowled. The boys were rocking from side to side, bumping shoulders and giggling as if the game were the funniest in the world. The youth sitting in front had his hand over his mouth, trying to smother laughter. "I've noticed bad feelings at Djeser Djeseru, and I've suspected Montu of being the culprit. If he was the troublemaker I believed him to be, would his slayer not stand among the many men he alienated?"

"A possibility I've not cast aside," Bak acknowledged.

Merry laughter erupted, and Kaemwaset clapped his hands, reminding the boys he was not so far away he could not discipline them. "I've also noticed an uneasiness at times, and that I attributed—rightly, I suspect—to the malign spirit. I know how the poor and uneducated are, superstitious to the core, and I thought their tales the creation of their imagination. Now, it seems, I erred."

"To a degree. The malign spirit is real, but without doubt a man."

"I don't disbelieve you, Lieutenant, but what do you hope to gain by airing the belief?"

"The workmen must see the truth. I want none of them so angered by the deception that they'll go out and invite injury or death, but should I need their help, I don't want them paralyzed by fear."

"I applaud your intent, but I'm not entirely convinced

you're doing the right thing. Would it not be wiser to let the man you seek believe you know nothing of him? Wiser and safer?"

"You sound like my father," Bak said, not bothering to hide his irritation.

Kaemwaset bowed his head, acknowledging the mild rebuke. "Forgive me, sir. I've taught for many years and can't resist speaking to other young people as I do to my students."

A boy yelled. Bak's eyes followed those of the priest. A small redheaded child had risen to his feet and gone down the row to strike a larger boy on the head with his scribal pallet. The youth Kaemwaset had left in charge grabbed the pallet, caught the boy by the ear, and forced him to return to his seat.

Bak could see he was about to lose the priest to his responsibilities. "Did you know Montu well or merely in passing?"

Kaemwaset tore his eyes from his students. "Our paths crossed at Djeser Djeseru, nowhere else. I found him a small man who believed himself large in all respects."

"Would he take what by rights belonged to another?"

"Would he steal?" Kaemwaset appeared surprised by the thought. "Hmmm. An interesting question." When Bak failed to explain further, he shook his head. "I can't answer with certainty; I didn't know him that well. If I had to make a guess, I'd say he would—if he believed he could get away free and clear. As I said before, he was a small man."

Bak left the priest, thinking of the shard he had found in Montu's office and the new path he had been following since. Sitre had accused the architect of having a convenient honesty. Menna thought him likely enough to be a tomb robber that he had vowed to dig deeper in search of the truth. Kaemwaset thought him a likely thief given the proper circumstances. But had he been a thief? The shard was suggestive, but it was far from proof. True, the sketch had not been made with the same skill as the others in the basket, but that indicated only that the artist was inexperienced, not necessarily that it had been drawn by Montu.

Even if Menna did discover that Montu had been robbing the old tombs, he might not learn the names of those who had helped him or the location of the disturbed sepulchers. Maybe later, when Hori had the time . . . . Well, it wouldn't hurt to plan ahead, he decided.

A quick glance at the lord Re told him he had at least another hour before his father would sail back across the river. He hurried around a corner, where a burst of wind caught him full force. He snapped his eyes closed and shut his mouth tight to keep out the dust blowing down the narrow lane. A few people passed him by, all rushing as he was toward a quiet and dust-free haven. Not a cat nor dog was anywhere in sight; the few donkeys allowed to stray were standing in sheltered corners, their rumps to the wind.

Another turn and a wider street took him to a square complex of buildings that served as the house of records, where the archives were located. Stepping through the wide entry portal, he found himself in a pleasant courtyard shaded by sycamores and palms and fragrant with bright blossoms. More than a dozen scribes had brought their tasks outside so they could enjoy the breeze beneath the surrounding portico. They had, however, misjudged the growing strength of the wind. Those without the foresight to weigh their scrolls down with stones were scurrying about, collecting documents rolling before each gust. The rest were grabbing up their scribal implements, preparing to retreat inside.

Bak scooped up several scrolls and handed them to the nearest scribe, an older man with the harried look of a minor bureaucrat.

"I've a question," Bak said. "Can you help me, sir?"

The man dropped the scrolls into a basket and lunged to grab another rolling cylinder. "Of course I can, but be quick about it, young man. I've much to do before day's end."

"I'm a police officer, assigned to look into a problem at our sovereign's new memorial temple in western Waset. Sometime in the near future I wish to send my scribe here to search the archives for information I need. Will he be welcomed or spurned?"

"We don't admit just any man," the scribe said officiously. "He'd need higher authority than you to gain admission." He scurried after another scroll, diminishing the effect he had intended. "No less than the chief archivist himself."

Smothering a smile, Bak tapped his baton of office against his calf and spoke in an offhand manner. "Would Amonked, Storekeeper of Amon and our sovereign's cousin, be of sufficient rank?"

"He would, sir, yes indeed."

Bak pretended not to notice the man's sudden obsequiousness. "My scribe is called Hori. He'll come when he has the time, authority in hand."

By the time Bak reached the small quay where his father moored his skiff, the wind was blowing hard and cold, negating the warmth of the setting sun. He found the vessel empty, Ptahhotep nowhere in sight. The light craft was bumping against the revetment, thrown cruelly at the stone by waves driven by the wind. If he had not expected to leave right away, he would have moved it, dragging it high up onto the riverbank where twenty or more vessels of all sizes were already laying, left there by men who had foreseen the heavy weather.

Two vessels moored farther along the revetment were much larger than the skiff, better able to endure the storm. A traveling ship laden with locally made red pottery shared the space with a small cargo vessel on which every cubit of deck space was mounded with chunks of fine white limestone. Unlike the skiff, fenders protected their wooden hulls. Fittings rattled in the wind, a loose corner of sail flapped against a yard. Neither was manned, their crews most likely warm and snug in some nearby house of pleasure. A short way upstream an unimposing fishing vessel, weathered to a deep brown, was moored to posts pounded into the river-bank. Its hull repeatedly ground against the rocks buried beneath the mud.

Shivering in the chill, Bak regretted that he wore no tunic. Nor could he buy one. The casual market that usually lined the waterfront was empty of both sellers and buyers, the lean-tos designed for shade offering no shelter from the wind. Most, in fact, had blown over and lay in scattered heaps of spindly poles and roofmats against the buildings facing the quay. Wind whistled across rooftops, a dog slunk into a dark, narrow lane. A man darted from one doorway to another and vanished around a corner.

Bak entered the only place of business still open, a dark and dingy house of pleasure. There, as had been the case several times in the past, he found Ptahhotep awaiting him. The older man wore a tunic of heavy linen and carried a second one for his son. It was too snug across the shoulders, but better than crossing the open water with nothing to hold off the cold.

They hurried out of the building and crossed to the skiff, pummeled by a gust of wind. Bak thanked the lord Amon that the sky was clear. At least they would not be drenched to the skin by one of the rare rainstorms that struck the area. "Do you wish to remain in Waset tonight? The storm is sure to blow over by morning."

A strong, cold gust made the older man irascible. "What do you take me for? A man who's grown cowardly in my old age?"

Bak refrained from pointing out that, rather than sailing off by himself, his father had waited, hoping he would come so he would have someone to help with sail and rudder when he crossed the river. "You are cautious, my father, in no way a coward."

"What kind of physician would I be if I failed to respond when summoned to an individual who could be reached in no other way but by boat?"

Bak knelt at the quay's edge, caught the rope that bound the skiff's prow to a mooring post, and pulled the bucking, tugging vessel close. His father released the stern rope. The vessel was similar to the one Bak had grown up with: sleek, fast, and practical, befitting a physician.

"Hurry, Father. Night will fall before long and the lord Amon alone knows where we'll touch shore on the west bank. If we're blown too far south, we could have a long trek back home."

The older man, no novice at boarding a boat in bad weather, waited for the most opportune time and leaped aboard. Bak untied the rope from the mooring post and, with the prow hard against the quay, wound it around the post. Scrambling aboard, he jerked the cord free. Ptahhotep shoved an oar into his hands and together they pushed the craft away from the quay and rowed like madmen toward open water.

Clear of the shore and other ships, the river ran free of obstructions. It flowed in a northeasterly direction, while the wind and the waves came out of the north, two powerful forces vying for control of the small vessel and all it contained. Low but fierce waves raced across the surface, lifting the skiff and dropping it hard, throwing a spray of chill water over its occupants.

Bak knew a man accustomed to sailing the Great Green Sea would say these waves were nothing, trifling bumps on the water's surface, but to him and all who sailed on the normally benevolent river, they were harsh reminders that the lord Hapi was not always a kind and generous god. He had sailed in similar conditions and was not afraid, but he felt a healthy respect for the combined forces of wind and water.

With his father manning the tiller, Bak struggled to raise the single rectangular sail. The moment the heavy linen rose above the lower yard, the wind caught it. The higher he lifted it, the stronger the force that filled it, threatening to tear the halyard from his hands or the cleats from the deck. Threatening to capsize the vessel. His father, who had sailed all his life and had taught his son the art, eased the boat around, attaining a fine line between letting too much wind into the sail and letting the skiff founder in the waves. At times the craft literally stood still.

At last the upper yard reached the masthead. Working together with sail and tiller, father and son turned the wind and current to their advantage. In a short time they were on course, not following a direct line, for the wind demanded a zigzag route, but they felt confident they would reach the opposite shore not far from the path that would take them home. They sped across the water, their journey strenuous and cold, but invigorating.

The lord Re hovered above the western peak behind Djeser Djeseru, dappling the surface of the rough water in reds and golds. Some distance upstream, a large traveling ship was coming toward them, its sail tucked away, its oarsmen holding the vessel on a course midstream of the current carrying them northward. Other than that, the sole vessel in sight was a fishing boat sailing some distance behind them on a course similar to theirs. Like the vessel Bak had noticed near the quay in Waset, its hull was weathered a deep brown. Assuming it was the same boat, it must have left not long after they did.

Bak dismissed the two vessels from his thoughts and concentrated on keeping the skiff on course. For all practical purposes, he and his father had the river to themselves. They could go where they pleased, sail as fast as they wished. The world was theirs alone.

Keeping in sight the mouth of a canal on the opposite shore, using the lord Re as a beacon, they sailed roughly in a northwesterly direction. After attaining a heady speed that would set the fastest chariot horse to shame, Bak would adjust the sail, spilling the wind, holding barely enough to maintain western movement while the current carried the skiff downstream. He was exhilarated by the speed, by the challenge of competing with the storm and the river. The wind tugged at his hair and the fabric of his tunic. It whistled through the lines and rattled the fittings atop the masthead. Gulls soared above, wings spread, letting the wind carry them south, squawking as if making light of the men below.

About midstream Bak tore his eyes from the goal ahead to see how his father was faring in the stern. He was startled to see the fishing boat behind them, coming up fast. Too fast. His heart leaped into his throat and he spat out a curse.

Though a far more cumbersome vessel, it was twice as large as their own and much heavier, with considerably more sail. The master of the vessel was using that sail to great advantage, allowing the wind to push the boat at an excessive speed.

"Father! Behind us!" Bak yelled. "He doesn't see us! Swing the tiller!"

Ptahhotep glanced backward and at the same time did as he was told. Bak filled the sail as much as he dared. The skiff swung partway around, climbed a wave, dropped with a thud into the hollow beyond. The fishing boat appeared to turn, as if deliberately following them. Denying the thought as ridiculous, he signaled his father for more rudder and let the sail balloon. The keelless skiff, leaning at a precarious angle, bumped across the waves, out of the fishing boat's way. Bak turned forward, thinking to set the vessel upright.

His father yelled, "He's turning with us!"

Bak swung around. The larger hull was fast approaching, too fast to escape. "Jump, Father!"

His face white with shock, Ptahhotep let go of the tiller and threw himself overboard. Praying his parent would get safely out of the path of the larger vessel, Bak let go of the sheets. As they slipped out of the cleats and snaked across the deck, the prow of the fishing boat loomed over the stern. The sail billowed furiously, slapping Bak's face. The skiff tipped over farther and began to skid on its side, taking in water. Bak jumped. The larger vessel struck the smaller, sending him sprawling into the river. The hull of the fishing boat struck him across the back.

Chapter Ten

Stunned by the blow, Bak felt as if he had been struck on the back by the fist of a god. The impact knocked the air from him and shoved him downward. Arms and legs limp, moving where the water took them, he vaguely saw the hull slide over him. Unable to think, he sucked in a breath, filling his lungs with water.

Coughing, taking in more water, desperate for air, he came back to his senses. He knew he was sinking and the current was carrying him downstream. Terror struck. His limbs flailed, too fast, out of control. Recognizing panic and how close he was to drowning, he forced himself to calm down. He held back a cough, made his arms and legs respond, and swam upward. His body felt heavy and stiff. His chest burned. He saw light through the water, beckoning him.

He broke the surface. The water was rough around him. Cold wind and heavy swells washed over his head. He coughed and coughed again, spewing liquid, making room for the air he needed.

Then he thought of his father and the boat that had struck the skiff.

"Father!" he yelled, looking around in all directions.

The sun had vanished, throwing a golden glow into the sky that reflected on the roiling water like broken shards of light, heaving and falling, appearing and disappearing, making it impossible to see any object as small as a man's head. He did glimpse a boat off to the right, making its way toward the west bank. It could have been the fishing boat that had run them down, but it was too far away for him to be sure.

He coughed hard, bellowed out, "Father!"

"Bak!"

Had to be Ptahhotep, he thanked the lord Amon. Hard to hear with water filling his ears, a strange hollow sound that made the man he heard difficult to locate. He called again, received an answer. Swimming in the direction from which he thought the response had come, he quickly found his father clinging to a long curved section of hull, all that remained of the skiff. A stub of mast was attached and a portion of the torn sail floated on the waves.

"Are you all right, Father?"

"Wet and angry but unhurt. And you?"

Bak tried a grin, but his teeth were clenched so tight it looked more like the grimace it was. "My back feels as if it's been peeled, and I sucked in a chestful of water. Other than that, I'm ready to do battle with the malign spirit himself." A gross exaggeration, one intended to make them both feel better.

"That boat struck us on purpose." Ptahhotep's eyes flashed with fury. "The son of a snake, the . . ." He ranted on, spouting invectives even his policeman son had never heard.

Bak looked toward the west bank, searching for the boat he had seen. The lord Re had entered the netherworld, taking with him the glow from the sky. Darkness was falling fast. The vessel had vanished, hidden by the gloom, probably nestled against a mudbank, its sail furled, its weathered hull blending into the background.

The waning light told him they must not tarry. He had every confidence that he could swim to the far shore, but his father was no longer a young man. "We must go, Father. We've a long swim ahead of us."

A movement caught his eye, a traveling ship coming downstream at a fast pace. The vessel he had seen earlier but

had forgotten in the struggle to survive. With the light so uncertain, he feared it might pass them by, but a member of the
crew spotted the torn sail. The oarsmen slowed the craft and
maneuvered it close with practiced ease. Ropes were thrown
and the crew hauled them on board.

Bak glanced at the lord Khepre, a sliver of gold peering
over the eastern horizon. He had awakened angry and impatient to get on with the new day, but Hori and Kasaya had yet
to come. The bandage his father had bound around his upper
torso chafed, the musky smell of the poultice tickled his
nose, and the bandage around his thigh was too tight. He untied the latter, decided the abrasion was healing properly,
and threw it away. His father, called out to tend an infected
foot, need never know.

When he went outside to care for his horses, he found Defender lame. A cursory inspection revealed a small stone
embedded in the animal's hoof, a problem easily fixed and
best not left to the end of day. But first the team had to be fed
and watered. As he finished the task, he spotted the scribe and
Medjay hurrying along the path toward the house. The bandage roused their concern and questions. While the horses ate
their fill, he sat with the pair beneath the sycamore, where he
shared their early morning meal—bread, cheese, and dates
Kasaya's mother had provided—and told them how the fishing boat had run down his father's skiff.

"The malign spirit," Hori said, his face grim. "The boat
had to be his. Or under his control."

"I'd wager my iron dagger that you're right." Bak did not
make such a statement lightly. The weapon was a treasured
gift, given to him by a woman he had met when first he had
gone to Buhen, one he had never ceased to hold close within
his heart.

"Who else has reason to want you dead?" Hori's question
required no answer and received none.

Bak retrieved a basket of instruments his father kept in the
house in case he was called out to care for an animal and

knelt before the lame horse. While he examined the gelding's hoof, Kasaya held the rope halter and rubbed his head. Hori hoisted himself onto the mudbrick wall, well out of the way of flying hooves should the creature strike out. He made no secret of the fact that he rued the day his father had insisted he follow him as a scribe, and he longed to be a man of action—if not a police officer, the chariotry officer Bak had been—but he did not quite trust the large, swift animals.

"I'm surprised you two weren't attacked when you climbed the cliff," the youth said.

"Maybe our so-called malign spirit wasn't at Djeser Djeseru then and didn't know we went up to investigate." Bak probed gently around the stone, trying to see how deep it was and loosen it if possible. Defender nickered softly but stood still. "Or he may've been there but couldn't get away unnoticed. Or, more likely, he feared being seen unless he took a roundabout route that would get him to the top too late."

The gelding's withers twitched in silent complaint. Kasaya distracted him with a handful of grain. "I suppose a man could climb up a different crevice than the one we did, but could he cross the tops of those tower-like formations without being seen from below?"

"I don't know, but I assume so." Deciding the stone could easily be removed, Bak took a pair of long-nosed tweezers from the basket and pulled it free. He laid the instrument aside and examined the hoof to see how deep the injury went.

"The malign spirit must fear you greatly." Hori held out a small bowl of salve Ptahhotep had prepared. It smelled much the same as the poultice on Bak's back. "First he made the cliff face fall upon you and now he's wrecked your father's boat."

"He'd better fear me." Bak's voice was harsh, angry. The horse, snorting surprise, jerked backward. "I'm a policeman, trained as a soldier. I can take care of myself. But my father's a physician, a man no longer young and vigorous. I'm very much troubled by the fact that he's been brought into this."

"He was an innocent bystander, surely!"

"Was he?" Wrinkling his nose at the strong, musky odor of the salve, Bak gently rubbed it into the tender spot. "The fishing boat was moored near the quay where he always leaves his skiff. Was it waiting in the expectation that I would sail home with him? Or was it waiting for him alone and I was an added bonus? Was he meant to be injured or slain as a warning to me?"

"I want my father guarded at all times, sir," Bak said, concluding his tale of the previous evening's events.

"Why do you come to me?" Commander Maiherperi, a slender man of forty or so years, eyed Bak with an intensity that would have made a younger, greener man uneasy. His woolly hair and dusky skin spoke of mixed blood; the scar across his cheek told of a man who had earned his lofty position. "Amonked brought you into this. Why not go to him?"

"I did. He suggested I speak with you. You stand at the head of the men who guard the royal house; therefore, you stand apart from all other forms of military and civil authority." A wry smile formed on Bak's lips. "He also believes you owe me a favor."

The commander, seated on a chair on a low dais, allowed himself a slight smile. "Because I tore you from the army to place you at the head of a company of Medjay police? Because I sent you to Buhen when our sovereign ordered you exiled? Has he not seen how you've thrived on the frontier?"

The chamber, central to the guards' barracks inside the walls surrounding the royal house and grounds in Waset, was of imposing proportions. Its lofty ceiling was supported by four tall pillars, and air circulating through high windows kept the space cool. The odors of leather and sweat served as a constant reminder of generations of armed and armored men who had come to report to and receive orders from their commander. Other than two tough-looking guards flanking the wide, double doors behind him, Bak and Maiherperi were the sole men present. Their words resonated through the huge, almost empty space.

"We spent more than a month together on the Belly of Stones, sir. We came to know each other quite well."

"So I've been told."

Bak was not surprised the commander knew of Amonked's adventures in Wawat. The officer's knowledge was legendary. It had to be, for he was responsible for the safety of the royal house and the well-being of their sovereign and all she held dear.

Maiherperi adjusted the pillow behind him and leaned back in his chair. "I don't know your father, Lieutenant, but from what I've heard of him, he'll not be pleased to have an escort keeping him company day after day."

"I can see no other way. If the man I seek thinks to hurt me through him, or to intimidate me, he and our small farm must not go unprotected."

"I agree. The accidents at Djeser Djeseru must be stopped, and what your father desires is of no importance. He'll have to put up with a guard until you succeed in your mission."

Normally Bak would have urged caution, warning the commander that he sooner or later might fail to lay hands on a man he sought. Not this time, however. He would catch the malign spirit if it took all his remaining days.

"I wish you to have a lean-to set up in the old temple of Djeserkare Amonhotep and his esteemed mother Ahmose Nefertari," Bak said to Hori. They were walking with Kasaya up the causeway that would take them to Djeser Dje-seru. "You must position it in a place of privacy, where no man can come close without being seen. Equip it with a low stool, a mat upon which a man can sit, and plentiful jars of beer."

"Yes, sir?" The question in the scribe's voice mirrored the curiosity on his face.

"You've talked with many men who've seen or been a victim of an accident here at Djeser Djeseru. While you set up the lean-to, I'll speak with your friend Ani. Then you must bring those men to me one after another. I wish to learn more of these mishaps firsthand."

"Yes, sir." Hori hurried on up the causeway and across the terrace, passing a gang of workmen towing a sledge on which lay a twice-life-size limestone statue of Maatkare Hatshepsut wrapped for eternity. How they could toil so hard on so hot a day, Bak could not begin to guess.

"Now, Kasaya, untie this bandage. It'll draw too many curious eyes, too many questions."

"Yes, sir. Montu was always after me to do things for him. Run errands mostly." Ani, seated on his mat beneath the scribes' lean-to, poured a couple drops of water onto a cake of black ink and mixed it in with a stiff brush. "I sometimes gathered broken bits of pottery and limestone chips for him, but I've no way of knowing if those you found in his home were those I gave him."

Bak, seated on the stool, was glad he had found the boy alone. He doubted Ramose would have interfered, but the garrulous old man Amonemhab would have added his thoughts, wanted or unwanted. "I was told he took them home a week or two ago."

The boy screwed up his face, thinking. "I'm not sure, sir. Could you describe some of the sketches? I might remember them."

As Bak complied, a drop of sweat trickled down the side of his face. Not a breath of air stirred across Djeser Djeseru, and heat lay over the valley like a heavy pallet stuffed with wool newly cut from a sheep. His back itched, the abrasion irritated by sweat. With the bandage gone, few men had commented, and those who did had assumed his back, like his thigh, had been scraped raw during the rock slide.

The trial copies of gods and offerings were commonplace, it seemed, with few special enough to remember, but the moment Bak began to describe the comic sketches, Ani's frown cleared and a smile broke across his face. "I remember! I took them from the trash heap between the foundation of the new shrine to the lady Hathor and the old temple of Nebhepetre Montuhotep."

Bak smiled with him, momentarily sharing the boy's enjoyment of the rough humor, but quickly sobered. "Do you remember seeing the neck of a broken jar with a sketch of a honey bee on it? Similar to this?" With the tip of his baton, he drew in the sand by his feet a crude jar with a necklace from which hung a pendant bee.

Ani studied it, shook his head. "It might've been there, sir, but I didn't notice it."

"Tell me of the accident." Bak sat down on the low stool and pointed with his baton at the reed mat on the ground in front of him. "Leave nothing out. The smallest detail could be important."

The man, a workman named Mery, looked wary of sharing the shaded space with the officer, not because he feared questions, Bak suspected, but because he was unaccustomed to the company of men of authority. He was one of the multitude who toiled day after day, moving heavy and unwieldy objects from one place to another.

With visible reluctance, he ducked low and seated himself before Bak. Dust clung to the sweat on his body, making him look a part of the earth. "What can I tell you, sir, that I've not already told your scribe?"

Bak kept his breathing shallow, measured. Mery was much in need of a swim. The faint breeze that had arisen could not clear away the smell of the man. It completely overpowered the faint musty odor of the broken mudbrick walls of the small temple of Djeserkare Amonhotep and his mother Ahmose Nefertari.

Laying his baton across his knees, he pulled a beer jar from the basket beside his stool and handed it to the workman. "I want to hear of the accident from your own lips, Mery, not from those of another man."

"Yes, sir." Surprised by the offering, Mery rearranged his thin buttocks on the mat, broke out the dried mud plug, and gulped noisily from the jar. "We were pulling a statue of our sovereign, a big one. Big and heavy. A twin to the one we were moving when your scribe came to get me a short while ago. Finished except for being painted. Ready to raise in its assigned place."

"It was meant to stand in the temple?"

"Yes, sir. Outside the sanctuary door." Mery drank again and licked the moisture from his lips. "We'd hauled it as far as the bottom of the ramp and left it there overnight. It was on a sledge, like the one we're using today." His hand tightening around the jar, he cleared his throat. "That morning, the morning of the accident, a man poured water on the ramp ahead of the sledge, making the slope slick, and we began to pull it. I'd guess there were twenty or so of us and we were moving right along. It happened when we were more than halfway to the top."

"Go on," Bak prompted. The tale was hard to tell, he could see, but he had to hear it.

"Yes, sir." Mery moistened his mouth, but this time he took no joy from the brew. "I was one of the closest men to the sledge and I had a better look than most." He shivered in spite of the heat. "I tell you, sir, it was . . . It was awful."

Bak thought to touch the man's arm, but the small show of sympathy would most likely rattle him, breaking the flow of his tale. "Tell me exactly what you saw, Mery, every detail."

"I heard a loud crack, the breaking of a dowel, I figured later. When I turned around, I saw that the front crossbeam was no longer snug against the runner on the right. I heard another crack, the dowel holding the second crossbeam breaking. The statue was heavy, the strain great, and one after another the rest of the dowels broke and the sledge collapsed. The statue, still roped to the pieces, slewed partway around on the wet slope. Dragging runners and crossbeams and rope along with it, it slid down the slope and toward the side of the ramp. We tried to stop it, but it was too big and heavy. It knocked one of our mates off the ramp, tipped over the edge, and fell on him, killing him and breaking into a dozen pieces."

He rubbed his face as if trying to eradicate the memory. "I tell you, sir, it was awful. If not the work of the malign spirit, it was that of a malevolent god."

No god caused the accident, Bak was convinced. Sledges were strong, made to hold extraordinary weights. This one had been tampered with, the dowels weakened.

"I tripped over a rope, sir, and fell into the quarry. Thanks to good luck and the will of the gods, I landed on a ledge not far below and suffered nothing more serious than a bump on the head." The fresh-faced young apprentice stonemason fussed with the nail on his big toe, refusing to meet Bak's eye. "I should've been watching my step, I know, but something distracted me."

"What exactly?"

"I . . ." The boy's eyes darted toward Bak and away. "I don't know, sir."

Suspicious, recalling his own youthful digressions, Bak asked, "How much beer had you had that day?"

The answer was slow in coming, given with reluctance. "The morning was hot—like today—and I was thirsty. I . . . Well, my head was spinning, sir, and an evil genie had invaded my stomach. It must've made me careless."

An accident, pure and simple. A man too besotted to place one foot in front of the other.

"I didn't see it happen, sir." The guard Ineni stood at the edge of the lean-to, looking uncertain as to whether the tale he had to tell warranted Bak's attention. "I can only speak of what I found."

"His death was attributed to the malign spirit, was it not?"

"Yes, sir."

"Then you must satisfy my curiosity."

Ineni brushed several small pebbles off the mat, settled down, and accepted a jar of beer with gratitude. "He was a guard, sir, his name Dedu. He was a big man, young and strong, rather like your Medjay Kasaya. Nothing less than a malign spirit could've caused the accident that made him fall, striking his head as he did."

Bak laid his baton on the ground by his feet, putting Ineni at ease. The guard needed no reminder of his authority. "He fell where, Ineni? And when?"

"About two years ago, sir. From the upper colonnade, down into the area where the new chapel of the lady Hathor is being built. He fell on a pile of stones waiting to be placed beneath its foundation."

"You found him at first light?"

"Yes, sir. I'd gone out to take his place. He usually waited for me at the top of the ramp, but this time he wasn't there. So I went in search of him."

Sipping from his jar of beer, Bak wondered why Menna had removed Ineni from the old tomb and put Imen in his place as a guard. He seemed a dependable man, and conscientious. "You went to him as soon as you saw him there?"

"Yes, sir. I hoped to find him alive." Seeing Bak drink, Ineni followed suit. The accident had happened too long ago for him to be upset, but he could not help but be moved by the memory. "Dedu was no longer among the living, that I saw right away. He had an ugly gash behind his left ear. His flesh held no warmth and his skin was pale and waxy looking."

Bak gave him a sharp look. "You rolled him over to see the wound?"

"Oh, no, sir. He was lying facedown when I found him."

How could a man strike the back of his head when he fell forward? The thought was not a question, the answer too evident. "Where was the rock he struck?"

"It was there, close by his head. I saw the blood on it."

"Had blood pooled around his head, or was it on the one stone? How big was that stone?" The words tumbled out too fast, too insistent.

Ineni, who failed to notice Bak's agitation, looked thoughtful. "The rock, about the size of a small melon, was stained and . . . No, I don't remember seeing blood anywhere else." His eyes opened wide as the truth hit him. "You don't believe he fell, do you, sir? You think someone struck him from behind."

"I suppose you didn't think to look for blood among the columns above."

"No, sir," Ineni said in a small voice.

Bak sat quite still. Montu's murder was not the first to occur at Djeser Djeseru. Dedu had suffered a similar fate.

"We were hurrying, sir. That was the problem."

"You picked up the ladder, swung it around, and it hit the scaffold." Bak crossed his arms over his chest and scowled at the stout, ruddy-faced sculptor of reliefs. "Did you not think of the men toiling on top?"

"I did, sir, but by then it was too late. Ahmose had fallen and broken his wrist."

Another accident, a simple act of carelessness.

"I was sweating, sir, and my hands were slick. When I bent over the retaining wall, my mallet slipped out of my hand. A mischievous god made it fall on Ptahmose's head."

Bak threw a pained look at Hori. This was the eleventh individual he had interviewed. He had never heard so much mention of spirits and genies and mischievous gods, most malevolent, a few merely playful. Not a man among them had failed to hear that he had found signs of a man on the cliff face, but for some reason he could not comprehend, it was far easier to believe in the vague and mysterious rather than the proven and ordinary.

* * *

"We'd raised that portion of the retaining wall to about shoulder height the previous day and were getting ready to lay the facing stones in front of it."

"Why had the space between the retaining wall and the terrace been filled?" Bak asked. "Shouldn't that have been done after the wall was nearer completion, with the facing in place to strengthen it?"

The short, muscular workman, Sobekhotep, wiped with the back of his hand the sweat from his upper lip, streaking dirt across one cheek. He smelled no better than Mery had. "That's right, sir. Montu warned the debris bearers many times to add the fill later."

"Yet his instructions weren't followed."

"They were, sir, but we didn't know that at the time. When we returned to the wall that morning, we found a lot more debris behind it than had been there the day before, and we even saw the end of the limb pressing against it. We assumed he or Pashed had ordered the fill thrown in and thought no more about it."

Bak cursed beneath his breath. Workmen were the same everywhere: accepting without question what should always be questioned. "Did you suspect the malign spirit of adding the fill?"

"Oh, no, sir." Sobekhotep shook his head vehemently. "The accident happened before that wretched creature made itself known."

"To what did you attribute the mishap? You must've thought up some explanation."

"We didn't, sir. Didn't think, that is."

Bak did not know whether to laugh or cry. The man's sincerity was admirable, his innocence a danger to himself and all who toiled near him. "You must tell me what happened."

"We added another course of casing blocks. Ahotep—our foreman, my father's brother—climbed up to make sure the blocks were seated properly. He bumped against the retaining wall." Sobekhotep licked his lips, blinked hard. "That's all it took. One bump. Without warning, the wall burst outward, stones flying. Ahotep was struck in the face by the limb and the wall collapsed around him. We pulled him free, only to discover that a smaller limb coming off the larger had gone through his eye and deep into his head. He breathed his last in my arms."

"You told my scribe that Montu was angry when he saw what had happened."

"Yes, sir. He believed the limb had been bent, putting it under tension, and dirt and debris thrown around it to hold it in place temporarily. He thought it was meant to spring forward and break the wall. As it did." Sobekhotep's mouth tightened at the memory. "Montu thought it a prank. A mean, vile prank."

"Later, I suppose the accident was laid at the feet of the malign spirit."

Sobekhotep nodded. "Now you say that vile specter is a man."

"More than one, I think. It would take at least two to set up the accident you've described."

The accident had been planned, without doubt. No man could have predicted Ahotep's death, so the goal had been to damage the wall and the men's morale. If anyone was struck down, so be it.

By day's end Bak had interviewed almost thirty men, sorting out obvious accidents from those that were suspect. A few lay somewhere in between, impossible to place in either category. Those he believed to be deliberate had almost all occurred early in the morning, which led him to believe the scene had been set during the night, a time when the men feared to leave their huts, when Djeser Djeseru lay deserted and the malign spirit could set the scene for destruction with little fear of discovery.

The malign spirit. He let out a cynical laugh. With few exceptions, the men he had talked with continued to cling to their belief that an evil specter was responsible for each and

every accident, including the rock slide onto the northern retaining wall. The tale Hori and Ani had spread had fallen on
deaf ears. Since no man had been seen on the cliff above the
wall, Bak had misinterpreted the signs he found there. Or so
the men believed.

Bak entered the lean-to beneath which Ramose and his
scribes toiled, dropped onto a shaded wedge of sand, and set
beside him the empty basket that had earlier been filled with
beer jars. He was hot and tired, badly in need of a swim.

Looking up from the scroll on his lap, Amonemhab asked,
"No luck, Lieutenant?"

"The day's not been entirely wasted."

"Nor a complete success, I gather."

"Did anyone tell you of the scribe who fell to his death?"
Ani asked, speaking quickly, as if wishing to silence his
grandfather. "An accident, they say, but I don't believe it."

Amonemhab snorted. "Don't bother the lieutenant with
trivialities, boy. Huni didn't die at Djeser Djeseru."

"Near enough," the youth said, a challenge in his voice.
To Bak, he added, "He was found in the canal along which
barges bring hard stone and other materials from the river to
the causeway."

Bak saw skepticism on the older man's face and utter conviction on that of the boy. "Tell me what happened, Ani."

"As far as I know, no one saw Huni fall," Amonemhab
said, indifferent to Bak's cue. "He was one of our own, a
scribe here at Djeser Djeseru. After he died, Ramose brought
me out here to take his place."

Ani glared at his grandfather, who seemed intent on spoil-
ing his tale. "He was found in the water beside a barge carrying a load of granite. It was moored at the end of the
causeway, waiting to be unloaded. The back of his head was
crushed in. Those who found him thought he had fallen off
the barge or the bank of the canal, striking his head on some
unknown object as he fell." The boy's face took on a stub-

born look. "I don't believe it. He wasn't a careless man, sir,
nor was he clumsy. He'd never have fallen backward unless
he was pushed."

"You seem quite certain he was slain. Did you tell anyone
at the time?"

"No one would listen to me, sir, but I knew something
wasn't right. I knew it!"

Bak accepted a jar of beer from Amonemhab. While he
sipped the thick, bitter brew, he thought over Ani's tale. The
boy could be mistaken in thinking the death a murder, but he
could as easily be right.

Other than the accidents caused by carelessness or the
whims of the gods, most had been well thought out, set up in
such a way that they would be accepted as mishaps, as the
wrath of the malign spirit and not the work of a man. But,
assuming the scribe had indeed been slain, as he felt certain
the guard Dedu had been, he had found two men whose
deaths had not been so neatly planned or carried out. Two in
addition to Montu, all three struck on the back of the head.

Why, he wondered, had these three deaths not been
planned out as the others had been? Had the victims actually
seen the malign spirit or guessed his name, making their immediate demise essential?

"When did the rumor of a malign spirit start?" Bak asked.

Ramose, Amonemhab, and Pashed looked at each other
and shrugged. Their faces reflected the reddish glow of the
fire around which the four of them sat. Hori, Kasaya, and
Ani, though they could barely see in the growing darkness,
were playing catch with a leather ball on the open stretch of
sand between the huts and the ancient temple of Nebhepetre
Montuhotep. Hori had sluffed off his veneer of a serious
young man to play with the same unbridled zest as the boy.
Kasaya never lost his youthful enthusiasm.

"The tale had started before I came here," Amonemhab said.
"Two years ago, that was. When Huni died, as we told you."

"It started before then." Pashed dunked a chunk of bread into the bowl setting on the fiery coals. The stew smelled of mutton and onions and tasted slightly burned. "Three years ago at least."

Ramose nodded. "Longer even than that, I'd guess."

"How did it get started?" With his father well guarded, Bak had decided that he and his men would spend the night at Djeser Djeseru. Through the day, he had learned a considerable amount; a few more hours might add to that knowledge.

The architect shrugged. "The men pursue an excuse for superstition and build on it. The old tombs we've come upon fuel the fire, so I suspect the first one we found set the rumor alight."

"That would've been about four years ago," Ramose said. "I doubt we knew of him so long ago."

"They're always seeking something to fear," Amonemhab agreed. "It gives them an excuse to leave their places of work long before dark."

"I've never known them not to give fair measure," Useramon said, coming out of the darkness. The tall, bulky chief sculptor knelt between Amonemhab and Ramose and edged sideways, making room for his small friend Heribsen, tagging close behind. "Talk of the mysterious brightens their lives, adds zest to an otherwise bland existence."

Bak doubled over his bread and picked up within the fold a chunk of meat. "You speak lightly of a deadly game, Useramon."

"He pretends indifference, Lieutenant. I, for one, can't feign such nonchalance." Heribsen accepted a jar of beer from Ramose and took a sip. In the erratic light of the fire, the deep furrows in his broad brow emphasized his worry. "I know you say the malign spirit is a man, and perhaps it's true. But man or spirit, will it sit back and let you drive the fear from the hearts of men it's so carefully made afraid? Or will it retaliate with more death and destruction? Will it reserve its vengeance for you, or for all of us who toil here? A few at a time or all at once?"

"Lieutenant Bak!" Hori, letting the ball pass over his head, pointed toward the temple of Nebhepetre Montuhotep. "Look, sir! The malign spirit!"

The youth's call rang loud and clear across the sand. Bak leaped to his feet and looked toward the ruined structure. The other men around the fire followed suit, as did those sitting in front of the nearby huts. He thought he glimpsed a light among the broken columns behind the terrace that faced them, but it vanished so fast he could not be sure.

"I see nothing," Pashed said.

Ramose shook his head. "Nor do I."

Kasaya scooped his spear and shield from the sand. "Shall we go after it, sir?" He stared at the temple, apparently seeing nothing. Each word he spoke was more uncertain than the one before.

"I didn't see anything," Ani said.

His grandfather scratched his neck. "I don't know if I did or not. These old eyes sometimes play tricks on me."

Bak stared at the ruin, its broken stones and fallen columns vague shadows in the sparse moonlight. By shouting so loud, Hori had unwittingly warned whoever was there—and he was fairly certain someone was there. He was equally sure the man would not be caught—not this night, at any rate. If his light had been seen in the valley as often as the workmen claimed, the man knew every square cubit far better than he.

That deficiency must be corrected.

Chapter Eleven

Bak stood at the south end of the upper colonnade, looking down into the new chapel of the lady Hathor that would one day replace the old. The rocks on which Dedu's body had been found were gone, used as fill beneath the foundation. Though the day was new and the lord Khepre had barely risen above the eastern horizon, a gang of workmen toiled in the spot where they must have been piled, shoving a paving stone into position, grunting and groaning at the effort. Sweat glistened on their faces and hard-muscled bodies. The day promised to be as hot as the day before.

At the back of what would one day be a columned court, other men were lengthening a sand and debris ramp and making it higher, taking care that the grade was not too steep. They were building a retaining wall to either side of the door into the sanctuary, which was being dug into the steep slope behind the temple. From inside the small cavern Bak could hear the thud of mallets on chisels and the bark of the stone breaking free, the clatter of flying chips and the workmen talking among themselves.

His gaze shifted southward, across the sandy waste on which the workmen's huts stood. There lay the memorial temple of Nebhepetre Montuhotep, providing a picturesque if ruinous background for the small, mean dwellings. There he had glimpsed the tiny, flickering light the workmen had so often reported as the malign spirit. Had the man who pretended to be the spirit known Bak had remained at Djeser Djeseru and walked through the old temple, thinking to lure him to his death in the dark? Or had he come on a secret errand, unaware that he and his men had not gone home for the night?

When Bak had accompanied his father's housekeeper to the valley as a child, she had told him many tales of ancient kings, including a long-held belief that Nebhepetre Montuhotep lay buried beneath his temple. Later he had heard that the entrance shaft of the king's tomb had been tunneled into by thieves, who had been forced to cut short their effort to reach the burial chamber when the ceiling collapsed. Pashed had verified the tale, adding that the mayor of western Waset had ordered that the shaft remain open, hoping to discourage further excavation by demonstrating how futile the first had been.

Surely the malign spirit was not trying to reach the king's tomb. Certainly not over a period of three or four years. More likely, he was hoping to find tombs of royal women or children. The jewelry in the honey jar had been that of a queen. Would not one success result in a thirst for more?

Bak had been sorely tempted to give chase the previous evening. He regretted his failure to act, but knew in his heart he had made a wise decision. He could tell by the way the workmen failed to meet his eye, however, that they thought less of him because he had not. A conclusion he must reverse.

"Everyone liked Dedu," Imen said. "Why would anyone slay him?"

Bak heaved a long and impatient sigh. "His life was taken much like Montu's: he was struck on the back of the head. He was probably thrown onto the mound of rocks after his death, and the stone used as a weapon was thrown after him. An uninspired attempt to make his death look like an accident."

"Huh!" Imen said with a frown.

A dozen or more guards stood or knelt around them in the long, early morning shadow of the rough stone hut used by the men who patrolled the construction site. To a man, they looked uncomfortable with the reminder that one of their own had been slain. Dedu's death had occurred long enough ago that they had set aside their anxiety; now Bak had brought it back. What had happened to Dedu could as easily happen to any of them, whether caused by an ethereal being or a man.

A scrawny guard with knotty muscles, who had been drawing circles in the sand with the butt of his spear, glanced up from his artwork. "The malign spirit. Had to be."

"Dedu saw it once, you know," an older, lanky man said.

His fellow guards turned as one to look at him, surprised at news they had apparently never before heard.

"So've a lot of other people," Imen grinned, "and they've not been slain."

A few of the men around them nodded, trying to convince themselves they were safe. The rest looked less certain.

Bak leaned back against the rough stone and smiled encouragement. The lanky man seemed eager to talk. Better to let him believe the malign spirit was something other than a man than to deflect his thoughts in the hope of convincing him otherwise. "Did he see more than merely a light from afar?"

"I recall his very words. He said: 'I practically bumped into the thing in the dark. It was kneeling in a deep shadow behind one of those big lion-like statues of our sovereign. Took off like a hare when it saw me.' "

Yes, Bak thought. As must have happened with Montu, Dedu saw the malign spirit and it slew him, but why run away that night and come back later? Why give Dedu a chance to tell others what he had seen? "Did he say what it looked like?"

"I asked him, and all he did was laugh. I decided the story was a joke, a tall tale made up so he could have a good laugh at my expense."

"Did he give any of the rest of you a similar account?"

A man with a black mole on his nose nodded, the rest shook their heads.

"Dedu talked with no qualms before going to his sleeping pallet," explained the man with the mole. "When he awoke, I guess he had second thoughts. He denied the tale, agreeing with Mose that he'd been jesting." He paused, scratched his stubbly chin. "I'd wager he was afraid."

"I'd be," a stocky youth said. "Wouldn't you?"

Afraid of what? Bak wondered. The malign spirit or a man he recognized? "How long after he saw the spirit was he slain?"

The lanky man grew somber. "That's the queer part. He fell to his death the next night. I knew then he'd told the truth. I figured the malign spirit hadn't liked him spreading the tale and had struck him down to silence him through eternity."

"So you repeated the story to no one?"

"Better safe than dead," said the man with the mole.

Which explained why Ineni had not heard the tale.

"Huni's dead, isn't he?" The artist, a tough-looking man of medium height and middle years, spat out the words almost in a whisper so no one in the half-finished court outside the solar chapel would hear. "Do you wish the same fate to befall me?"

"You just said he didn't tell you anything." Bak did not bother to hide his annoyance, but he, too, spoke softly. "You can't have it both ways. Either he confided in you or he didn't."

"He was a good friend. As close to me as a brother. He'd not want me to die because of what he told me."

Bak rested his shoulder against the altar where the priest would ascend the steps, after Djeser Djeseru was dedicated, and face the lord Khepre rising in the eastern sky. From where he stood, he could see the door to the anteroom. He doubted the malign spirit would slay this man—too much time had passed since the scribe had died—but he did not want a death on his conscience should he err. "Then you do believe Huni was slain so his lips would be sealed forever."

"I've never doubted it. I never fail to thank the lord Amon that he told me in confidence, with no other man to hear or to know I knew what he saw."

"What did he see?"

The artist gave him a wary look. "How can I be sure you'll not pass my words on to anyone else?"

"I'll tell my scribe and my Medjay. No one but them."

The artist stared at a bright relief of Maatkare Hatshepsut making offerings to the lord Amon. His face revealed his inner turmoil: he wanted to speak out and was sorely tempted, but was afraid. At last he shook his head. "No. One of them might talk. A single word and I'll be slain as Huni was."

Bak's mouth tightened. "I could leave this temple and within the hour tell ten or more men that Huni confided in you. How long do you think it would take for the tale to spread throughout Djeser Djeseru?" He did not like himself for making the threat, nor did he have any intention of following through, but the man must be made to talk.

The artist's face paled. "You wouldn't! My death would lie at your hands."

"How many men have been slain by the one who calls himself the malign spirit? How many has he injured? If I don't lay hands on him, how many more will be hurt or killed?"

The artist clapped his hands over his ears, refusing to listen.

Bak stepped forward, grabbed his wrists, and pulled them away from his head. "If you can help me snare him and you refuse, will not all future deaths and injuries prey on your conscience?"

The artist slumped to the floor, buried his face in his hands. "Don't you realize how much I ache already? Each time an accident happens, each time a man dies or is hurt, I feel as if a red hot brand has been placed on my heart."

"Tell me what Huni told you. It might ease your pain."

Bak knelt before the artist and laid a hand on his shoulder. "Together let's stop this death and destruction."

The artist looked up, wiped tears from his cheeks. "Will you ask Pashed to send me away? To a place of safety? I've a brother in Mennufer. He's an artist as I am, and he toils on the mansion of the lord Ptah. I could rest easy there."

"I'll speak with Amonked, our sovereign's cousin." Bak prayed the information this man held within his heart would be worth the effort of digging it from him.

The artist sucked in several deep breaths, calming himself. "Huni dwelt in the village where I live, at the base of the ridge to the north, near the cultivated land. He usually walked home with the rest of us, but now and again he'd remain behind, eat with the workmen, and sleep in Ramose's hut. And so he did the night he saw the malign spirit."

A swallow darted past Bak's head, carrying an insect to a nest in the anteroom. He heard the faint cheeping of baby birds demanding sustenance. "The workmen won't leave the huts after dark, and the malign spirit never draws near. What prompted him to strike out alone?"

"While sharing the evening meal, he remembered that he'd left his scribal pallet on a statue on the terrace. The white limestone, seated statue of our sovereign. He told me he drank much too much beer during the meal and after. It made him drowsy, but when he lay down on his sleeping mat, he couldn't slumber. He kept thinking of his writing pallet. He finally decided he couldn't leave it there overnight; he must get it."

"The beer thinking for him."

"Yes, sir." The artist lifted himself off the floor and sat on the bottom step leading up the side of the altar. "He climbed the ramp to the terrace, taking nothing with him but a jar of beer. At the top, he felt in need of a drink."

"He took no torch or lamp?"

"No, sir. The moon was full, the night bright. And he knew exactly where he'd left the pallet."

Bak nodded, well able to imagine the scene. A man besotted, a moonlit night, a terrace inhabited by unfinished statues, and tales of a malign spirit filling his heart.

"He tipped the jar to his lips," the artist went on, "and suddenly he saw a white ghostly figure flitting among the statues and architectural elements."

"The white statue would look ghostly in the dark."

"A fact I pointed out." The swallow sped by, but the artist failed to notice its sharp, commanding twitter. "He swore he wasn't so witless that he couldn't tell the difference between a moving figure and one sitting still."

As a youth, Bak had a few times imbibed enough to see a room revolve around him, but the artist's next words dispelled his skepticism.

"The figure darted past him and down the ramp. Filled with brewed courage, Huni followed. It stayed deep in the shadow of the southern retaining wall, and so did he. Once out of the shadow, it hurried past the slope below the cliff and along the base of the platform on which the old temple of Nebhepetre Montuhotep stands. He pursued it through the moonlight, fearing the whole time it would see him."

"It stayed well clear of the workmen's huts."

"Yes, sir. As it always does."

"He's sure it didn't know he was following?"

"He was very quiet and it never looked back, he swore." The artist rubbed his nose with the back of his hand. "It climbed up a pile of rubble and onto the terrace of the old temple. Huni was close behind by this time. He'd regained a portion of his wits, he told me, but not the use of his feet. As he followed it up the rubble slope, he stumbled and a rock clattered behind him. The malign spirit heard.

"It turned around, spread its arms wide, curled its fingers like claws, and raced toward him. He leaped off the edge of the terrace. Fortunately, the sand below was soft and he broke no limbs. He ran toward the workmen's huts, certain that at any instant he would die. He was nearly there when he worked up the courage to look behind him. He was alone; the specter had vanished."

Bak could understand why the malign spirit might think Huni a threat, but he could see no reason why this man was afraid for his life, unless . . . "Did Huni see the figure well enough to know it was a man and not an apparition? Did he have any idea who it was?"

Fear once again filled the artist's eyes. "He was sure it was a man, one driven to madness by the night. He may've guessed its name."

"But he didn't tell you?"

The artist, looking miserable, shook his head. "Since his death, I've lived in fear that the madman will think I can point a finger at him. I swear to the lord Thoth that I can't."

Bak was fairly certain he was telling the truth. If not, nothing less than a god would get it from him. "When did he tell you of his adventure?"

"At first light the next morning."

"How much time passed before his death?"

"He died late that afternoon or early in the night, so Pashed believed."

Convinced the so-called malign spirit had slain both Dedu and Huni in fear of his identity being aired—and no doubt Montu as well—Bak decided to use the remainder of the daylight hours to explore the ruined temple of Nebhepetre Montuhotep, the place where lights were so often seen in the night. Taking Hori and a none too eager Kasaya with him, he climbed the long ramp the workmen had built to remove the stone being scavenged from what had once been a large cov-ered main court and the colonnades surrounding three of its four sides.

They crossed the broad strip of terrace that fronted the northern colonnade, the terrace from which Huni had jumped. The colonnade, an open structure whose stone roof had been supported by two rows of square columns, stood in front of the partially ruined wall that enclosed the main court. The roof was almost entirely gone, the broken slabs and architraves lying where they had fallen among damaged and overturned columns.

"How many years has this building stood?" Kasaya asked, looking at the ruined colonnade as if not quite sure the malign spirit had vanished with the night.

"I'm not sure," Bak admitted. "Five hundred or more, I suppose."

The young Medjay whistled. "No wonder so much damage has been done."

Hori pointed to a gang of men struggling with a broken architrave that would be reworked for use in the new temple. "Our sovereign's need for stone isn't improving its appearance."

"Why shouldn't she take material from here?" Kasaya asked. "It saves the effort of quarrying. Just think how much grain and supplies will remain in the royal storehouses that would otherwise have been handed out to workmen."

"Savings isn't everything. Should not Maatkare Hatshepsut have some respect for the past? For the long ago dead?"

"One of the workmen told me Nebhepetre Montuhotep isn't even her ancestor."

"What difference does that make? He was someone's ancestor, wasn't he?"

Followed closely by the squabbling pair, Bak walked among the fallen stones, looking for a breach in the ruined wall. He soon found a place low enough to climb over and they entered what had once been the huge enclosed main court. They looked around, awed by what they saw. Stones were strewn everywhere, as if the edifice had been struck by the wrath of the gods.

Small stones and rubble lay scattered around a squarish structure in the center, its original height and exact shape impossible to deduce. Broken roof slabs and architraves lay among this lesser debris and among dozens of eight-sided columns, about half of which stood whole or in part. The remainder lay broken where they had fallen on the sandstone

pavement around the center structure. Bak could not begin
to guess how many columns and slabs had been removed for
reuse. A small rock slide had spilled over the rear wall.

"Do you suppose Djeser Djeseru will one day look like
this?" Hori asked in a voice humbled by the destruction.

"Five hundred years into the future?" Bak shrugged. "If
the king of that time has no more respect for our sovereign
than she does for her worthy predecessor, it might well be
torn asunder."

Kasaya stared, his eyes wide with amazement. "No wonder the malign spirit treads this pavement."

"Watch your feet," Bak said, refusing to point out once
again the exact nature of the malign spirit.

The walking was difficult. He was glad he had refused to
be enticed into the temple the previous night. Someone
could easily have broken an ankle. Not the malign spirit,
who knew the structure well, but he or his men.

An opening through the ruined wall at the back of the
main court took them into an open court surrounded by a
colonnade. Above, soaring high in a deep blue sky, Bak saw
a falcon making a sweeping circle over the valley, searching
for its evening meal. At the far end of this colonnade court, a
veritable forest of eight-sided columns had once graced the
temple. Here, the cliff face closed in on the structure. The
wall of the building, instead of standing free, became a retaining wall, holding back the slope at the base of the cliff,
where a huge chunk had been cut out to provide space for
these rear chambers.

The front portion of the colonnade court had weathered
the years fairly well, while the southwest corner of the outer
wall had been felled by a rock slide and the eight-sided
columns toppled and broken. The hall of columns beyond
had not been so fortunate. Many of the columns still stood
and a portion of the roof was in place, but these had suffered
a battering from above. For over five hundred years, rocks
had fallen from the towering cliff, racing down the slope at a
frenzied speed and with immense force. As a result, the back

of the building was a chaotic landscape of standing and fallen columns, architraves, and roof slabs, of broken stone, fallen rock, and sand. A rough hole, about as wide as Bak's arm was long from closed fist to shoulder, marred the pavement near the damaged end of the colonnade court. Pashed had warned of the opening, the tomb robbers' hole.

Bak and Kasaya explored the columned hall as best they could and managed to enter the sanctuary, cut into the living rock behind the temple. They found nothing but chaos, no recent footprints on the dusty floor.

Returning to the colonnade court, Bak glanced at the long shadows cast by the standing columns. "Tonight we'll return to this temple. The workmen are no less likely to lay down their tools and flee than they were when the rock slide felled the northern retaining wall. We must once and for all convince them that the malign spirit is a man and not an apparition." Hands on hips, he surveyed the tumbled stones around him. "First we must learn our way around. We've another hour of daylight, plenty of time. I want no broken limbs because we stumbled over a fallen stone we should've known was in our path."

"You know what you're to do," Bak said.

Pashed gave him a wry smile. "The moment we spot you, Ramose, Ani, and I will direct the men's attention to the old temple. They'll be certain they're seeing the malign spirit. We'll give them some time to work themselves into a state, then Ani will climb onto the roof of our hut with a torch. When you see his signal, you'll light your torches and let the men see who you are."

"If that doesn't convince them they've been duped, nothing will."

As darkness settled on the valley, Bak, Hori, and Kasaya slipped through a gateway in the stone wall that enclosed a vast expanse of sand in front of the ruined temple of Nebhepetre Montuhotep. They loped across the low dunes that filled the space, passed through another gateway near the southeast corner of the structure, and hurried alongside the platform on which the temple had been built. With the workmen's huts on the opposite side of the building, they had no fear of being seen.

They had discovered, during their daytime visit, a pile of rocks they could use to climb up to the temple. The steps were so regular that Bak wondered if the mound had been built by the malign spirit to ease his path onto the platform. They stopped there to prepare for the night's excursion.

Hori set down the basket he carried and took from it two baked clay oil lamps sized to fit in the palm of a hand. Using a hot bit of charcoal stored in a small pottery container, he set the wicks alight and handed one to each of his companions. Bak handed to the scribe the three torches he carried, each soaked in oil and ready to fire. With great reluctance, Kasaya left his spear and shield with the basket Hori hid in a dark space at the base of the platform. By the time they were ready to move on, the quarter moon had risen as if on command and the stars shone as bright as tiny suns, reborn mortals emulating the lord Re. The night could not have been more ideal for the malign spirit to show himself.

"Shouldn't Kasaya bring along his spear?" A slight tremor of Hori's tongue, the question itself, betrayed his nervousness.

"Are you certain we're doing the right thing?" the Medjay fretted. "What if the malign spirit takes offense?"

Bak gave no answer. If he could not convince Kasaya, who had seen with his own eyes several proofs of the truth, dare he hope this charade would convince the workmen?

Shielding the small flames with their hands so they wouldn't be seen from afar, they climbed onto the platform. They stepped over fallen columns and walked around piles of rubble, and soon they reached the north colonnade, which faced the workmen's huts. There they turned west and walked slowly toward the rear of the temple. Clinging to the shadows, Bak and Kasaya wove a path among the twin rows of partly fallen columns, giving the men at the workmen's huts glimpses of their lights, sporadically shielding them so they would seem from a distance to vanish and reappear. Hori remained close to the wall, seeking its security. Kasaya's heavy breathing betrayed his uneasiness.

The moon aided their journey, but also hindered them. The shadows were deceptive, hinting at foreshortened distances and deeper depths. Bak prayed the effect looked equally dramatic from afar. Either the lights had struck the workmen dumb or the breeze was carrying their words in another direction.

They reached the low spot in the wall where they had crossed into the main court during the day. Bak, expecting at any time to see Ani's signal, stopped to shield his lamp before turning back. Murmuring voices teased his ear, voices carried over the wall behind him by the slight breeze. The malign spirit, he thought, and cold fingers of fear crawled up his spine.

Nonsense!

Shrugging off so preposterous a thought, he raised his hand, signaling his companions to stop, and placed a finger before his lips. Hori, paying no heed, stubbed a toe and muttered an oath, silencing the voices—if voices Bak had heard.

"There's Ani's signal," Kasaya said loud enough to awaken the dead.

He set his lamp on the pavement, grabbed a torch from Hori, and touched it to the burning wick. The oil-soaked linen burst into flame with a whoosh. He grabbed another torch, set it alight, and shoved it into Bak's hand. As Kasaya lit the third torch for himself, Bak stepped back close to the wall. Not sure of what he had heard—if anything—he tilted his head, listening. All was quiet.

Holding the burning torches aloft, he and his men strode out of the ruined colonnade to stand on the open terrace that faced the workmen's huts.

"You see!" they heard Pashed bellow. "That's Lieutenant Bak, his scribe, the Medjay. Men no different than you and I.

Now maybe you'll lay blame for the accidents where blame belongs: at the feet of a man, not a being without life or substance."

"What the . . . ?" A deep and surprised voice behind Bak.

He swung around, saw a man standing at the low place in the wall, glimpsed short-cropped hair, a flattish face, and a small nose. The man slipped back into the shadows beyond the wall.

"We've company, my brother!" the man shouted through the darkness. "Let's go!"

"Kasaya!" Bak yelled, running to the broken wall, hurdling it, and racing after his quarry through the maze of fallen columns, roof slabs, architraves, rubble. Sparks flew from his torch. The flame, blown backward by his speed, made the shadows ahead dance and change shape and the path he followed elusive, his flying steps perilous. Once, he thought he glimpsed a man off to his right, decided it was cavorting light and shadow.

The man ahead sped through the opening into the colonnade court. Bak, close behind and with no better weapon, hurled the torch at him. It struck his back, drawing forth a furious snarl, and dropped to the pavement. Bak leaped the sputtering light, flung himself at his quarry, and they grappled. The man was slightly taller than Bak and broader. He was slick with sweat and not easy to hold on to. They flung each other from side to side, each trying to throw the other. Their feet slid across the paving stones. They stumbled on rough joins between the stones, their feet struck fallen chunks of rock, but neither dared allow himself to fall.

They struggled along an erratic path, gradually working their way toward the columned hall. They were within a half-dozen cubits of the hole in the floor when something hard struck Bak on the back of the head. He fell half-senseless to the pavement.

"He's not alone," he heard. "We have to get out of here."

"Let's get rid of him first." A different voice, a second man, the one who had hit him.

"We've no time."

"Throw him down there. That won't take long."

There. What did they mean by *there*? Bak wondered.

"Lieutenant Bak!" he heard Kasaya yell. "Where are you?"

Strong hands gripped his upper arms and dragged him belly-down along the paving stones. He opened his eyes, saw before him the hole cut through the stone, the old tomb robbers' shaft. His heart leaped into his throat. They were going to drop him into the tunnel.

Chapter Twelve

One man grabbed his feet and dropped them into the tomb robbers' hole. The man holding his arms stepped close to the edge, letting him hang, and released him. He plunged downward. The lord Amon and the will to survive came to his aid, clearing his head. Both his arms shot out. His right elbow bumped the rim of the shaft. He flattened his arm on the pavement and caught with his fingertips a broken edge of paving stone. At the same time, his left arm slid over the rim, grating away a layer of skin. He managed to grab hold of the edge and cling with the fingers of that hand. His bottomward flight stopped with a jolt that threatened to tear his arms from their sockets.

"Lieutenant Bak!" Kasaya bellowed.

"Let's go!" one of his attackers hissed, and they ran.

Bak offered a hasty prayer to the lord Amon, thanking the god that the tomb robbers had cut the hole small to save themselves unnecessary labor. His position was precarious, but he thought he could hang on until help arrived.

Barely aware of a frustrated oath and the pounding footsteps of his assailants racing away, he pushed his left hand hard against the side of the hole, using the pressure to hold him in place, and scrabbled on the wall below with his feet. One foot found a minuscule ledge. With the other, he could feel slight projections, but the woven reed sole of his sandal was too slippery to allow a firm hold. He shook it off, heard it strike the stone below with a slight *thunk*, planted his toes on a protrusion.

"Lieutenant Bak!" Hori's alarmed call.

"The colonnade court!" he yelled. "Come quickly!"

He heard the swift flight of his assailants, retreating through the main court toward the front of the temple, and the thudding feet of Kasaya and Hori speeding toward him.

"Sir!" Kasaya burst through the doorway and looked around, confused by the torch sputtering on the pavement, the rapidly fading sound of running feet, and what on first glance looked to be an empty court. "Where . . . ?"

"There!" Hori pointed. "The robbers' hole!"

"Get me out of here," Bak called. "Quick! They'll get away."

The two young men leaned their torches against a fallen column and ran to him. Each grabbed an arm and, with Bak using the rough surface of the shaft wall to help himself, they pulled him to safety.

He scrambled to his feet and picked up his torch, giving it new life. "Come on! There were two of them."

He dashed into the main court, though he had little hope of catching the pair. They had too much of a head start and knew the temple and its environs far better than he and his men. The birds they had flushed had flown away.

"Did you see a light other than the two we carried?" Bak asked, looking up at Ani, standing on the roof of the scribes' hut. The boy would have had the best view of the old temple.

"No, sir. I saw no one but you. The way you made the lights vanish and reappear was confusing, and if I hadn't known there were two lamps, I'd never have guessed. But your lights were always in one small area. I saw none anywhere else in the temple."

"We didn't see anything either," Pashed said, speaking for himself and everyone else within hearing distance.

A rumble of assent arose from the large group of workmen standing in the darkness around them.

Ramose, Seked, and Useramon nodded agreement. The light of the boy's torch played on the planes of their faces and deeply defined the muscles of their arms and torsos. The sharp smell of the flame tainted the air.

"So whatever the intruders came for, they never got to it," Bak guessed, "or they were in some part of the temple not visible from these huts."

"Or they can see in the dark," Kasaya muttered.

A voice came out of the darkness: "I'd wager my month's ration of grain that they're tomb robbers. That they have nothing to do with the malign spirit. I bet they've been taking advantage of our fear of him to roam around at night, trying to find an old tomb to break into."

"Yes," another man agreed. "The malign spirit always makes himself seen."

A third said, "I, for one, wouldn't walk around this valley at night for any reason at all. Look what happened to Montu."

The men's faces were pale ovals in the darkness, their features ill-defined, their bodies lost among their mates, each voice one among many but speaking for all.

"Some of those old tombs are filled with gold," yet another said. "Would it not be worth the risk?"

A grizzled oldster at the front of the crowd spoke up. "A lot are empty, too, long ago rifled by men who've defiled the dead to satisfy their greed."

"I'd wager my father's donkey that the malign spirit is one of the disturbed dead," said the water boy standing beside him. "Who else would wish us ill simply because we spend our days toiling in this valley?"

The surrounding men murmured assent, their voices rising in a chorus of agreement.

Bak muttered an oath under his breath. His plan to set to rest the workmen's belief in a malign spirit had gone badly awry. "Are you certain, Pashed, that the old shaft in which they threw me leads nowhere?"

The chief architect stood, hands locked behind his back,

looking toward the ruined temple. "There is a burial chamber, I feel sure, but it's long since been closed. The mountain above has settled through the years. It collapsed the robbers' shaft and I'd guess the tomb itself. A man braver than I—or far more foolhardy—might venture inside with mallet and chisel, but I've no wish to be buried alive."

"You've never been inside?"

"Perenefer has crawled to the end, but no one else, and he only the one time."

"I suggest you send him down in the morning to be sure no new attempt has been made to reopen the tunnel. I'll go with him." Bak made the offer reluctantly. For a task so perilous, he could not expect another man to go alone.

He doubted they would find any sign of fresh digging. If the intruders had been excavating there, trying to reach the burial chamber, they would not have thrown him into the hole, drawing attention to the tomb and losing their chance to continue within. An inspection must be made nonetheless.

"Also, assign the crew who've been removing stones from the old temple to another task elsewhere. I mean to seek for signs of the intruders; and I want no fresh disturbance to destroy or hide any traces they might've left."

"Who do you think they were, sir?" Hori opened his mouth wide in a deep yawn. "Tomb robbers or men pretending to be a malign spirit?"

Bak spread his borrowed sleeping mat on the rooftop of Ramose's hut and sat down on it. He much preferred slumbering under the stars to sharing the crowded and smelly quarters of the workmen. "I'm too tired to guess, Hori."

The scribe got down on his knees before him and wrapped a swath of linen covered with a sour-smelling poultice around his skinned arm. "If they were the malign spirit, wouldn't they have been carrying a light to frighten the workmen?"

"You'd think so, wouldn't you?" Bak spoke through gritted teeth. The salve burned like fire.

"If they were tomb robbers, do you think they found a likely target?" Kasaya asked.

"Other than the shaft they threw me into, I noticed no signs of burials when we explored the temple today. Tomorrow we'll look again."

Finished with the knots that held the bandage in place, Hori plopped down on his sleeping mat, took off his broad collar and bracelets, and laid them with his scribal pallet. "Would you recognize them if you saw them, sir?"

"I'd recognize only the one. The second man struck me from behind." Bak heard again the words "Let's get rid of him" and his expression hardened. "If ever we meet—and I vow we will—I'll look forward to repaying him in kind for dropping me into that shaft."

The next morning soon after first light, Bak returned with Hori and Kasaya to the ruined temple of Nebhepetre Montuhotep. They found Pashed and Perenefer there ahead of them, waiting beside the old tomb robbers' hole. The foreman did not hesitate to let himself down into the shaft, taking a torch with him. It was no more than two and a half times the height of a man, he assured them, and so Bak found it when he allowed himself to be lowered. Which made him wonder if the previous night's intruders had wanted him dead or had simply used him as a distraction while they made their escape.

At the bottom, the tomb robbers had cleared a rough chamber in which to stand while they excavated deeper and raised the dirt and rocks to the surface. A pitch-black hole about the size of the one above led off at a downward slope in a westerly direction. A close examination around its mouth revealed that the material through which it had been cut was the debris used to fill the tunnel after the ancient king's burial. A slight discoloration off to one side hinted at an earlier attempt to reach the burial chamber.

Other than the sandal Bak had let fall the night before and Perenefer's footprints, the light sprinkling of sand on the floor showed no sign of intrusion. Both men were convinced no one had been inside the shaft since the foreman's last expedition, but they agreed that one of them should go on to the end while the other remained behind to call for help if he became stuck or if the tunnel collapsed. Perenefer, who had been there before and knew what to look for, was the most suitable of the pair to enter the hazardous tunnel, and he took for granted that he would be the one to do so. Bak made no secret of his relief.

"If the tunnel's as it was when last I saw it, it's not very long. Only six or eight times the height of a man." Perenefer handed a coil of stout rope to Bak and tied one end around his own waist. "If I yell, pull as if the lord Set himself was after you. If you can't pull me out, call for help. I'd not enjoy spending my last moments buried alive."

The thought made Bak's skin crawl.

Taking an oil lamp with him, Perenefer got down on hands and knees and crawled head-first into the dark, confined passage. Bak knelt at the entrance, paying out the rope as the foreman moved forward. All the while, he prayed to the lord Amon that the tunnel would not collapse.

The chamber where he waited was hot and smelled musty. The torch sputtered, giving off the noxious odor of rancid oil. At times bats would squeak somewhere within the tunnel and several would fly out, their daytime slumber disturbed by the man who had invaded their dwelling. Bak could not begin to imagine how uncomfortable Perenefer's passage must be, how many other denizens of the darkness he must be encountering.

The time seemed endless, but finally Bak heard Perenefer's muffled words. "I'm coming out. Keep the rope taut."

Bak had not realized how long he could hold his breath until the foreman backed out of the tunnel and he allowed himself to breathe once again. Perenefer rose to his feet. Neither he nor Bak said a word; they just looked at each other and grinned.

"Has the tunnel been extended?" Bak asked.

Perenefer shook his head. "No, as you thought. You'll have to look elsewhere for whatever those men were after."

Pashed and the foreman returned to their duties at Djeser Djeseru. Bak, Hori, and Kasaya spent the morning searching the ruined temple, repeating their previous day's effort, but looking now for signs of a tomb and for minute traces of the intruders. In the end, they summoned Perenefer and Seked, who brought a team of men to help. They found nothing. Whatever the two men had been doing the night before, they had left no visible sign. If a tomb other than that of the long dead king had been dug beneath the temple, it was too well hidden to find.

"If the malign spirit always makes himself known, as the workmen believe, either carrying a light or somehow making himself look . . ." Lieutenant Menna paused, frowned. "What did the artist say his friend Huni saw? A white ghost-like figure?"

Bak walked with the guard officer along the river's edge, looking at the dozen or so skiffs drawn up on the narrow beach. "He's probably wearing a white tunic. Made of a sheer linen, I'd guess. Something that picks up the light of the moon and makes it appear to glow."

"Here's the skiff I thought your father might like." Menna stopped in front of a nearly new boat much like the one the fishing boat had destroyed. As usual, he looked superb, making Bak wonder how he managed to stay so neat and clean on so hot a day. "One man should be able to sail it easily. Ideal for a physician, I'd think."

Bak walked around the small vessel, pleased with what he saw. Most of the men and women who summoned his father with ailments or injuries dwelt on the west bank of the river within easy walking distance of his home, but six or eight times a week he was called to aid someone who lived across the river in Waset or far enough north or south to make sailing a necessity.

He thanked the lord Amon that Menna no longer resented his help. The officer had actually expressed appreciation when he had come with his tale of the nighttime intruders in the old temple of Nebhepetre Montuhotep. If this skiff proved to be acceptable, their friendship would be sealed.

"What could your intruders have been doing there?" Menna asked. "Searching for a tomb to rob? Robbing one they'd already located?"

Bak spread his hands wide and shrugged. "We found no sign of an open sepulcher—or any other tomb, for that matter—and we searched that temple from one end to the other."

"It seems a likely source of the jewelry you confiscated at Buhen. The objects are of a style from that period and once adorned a woman of royal blood. But surely you'd have found some sign of digging or a similar disturbance."

"Where are the other kings of that period buried?" Bak asked, aware that there was a slight chance the jewelry had been taken from an earlier or later king's tomb.

"Most were laid to rest in a cemetery at the north end of western Waset. We may not know of them all, but of those we do, their burial places were robbed and desecrated many generations ago."

No surprise there. Bak studied the skiff, which was half lying on its side, with much of its keelless hull visible. The bare wood glowed with oil painstakingly rubbed in. A bouquet of flowers with intertwined stems had been painted on its prow. He thought his father would like it.

"Tell me again what the men looked like," Menna said.

"The one I saw was slightly taller than I am and heavier. His face was broad, his hair short, his voice deep and grating, although the harshness may've been because he was angry."

"Would you recognize him again?"

"Without a doubt."

"Do you think they were deliberately trying to slay you?"

"I thought so at the time, but when we went down into the old robbers' shaft, I wasn't so sure. It's not very deep." Bak walked to the stern and knelt beside the rudder. Cool rivulets of water splashed against his heels. "Of course, they may not have known its depth. They may never have gone inside."

"I doubt tomb robbers would turn their backs on the promise of wealth," Menna chided, "especially the vast amount likely to be found in the sepulcher of a king."

Bak smiled, accepting the teasing for what it was: good-natured and well meant. "Pashed assured me that every workman at Djeser Djeseru knows how dangerous it would be to dig deeper. If they know, you can be sure everyone who dwells along the west bank knows."

"I've been told," Menna admitted. "More than once."

"I'd not like to dig down there." Bak walked around to look into the open hull, to examine the crossbeams. "Perenefer knows the tunnel well, and I could see the relief on his face when he came out. He was truly afraid."

"The sail's practically new and so are the lines." Menna pointed to the tightly furled white canvas and to various places where the ropes usually wore out first, demonstrating how free of wear they were. "If your intruders were indeed tomb robbers, perhaps they were involved with Montu. Maybe he kept the source of his spoils a secret, and now that he's dead, they're searching for it."

"Have you unearthed anything new to indicate he was the man you've been seeking?"

"I haven't," Menna admitted ruefully. "I made the mistake of telling mistress Mutnefret what I sought and why. She's adamant that he wasn't a tomb robber and refuses to cooperate in any way. Each time I go to their dwelling, she watches me as if I were a mouse and she a falcon ready to swoop down and eat me."

Bak flashed a sympathetic smile. "There goes your chance to pay court to Sitre."

"I fear you're right," Menna said unhappily.

"I hope the woman's annoyance with you doesn't extend to me. I mean to go today to her country estate in western Waset. If she's there, I want no confrontation." Bak reached inside the boat and pulled out the oars, which were not new but showed few signs of wear. "I think that a good place to begin my search for the men we disturbed last night."

"So you're coming around to my way of thinking, eh?"

"That Montu was a tomb robber? I'm not entirely convinced, no, nor will I be without further proof, but I'd be remiss if I didn't look there for last night's intruders."

"I wish you luck," Menna said fervently. "I'd like to clear this problem away once and for all. Each time a new piece of jewelry surfaces, I feel like a man having a nightmare that occurs again and again and again."

"One day you'll lay hands on the thief—or find proof that Montu was rifling the old tombs." Bak clapped the officer on the shoulder. "Now tell me of the owner of this skiff. My father must see it, of course, but it looks to be exactly what he needs."

"Montu was a lot of things, Lieutenant, not all of them appealing, but he was not a man who would steal from the dead." Mutnefret stood in the courtyard of her country house. Her greeting had been neither warm nor cool. Impatient, rather, typical of a woman distracted from a busy day.

Six women sat before tall vertical looms protected from the sun by a heavy linen awning. A seventh loom stood idle, testifying to the task Bak had interrupted when he had asked to speak with the mistress of the house. Doors leading into the dwelling, which was of considerable size, opened off all four sides of the court. Mutnefret seemed not to care what her servants heard.

The shuttles whispered softly as they shot back and forth, creating fabric of exceptional quality. Fabric to be traded, he felt sure, rather than used within the household. An additional source of income. No wonder the estate appeared so prosperous.

"Your daughter must've told you of the neck of a broken jar I found in his place of work."

"The honey jar. Yes." She put her hands on her ample hips

and scowled at him. "He could've picked that up anywhere."

"All the other shards in the basket in which I found it came from Djeser Djeseru."

"There!" She flashed a triumphant look. "You see? You've proven my point."

Bak gave her a genial smile. "As I told Lieutenant Menna earlier today, I'm not as convinced as he that your husband was robbing the old tombs."

Mention of the guard officer's name brought the frown back. "How convenient for him if he could lay blame on a dead man!"

He ignored the sarcasm. "I'll need more proof than a broken bit of pottery before I blacken Montu's name—or that of anyone else. Nevertheless, I must see the men who toil on this estate."

The shuttles grew silent; the servants turned around to stare, their hostility clear. Their husbands, brothers, and sons would be among the men he had asked to see.

Mutnefret flung her chin high, cool and haughty. "I can assure you, Lieutenant, that my servants spent the whole of the night sleeping peacefully with their wives and families."

The servants muttered a resentful agreement.

"You must see that I can't accept your word for their whereabouts. Were you not in this house, in your own bed-chamber, while they slept elsewhere?"

"I didn't see them with my own eyes, I must admit, but the women you see here . . ."

"Devoted mothers and wives and sisters, women who would say what they must to protect those dear to them." He softened his voice. "If I don't see a familiar face, you'll be done with me."

She had no choice but to acquiesce, and she knew it. "Oh, very well."

To be certain he missed no one, he asked, "Have any of your servants moved away since your husband's death?"

She flung her head high. "None have left, nor will they. They toiled on this estate for my first husband and for his father before him. This is their home, Lieutenant, and so it should be."

Mutnefret summoned the scribe who managed the estate. Teti was a rangy man of thirty-five or so years, with the deep tan of one who spent more time beneath the sun than indoors with his writing implements and scrolls. Bak saw right away how quick the household servants were to obey him and the high degree of respect they showed him.

The scribe listened to his mistress's order that Bak should see all the male servants. Stifling a visible curiosity, he took him outside the walled compound to a mudbrick bench, where a slight breeze stirred the air beneath one of four sycamore trees that shaded several outbuildings built against the wall. He told a boy of ten or so years—his son, Bak suspected—to summon the men of the estate. The boy hurried off, racing across a field of yellow stubble to speak with two men who were tending a mixed herd of cattle, sheep, and goats.

While they waited, Bak explained that he had been attacked and assumed the assailant dwelt on the west bank. He provided no specific details.

"My mistress told true, sir. Our servants were here through the night."

"I must see them nonetheless."

"Yes, sir." Teti wove his fingers together and laid his hands in his lap. His thumbs chased circles around each other. He looked like a man uncomfortable with the silence but at a loss for words.

"What did you think of your master, Teti?"

"I thought our previous master the finest of men. As for Montu . . . Well, they say if you've nothing of note to say about a man, it's best to say nothing."

"I've been told he shirked his duty at Djeser Djeseru." Bak smiled, inviting confidence. "I've yet to see a black goat turn white overnight."

A faint smile touched Teti's lips, but still he chose his

words carefully. "I've thanked the lord Thoth many a time that our mistress trusts me to manage her properties. Hers and mistress Sitre's."

Bak eyed the scribe thoughtfully. "Are you inferring that Montu would've taken what was theirs and used it for his own purpose?"

"Not at all," Teti said with conviction, "but he would've liked to control their holdings."

"I don't understand. If he didn't want their wealth for itself, why would he . . . ?" Even as he formed the question, Bak remembered the way Montu had demanded that the paintings and sculpture at Djeser Djeseru be altered. "I see. He wanted to be in authority and to demonstrate how important he was."

"Yes, sir." Teti seemed surprised by Bak's perspicacity, and pleased that he understood. "When first our mistress wed him, she let him make a few decisions concerning the running of her estate. He used no common sense whatsoever. She recognized the failing and saw how dangerous he could be to the well-being of all that was hers and her daughter's. She said nothing to him, but quickly guided his interests elsewhere and told me to continue as before."

Bak smiled. In her own way, Mutnefret had used a tactic similar to that of the craftsmen at Djeser Djeseru.

He shoved the thought aside as the first of the farmhands approached. While he and Teti had talked, he had seen the boy running from field to palm grove to field to pigeon cote to paddock, sending men striding toward the house. One man came to stand before Bak, followed by the rest in rapid succession. As on any prosperous estate, they were men of all ages who carried on a multitude of duties. He spoke a few words to each, letting them know they had no reason for fear, then allowed them to return to their tasks. The man with whom he had fought at Djeser Djeseru was not among them.

Where the intruders' presence on the estate might have suggested Montu was a tomb robber, the fact that they were not to be found here told him absolutely nothing.

As the last man walked away, Bak said, "Are you aware, Teti, that Lieutenant Menna suspects Montu of being a tomb robber?"

"So my mistress has said." The scribe shook his head. "I don't believe it. He was indolent and authoritarian and thought far too much of himself, but I truly believe he was no thief."

Bak described the shard he had found among Montu's possessions, the sketch.

Teti laughed. "He could've picked that up in a dozen different places. A neighboring farm. A village garbage dump. A vacant plot of land in Waset." He paused, struck by a thought. "If the jar was from olden times, he may've found it in one of the old cemeteries on the ridge north of our sovereign's new temple. I saw him two or three times, walking among the hillside tombs and those on the plateau just above the floodplain." He spotted Bak's sudden interest, smiled. "Those tombs are empty, sir, with nothing left to steal. Nomads sometimes camp in them when they bring their herds to the river."

Were those the same tombs Menna mentioned? Bak wondered. Tombs long ago plundered, the guard officer had said. "Isn't that a bit farther afield than you normally travel, Teti? Especially after toiling here from dawn to dusk. What were you doing? Did your mistress tell you to follow him?"

"Oh, no, sir." The scribe looked sincerely surprised by the question. "When he didn't come home as expected, she always assumed he was visiting a house of pleasure he frequented, amusing himself with a young woman whose company he enjoyed."

"I've an idea that you're a man who'd go out of your way to look after her interests, if you felt the need."

"In this case, sir, I was looking after my own interests." Teti spoke with an indignation that melted away as fast as it had formed. "You see, sir, I lost my wife last year, and I've three children to raise. Oh, they'll get plenty of mothering from the women who dwell on this estate, but they need a true mother and I need someone to share my sleeping pallet. I've found a young woman, daughter to an artist who dwells in the village below the ridge. My mistress has given me leave to visit her there."

Bak gave the scribe a long, speculative look. "What's the artist's name?"

"Heribsen, sir."

Bak could not help but smile. "Was he the man who gave your mistress—or, more likely, you—the idea of letting Montu believe he was the master of her estate when in reality you manage her affairs quite well?"

A quick smile flitted across the scribe's face. "I don't know what you're talking about, sir."

Poor Montu, Bak thought. Could a man of such arrogance that he allowed himself to be made a fool of be clever enough to rob the old tombs and dispose of the jewelry in complete safety? Would he have had the patience to smuggle jewelry out of the land of Kemet a few pieces at a time over an extended period? Or had Montu been smart enough to make himself look the fool?

Chapter Thirteen

Bak did not reach Djeser Djeseru until late in the day. He found Pashed seated, elbows on knees, head in hands, on a stone cube at the end of the partially completed southern section of the upper colonnade. The chief architect was alone, with no other man nearby. Workmen at the opposite end of the incomplete colonnade had just hauled an architrave up the construction ramp and were preparing to position it across the space between two columns. The foreman was cursing, urging the men to greater effort before the lord Re entered the netherworld and darkness fell. The men were grumbling because they wished to postpone the task until the next morning.

The crunch of Bak's sandals on grit roused Pashed, who raised his head to see who was approaching. Bak was alarmed by how distraught the architect looked. His face was drawn, lines were deeply etched around his mouth.

"Pashed! What's troubling you?"

Pashed rubbed his eyes, as if trying to wipe away whatever adversity had brought about such worry. "Each time I feel the gods have chosen at last to favor me, they once again turn their backs."

"Not another accident, I pray!"

A bitter smile flitted across the architect's face. "No accident, Lieutenant. Only an inspection by Senenmut himself. Our sovereign's favorite and the man to whom I'm responsible."

191

Bak could not understand why Pashed was so upset. True, Senenmut was the Overseer of Overseers of All the Works of the King (as Maatkare Hatshepsut had begun to call herself), and he claimed Djeser Djeseru as his creation, but . . . "This can't be the first time he's come."

"He comes monthly, and more often if a decision of import must be made."

The cheeping of baby birds drew Bak's eye to a nest built in a crack at the join of the roof and the retaining wall behind the colonnade. He glimpsed a swallow feeding its voracious young. He never ceased to be amazed at how fast the wild creatures took as their own the dwellings of man. "Why is this inspection different?"

"Montu is dead and I stand alone at the head of this building effort. You, who were brought specifically to put an end to the accidents, have been here six days, yet they continue as before. The malign spirit, or the man I'll always think of as that vile specter, continues to walk this valley, wreaking havoc wherever he treads, and you seem unable to stop him. Now tomb robbers have come."

Bak was irritated by a charge he felt unfair, but he spoke with the patience a mother must show a whimpering babe. "You're not a man alone, Pashed. Except for designing the temple and seeing that the men do what they must to build and adorn it, Amonked shares your burden of responsibility. You've also Lieutenant Menna and me. He'll sooner or later lay hands on the tomb robbers, and I'll snare the malign spirit and stop the accidents—and I'll catch the man who slew Montu." He thought it best not to reveal that he believed the deaths of Dedu and Huni to be murder.

"The men talk of laying down their tools and walking away from this valley," Pashed said, as if he had not heard. "They vow never to return, letting the temple remain as it is, allowing it to languish through eternity."

Bak felt like shaking him. He had reason to be troubled, to be sure, but he had no need to exaggerate. "My scribe and my Medjay have spoken with many of the men in the past few days. True, the threat to flee hovers at the edge of their thoughts, and they cling to their belief in the malign spirit, but so far common sense has prevailed."

"For how long?"

Bak knelt before the architect and laid a hand on his lower arm. The mother swallow hurtled past their heads on her endless quest for insects. "You must not allow yourself to fall in defeat, Pashed. Your problems will be resolved."

The architect refused to meet his eyes. "You told me of the accident on the river and I saw for myself the rock slide. I didn't see you thrown into the old robbers' shaft, but I heard of it. That's three attempts to slay you in three days. What's to prevent the malign spirit—the man posing as that vile being—from slaying you while Senenmut is here?"

So that was the problem. Pashed feared another death, this one right before Senenmut's eyes. The thought was disconcerting, chilling. Rising to his feet, Bak formed a reassuring smile. "I can assure you I'll do everything in my power to see that nothing happens to me."

"What's to prevent some other catastrophe from occurring? What if an attempt is made on his life?"

Bak hesitated before answering. He hated to go again to Maiherperi, but was very much aware that thus far he had been unable to stop the incidents at Djeser Djeseru. On the contrary, the situation seemed to have escalated. If the goal was to stop construction, as he was beginning to suspect, what better way than to do harm to Senenmut? "I'll speak with Commander Maiherperi and ask him to send an extra company of men with Senenmut. With luck and the favor of the gods, the malign spirit won't dare strike."

The architect was not consoled. "If a scandal rocks this project, he'll send me far away to the desert wastes of Wawat, making me stand at the head of a gang of prisoners working a remote gold mine."

One thing Bak knew for a fact: with Pashed so frightened

for his future, he could not possibly be a party to any effort to disrupt construction at Djeser Djeseru. "When will Senenmut's inspection take place?"

"Three days from now."

Bak muttered an oath. Not much time, he thought. Not nearly enough time to lay hands on a man when he had not the vaguest idea who he was. "I'll go see Maiherperi right away."

"Where a king lies through eternity, his family and courtiers are nearby," Bak said, airing the thought for what he feared was the hundredth time. He stood beside the white seated statue of Maatkare Hatshepsut, staring at the ruined temple beyond the sandy waste on which the workmen's huts stood. "The men we came upon last night undoubtedly believe so, too."

Hori, looking glum, eyed the temple whose pavement he had trod for so many long hours through the morning. "We found no sign of a tomb, sir, and not for lack of trying."

"I know." Bak eyed a gang of men on the terrace where he, the scribe, and Kasaya had revealed themselves to the workmen the night before. The crew was using a large wooden rocker to raise a heavy stone onto their sledge. "Nonetheless, their presence and the fact that the malign spirit frequents that temple has convinced me a tomb is yet to be found somewhere within."

"Maybe the men taking stone from the ruins will uncover it," the scribe said. "We won't. We searched the building so often and know it so well that we'd not recognize a tomb if the deceased leaped out and dragged us inside."

Smiling, Bak laid an arm across the youth's shoulders and ushered him toward the ramp. "I must go to Waset and you must go with me."

"Waset?" Hori looked crestfallen at the sun, peering over the western peak, signaling that within an hour or so he could go home to his evening meal.

"We must seek out the priest Kaemwaset. I've a task for you, which you must begin tomorrow, but you'll need help."

"You wish the boy to search the archives." Kaemwaset, seated on a low stool in the murky light of a storage room that smelled strongly of fish, let the scroll in his lap roll closed. He pursed his mouth, thinking it over. "I don't see why he can't, but he'll need the approval of the chief archivist."

"Amonked will see he has it," Bak said.

"What does he look for, may I ask?"

Bak stepped inside the door and pulled Hori with him. The room was dark enough without the two of them blocking what little light came through. "Records of the old temples and tombs, specifically those of the reign of Nebhepetre Montuhotep and his immediate family."

"Hmmm." The priest's eyes leaped toward the boy, but he spoke to Bak. "You're asking a lot, sir. The task could take days without number and still he could come up empty-handed."

Bak had often heard his father complain about the archives, thrown into disorder by years of neglect and wanton destruction when the rulers of Kemet had weakened and lost a portion of the country to the vile foreign princes from far to the east. It had been the worthy ancestors—or so she claimed—of Maatkare Hatshepsut who had waged war on the wretched intruders and consolidated the kingdom. Surely after so many years had passed, the situation had improved. "Aren't the records in some kind of order?"

Kaemwaset laid the scroll on the floor with his writing implements. They had found him taking inventory in a room stacked high with bundles of dried fish. Unless the priest had lost his sense of smell altogether, Bak felt sure he and Hori were doing him a favor by interrupting.

"Most are in excellent order, but have you any idea how many scrolls are stored there?"

"When I was a boy, my father spent many hours in the archives. I remember well my impatience to be gone, while he went from room to room and from jar to jar, seeking some obscure text about healing."

Kaemwaset motioned toward the door, signaling them to precede him out of the room. "Ah, yes. Your father is the physician Ptahhotep. He's been a frequent visitor to the archives for as long as I can remember."

"You know him?" Bak asked, surprised.

"Very well indeed. I toiled in the hall of records for several years when first I came to the mansion of the lord Amon. Before you were of an age to come with him." The priest glanced at Hori and smiled. "I think the idea was to eliminate my childish exuberance by giving me tasks of an exceedingly boring nature."

Hori grinned. "I thank the lord Amon time and time again that my first task was with Lieutenant Bak and his company of Medjays and we were sent far away to the southern frontier." No one could mistake the sincerity in his voice.

Bak ruffled the young scribe's hair. "Will you help Hori, Kaemwaset? Will you show him around the archives? Show him the system for filing the documents and how to find them?" Bak, aware that the lesser priests were assigned tasks they had to complete and were not always free to do as they liked, added, "If you can't help him, can you tell me who can?"

"I must get permission from the fourth prophet, of course, but I'd be delighted to aid him." Kaemwaset glanced at the doorway behind him and wrinkled his nose in distaste. "You've no idea how weary I am of the mundane tasks I'm given each time I've finished my regular duties."

He offered to help them obtain permission right away, then smiled and rubbed his hands together, demonstrating his eagerness. "Your task promises to be most interesting, Lieutenant, and rather daunting."

"In what way?"

"Many of the old records were lost during the time of

chaos, before our sovereign's ancestors gained control of the land of Kemet. We ofttimes find one or two related documents where originally there may've been ten or twenty scrolls. Sometimes we find none and sometimes we find them all. We never know."

"I ask only that you do the best you can."

"I agree," Maiherperi said, pacing the length of the shallow reflecting pool, Bak by his side. "We must do all within our power to see that no attempt is made on Senenmut's life. You were wise to come to me."

"I pray an extra company of guards will be sufficient."

Maiherperi gave him a sharp look. "Do you know something you're not telling me, Lieutenant?"

"No, sir, but . . ."

"Speak up! I detest men who seal their lips, forcing me to discover unpleasant truths for myself."

His sharp voice startled a brown goose, which took to the air and flew low over the pool, throwing its shadow across several clusters of water lilies growing from pots scattered around the bottom. A frog sitting on a pad leaped into the water with a splash. Alarmed, a flock of egrets skimmed the surface of the flooded garden with a whir of wings, wheeled around, and settled back down to feed. A slight breeze carried the strong, sweet scent of the lilies, whose petals were closing at the end of day.

Bak smiled to himself. Maiherperi had not changed since first he had met him. He was a straightforward, honest man and he demanded the same candor from others. "Several days ago, a priest suggested that the malign spirit was created to discredit our sovereign, to make her look weak in the eyes of her people. I've never taken the idea seriously, and if you ask me why, I can't give you a good reason. But if I've erred . . ."

"Why would a man injure and slay so many people if not on a matter of import?" The commander looked puzzled, more by Bak's doubts than by the question itself.

"I'm not sure, sir."

"You must realize that the most likely individual to wish our sovereign ill is her co-ruler and stepson Menkheperre Thutmose."

"He's not that kind of man, sir." Bak, like many men in the army the young king had begun to rebuild after years of neglect by Maatkare Hatshepsut, truly believed he should be the sole ruler of the land of Kemet, wielding the power of office his father's sister-widow had grasped while the boy was hardly more than a babe.

The commander's voice turned wry. "One never knows how low the best of men will stoop when the object they desire is tempting enough. However, I'm convinced that young man is much too preoccupied with playing soldier in Mennufer. The thought of wreaking havoc at Djeser Djeseru would never enter his heart."

"I agree, sir," Bak said vehemently.

"One of his followers might—or hers, for that matter—if they wished to cause trouble. But why spill a jar of wine when it holds considerably more pleasure when drunk from a bowl? Especially since both Maatkare Hatshepsut and Menkheperre Thutmose seem content with the situation as it is."

Relieved that the commander had chosen to remain neutral rather than side with the woman to whom he reported, Bak decided to air a thought that had been nagging him throughout the day. "I've begun to think the malign spirit is more interested in personal gain than in who holds the reins of power in the land of Kemet."

Maiherperi conferred upon him a long, speculative look. "Tell me."

"Are you aware of the old jewelry that's been found on ships bound for far-off lands? Jewelry that had to have been taken from tombs dug during the reigns of Nebhepetre Montuhotep and his family?"

"Amonked has told me, yes."

Bak went on to tell the commander of all that had occurred

since he had first set foot on Djeser Djeseru. While he talked, they walked side by side along the white graveled paths that ran through the lush garden behind the royal house. Flowers in a multitude of colors, herbs, and shrubs graced walkways shaded by palms, sycamores, acacias, and tamarisks. Monkeys swung through the trees, setting bright birds to flight. Gazelles, too shy to draw near, shared the flooded garden with egrets and ducks and other wading birds.

Ending his account, he asked, "What better way for tomb robbers to direct our thoughts away from their nighttime activities than to create a malign spirit who's not merely frightening but dangerous as well?"

"What better way?" Maiherperi agreed. "If you're right, if this is a simple matter of tomb robbery, Senenmut's life is not necessarily at risk."

"Such would be my guess. However, if the robbers have found—or believe they're close to finding—a tomb of great potential value that they don't dare break into as long as the workmen remain at Djeser Djeseru, they might well bring about a fearsome accident while he's there. One so horrendous he'll recommend to our sovereign that the project be stopped and the valley abandoned."

"She'll never stop construction of her memorial temple. It means too much to her. Not simply for the continued offerings it will glean for her journey through eternity, but for the message it will carry of her divine birth and all her accomplishments while she sits on the throne."

"I'd wager she'd stop the effort for a month or two, given sufficient reason."

"Such as?"

"If she could be led to believe that, to stop the accidents, she must propitiate the lord Amon during some important occasion." Bak paused, building his thoughts, nodded. "For example, during the Opet festival, which will take place in a few weeks. Construction would be delayed, not stopped entirely, and would give the robbers time to enter and rifle the tomb without fear of being caught."

"Have you heard such a rumor?"

"No, sir, but any similar tale would do. Or another serious accident where men are injured and lives lost. The workmen are already talking of laying down their tools and leaving the valley. They came very close to doing so after the last rock slide."

"You've given this some thought, I see." Maiherperi swung around and headed back to the building that housed the royal guards. "I'll make sure Senenmut's well guarded while at Djeser Djeseru, and warn the officer in charge to expect the worst. Then we must all bend a knee to the lord Amon, praying the worst doesn't happen."

Later, as Bak prepared to leave, he paused beneath the portico outside the building where Maiherperi toiled. "I've yet to thank you, sir, for sending a man to look to my father's well-being."

The commander smiled. "Sergeant Huy is one of my best men, awaiting reassignment to the royal house in Mennufer. You've nothing to worry about with him standing guard."

The sky had darkened, Bak saw, and the lord Re had long ago entered the netherworld, allowing the stars to show their faces. He hoped he could find a boatman to ferry him across the river in the night. "I've spent the last two nights at Djeser Djeseru, so I don't know how my father feels about having a man in constant attendance."

"From what I've been told, he made no secret that he resented the need for a guard, but he doesn't hold the sergeant responsible. In fact, he treats him as a friend and companion rather than holding him at a distance."

Thanking the lord Amon for small favors, Bak trudged down the lane to the gate, bade good night to the sentry, and walked out into the darkened city.

The world was black, with the quarter moon pale and weak. Stars were sprinkled like bright grains of salt across the sky. Bak heard the rustle of a small unseen creature slipping through the tough dry grass that grew along the irrigation channel. A hare bounded across the path in front of him, leaving a melon patch to hide within a field of henna. Indistinct images off to his right were all he could see of cattle resting in a neighbor's field of stubble. The distant cry of a jackal set off a chorus of barking dogs. The air was cool and smelled of the manure spread across a fallow field.

His father's house was dark, Ptahhotep no doubt asleep. He saw no sign of the guard, but assumed Sergeant Huy would show himself when he spotted him approaching in the dark. To make sure the sergeant did not set upon him, thinking him an intruder, he began to whistle.

He approached the paddock where his horses lazed away their days, fully expecting the guard to appear. He saw no one. The shed, a small and unattractive but sturdy structure at the other end of the paddock, was dark, the horses safely inside for the night. The back of the structure and one end were mudbrick, the remains of a partially fallen building. A wooden front and second end had been tacked on and a new roof built when Bak had brought the animals from the garrison stables. They were much too valuable to leave outside each night, risking theft.

Walking along the paddock wall, he began a livelier refrain. Still the guard did not appear. A sense of unease washed through him. He stopped whistling and stepped up his pace, trotting past the wall and across the plot of grass in front of the house. The silence was unnerving, the failure of the guard to appear disturbing.

He ducked beneath the portico, his eyes on the wooden door. As dark as it was, he could see that it stood slightly ajar and a man lay crumpled on the ground before it. Alarmed, he took a quick step forward. His foot struck something and he lost his balance. He grabbed a wooden column to save himself, spotted the long spear he had stepped on, dropped onto a knee to see who the man was. The face was unknown to him, but the spear and the white cowhide shield beside the limp body identified him as a guard of the royal house.

Sergeant Huy, the man Maiherperi had assigned to keep his father safe!

The guard was breathing. Bak found no open wounds on his broad back or chest, but when he ran his fingers over the thick short hair, he discovered a large wet lump on the back of his head. The sergeant had been struck down by a hard blow. As he could do nothing for the man, he rose to his feet, stepped over him, and pushed the door wide.

The loud, terrified scream of a horse and the clatter of hooves on a hard-packed earthen floor sounded in the shed. He stiffened. His father could as easily be with the horses as within the house, trying to save the animals from . . . From theft or worse?

Snapping out a curse, he leaped from beneath the portico and raced across the scraggly grass toward the paddock. Vaulting the wall, he veered around the water trough and sped toward the shed. Another shriek of equine panic gave wings to his feet, as did thoughts of his father alone and in desperate need of help. Bursting through the doorway, which should not have been open but was, he stopped abruptly.

A minimum of light came through the high window on the mudbrick end of the building, but his eyes were as accustomed to the darkness as they would ever be. Both horses, tied to stone hitches near the manger, were screaming, bucking, kicking out, trying to break free, trying to escape from whatever they feared. Ptahhotep was not there.

Bak's first thought was a snake, perhaps a deadly cobra or some other poisonous reptile crawling through the straw strewn across the floor. Before he could dwell on the thought, a loud crack sounded against the doorjamb beside his head. Another struck somewhere inside the shed, adding to the horses' frenzy.

A sling! Someone was pelting the animals with rocks. Not large killing rocks, but smaller stones designed to sting and make them panic. He glimpsed the head and shoulders of a man at the window. The image vanished at the blink of an eye. He swung around, thinking to give chase, but stopped himself. In their hysteria the horses could break a leg or injure themselves or each other in some other fashion. They must be calmed quickly so he could go back to the house and his father.

Forcing himself to be patient, to appear unruffled—at least to the horses—he left the doorway and sidled around those flying hooves. He approached Defender, the horse farthest from the window, slowly from the side, careful to make no sudden or threatening moves, murmuring words that had no meaning. The sound of his familiar voice, his cautious approach, the absence of further flying stones, quieted both animals' screams and stilled their frantic bucking. As poor as the light was, he could see their trembling limbs, and when he reached out to catch Defender's rope halter, he felt his flesh quiver.

Without warning, the horse jerked his head. Victory snorted in terror and at the same time Bak smelled smoke. He pivoted, spat out a curse. The door was closed and fire curled under the bottom edge. The straw!

He raced toward the door, tried to shove it open. It held tight, barred, he felt sure, by the man he had seen at the window. He stamped out the flames reaching out beneath it, but other bits of straw fueled the spreading fire. The horses screamed hysterically, bucked and kicked out, shook their heads and jerked backward, trying to free themselves of the ropes that held them fast.

Bak checked his own fear, the desperate need to escape that stifled common sense and straight thinking. He knew the shed well. He had helped build it. And he knew its weaknesses.

He darted around Defender, the flying hooves, and grabbed a wooden rake standing in the corner. Using its butt end as a battering ram, he struck out at the join between the wood and the mudbrick. A crack formed between the two.

He forced the rake handle into the gap and pried the wood farther from the brick. The dowels connecting the first two boards broke with a loud crack.

He flung the rake aside, raised his foot, and kicked the board as hard as he could. The cords binding it to the roof tore away and it crashed onto the ground. A family of rats scurried out through the hole and disappeared in the darkness. Trying not to breathe the smoke that filled the shed, ignoring the crackle of the fire sweeping across the floor, the clatter of hooves, the terrified equine screams, Bak kicked another board loose and another and another until the space was wide enough for a horse to go through.

Satisfied with the hole, he swung around and stared, appalled. The straw was burning all across the floor, and flames were licking the legs of the frantic horses. He could smell their singed hair. He scooped up the rake and swung it from side to side, sweeping a path through the burning straw, pushing as much as he could away from the panicked animals.

Dropping the tool, he tore his dagger from its sheath and cut through the knot that held his kilt in place. He lunged at Defender, flung the kilt around the horse's head, blinding it, and slashed through the rope that held it captive. Catching the halter, he led the trembling, terrified animal through the hole in the wall and away from the burning shed, jerked the kilt off its head, and slapped it on the flank to send it to the opposite side of the paddock.

He raced back inside. The grain in the manger had begun to smolder, making it hard to breathe, and all the bits of straw scattered across the floor were flaming like tinder. The palm frond roof was burning, snapping and popping and shooting out sparks. Ignoring the heat, the smoke, the stench, he hurried to Victory. The horse sidled away, as afraid of him and the cloth in his hand as it was of the fire. He grabbed the rope holding the animal in place. It reared back, flung its head, flailed out with its front hooves.

Bak ducked, saving himself, and lunged at the horse to

grab its halter and throw his kilt over its head. Holding both with one hand, he severed the restraining rope, got a better grip on the halter, and urged the trembling horse across the shed and through the gap in the wall. Outside, he jerked the kilt from its head and slapped its flank with the fabric to send it across the paddock to its mate.

He looked back at the shed. Its blazing roof collapsed, setting off a shower of sparks, and flames were leaping out of the cracks between the boards. Soon nothing would be left but the mudbrick walls, and they would probably fall.

Turning away, thanking the lord Amon for standing beside him while he saved himself and the horses, he walked slowly to the water trough. He dipped his kilt in the none too clean water and wiped his sweaty face. Tension and effort had worn him out.

A movement beneath the portico in front of the house caught his eye. The guard hoisting himself into a sitting position, staring at the burning shed.

Father! Bak thought. Forgetting his exhaustion, half sick with worry, he raced across the paddock, leaped the wall, and sped to the house.

Chapter Fourteen

"My father!" Bak knelt beside Sergeant Huy. "Where is he? Is he all right?"

The guard, looking dazed, tore his eyes from the burning shed and lifted his hand to his injured head. He flinched, withdrew the hand, stared at the dark, wet stain on his fingers. "He went . . ." He frowned, trying to think. "He went to a neighbor's house, a man whose leg was cut by a scythe."

"Who came for him? Did you know him?" Bak heard the sharpness in his voice, the peremptory demand.

"No, sir, but your father did. The name was Amonemopet and he said they were longtime friends. Neighbors. He's a big man, looked as strong as a bullock."

Bak knew Amonemopet, a man to be trusted. "When? When did they leave?"

"Not long after sunset. Darkness was falling."

Some time ago, Bak thought. Close on two hours. "He hasn't yet come home?"

The sergeant looked again at the burning building, but his eyes were vague, puzzled. "I . . . I don't know. I don't remember seeing him, but . . ."

Fear raced into Bak's heart. The blow to the sergeant's head had been hard. It had clearly befuddled him and might also have stolen a portion of his memory. He leaped to his feet, ran into the house, sped from antechamber to main room to bedchambers to bath to storage rooms. The house was empty, his father's sleeping pallet on the rooftop smooth and unused. A hasty look at the cooking area outside revealed no one. He grabbed a short-handled torch his father kept for emergency use and lighted it on a bit of hot charcoal he found in the brazier. A peek at the lean-to where his father kept his two donkeys revealed one missing. The smell of smoke from the burning shed was making the remaining donkey uneasy, fidgety. The half-dozen goats lying on a bed of drying hay were calmer but wary.

He was not entirely reassured. The man who had trapped him in the shed and set the structure on fire could have waylaid Ptahhotep in the dark somewhere away from the house. Or he may have had no designs on the physician's life. The man's intent had clearly been to slay Bak. Once that purpose was accomplished, why take the life of an innocent party? So Bak told himself.

He hurried around the corner to the portico, where the sergeant was trying to stand, hanging onto a column for support. He took the guard's arm and pressed him back down. "Sit, Huy. You've a nasty wound. When my father comes, he'll never forgive me for allowing you to move about." When my father comes. The words were spoken in hope, a prayer.

Huy stared dismally at the shed, where the fire was beginning to burn itself out. "I should've been more alert, sir. You've no idea how sorry I am."

Bak knelt beside him. "Do you remember what happened?"

"I was angry with myself for letting Ptahhotep leave without me. Commander Maiherperi had ordered me to stay with him, but when he insisted that I remain here, assured me his friend would not let him out of his sight, what could I do? Then I sat where you see me now, upset because I'd failed to obey orders. I was worried, too. I like your father, you see, and . . ."

"My father can be a most persuasive man," Bak said, his wry tone betraying his own past experience.

"Yes, sir." Looking rueful, Huy reached up to touch his head but stopped himself before his fingers reached the wound. "I've no clear memory of what happened, sir, but I must've relaxed my guard, and the man who struck must've come upon me from behind."

"How long did this happen after my father left?"

"I'm not sure. A half hour at most."

"Do you remember the name of the man he went to help?"

"Djehuty." Huy smiled, pleased that he could answer one question, at least, with certainty. "He dwells on the farm adjoining Amonemopet's property to the south."

Convinced the assailant was nowhere near and the sergeant in no danger, Bak stood up. "I must see that my father has come to no harm. Can I trust you to stay where you are and rest?"

"Listen!" Huy stared into the darkness toward the path that ran along the paddock wall.

Bak heard the quick thud of hooves and men's excited voices. A donkey came trotting at its fastest pace into the circle of light cast by the torch. Two men ran alongside the sturdy beast: Ptahhotep and Amonemopet. Both stared at the shed, where flames still spewed from what remained of the palm frond roof, casting light over blackened wooden beams sagging onto the few charred boards of the wall left standing. Red glowed where the wood smoldered, and flames sporadically darted upward.

Bak offered a silent prayer of thanks to the lord Amon that his father was well, while the sergeant spoke his prayer aloud.

Ptahhotep looked with a critical eye at the sergeant seated on the ground and Bak standing over him. "What, in the name of the lord Amon, has happened here?"

Bak suddenly remembered that he wore no kilt, merely a loincloth, and that he was smeared with soot. "Are you all right, Father?"

"Of course I am," Ptahhotep said in a gruff voice. "Now tell me what's happened."

"No one tried to attack you either coming or going to Dje-huty's farm?"

"No." Ptahhotep knelt beside the sergeant, who turned his head so the physician could see the wound. "Bring that torch closer. Can't see a thing." He gave his son a stern look. "How many times must I ask? What happened here?"

Bak thanked the lord Amon that he rather than Ptahhotep had been meant to die. The assailant had come to his father's small estate, either intending to slay him during the night or to check out the lay of the land for another time. When Ptahhotep had been called away and Sergeant Huy had grown careless, the assailant had taken advantage of the moment, thinking to disable the guard and await his arrival. Luck, or that wretched lord Set, had been with him, and he had walked into the assailant's snare not in silence, but whistling a loud and spirited tune to announce his arrival.

"Defender's burns are insignificant." Ptahhotep dropped a rear hoof of the first horse Bak had saved from the burning shed and rose to his feet. "His legs should heal in a few days."

Bak, who was holding the animal's head, nodded toward the horse Amonemopet was holding. "What of Victory?"

The physician picked up a bowl containing a thin greenish substance and walked around the flank of the horse that had remained in the burning shed a longer period of time. Sergeant Huy, seated on the edge of the watering trough, shifted the flaming torch so Ptahhotep could see his second patient. The guard's head was swathed in a white bandage, and he looked bleary-eyed from the medicine Ptahhotep had given him for his headache. He should have been on his sleeping mat, but had insisted instead on helping with the late night doctoring.

"This may sting, Amonemopet, so hold him quiet." Ptah-hotep knelt, lifted a hoof, dipped a soft cloth into the poultice, and daubed the burned area. "His front legs are no worse than Defender's back ones, but the rear legs will take

a while to heal. You've no need to worry, though. Unless the
gods turn their backs to him, he'll fully recover."

Bak watched, puzzled, while his father wrapped a soft
cloth around the scorched leg and tied it in place. "You've
always told me a burn heals best when left open to the air.
Why bandage Victory?"

"The gods will look more kindly toward him if we keep
the flies away from the wound."

Soon after daybreak the same young apprentice scribe
who had summoned Bak the first time he had met with the
Storekeeper of Amon hurried up the path to Ptahhotep's
small farm. Bak was preparing to go to Waset to report to
Commander Maiherperi and ask that he replace Sergeant
Huy, who would be in no condition to guard anyone for the
next few days. Kasaya would remain with his father until the
new guard arrived, then go to Djeser Djeseru.

"Amonked wishes to see you, sir," the scribe said.

"Surely he's not heard of the fire!" Kasaya exclaimed.

"Did he tell you why?" Bak asked the apprentice.

"Something important has turned up, he said, something
you should know about."

The scribe escorted Bak to Amonked's home in Waset.
The dwelling was located in an even older and more desir-
able neighborhood than that in which the architect Montu
had dwelt. The property was larger and therefore the house
more spacious. The street was as narrow and dark and had
the same musty odor, but here guards stood before each entrance, holding at a distance unwelcome visitors.

Bak was rather intimidated. He had known that Amonked,
in spite of his lofty lineage, had no wealth to speak of and
that his wife, a woman of substance, had brought this
dwelling to the marriage. He had not expected the unpreten-
tious man who treated him as a friend and toiled daily in the
storehouses of the lord Amon to live in such grand circumstances.

A servant admitted him and the apprentice. The young scribe ushered him up a zigzag flight of stairs, across a courtyard lush with potted trees and shrubs, and into Amonked's spacious private reception room. The Store-keeper of Amon, looking very much the scribe, waved away the youth and told Bak to be seated on a stool whose hard surface was covered by an embroidered pillow. A pillow on a stool! Unheard of in the fortress of Buhen.

The room, cooled by a breeze wafting through high windows, was sparsely furnished, but each low table, wooden chest, and stool was a masterpiece of the furniture maker's art. Tightly fitted woods of different colors and grains formed designs inlaid with ivory. The thickest pillow Bak had ever seen lay on the seat of Amonked's armchair. Colorful murals adorned the walls, showing fish swimming in deep blue waters and birds flying through the emerald branches of trees. A bowl of dried flower petals on a chest near the door scented the room.

Bak was clearly out of his element. "You summoned me, sir." The words sounded as inane as any he could recall ever uttering.

If Amonked thought so, he offered no sign. "Help yourself to a small repast." He nodded toward the low table beside the stool, which was laden with bread and honey, grapes, and a jar of milk.

Settling gingerly on the thick, soft pillow, Bak poured milk into a bowl and helped himself to a chunk of honeyed bread.

Amonked leaned back in his chair and wove his fingers together across his thick waist. "Three days ago I had occasion to go to the harbor to receive a shipment of cedar from the land of Amurru. I spoke with the harbormaster of the jewelry you confiscated in Buhen and suggested the objects came from the same source as the pieces his inspectors have stumbled upon over the past few years." A shadow of a smile flitted across his face. "Needless to say, he was not pleased with my use of the words *stumbled upon.*"

"I'd think not," Bak agreed, returning the smile.

"He was quite interested when I mentioned the jar of honey in which the jewelry was being smuggled. In fact, he summoned his inspectors then and there. They'd already begun to gather in the courtyard when I left, and he could barely wait for my departure to tell them of the sketch on the neck of the jar, the honeybee."

Bak noted the glint in Amonked's eyes, a hint of excitement on his face. "Your talk bore fruit, I gather."

"Late yesterday." With a smile so satisfied it bordered on smug, Amonked opened the drawer in the chest beside his chair. He withdrew a reddish pottery jar, ovoid in shape, exactly like the one found in Buhen, and handed it to Bak. Around the neck was a sketch of a necklace with a pendant honeybee. "This, I believe, is what we've been seeking. An inspector found it on board a merchant ship bound for the land of Keftiu. The drummer who maintains the oarsmen's rhythm had it among his personal possessions."

Bak flashed a congratulatory smile at his host. "Did he reveal where it came from?"

"He's a simple man, the harbormaster told me, one who accepts what others tell him without question. He claims a youth he'd never seen before paid him to pass the jar on to a man who would meet him at the harbor at Keftiu's capital city. The Medjay police who questioned him didn't spare the cudgel and still he clung to his tale. They believe he told the truth."

Bak studied the sketch, almost identical to those he had seen before. The jar was empty, as clean as if it had never been used. "Did the inspector find honey inside? Or jewelry?"

"There was honey, yes." Amonked pulled from the drawer a square of linen much like the one in which Bak had carried the jewelry from Buhen. He spread wide the fabric and, with a broad smile, held out the open package. "And these."

Bak took one look and his breath caught in his throat. Laying in the palm of Amonked's hand were two bracelets,

two gold rings, and a rock crystal heart amulet. He had never
seen the rings or amulet before, but the bracelets were all too
familiar. Tiny inlaid butterflies adorned one, the second was
a wide gold band with three miniature golden cats lying in a
row along the top. Their likeness to those in the tomb he had
seen opened and closed at Djeser Djeseru was too close to
be a case of similarity. They were the same bracelets.

They had been stolen from the tomb right before his eyes.

A sightless man could have seen how shocked he was,
and Amonked was not blind. "What's wrong, Lieutenant?
You look like a man who's seen a dead man walk."

"In a sense I have," and Bak went on to explain.

"How can this be the same jewelry?" Amonked shook his
head, unable to believe, unwilling to accept. "The tomb was
guarded without a break. No man could've entered unseen."

Bak swallowed the last of the honeyed bread and washed
it down with a gulp of milk. He wished he could wash away
Kasaya's well-meant blunder as easily. "Kasaya spotted a
light, what he believed to be the malign spirit, and gave
chase. Imen, the guard assigned to watch the shaft, could've
climbed down while he was away. Kasaya thought he saw
him there the whole time, but he might well have become so
involved in the chase, so afraid of catching the malign spirit,
that he lost track of passing time."

"Imen. The guard. A tomb robber." Looking dismayed,
pained, Amonked shook his head once more. "I've heard
tales that the men who cared for the old tombs, who dwelt in
towns built close to the sepulchers to which they'd dedicated
their lives, robbed their deceased charges during times of
need. But today? In this time of prosperity? Why, Bak?
Why?"

"Many of the tombs are filled with wealth, sir, a powerful
incentive to a greedy man."

Amonked's face clouded with anger. He dropped the jewelry into the drawer and slammed it shut. "Go find Lieutenant Menna. Take him with you to Djeser Djeseru and
snare Imen before he hears we've found the bracelets and

tries to flee. I wish that vile thief to stand before the vizier as quickly as possible. We must make an example of him."

Bak picked up the honey jar he had set on the floor by his stool. An unexpected thought welled up in his heart, a suspicion. "Does Menna know of this discovery?"

"He does. I sent a messenger to him the instant the harbormaster brought the objects to me—as darkness was falling yesterday."

"He saw the bracelets in the tomb, sir. I pointed them out to him. I can't believe he didn't recognize them."

"Rest easy, Bak. I provided no details about the jewelry, and he's had no opportunity to see the pieces."

Bak let out a long sigh of relief. He had come to like Menna and was not happy at suspecting him of stealing and worse.

"Imen." Menna, striding up the causeway beside Bak, appeared bewildered by the guard's duplicity. "I've known him for years. I'd have trusted him with my life."

"You can never tell what lies within another man's heart." Bak hated clichés, but could think of no words more appropriate.

"Still, the deceit hurts. I thought him an honest man, not one to rob the dead."

They veered around a sledge on which a twice-life-size, rough-cut limestone statue of Maatkare Hatshepsut in the guise of the lord Osiris was being pulled up the causeway. Moisture rolled down the faces and bodies of the men pulling the sledge beneath the harsh midday sun. The bitter odor of sweat lingered in Bak's nostrils long after they passed by.

"What will people think of me?" Menna asked. "How will this affect my future?"

"You'll look no worse for Imen's deception," Bak said in a neutral voice.

"I should've seen a problem. I should have."

Bak could find no words to set Menna's heart at rest. His first inclination was to blame the officer for not being more aware of his men's inclinations. If he walked in the guard officer's sandals, he would tour the cemeteries each day to see that the men were at their assigned posts and remained alert. He doubted Menna left Waset more than once or twice a week. Would such diligence have mattered, though? Would he, Bak, spot a dishonest man among his Medjays or would he turn a blind eye to one he knew and liked, as Menna had done?

"Caught at the wrong time, he could have a foul temper," Menna said. "Do you think he slew Montu? A falling out of thieves?"

"We'll soon know."

They strode past a second sledge, this one carrying two large rectangular blocks of pinkish granite, and hurried onto the terrace. A crowd of men standing at the unfinished end of the northern retaining wall immediately caught their attention. Pashed had stopped all work on the wall after the rock slide and had vowed to keep the men away until the malign spirit was snared. Something had to be wrong.

"Hurry," Bak said, breaking into a run.

Menna put on a burst of speed to catch up. "Another accident?"

So Bak feared. Side by side they sped across the terrace, swerving to left and right around rough-finished statues and architectural elements. Someone at the edge of the crowd spotted them and called out. Men stepped aside to let them through.

They found Pashed and Kasaya standing at the leading edge of a small landslide. The prone form of a man lay on his back on the pavement between them, covered below the shoulders by rocks and debris that had rolled down off the slope. A spear point and part of the shaft lay uncovered to his right, while a red and white spotted cowhide shield lay well clear of the debris. Perenefer knelt near the head, concealing the man's identity. As the two officers came forward, he turned around, shifting his position, revealing the face of Imen.

Snapping out an oath, Bak knelt beside the foreman. He touched the body, seeking warmth, though its pallor told him Imen was dead. A bloody mess on the side of the head was covered with flies in spite of Perenefer's efforts to wave them off. "When did this happen?"

"Sometime in the night," Pashed said. "His body has grown stiff."

"If only I'd seen the jewelry," Menna muttered to himself. "If only I'd gone to Amonked's house the moment I heard of its discovery."

"Who found him?" Bak asked.

"We did," Perenefer said. "A few of my men and I. We spotted the slide at first light and came right away to clear it. This is what we found."

"It wasn't a big slide," Pashed explained, "but enough of the slope had fallen to remind the men of the last one. Of the injured and dead. They didn't need another reason to fear."

Bak studied the disturbed hillside and the fallen stones and debris that nearly covered the remains of the wall that had partly collapsed a few days earlier. From the hole left higher up the slope, about halfway to the base of the cliff, a large boulder had come loose and begun to roll, setting off the slide. He could see its upper surface behind the fallen wall, which had stopped its descent and that of the debris that nearly covered it. He was willing to bet his best beaded collar that the slide had been no accident.

"Get rid of these flies," he said to Kasaya. "Water will do." A boy stepped forward with a goatskin water bag and flooded the wound, washing away the insects. They rose in a swarm and buzzed around all who were close, refusing to abandon so tasty a meal. Waving off the most persistent, Bak bent close to inspect the wound. Or wounds, he discovered. Above Imen's right ear he found a shallow injury that had broken the skin. A bit lower and farther back was a much deeper indentation that resembled the injury to Montu's head. The guard had first been struck down and had later been slain.

Without a word but with an expression so grim every man in the crowd understood, Bak circled the end of the half-collapsed retaining wall and climbed the slope. Kasaya, unbidden, went with him. When they reached the hole where the boulder had been, they saw right away that it was too deep for the huge block of stone to have come away without the help of a man.

"Someone's tried to cover his tracks," the Medjay said, pointing to what looked like a fresh layer of dust, sand, and pebbles on the uphill side of the hole.

Bak brushed away the loose dirt. Beneath, he found the normally hard-packed sand and rocks greatly disturbed, as if the man who had loosed the boulder had dug up the ground to conceal all signs of himself and the lever he had used to pry it loose.

"What do you think happened, sir? Someone struck Imen on the head, then tried to make his death look like an accident?"

"He got away with murdering Huni and Dedu, and no one the wiser. Or so he believed." Bak rose to his feet and looked down the slope at the dead man. "I guess he thought to try his luck a third time."

"He must've come here right after he tried to slay you."

Bak's smile held not a trace of humor. "He's worried, Kasaya. He's covering his tracks in the hope of getting away free and clear, with no suspicion touching him. We'd best move quickly before he slays all who can point a finger at him."

"I must go back to Waset to report to Amonked." Bak stood with Kasaya within the ruined mudbrick temple of Djeserkare Amonhotep and his esteemed mother Ahmose Nefertari, with no one else nearby to hear. "While I'm gone, and for as long as it takes, I wish you to search out the source of the jars of honey containing the smuggled jewelry."

"But sir! You said yourself the sketch of the bee was most

likely a symbol to attract the attention of the man destined to receive the jewelry. One jar in a hundred might be so marked, one in a thousand, and those not seen by the multitudes."

The plea had some merit, but Bak could no longer justify his failure to follow up on the symbol. "The fishing boat that ran down my father's skiff vanished from view on this side of the river. Therefore, you must begin here, going from one farm to another, one village or hamlet to another, one place of business to another." Bak handed the young Medjay the upper portion of a broken jar similar to the one he had found in Buhen. On it he had sketched a necklace with a pendant honeybee. "Take this with you and show it to every man and woman you meet."

Kasaya groaned. "You ask the impossible of me, sir."

"You know how country people are, Kasaya. They tend to each other's business. Someone will have seen a jar with that symbol around its neck."

"Hori would be much better at this."

Bak agreed, but did not wish to hurt the young man's feelings. The scribe would be far more subtle in his questions, far less likely to attract undue attention. "Can you search the archives in his place?"

The Medjay hung his head in defeat. "You know I can't read, sir."

"Do you have any idea who slew that guard?" Amonked, seated on a stool beneath a portico in front of a storehouse that reeked of newly tanned hides, looked as frustrated as Bak felt.

No thick pillows on this stool to soothe the noble backside, Bak noticed. "I feel confident the malign spirit took his life."

"The malign spirit." Amonked snorted. "Could not Imen have been your so-called malign spirit?"

Bak, leaning a shoulder against a wooden column, eyed the long line of sweating men carrying the large, unwieldy bundles of hides from the cargo ship moored at the quay. Beneath the portico, they dropped the hides, which exuded a strong odor of the urine in which they had been cured, and went back for more. Scribes counted the individual hides within each bundle and called out the total to the chief scribe, seated on a stool near the storehouse door. Other men carried the counted bundles into the building. He marveled at Amonked's ability to move so easily between his luxurious household and the everyday world of a senior scribe.

"The malign spirit, I feel certain, is several men. Imen may've been one of them, but more likely he served as their lookout."

"So he was but a tool of the man who slew him."

"I believe so, yes."

"And he was slain because he could name that man."

"Yes, sir." Bak rubbed his nose, trying to banish a tickle brought on by the stench of the hides. "I've sent Kasaya out in search of the source of the honeybee symbol. We must lay hands on any other men who may be involved before they, too, are found dead."

"Leaving behind who? Their leader?"

Bak nodded. "A man who walks among those who toil at Djeser Djeseru. A face so familiar no one would ever suspect him of the vile deeds he's committed."

"Can you name him?"

"No, sir," Bak said, unwilling to acknowledge the tiny suspicion that had begun to lurk in his heart.

Chapter Fifteen

Bak hurried back across the river, reaching his father's house shortly after midday. He found Sergeant Huy there, but not Ptahhotep. The physician and a new guard assigned by Maiherperi had gone to a nearby village to tend to the aged headman, who suffered from a painful stiffening of the joints in his hands and upper limbs. They also planned to visit several other patients in the general area. Huy, though he swore he was fully recovered, had been left behind to stay quiet and see that no harm came to the house and animals.

Assured Ptahhotep would not be needing his new skiff, the one Lieutenant Menna had found for him, Bak hurried to the river and borrowed the small vessel. He shoved it into the current, raised the sail, and began a quest he suspected was no less challenging than that on which he had sent Kasaya. He had not gotten a good look at the fishing boat that had run down his father's skiff, and had paid no attention to the one moored at Waset, so was not even sure they were one and the same. But if he was right, if the head of the tomb robbers was slaying all who could name him as a thief, the fishermen who had manned that boat must be found before they met a fate similar to that of Imen. With uncommon luck and a benevolent smile from the lord Amon he might locate the vessel and therefore the men.

Filling the sail with the northerly breeze, he sped upriver to a point some distance south of where the fishing boat had vanished from sight. He let the current carry him back downstream, using the oars only to ease the skiff to the shore so he could examine a vessel pulled out of the water for the night. The day was glorious, the heat tempered by a breeze ideal for sailing. If he had not been so intent on his mission, he would very much have enjoyed his journey.

He rarely spotted a lone fishing boat. Most lay on the beach in groups, the nets spread out to dry. The day's fishing had been good, and the vast majority of the fishermen had come ashore by midday to sell the day's catch if they earned their bread on the water or to take the fish to a country estate if they toiled for a man of property. Inevitably, one or two had remained behind to mend a net or repair a wooden fitting or clean a few fish to take home. These, like most men who toiled day after day for small gain, were a convivial lot and were as aware of each other's business as men who toiled on the land. And that was what he counted on.

He must have stopped six or seven times before he entered a side channel that separated a narrow beach from a low island, a sandbar that had survived the yearly floods long enough for tall grasses and brush to take hold. More than a dozen boats of modest size had been drawn up on the beach, which ran along the base of a nearly vertical mudbank. Two men wearing skimpy loincloths sat in the shade of an acacia atop the bank, mending nets. He rowed his skiff close, jumped out, and pulled it half out of the water below them.

"I'm Lieutenant Bak of the Medjay police." He saw no need to explain that his Medjays were far away in the land of Wawat. "I seek a boat . . ."

"A boat!" Laughing merrily, the older man slapped his thigh. Like the nets they were repairing, he and his companion reeked of fish and the musty smell of the river. "That's a good one. Best I've heard all day."

The younger one sputtered. "There you are, sir." He pointed at the row of vessels lined up on shore. "Or how about out there?" Guffawing, he swung his arm wide, indicating the many boats out on the river.

"A fishing boat," Bak said, half smiling to let them know he held no rancor. Sobering, making his voice stern, he added, "Men's lives may well depend upon whether I find it. Can you help?"

Their laughter faded away and they exchanged a look easily read: they would help, but would not go out of their way, nor would they answer questions he failed to ask. This was not the first time he had faced a similar attitude, nor would it be the last.

Laying aside the nets, the fishermen rose to their feet.

"Anything we can do, sir," the younger man said, winking at his companion.

Ignoring the mockery, Bak walked with them along the shore, studying the wooden hulls of the vessels, looking for signs of collision. More than half were skiffs used for ferrying people, produce, and animals across the river and were of no concern to him. The remaining five were fishing boats. None looked any different than the twenty or so he had already examined farther upstream. All were scarred from striking small hazards floating on the water and from careless mooring. In most cases the wounded wood had darkened with time, proving the damage old. Where the scar was bright and new, it was too high or low on the hull or too far astern or its shape was wrong. He walked back along the line for a second look, scowling at his failure.

"None among them is the one you hoped to find?" the younger man asked, exchanging grins with his companion.

"I can't be sure, but I don't think so."

"You're not a man of the river, I see," the older one said.

Bak caught the inference that he did not know boats; therefore, did not know what he was looking for. He gave the man a cool look. "Don't underestimate me, old man. I grew up near here. Boats have always been a part of my life."

The younger fisherman stepped forward, formed a smile.

"If you tell us what you hope to find, sir, we'd be better able to help."

"Yes, sir," the older one said, making a too elaborate show of eagerness. "Exactly what did the vessel look like?"

"All I know for a fact was that its hull was dark and weathered," Bak admitted. From the way the pair looked at him, he could see they thought him less a man than they, for they could without doubt easily distinguish every vessel on the river. "It came upon us from behind and ran us down, sinking my father's skiff midstream. We were too busy saving ourselves to get more than a glimpse of the boat."

The younger man's eyes widened. "Your father? The physician Ptahhotep? We heard of his accident."

"You know him?"

"Oh, yes, sir!" Warmth filled the man's voice. "If not for him, my wife and newborn son would've died. A year ago it was, a time I'll never forget."

The older man eyed Bak with interest. "You came a few days ago from the southern frontier, they say. You're trying to stop the accidents at Djeser Djeseru."

"You've heard . . ." Bak chuckled. "Of course you have. You know everything that happens along the river."

Both men beamed. "Come along, sir," the older one said, "We've a brew we can share and a patch of shade."

Bak hated to spend the small amount of time he had in this one location, but he was thirsty and there was a slight chance that, given more information, they might recall something of use. He settled down with them beneath the acacia, beer jar in hand, and told them of the accident and all he remembered of the vessel. Even downwind, the musty-fishy smell was strong, abbreviating his tale.

When he finished, the younger man looked at his companion. "Could be the boat belonging to Pairi and Humay. There's a fresh scar on the hull. But why would they wish to run down the physician?" His eyes darted toward Bak. "Or you, sir."

"Who are Pairi and Humay?" Bak cautioned himself not

to let his hopes build too high. Their vessel could as easily have struck a log floating on the water as his father's skiff.

"Brothers." The older man busily scratched an itch on his inner thigh. "They usually draw their boat up here when the day's fishing is over." His eyes darted toward the row of vessels on the beach and his expression turned thoughtful. "Strange they've not yet come."

"Their father died several years ago, leaving them a farm," his friend said. "They're often the first to bring in their catch so they can get home in time to tend the flocks. Why, I'm not sure. They've a shepherd boy who does the task well enough, so I've heard."

A farm. A place where bees were no doubt cultivated. Bak's interest in the tale multiplied tenfold.

"Their boat struck something a couple days ago. No question about it. It left a long gouge down one side of the bow." The older man frowned. "Come to think of it, the scar was at about the level where it would've struck the stern of a skiff like your father's."

"We should've paid more heed, wondered more about what happened," his younger companion said. "They're not men to have an accident. They're cautious sailors, careful of their possessions—especially that boat."

Barely able to believe his good fortune, Bak set his beer jar on the ground by his side. "It wasn't here the night we were struck?"

After a short argument with his friend about who did what on which evening, the older man concluded, "It wasn't here when I left. These nets are old—my master's a stingy swine—and I often stay until close on sunset. And so I did that day."

Bak offered a silent prayer of thanks to the lord Amon. Against all odds, he had most likely found the men he sought, not mere fishermen but probably beekeepers as well. "Are they men who would take what by rights belongs to another?"

The older man chortled. "Wouldn't every man be tempted if the prize was rich enough?"

"They toil from dawn to dusk to better themselves, but would they steal?" The younger man shrugged. "Maybe. Maybe not."

Bak rose to his feet, preparing to leave. "Can you describe the two of them?"

"Hmmm." The older man picked up the net he had been repairing and located the tear he had yet to mend. "Pairi's a big man, broad across the shoulders, taller than you are. His face is square, not much to look at."

His younger companion chuckled. "His face is as flat as the sole of a leather sandal."

A flat face. Bak resisted the urge to shout for joy. He owed these two men more than he could ever repay. In addition to their other revelations, they had identified the men who had dropped him into the shaft of Nebhepetre Montuhotep's tomb.

"Humay looks a lot like his brother," the older fisherman said, "but he's not as big and his face is rounder. Kind of like an egg."

Bak thought of the many places along the river where a boat could be drawn onto the shore and of the time he might waste searching for the vessel when he wanted instead to lay hands on the men. "How can I find their farm?"

Wishing he had Kasaya to back him up, Bak hurried along a narrow path raised above the fields on a ridge of dirt cleaned out of the dry irrigation ditch beside it. The farm ahead looked to be small like his father's, but the house needed whitewash, and the two mudbrick sheds were in an advanced stage of decay, their walls partly fallen down. A large flock of sheep and goats grazed on the scant remains of harvested crops in the field to the east. A boy of eight or nine years sat in the shade of a clump of tamarisks, keeping an eye on the animals and watching Bak. The yellow dog beside him rose to its feet and barked, but grew silent at a sharp command from its master. A donkey grazed nearby unconcerned.

A few clumps of vegetation not yet eaten by the voracious animals told him what the harvested crop had been. Clover, a good source of nectar for bees. He saw no hives at the edge of the field, but spotted them on the roof of the house. A large grouping of cylindrical pots held together by dried mud.

Yes! he thought, gratified beyond measure. He had come upon the beekeepers he had sent Kasaya out to find. Beekeepers who were also fishermen and tomb robbers. A few hours' effort well worthwhile.

He stopped at the edge of the field. Other than the bleating of a lamb lost from its mother and the distant howling of a dog, he heard not a sound. The house ahead looked empty. Appearances, however, could be deceiving. The fishermen could have seen him approach and recognized him. They might well be lying in wait, hoping to catch him unaware.

Where? The house and sheds stood in the open. From the manure dotting the grass and weeds, Bak guessed the livestock was allowed to graze where it would. The small garden was surrounded by a wall of sorts, dried acacia branches bristling with needles. He could see through the fence, and the interiors of both sheds stood open to view and empty. He glanced toward the stubble field. Boy and dog had gone in among the animals and were paying him no heed.

Clutching his baton of office as he would a club, he strode to the house. Pausing ten or twelve paces from the door, he called, "Pairi! Humay! I must speak with you."

He received no answer.

Trying not to step on dry grass that would crunch beneath his sandals, he crept to the door and stopped to listen. All was quiet. He remained where he was, waiting. He heard not a sound. Tamping down his impatience, he counted out the moments as a woman would do when awaiting the birth of a child. Halfway to his goal of two hundred, his patience paid off. He heard a faint rustle just inside and to the right of the door. The noise could have been made by a mouse or a rat—but he did not think so. He took a silent step forward, bringing him close enough to touch the doorjamb.

He leaped across the threshold. Through eyes unaccustomed to the darkness, he glimpsed a figure where he had expected it to be. He swung half around, knocked something from the man's hand, and with his free fist struck the man hard in the stomach.

"Oof!" he heard, and the man fell at his feet, dropping spear and shield with a clatter, clutching his stomach. The light from the open door fell on his face.

"Kasaya!" Bak dropped to his knees beside the young Medjay.

"Lieutenant Bak?" Kasaya, his face screwed up in a grimace of pain, heaved his shoulders off the packed earthen floor and sat up. "What are you doing here, sir?"

"Why didn't you answer when I called out?"

"I didn't recognize your voice. I didn't expect you."

Bak helped the Medjay to his feet and seated him on a stool in the center of the sparsely furnished room. "I might've killed you."

Kasaya gave him a wan smile. "If you'd given me the chance, I'd have brained you with my mace."

Bak had told his Medjays time and time again that they must not slay suspects before they had a chance to talk. Kasaya, he saw, had not altogether taken his words to heart.

The young man rubbed his stomach gingerly. "I must warn the other men in our company not to anger you, sir."

"I expected to fell an enemy, not a friend." Bak's smile waned. "Now tell me what brought you to this farm."

"I met a man at a house of pleasure a short walk south of here. When I showed him the sketch you made, he remembered seeing the fisherman Pairi with such a jar. I came here to ask who'd given it to him. By great good fortune, I stopped first to talk with the boy watching the flocks. He knew of the jars; his mother makes them. Pairi and the brother Humay give her fresh fish in exchange for a few newly formed and dried jars. They add the design and return them to her so she can place them in her kiln."

"What's she to these men? Sister? Mother?"

"Neither. She dwells on the adjoining farm. The boy's father died two years ago and he has several younger brothers and sisters. They earn their bread the best way they can. He tends the flocks of Pairi and Humay and in return his family's flocks graze with theirs."

Bak looked around the dwelling, which was none too clean and smelled strongly of unwashed bodies and fish. A quick search revealed nothing of value and no clothing. Either the two brothers had taken all they had of value and fled or they lived in squalor with the most meager of possessions.

"Not much to show for the lord Amon alone knows how many years of tomb robbing."

Kasaya, looking doubtful, eyed the room. "If they're the robbers, sir, where's the wealth they've been getting in exchange for the ancient jewelry?"

"Perhaps the man we call the malign spirit is keeping it."

"For them or for himself?"

"Yes, sir, I've seen them go out at night." The boy, wide-eyed with curiosity and excited at such an interesting distraction from his lonely vigil over the animals, rubbed the soft ears of the baby lamb he held in his arms. "The two of them most of the time, but sometimes another man goes with them."

"What does he look like?" Bak asked.

"He's taller than they are and not as broad, but otherwise I don't know. I'm always out here with the animals, too far away to see in the dark."

"Do they go out often?"

"Not that I've seen, sir, but I might've been asleep when they left. My dog barks at strangers, not men he knows. Or at jackals or some other predator. Or when a sheep or goat gets itself in trouble."

"Is there a pattern to their nighttime journeys? For example . . ." Bak hesitated, not wishing to put thoughts into the boy's heart. "Do they leave early or late? Do they go often or seldom? A day at a time or several days in a row?"

The boy set the lamb beside its mother and scratched his bony chest, thinking. "They usually go not long after darkness falls, during nights when the moon isn't very bright. Sometimes they go several nights in a row with a long gap until the next time, and sometimes they just go. No pattern that I can see."

"Do you know where they are now?"

"No, sir. They left early this morning, as they always do, and I haven't seen them since."

After a few more questions that led nowhere, Bak thanked the boy with a plaster-covered wooden token, which his mother could take to the local garrison quartermaster and exchange for grain or some other item she needed. He and Kasaya headed toward the river and Ptahhotep's skiff.

"Someone—our malign spirit, I suspect—finds the tomb," Bak said to Kasaya, "and these two, possibly the three of them, dig it out."

"And Imen, while still he lived, watched to see that no one stumbled upon them in the night."

Bak nodded. "Once they've dug their way in, they take a night or two to clean the sepulcher of all its valuables. That done, they close the mouth of the shaft to deceive the guards who patrol the cemeteries."

"I'd not be surprised to learn that Pairi and Humay have gone for good." Kasaya's brow furrowed. "Or have they been slain as Imen was?"

"If I trod in their sandals, I'd have fled the instant I learned of Imen's death."

Chapter Sixteen

"Well done, Lieutenant. You've accomplished in a week what that guard lieutenant—What's his name? Menna?—has been unable to do in more months than I can guess."

"Yes, sir. Now all we have to do is snare them."

"You can leave that to me." Maiherperi snapped his fingers and beckoned. A young officer who had been talking with several scribes at the back of the room hastened to the dais. The commander sent him off to summon the head of the garrison at Waset. "Or, rather, to my colleague Commander Ahmose. Within the hour he can have soldiers across the river watching the farm and send out couriers to have the boat stopped should Pairi and Humay travel beyond the borders of this province. At first light tomorrow he'll have men on the river searching for their boat nearer to home."

Bak nodded, well satisfied. He had hurried directly to Waset after leaving the farm of Pairi and Humay, thinking to relate his tale to a man with far more authority than he. Unable to reach Amonked, he had come to the commander. The decision had been a good one. Maiherperi was a man who wasted no time in setting in motion what had to be done.

"As I said before, sir, they may no longer be among the living."

"I'll tell Ahmose. Never fear; they'll be found whether alive or dead." The commander waved away a ribbon of smoke wafting across the dais from a torch mounted on the wall. "Does Amonked know of your success?"

"No, sir. I thought to bring him with me to see you, but he was away from his home, summoned by our sovereign to the royal house. Something to do with Senenmut's inspection tomorrow of Djeser Djeseru."

"Ah, yes. The matter of providing additional guards. I suppose I should've gone to the royal house, too, but I've no patience with discussing over and over again a problem that's been resolved. The guards will be provided and they'll be on the alert for trouble. If Senenmut insists on going. And knowing him, he will."

Maiherperi had to be very secure in his position, Bak thought, to take a summons from their sovereign so lightly.

The commander waved his hand again, breaking up the smoke. A guard grabbed a torch mounted beside the door, hastened across the room, and substituted the one for the other.

"Have you told that guard officer—Menna—that you've resolved his problem for him?"

"No, sir." Bak hesitated, added, "I'd rather he didn't know yet."

Maiherperi gave him a sharp look. "Why not?"

Bak was not sure what he should say. He did not want to lay blame where no blame was due. "He was very resentful when first I came to Waset. His attitude has since improved and he's readily accepted my recent suggestions, but he won't like the fact that I've achieved what he has toiled so long and hard to accomplish. And now, instead of going to him and sharing the success, the glory, I've come straight to you."

"He has no one to blame but himself." Maiherperi frowned at the scribes, whose voices had risen in a mild squabble. "This so-called malign spirit . . . Do you have any idea who the vile creature might be?"

"If Pairi and Humay are found alive, they can be made to point a finger. If not . . ." Bak hesitated, unwilling to commit himself, but finally said, "I could guess, sir, but I wish to be more certain before I name him."

Not long after daybreak the following morning, Bak strode into the courtyard at the hall of records. There he found Hori and Kaemwaset seated on woven reed mats beneath a portico, dipping chunks of fresh, warm bread into a bowl of duck stew resting on a hot brazier. To Bak, who had spent the night in the garrison and shared with the duty officers a morning meal of hard day-old bread and cold fish stew, the mingled smells of yeast and duck were as the food of the gods. Fortunately, they had enough for three, and the respite allowed him to tell them of his previous day's successes.

After nearly emptying the bowl, they cleaned their hands with natron and a damp cloth so they would not damage the aged documents they would be handling. No sooner had they turned away from the remains of their meal than a yellow cat and five kittens crept out from beneath a bush to lick the bowl clean. Kaemwaset lifted a scroll from a shallow basket containing a dozen or so others. The seals were broken and the strings that had once bound them had in many cases rotted away.

Unrolling the scroll, the priest held it out for Bak to look at. "You see what we must contend with." The papyrus had turned brownish with age, was torn, riddled with holes, and dotted with splotches large and small. "This document is no worse than many others we found," he added, tapping the basket with a fingernail.

Bak took the musty-smelling scroll from the priest and, holding the brittle papyrus carefully, studied the uppermost lines of symbols. "Not easy to read."

"No, sir. And errors can creep in through misunderstanding of the partial lines we can read."

"Did a plan survive of Nebhepetre Montuhotep's temple?"

"You should see it, sir!" Hori plucked a scroll from the

basket. "It doesn't look at all like the ruined temple. You wouldn't know it's the same building."

Bak had hoped for more but was not surprised. "The mansion of the lord Amon in Waset has been altered many times through many generations. Even the initial plan of Djeser Djeseru has been changed during the few years since construction began. Can we expect less from a provincial king who pulled together a fragmented land and made it into a single grand whole?"

"He would've wanted better for himself as his power increased," Hori agreed.

Taking the scroll from the young scribe, Kaemwaset unrolled it across his lap.

Laying aside the document he held, Bak bent close to look at the sadly decayed papyrus, whistled. "How certain are you that this was planned for Nebhepetre Montuhotep?"

"Some doubt arises," the priest admitted. "It contains the name of Montuhotep and was found among the other scrolls we know were prepared during Nebhepetre Montuhotep's reign. We must face the fact that it could've been drawn during the reign of a different Montuhotep—the name is slightly different—and placed with the wrong documents at a later time."

"But you don't think so."

"Nebhepetre Montuhotep ruled for some years and he'd have wanted to display his expanding authority. I'd be less surprised to find his temple altered than a few others I've seen."

Bak stared at the plan, so different from the temple he, Hori, and Kasaya had so painstakingly searched days before. "Have you finished with the archives? Or do you have more old records to go through?"

"We've one more section," Kaemwaset said, "another fifty or so storage pots that have no labels denoting their contents. I suspect they contain documents thrown asunder during the years of chaos and gathered together later in too much haste to store and label properly. Between the two of us, it'll take much of the day to go through them all, reading a sufficient amount of each document to be certain it is or isn't what we seek."

Kneeling to scratch the mother cat's head, Bak scowled at the ancient plan spread across the priest's legs. He was not sure how helpful it would be, but it was all they had and might be all they would ever find. "Get a fresh scroll, Hori. I wish you to take time out from your search to redraw this plan. Draw as much as you can clearly see in black ink, then with Kaemwaset's help, fill in the missing or stained places with red ink. Maybe we can discover exactly what this is."

The priest smiled his appreciation. "A good idea, sir. If this is an early version of Nebhepetre Montuhotep's temple, a new and complete drawing might well be worth the effort."

"Keep a close eye on Hori." Rising to his feet, Bak grinned at the youth, letting him know he was teasing, at least partially so. "We spent many hours searching that temple and he knows it well. He must not add parts to the new plan that fit closer to his memory than does this aging papyrus."

"Welcome, Lieutenant. Amonked has told me of you." Mai, the harbormaster, a stout man with a fringe of curly white hair that surely tickled the back of his neck, ushered Bak into the room he used as his office. "He speaks highly of you, and with good reason if all he says is true."

"He's probably exaggerating," Bak said, smiling.

"I've known him for years and I've never known him to embellish a tale." Mai walked to a large rectangular opening in the outer wall and looked out upon the harbor of Waset, with its many ships moored along the river's edge and the bustling market where townsmen exchanged local products for the exotic objects brought by seamen from faraway ports. The opening reminded Bak of the window of appearances in the royal house, which served as a stage upon which their sovereign appeared before her subjects. "Did he ever tell you he once dreamed of sailing a large and imposing seagoing ship? One that would ply the waters of the Great Green Sea to Amurru, Keftiu, the southern shores of—" He stopped abruptly, laughed. "Suffice it to say, he's traveled no farther than the Belly of Stones."

"I stood with him on the battlements of the fortress of Semna, looking down upon the border between Wawat and Kush. I could see in his heart the wish to follow the river to its end."

"So he told me." Mai swung away from the window, motioned Bak onto a stool, and sat on a low chair that allowed him to look out at the harbor while they talked. "To what do I owe your visit, Lieutenant?"

"I've come to clarify something Amonked told me. Something I thought nothing of at the time."

"I assume this involves the ancient jewelry my inspector found?"

"Yes, sir." A harsh yell drew Bak's eyes to the street below, where a spirited pair of chariot horses had knocked a woolly fleece from a merchant's shoulder and trampled it. The charioteer flung what looked like a garrison grain token at the man and drove on. "He said yesterday, when he informed me of your discovery, that you'd grown very excited when he told you, three days earlier, of the jar I found in Buhen with jewelry inside. Especially when he described the sketch around the neck, a necklace with a pendant bee."

"That surprises you? It shouldn't. After months of fruitless searching here and there and everywhere, we had something specific to look for. Who would've thought of looking inside a honey jar? None of my inspectors. Nor I, for that matter."

"Lieutenant Menna didn't come to you seven or eight days ago, when I told him of the sketch?"

"He did not." Mai's eyes narrowed. "You told him when?"

"A few hours after I arrived in Waset. He vowed he'd tell you right away."

"Well, he didn't." Mai, obviously irritated, stared out the window at the many vessels moored there. The beat of a drum and the chant of the oarsmen announced the arrival of a cargo ship whose deck was divided into stalls filled with reddish long-horned cattle. Bak doubted the harbormaster saw the ship or its contents. "Menna seems a good-hearted soul, Lieutenant, rather touchy about what he perceives as the status of his assignment, but he's not a man one can depend on."

"Is he incompetent, sir? Or something else?"

Mai's eyes darted from the window to Bak, his expression censorious, directed not to his visitor but to the man about whom he spoke. "I've heard he seldom visits the cemeteries, that he spends more time writing reports than supervising the men who guard the dwelling places of the dead." His mouth tightened to a thin, critical line. "I've never seen him with a speck of dust on his kilt or sandals, and he always looks as if he's fresh from his bath. When I visit my venerable ancestors during the Beautiful Festival of the Valley, staying on the paths as much as possible, I return to my home dripping with sweat and with myself and my clothing stained brown by dust."

"I've felt he was lax in his duty, but tried to believe he had sergeants he could trust. As I trust mine."

"Do you leave your sergeants alone day after day, letting them do what they will with no word from you, no report from them?"

Bak smiled. "No, sir."

The smile Mai returned was stingy, weakened by censure. "Don't get me wrong, Lieutenant. I like him. However, I can't condone a man's failure to oversee the men responsible to him."

Bak liked this gruff, outspoken man. They saw their duty much the same. "How well do you know him?"

"Not personally. Our paths seldom cross. Only when my inspectors recover an object stolen from the dead. Also, if I have the time, I drop in to see him when I visit my chief inspector, who's housed in the same building."

"Where's Menna from, do you know?" Bak spoke casually, as if giving no special weight to the question.

He either failed in his purpose or Mai's thoughts were keeping pace with his, for the harbormaster gave him a long, thoughtful look. "His forebears were men of the river, as were mine, so that question I can answer. He was born in Iunyt, the son of a fisherman who died when he was three or four years of age. His mother was daughter to a ferryman who dwelt across the river. Upon the death of her husband, she returned to her family home in western Waset, bringing the child with her."

Bak's heart skipped a beat. The Lates fish was held sacred in Iunyt. "So he knows western Waset well, and the people who dwell there."

"Better than most, I'd say."

Bak drew in a breath, then released it with a whoosh. Though he had no proof, the tiny suspicion in his heart was rapidly turning into a conviction. "Would that I'd come to see you when first I came to Waset. Information flows from you as water from a spring, and each word more worthy than gold."

"You must've asked the right questions," Mai said, openly curious.

"As harbormaster, you must know or at least have met Pairi and Humay, two brothers who sail a fishing boat out of western Waset."

Mai must have detected the change from suspicion to certainty, for he turned away from the window, focusing his attention on his visitor. "Broad, strong men, one most notable for a squarish head and flat face."

"Are they in any way related to Menna?"

"Not that I've heard." Mai tapped his fingers on his thigh, trying to remember. "Their father was a farmer, I've been told, and their uncle a fisherman. They were apprenticed to him as youths, and when he died, they inherited his boat."

"Have you ever seen Menna with them?" Bak asked, not quite ready to reveal his thoughts.

"Not that I recall."

Bak was willing to bet that if the three men had been together at the harbor, Mai would remember. "Have you ever
seen the brothers with any of Menna's guards? His sergeants?"

"I fear you've lost me, Lieutenant. I know the Medjays
assigned to guard the harbor, and I'd recognize a palace
guard by his dress and weapons and shield. Other than those
two units, I can't tell one from another."

"One of Menna's men, a sergeant, was found dead yesterday at Djeser Djeseru. He'd been slain, struck down from
behind, and a small landslide set off to make his death look
accidental. I thought before we found him that he'd robbed
the tomb in which I saw the jewelry your inspector found in
the honey jar. I erred. Another man, the one we call the malign spirit, took the jewelry and slew the guard who helped
him take it." Bak went on to describe Imen.

"Several men answer to that description, so I can't be
sure, but I think I've seen him here at the harbor. Not with
Menna, but talking to Pairi and Humay."

Satisfaction erupted within Bak's heart. The various trails
he had been following had converged into one.

Mai eyed him curiously. "What are you thinking, Lieutenant?"

"I think Menna might well be the man we've been calling
the malign spirit, his goal to steal ancient jewelry from a
tomb or tombs in the valley where Djeser Djeseru is being
built."

"Menna?" The harbormaster chuckled. "He's negligent,
lazy, never follows through on a task. Does that sound like
your malign spirit?"

"He could be a man of two faces. On the surface, a quiet,
perfectly groomed, and rather incompetent guard officer.
Beneath the skin, a cold-blooded and vicious slayer of innocent men, one whose sole purpose is to safely rob the dead."

Mai laughed so hard tears flowed from his eyes. "Your
imagination does you credit, young man, but I fear you must
look elsewhere for your malign spirit. Menna simply doesn't

have the will or competence to pursue a task as dangerous and difficult as robbing tombs."

With Mai's laughter ringing in his ears, Bak hurried along the busy streets to Menna's office. The harbormaster's certainty that the guard officer was incapable of carrying out a long-term, complicated, and difficult task had seriously placed in question his suspicion. For one thing, Mai's impressions of Menna were much in line with his own over the past few days.

If not Menna, then who could the malign spirit be? More than one man, he had already concluded. The fishermen, certainly. They would be as likely to wear amulets of the Lates fish as a man from Iunyt. They had had Imen's help and that of at least one other man. One who could walk unimpeded and unnoticed across the sands of Djeser Djeseru, one who knew the building site well.

No man would have had more freedom or knew the site better than Montu, and Bak had found the shard with the sketch of the bee in the architect's office. True, Montu had expressed anger when the workman Ahotep had died while toiling at the southern retaining wall, but what better way to draw attention to an accident that was not in fact an accident than to point it out?

But Montu had been slain. Perhaps there had been a falling out of thieves and the fishermen had taken his life. The architect would have been the leader, the one who thought and planned for the gang. Maybe he had demanded too large a portion of the spoils, thinking himself indispensible. Maybe the others had disagreed. After many months of working with him, they would know exactly what to do and how to go about it, with or without him.

Lieutenant Menna was not in his office. He had gone to the garrison, a young scribe said, to arrange for a replacement for Imen. While there, Bak felt sure he would hear of the search for Pairi and Humay. If he was the vile criminal,

the news might well set him to flight. Or would it? Flight
would be an admission of guilt. If he thought the fishermen
free and clear—or dead—would he turn his back on his life
in Waset unnecessarily? Would he want to look guilty before
he was certain he had been identified as the malign spirit?

Bak was torn. He wanted to go to the garrison, to question
Menna right away, to satisfy himself of the officer's guilt or
innocence. But dare he? The fishermen might not be dead.
No matter who their leader, the deceased Montu or the living
Menna, they could be hiding somewhere near Djeser Djeseru, planning a spectacular accident with Senenmut as a
witness or, far worse, a victim. He might still have time to
stop it—if it was not already too late. The barque of the lord
Re had climbed halfway up the morning sky, and the inspection should be well on its way. Worse, to Bak's way of thinking, was the certainty that Amonked, escorting Senenmut
around Djeser Djeseru, was as much at risk as Maatkare
Hatshepsut's favorite.

He must hurry to Djeser Djeseru. But before he crossed
the river, he must share what he knew with Maiherperi. Only
the most foolhardy of men would keep to himself knowledge so important. Of equal importance was the need to discover the identity of the man he had been calling the malign
spirit, and the fastest way was to draw Menna to Djeser Djeseru. How could he do so? With garrison troops searching
for the fishermen, the officer was bound to be wary—if indeed he was the malign spirit—but hopefully not so suspicious he could not be soothed.

What would put at ease a guilty man as well as one who
was innocent? After a few moment's thought, Bak borrowed
brush and ink from the young scribe and wrote a brief note:

*I think I know who's been causing the accidents at
Djeser Djeseru. If you join me there at mid-afternoon,
Senenmut's inspection should be completed and we
can snare him then.*

He handed the note to the scribe. "I wish you to take this message to Lieutenant Menna. I must go to the hall of records, so deliver his response to me there. Report to me also if you fail to find him."

If nothing else, the note's enigmatic nature should pique Menna's curiosity.

"They've not yet crossed the river," Maiherperi said. "Senenmut decided to use the morning hours to inspect the repairs being made at the mansion of the lord Amon here in Waset."

"I thank the gods!"

The guard at the door, alerted by the exclamation whose words he had evidently not heard, took a quick step forward, poised to act. The commander signaled that all was well, sending him back to his post. "Your optimism is unfounded, Lieutenant. When he's finished here, he plans to move on to Djeser Djeseru."

Bak slumped onto a stool unbidden. "It's not too late to stop him."

Maiherperi made a sour face. "Amonked tried to convince him he must not inspect Djeser Djeseru today—or until the malign spirit is snared. He refused to listen, saying no one would dare injure him. When I seconded Amonked's plea, he suggested we've something to hide, a wall that collapsed from shoddy construction perhaps or . . ." He paused, smiled with little humor. "The list is endless, it seems."

Bak muttered a curse. "You must somehow stop him, sir."

The commander raised his hands, palms forward. "No man can stop Senenmut when he sets his heart on an action. After all, he's Overseer of Overseers of All the Works of the King." A wry note crept into his voice. "He takes the task seriously."

"If he witnesses a terrible accident, if he's hurt or killed by chance or by design . . ." Bak could go no further. The thought was too appalling.

"He's blind to the risk. To his way of thinking, spirits malign or benevolent act at random, with no purpose. When we pointed out that this spirit is a man, he remained unmoved, thinking himself safe because no ordinary individual would dare touch a man so close to our sovereign."

Bak stood up. "I fear not only for Senenmut, sir, but for Amonked as well."

Maiherperi stepped down from the dais and laid a sympathetic hand on the younger officer's shoulder. "No more than I, Lieutenant. No more than I."

"Here it is, sir, the new plan we drew." Hori, looking as proud as a father showing off his firstborn son, handed the new-made scroll to Bak. "If this was an early temple built by Nebhepetre Montuhotep, I'm not surprised he changed it. It wouldn't have been half as imposing as the temple he completed."

Kaemwaset hovered close, as pleased with the drawing as Hori. "The plan makes no mention of the setting in which the temple was built. If it was built. It's smaller than the ruined building and could easily have been leveled and the new structure built over it."

Bak knelt beside the pair and unrolled the scroll. The drawing, while a long way from being a work of art, was exactly what he wanted. He prayed it would also be what he needed. "Excellent. Let's hope I can use this to good advantage."

Even with the blank spaces filled in, the plan in no way resembled the temple he and his men had explored cubit by cubit. The entrance to the king's tomb was some distance in front of the raised platform rather than at the back, as at present. The platform on the old plan, shorter in width and length and not as high, was surmounted by a small memorial temple rather than the solid structure and enclosed main court surrounded by a colonnade that lay in ruins on the existing platform. The colonnade court, columned hall, and sanctuary of the present structure were not shown at all. Six small chapels or shrines lined the rear edge of the smaller platform.

"Have you found anything else of interest?" he asked, rolling up the plan.

Kaemwaset pointed to a stained scroll lying on top of those in the basket. "One of the old documents we found makes mention of the sepulcher of a royal spouse named Neferu. It's somewhere east of the new temple, at the base of the slope beneath the northern cliff."

"In the path of the northern retaining wall at Djeser Djeseru?"

"Possibly. The exact location isn't clear." The priest offered Bak a rolled scroll made of fresh white papyrus. "The document was very fragile, so I copied it, filling in the missing or unclear symbols in red ink, as Hori filled in the plan."

"Good." Bak stood up, granted each a quick smile of thanks. "I can take it and the plan with me and study them on the ferry while I cross the river."

The pair glanced at each other, visibly disappointed, no doubt feeling he was not giving their considerable effort the attention it deserved.

"Lieutenant Bak." The young scribe he had talked with at Menna's office approached across the courtyard. "I've delivered your message, sir, and the officer said he'd meet you as you asked him to."

"How did he receive the message?"

"He was puzzled, sir, very puzzled."

Bak nodded, not at all surprised. Whether Menna would have second thoughts and not appear as promised was an open question. Even at the best of times he was not dependable. With Senenmut's inspection delayed, giving him more time, perhaps he should . . . "Where is he now? Still at the garrison?"

"No, sir, I caught him as he was leaving. I think he was looking for a boat to carry him across the river."

Bak thanked the scribe and sent him on his way. Had Menna crossed the river on an ordinary errand, or in an attempt to escape? Or to do further damage? He prayed fervently to the lord Amon that he had not missed the only opportunity he might have had to lay hands on the guilty man. "I must go right away to Djeser Djeseru. Senenmut has delayed his inspection until after midday, and I must do all I can to ensure his safety while he's there."

"Do you think Neferu's tomb is the one the malign spirit is seeking?" Hori asked, trying to hide his distress.

"It's impossible to say. We've no idea how many wives and daughters Nebhepetre Montuhotep had." Noting the gloom on both their faces, Bak realized he could not simply walk away from them after they had searched the archives with such diligence. "The two of you must come with me. If Lieutenant Menna turns up at Djeser Djeseru as I hope, you've every right to be there when I question him. While we await him, we can search out the tomb he's looking for."

Hori gaped.

Kaemwaset looked perplexed. "Lieutenant Menna?"

Bak realized they were ignorant of all he had learned since last he had seen them. "Lieutenant Menna may be the malign spirit. If he proves to be innocent, I fear we must look closer at a dead man: Montu."

"Menna?" Kaemwaset shook his head in denial. "He's the guard officer, a man above reproach."

"Come. I'll explain on the way."

Kaemwaset looked as sober as Bak had ever seen him. "The workmen and artisans must not be given the smallest hint of what you're thinking. If they convince themselves Menna is the one who's brought about so much injury and death, they'll tear him apart."

Chapter Seventeen

Bidding a temporary farewell to Hori and Kaemwaset, Bak hurried up the causeway to Djeser Djeseru about an hour before midday. The scribe and priest turned aside to walk to the ruined temple of Nebhepetre Montuhotep. At their heels, ranging from side to side as the urge struck, trotted a large white dog they had borrowed from a desert patrol unit garrisoned in Waset.

Bak stopped at the eastern end of the terrace, where it overflowed onto the ruined walls of the temple of Djeserkare Amonhotep and his revered mother Ahmose Nefertari. Standing quite still, concentrating fully on all he saw, he studied the cliffs around the valley and the rim above, where a path ran along the edge. With the sun striking the cliff high and from the front, the vertical surfaces looked flat and the crevices shallow. The tower-like projections merged into the background and much detail was lost. A thin haze, minute particles of airborne dust, turned the cliffs an unnatural pinkish purple, further obscuring all but the most outstanding features. The heat was pervasive, the sand hot beneath his sandals.

The malign spirit had twice used rock slides as a means of destruction, and Bak could think of no more spectacular a way of creating further devastation and fear than a slide originating high up the face of the cliff. Along much of the way, rock and debris would plunge harmlessly onto the tower-like projections, but he could see several chute-like places where a slide could fall unimpeded onto the memorial temple of Maatkare Hatshepsut. One had but to look at the ruined columned hall at the rear of Nebhepetre Montuhotep's temple to see what damage could be done.

"Menna." Pashed, standing in the sunlight at the top of the ramp leading to the temple, looked out across Djeser Djeseru, thinking of all Bak had told him. "Yes. I've always thought him a man who'd go to far greater lengths to attain his goals in a less than admirable fashion than to exert himself by earning his bread in a hardworking and diligent manner."

Bak gave the senior architect a surprised look. "You never said."

"You surely noticed he seldom visited Djeser Djeseru. Or any of the cemeteries of western Waset, for that matter. If I'd not taken control, the guards here would've spent much of each day playing knucklebones and throwsticks, drinking beer and wagering. As it was, they neglected their duty at night."

"Afraid of the malign spirit."

Against his will, Bak looked at the cliff towering above the temple. He saw no movement along the rim, no man poised to start a rock slide, but his skin crawled as he thought again of the possibilities for destruction.

"I could hardly blame them for that," the architect said grudgingly. "They were but a few among the many."

Laughter, a sound incongruous under the circumstances, tugged Bak's glance to the north end of the lower colonnade, where a gang of men were increasing the height of the rubble ramp in the expectation of hauling up another stone block and placing it on top of a partially completed column. "Montu would've known even better than Menna how best to do damage to Djeser Djeseru."

Pashed did not appear surprised by the suggestion, but gave it some thought nonetheless. "He was indolent, yes, selfish and arrogant, and cruel in his own way, but I never thought him so callous he'd slay men at random."

"Someone did, and I'd bet my best kilt it was either him or Menna." A darkness consumed Bak's heart, a feeling of sadness—and rage—that one man could be responsible for so much needless death and injury. "If one of them didn't, the fishermen or Imen did at their leader's instruction."

Pashed's voice turned harsh with anger. "I'd like to slay them all with my bare hands."

"Imen can do no more harm. If the fishermen haven't run away, they may well come today, drawn by Senenmut and the desire to do damage. And I've summoned Menna . . ." A wry smile flitted across Bak's lips. ". . . with a promise that the two of us will snare the malign spirit, he and I together. Whatever the truth, I'll find it, and your troubles will be over."

"I wish I could be as certain as you."

Bak tamped down his irritation. Over the past few years, Pashed had shouldered far too much adversity for any one man. He had every right to be pessimistic. "There've been four attempts on my life, Pashed. Whether Menna is the malign spirit or the fishermen are walking in the shadow of a dead man, they have to know their time is running out. If they're determined to bring about an accident serious enough to stop construction, they must do so without delay. What better time than when Senenmut is here?"

"Senenmut has the ear of our sovereign." The worry lines deepened in the architect's face, alarm seeped into his voice. "He's her right hand, much beloved. How can we let him walk into what could be a deadly trap?"

Bak had explained once that Maiherperi and Amonked had both tried to dissuade Senenmut from coming. He saw no need to repeat himself. "Move as many of the men as you can away from the cliff, and remove the craftsmen from the sanctuary and side chapels. I know, because of Senenmut's inspection, that you can't take everyone away from their tasks, but do the best you can."

Looking harried, pushed to the limit, Pashed nodded.

"You must go from one chief craftsman to another, from one foreman to another, and tell them to be extra alert for anything out of the ordinary, any problem. We may not be able to stop altogether what they plan, but with luck and the help of every god great and small, we should be able to contain the damage."

"Where will I find you should I need you?" Pashed asked, too worn down to offer further resistance.

"Utter not one word of what I've told you," Bak cautioned, not for the first time. "I must speak with Menna before the men learn he could be the malign spirit. I don't want them attacking an innocent man."

"I've always been one to behave in a right and proper manner, to obey the law of the land and do right by the lady Maat, but in this case . . ."

"No." Bak placed a hand on the architect's wrist. "What good is the law if men take punishment into their own hands?" He noted Pashed's troubled demeanor and said no more. The man's conscience would lead him to reveal nothing—or so he prayed.

He started down the ramp, remembered a question he had failed to ask, and turned back. "Do you know anything about the tomb of a woman called Neferu, spouse of Nebhepetre Montuhotep?"

"Neferu?" Pashed shook his head slightly, as if to clear away his troubled thoughts, at least enough so he could speak of a less bothersome subject. "Hers was the first sepulcher we came upon in this valley."

Bak gave him a sharp look. "Kaemwaset knew nothing of it until he found mention of it in the archives. Has he not been priest from the day construction began?"

"He wasn't assigned to Djeser Djeseru until after our sovereign laid the foundation deposits and the chief prophet consecrated the valley. We found the tomb a few months earlier, the day we inspected the landscape to learn the extent of the effort we must make to give the building a firm base."

Bak nodded his understanding. "You were here at the time?"

"Yes, sir."

"Where exactly is the tomb located?"

Pashed pointed eastward and a bit to the left of the temple of Djeserkare Amonhotep and Ahmose Nefertari. "At the base of the slope below the cliff, north of an old wall partly buried in sand that runs alongside the temple."

"How did you find it way out there?"

"The mouth of the tomb lay open." The architect eyed the terrace below them, the incomplete statues and architectural elements, the many men toiling there, and a look of pride blossomed briefly on his face. "You must remember that before this project began, this valley was seldom visited by man or woman much of the year. Only during the Beautiful Festival of the Valley. Oh, a few women came to bend a knee at the shrine of the lady Hathor, and the cemetery guards made random visits. The robbers must've felt they had the place to themselves."

Bak well remembered how empty and desolate the valley had been when, as a small boy, he had accompanied his father's housekeeper to the shrine of the lady Hathor. "What did you find inside the tomb?"

"As was apparent the moment we laid eyes on the open shaft, robbers had been there ahead of us. Not once, but several times. Much of the devastation we found in the burial chamber had occurred many years before, many generations ago, but a small niche looked as if it had been opened recently. What had been removed, we had no way of knowing."

Bak was willing to bet his iron dagger that the jewelry he had found in far-off Buhen had come from that niche. If so, the malign spirit and his gang had already entered Neferu's tomb and rifled it. It could not possibly be the one they were searching for—or had found but had been unable to clear.

"The tomb was quite lovely," Pashed went on. "Senenmut ordered it temporarily closed, to be reopened later. He's not yet decided if the terrace will be extended beyond its entrance, but he plans to make it accessible so all who come to Djeser Djeseru will be able to visit the sepulcher of our sovereign's worthy ancestor."

An admirable goal, Bak thought, especially since Maatkare Hatshepsut's forebears had no blood tie to Nebhepetre Montuhotep, and probably not to his spouse either. "I must leave you, Pashed, but I wish to be told the instant Senenmut appears."

"Should I need you, where will you be?"

With a grim smile, Bak pointed toward the ruined temple of Nebhepetre Montuhotep, where Hori, Kasaya, and Kaemwaset stood with the white dog among the broken columns on the northern terrace. "We'll be there, searching for the tomb of a royal spouse or child."

The architect flung him a startled look. "If Menna's the malign spirit, if the tomb he's been seeking is there, he'll not sit back and let you find it ahead of him."

"So I hope."

"How much time do we have before Senenmut arrives?" Kasaya asked.

Bak knelt among the broken columns and scratched the dog's head. The sturdily built animal, which stood higher than his knee, had slick white hair and a bushy tail that curled over its back. Its head was thick and flat, its brown eyes alert and intelligent. It wore a red leather collar studded with bronze squares. "I hope he'll take a pleasant noonday meal in the royal house before crossing the river. That'd give us about two hours free of worry."

Hori wrinkled his nose in disgust. "Why would he not listen to Amonked and Maiherperi? Why walk into the arms of a slayer?"

Bak gave the dog, trained as a tracker of men, a final pat and stood up; his eyes slid toward Kaemwaset. "It's time we began."

The priest untied the ends of a cloth bag he had hung on

his belt and withdrew the roll of papyrus on which Hori had redrawn the plan. He handed it to Bak, who climbed over the broken wall into the main court. His companions followed. Locating a column standing to waist height, facing the cliff behind the temple, he unrolled the scroll across the broken but relatively flat upper surface.

He and Kasaya glanced at each other, their thoughts alike, and both examined the vertical cliff face that loomed high above the temple. Here the tower-like projections were not as numerous or as tall, not as well-defined, as those behind Djeser Djeseru, and they would not shelter the temple as well. A significant break in this natural shield could be seen, and it occupied the worst possible location. It rose directly above what looked like a fairly recent slide that had partly crushed a portion of the columned hall near the sanctuary.

Menna had not been seen for some time, and the fishermen had vanished about thirty hours ago. Was one man or more somewhere high upon the cliff face even now? The most likely target for attack was the new temple and not the old, but . . .

Shoving the thought firmly aside, Bak signaled his companions to gather around his makeshift table. While they looked at the plan, the dog lay in a nearby patch of shade, licking a paw. A warm breeze ruffled their hair and dried the sweat the sun stole from their bodies. The odor of fish drifted to them from the workmen's huts, as did an acrid smell from the metalsmiths' furnace. A familiar, comfortable scene that made a lie of Bak's fears.

"We've no way of knowing for certain," he said, "but let's assume the temple in this plan was torn down and its foundations buried beneath the one in which we're standing."

Kasaya glanced around, skeptical. Hori eyed the ruin with distaste, reluctant to search again for something he had looked for twice without success. Kaemwaset nodded, his faith in Bak bolstered by prayer.

Bak turned his back to the cliff and studied the main court. Around the ruined block of rubble and stone in the center, a few paving stones had been removed and others were broken, but no gap was deep enough to reveal what lay beneath. If the need to know became imperative, they could dig a vertical shaft in the hope of finding the old temple, but such a laborious effort must be a last resort.

Turning slowly, he looked at the broken stone blocks and slabs among which he stood. Pairi and Humay had been somewhere here or in the colonnade court just beyond when he and his men had disturbed them. Had they been working their way around the temple and reached this point after many nights of fruitless searching? Or had they concluded the tomb they sought lay in this court or the next?

The dog growled, alerting them to a new arrival, the young scribe Ani.

"Lieutenant Bak!" Ani stepped over a chunk of rock and came to a halt before the makeshift table. "Senenmut is coming, sir. He's about halfway up the causeway."

"Already?" Bak moaned.

"Can we go see him, sir?" Kasaya asked.

"We've a task to do," Bak snapped, then relented. "All right. We can see him well enough from the terrace."

"Sir!" Hori looked pained. "The terrace is too low. We won't be able to see anything. Can't we go over to Djeser Djeseru?"

"We can't take the time." Bak's eyes darted toward the priest. "Should you be there to greet him, Kaemwaset?"

"I see no need. This is a simple inspection, with no part of the temple to be dedicated." Kaemwaset's eyes twinkled. "I'll stay here with you. Searching for a hidden tomb will be much more intriguing than walking around a construction site I've seen many, many times before."

Bak stood with his three companions on the edge of the terrace that faced Djeser Djeseru. Behind them lay the ruined colonnade they had walked through four nights earlier, carrying oil lamps and trying to look mysterious in the hope of proving to the workmen that the malign spirit was a flesh and blood man. The old temple was lower than the new and the view far from ideal, but it was good enough to satisfy Bak, who had no desire to attract Senenmut's attention.

He studied the cliffs towering over the two temples. The lord Re, high overhead, reached into the crevices and cracks that broke the face of the cliff, making them blend together as a single rough-hewn mass. He saw no sign of life on the rim above, and if anyone had climbed partway down the cliff face, he was safely concealed among rocks, impossible to distinguish in the deceptive light.

Uneasy, preferring to face an enemy he could see, he focused on the procession walking at a good fast pace up the distant causeway toward Djeser Djeseru. Sunlight glinted on bronze spear points. Leather armor glistened, polished to a high sheen. Ostrich feather fans waved back and forth, stirring the air above lofty officials. Though he heard, faint and far away, the hunting cry of the falcon streaking down from the deep blue sky, neither the words spoken by Senenmut's party nor the sound of marching feet carried across the sand.

Maiherperi had kept his vow and more, sending with Senenmut two companies of guards, one hundred men who carried the white shields of the royal house. One contingent marched at the head of the inspection party. Solely responsible for Senenmut's safety, they could not leave his presence. A second unit marched behind, men handpicked by Maiherperi and given red armbands to distinguish them from Senenmut's personal guards. These men Bak could call upon when needed. Whether the royal guards were setting the speed of forward movement or whether the Overseer of Overseers had deemed it wise to come and go as quickly as possible, Bak could not begin to guess.

The inspection party was larger than he had expected. At least fifteen men rode on carrying chairs held high above the ground on the shoulders of porters. Senenmut had to be the man in front, and Bak thought he recognized Amonked by his side. Their faces and those of the men behind them were hidden in the shadow of white awnings that sheltered them from the sun. The latter were lesser noblemen, he suspected, men who hoped to gain advantage by breathing the same air as that of their sovereign's favorite. Heralds, fan bearers, and scribes kept pace behind them.

Bak took a small, highly polished mirror from a square of cloth tied to his belt, caught the sun on its surface, and angled it toward the rear column of guards. Within moments a mirror flashed a response from the lieutenant in charge of the men wearing the armbands. Should one need the other, they each knew where to find him.

After taking another long, careful look at the cliff above the new temple, Bak turned away. He could find nothing out of order, but he was far from satisfied. Somewhere up there, he feared, a man lay hidden, waiting.

He walked to the fallen segment of wall where he had been surprised by Pairi. Warning the others to keep a wary eye on Djeser Djeseru and the cliff above, he scrambled over the broken stones and crossed the littered pavement of the main court to the opening in the rear wall, trying to re-create in his thoughts exactly what had happened that night.

Pairi had led him into the colonnade court, where he had been struck from behind. Another man, Humay no doubt, had been the one to fell him. Earlier, well before he had been struck down, Pairi had shouted, "Let's go, my brother," or something similar. He didn't recall seeing Humay, but had sensed someone's presence. Or had the frenzied shadows cast by the wildly flaring torch sent his imagination soaring?

He backed up to stand beside the column where the plan lay, both ends curled to meet in the center. He closed his eyes and tried to bring back that night. The man—Pairi—appearing out of nowhere. He, Bak, leaping over the fallen section of wall and racing after him, torch in hand. Sparks flying, erratic shadows flitting over and around the fallen columns, Pairi's fleeing footsteps.

Suddenly he remembered: While passing the block structure in the center of the court, he had glimpsed a man off to the right.

He eyed the right rear—northwest—corner of the main court. Both back and side walls rose higher than his head. A slope of dirt and debris fallen from the cliff over many years pressed against them from the outside and had spilled over into the main court. The two rows of eight-sided columns that had once supported the roof behind the central, ruined block were sadly damaged. A few stood to various heights, but most lay broken on the pavement among remnants of architraves and roof slabs. Again he asked himself: Had Pairi and Humay reached this point after many nights of searching? Or had they found a rich tomb?

Seeking some sign of fresh disturbance, he walked along the spill, turned the corner, walked a dozen or so paces farther. The pavement beneath his feet was covered with sand and littered with chunks of stone of all sizes and shapes.

Voices drew him on to the fallen segment of wall. Kasaya, Hori, and Kaemwaset stood where he had left them, looking toward Djeser Djeseru. Senenmut and Amonked, easier to see than before, were walking slowly along the fill above the southern retaining wall, watching the men below slide a stone in place. Kaemwaset was pointing out various men in Senenmut's party whom he recognized.

Bak turned away to retrace his steps. Rounding the corner and walking a few paces along the rear wall, thinking of the plan Hori had so painstakingly redrawn, he knelt to dig away the debris at the base of the spill. It was not as hard-packed as he had expected, betraying the fact that it had been recently deposited.

His expectations were small, a faint hope at best, but the lord Amon chose to smile upon him. The edge of his hand struck a hard projection. He quickly dug away more debris, revealing a slab of carved stone set into the pavement. Barely daring to breathe, he moved a few chunks of broken rock and dug away more of the spill, revealing several carved slabs between the one he had initially found and the corner of the court. They formed two rectangular shapes. Shrines,

he guessed, from their location at the rear of the court. Dedicated to the gods important to Nebhepetre Montuhotep. The
base of a fallen column caught his eye. It stood almost directly in front of the entrance to the shrine farthest from the
corner.

The shrines had been built during an earlier stage of construction!

Forgetting Menna, forgetting the likelihood of a rock
slide, he ran to get the plan and returned to the corner. Unrolling the scroll, he compared the six small structures that
lined the rear edge of the platform with what he could actually see. They might well be the shrines he had found—if the
original temple lay beneath the northern side of the present
building instead of being centered beneath it as he had assumed. If so, he had found the two northernmost shrines. He
saw no sign of the other four, but he had every confidence
that a diligent search would reveal them.

He wanted to shout for joy, but had he found anything to
shout about? The shrines of gods contained no wealth except
for the god himself and his accoutrements. Once removed,
as these had been many generations before, nothing remained to steal. That did not mean the tomb Menna—or
Montu—and the fishermen had been searching for was not
close by. But where?

Returning to the terrace, he saw that Senenmut and his
followers were walking among the rough-finished statues
and architectural elements on the opposite terrace, stopping
before first one image and then another. The porters had settled down with the carrying chairs near the old mudbrick
temple of Djeserkare Amonhotep and Ahmose Nefertari.
They, at least, would be safe should a rock slide occur.
Senenmut's guards stood at full alert around him and his
party, while the other guards had spread throughout the construction site, searching for trouble.

He saw no one on the rim of the cliff, nor any movement
on its vertical face. The lord Re had begun his descent to the

western horizon, and shadows filled the deepest crevices. The tower-like formations appeared to be separating themselves from the parent rock. Within the hour each individual formation would stand out in full relief against the cliff face.

"It's time we showed Tracker here . . ." He nodded toward the dog. ". . . the tunic we took from the fishermen's house."

"You've found something?" Hori asked, his eyes lighting up, betraying the fact that he was tiring of the activity at Djeser Djeseru.

While Bak quickly explained what he had discovered, Kaemwaset retrieved a torn and dirty linen tunic that smelled of fish and sweat from the top of a tall column where he had left it earlier. The priest had proved to be the most proficient of the four when the patrol officer who had loaned them the dog had instructed them on how best to use him.

Openly pleased at playing so important a role, Kaemwaset gave Tracker a good long sniff of the garment. Bak, Hori, and Kasaya stayed well clear. The officer had warned that the fewer men to touch the cloth, the less confused the dog would be by conflicting smells.

Tracker put his nose to the pavement. He immediately headed off in the wrong direction, trotting back and forth among the fallen columns as if confused by too many paths. Not surprising since the fishermen had frequently carried lights along the terrace, pretending for the workmen's benefit to be the malign spirit.

"Take the dog into the main court," Bak told Kaemwaset.

The priest grabbed Tracker's collar and scrambled with him over the wall. Hori followed.

Bak stopped the Medjay before he could cross after them. "You must stay on the terrace, Kasaya."

"But, sir!" the young man said, crushed.

"Someone must keep a close watch on the cliff above Djeser Djeseru—especially when Senenmut climbs up to the temple—and you've the keenest eye of any of us. Should you see movement of any kind, any sign of trouble, call me."

He handed over the small mirror. "At the same time, signal the officer in charge of the guards Maiherperi assigned to help us. The quicker you pass on the news, the more men he can get out of the way should a rock slide occur."

"Can I not go with you and still keep watch?"

"I fear you'd become too distracted." Bak laid a hand on the young man's shoulder. "Senenmut's life and the safety of many others, men we've come to know and like, may well depend upon your quick reaction."

Clearly not placated, Kasaya mumbled, "Yes, sir."

Certain the Medjay would do what he must, like it or not, Bak clambered over the break in the wall. Kaemwaset released the dog. Tracker was less confused in the main court, as if the fishermen had trod the same path time and time again. Following a trail no man could see, he trotted toward the rear of the building. Bak and his companions hurried after him. At the opening into the colonnade court, the dog ranged back and forth again, as if he had either lost the scent or had too many choices. Staying well back, they watched him explore with his nose each trail of invisible footprints in turn. He followed one path to the robber's shaft, another along the northern colonnade and into the ruined columned hall at the back of the temple.

Hori groaned. "Not in there, I pray."

"The heart of the temple is slowly collapsing," Bak explained to Kaemwaset, "not at all safe." He eyed the darkness into which Tracker had vanished. "We saw no sign of intrusion among the columns, no footprints in the dust. Why do you suppose he went in there?"

The dog loped out from among the columns and sniffed his way directly to Bak. Tail wagging, he looked to Kaemwaset as if expecting a reward for a task well done. Bak, grinning in spite of himself, suggested the priest move closer to the break in the wall, where the dog had seemed the most confused, and give him another good, long sniff of the tunic.

The response was immediate. Tracker followed the scent

to the corner where Bak had found the shrines, making him fear the dog was once again tracking the wrong man. He sniffed the paving stones in the area, retraced his steps, and went into the colonnade court. His nose drew him to the corner that lay behind the shrines. There he sniffed the floor and the intersecting wall, then stood up on his hind legs, stretching himself as high as he could. He looked at the men behind him, pawed the wall, barked. His meaning was clear: he wanted to cross the wall.

Bak's hopes shot upward. He had assumed the rocks and debris outside filled the corner where the walls intersected. Maybe not. "Let's go around," he said, sounding much calmer than he felt.

As they hurried to the main court, Tracker dropped onto all fours and paced back and forth in front of the wall, whimpering, not wanting to leave. Though torn, Hori turned back to stay with him.

Bak and Kaemwaset exited the main court, ran past a startled Kasaya, and hurried westward along the terrace, which disappeared beneath the high mound of dirt and rocks that had piled up against the thick sturdy walls of the temple.

The climb upward was fast and easy, the debris packed solid by time and weather. At the top and around the corner where no one could see from the front of the building, they found the surface to be soft and loose, newly placed. It had clearly not fallen from above. A few paces farther, they discovered where it had come from. In the corner, where the colonnade court joined the main court, they found a large excavation dug down to the paving stones of what had originally been an open platform facing the cliff.

"Hori!" Bak called. "Somebody's been digging here. Bring the dog."

"He's on his way, sir. He heard you out there."

Tracker raced around the corner and sped across the mound, flinging dirt in his wake. He half ran, half slid down into the excavation. Following his nose, he sniffed every square cubit of pavement, his tail wagging hard and fast.

From where he stood atop the mound, Bak spotted beneath the dog's feet a telltale sinking of the paving slabs. Underneath, he felt sure, lay a tomb.

If the shrine on the opposite side of the wall had been built for the deceased, six shrines most likely meant six tombs of six royal ladies.

"Lieutenant Bak!" Kasaya yelled. "I see a man on the hillside north of Djeser Djeseru, coming down the trail. I think it's Lieutenant Menna."

Bak ran to the corner of the building and looked out across the workmen's huts and Maatkare Hatshepsut's new temple. The man was a long way off, but the light was striking him at an advantageous angle. He looked like Menna, walked like him.

Why would he approach the valley by such an indirect route? he wondered. Had he had time to go all the way to the top of the cliff or had he met the fishermen somewhere along the way? Were they even now preparing a foul deed? Was he simply being cautious, approaching the valley by way of a high path that offered a good view of the temples?

Or was Menna merely coming from an old cemetery located farther to the north? An innocent man going about his business.

Kaemwaset came up beside him and shaded his eyes with his hand. "If we can see him, he can see us. If he's the malign spirit, he can't help but know we've found his excavation."

"Our timing couldn't have been better," Bak said, grimly satisfied.

"He must not have guessed you suspect him."

"Senenmut is climbing the ramp to our sovereign's temple," Kasaya called from the base of the mound.

Hori came running out of the main court.

"I must go meet Menna." Bak whistled to call Tracker, who came racing out of the hole. "You, Kasaya, must remain here and keep an eye on the cliff and Senenmut's party." To the priest, he said, "I'll send men to help you and Hori keep the tomb safe. In the meantime, all of you must go to the front of the temple where you'll be out of harm's way in case of a rock slide. I'll . . ."

A low growl grabbed his attention. Tracker, standing beside Kaemwaset, was poised as if for flight, head raised, ears cocked. The hair rose on the back of his neck and he began to bark, loud and frantic. Bak heard a faint rumble from above that rapidly increased to a roar.

"The cliff!" he shouted. "Run! Now!"

Chapter Eighteen

Tracker bolted. Kaemwaset, by no means old but not young either and certainly not a man of action, hesitated. Bak slipped his arm around the priest's lower back and half carried him down the mound. Hori was racing eastward along the terrace. The dog dashed past him, not stopping until he reached the front of the temple and certain safety. Kasaya, standing as if glued to the pavement, ignored an initial sprinkling of small rocks and dirt and held the mirror high, signaling.

Bak shoved Kaemwaset after Hori and glanced upward. The cliff high above the temple looked as if it had blown apart. A thick, yellow dust billowed out from the boulders, stones, pebbles, and dirt racing down the vertical surface. The roar was deafening.

"Kasaya!" Realizing the Medjay could not hear him, he grabbed an arm and pulled. "Come!" he shouted, leaning close. "You'll be buried alive!"

Running sideways, signaling, the Medjay stared at the top of the cliff above Djeser Djeseru and shouted something. The words were drowned by noise, but the excitement on his face directed Bak's gaze toward the top of the cliff.

A flash of light gleamed from the cliff-top trail. The response from the sergeant in charge of ten royal guards who had hidden above the new temple earlier in the day. Bak saw no other sign of life. Were Pairi and Humay hidden somewhere up there, preparing to send rocks down on Djeser Djeseru as they had on the older temple? Or had the guards snared them before they could do more damage?

A heavier shower of rocks and dirt began to fall around and on them, pelting their heads and shoulders. One razor-sharp stone sliced down Bak's back, drawing blood. He grabbed the mirror from Kasaya, taking away his purpose, and forced him to flee. They ran for their very lives along the edge of the terrace, where fewer broken stones lay to impede their escape. Their feet pounded unheard across the pavement, lost in the thunder of the rocks tumbling down the face of the cliff, buffeting the tower-like projections and the slope below, hurtling down upon the ruined temple and rolling among the fallen columns, architraves, and roof slabs through which Bak and his friends had so recently walked.

A boulder big enough to crush a man burst out of the dust cloud and rolled along the edge of the terrace, chasing them. Stones of all sizes came with it, and sand and dirt. The cloud billowed up behind, consuming everything in its path. Bak muttered a quick prayer to the lord Amon and put on an additional burst of speed.

The boulder tumbled over the edge of the terrace and dropped into the sand below. Dust erupted around it, merging with the larger cloud. The leading edge of the slide caught them and stones of all sizes came bouncing, hurtling, rolling around their legs and beneath their feet, threatening to topple them. The dust swallowed them, making their eyes burn, making them cough. Kasaya stumbled, fell. Bak grabbed an arm and tugged. The Medjay scrambled to his hands and knees, his feet, and they ran on. A stone struck Bak hard on the back, slamming him forward, knocking the breath from him. He sucked in the filthy air and ran on.

Suddenly the fall was behind them, the rocks losing their momentum. They slowed to a trot, looked at each other, exchanged relieved smiles. They were safe.

They walked on, legs wobbly, dust coating sweaty bodies, neither man speaking. Each thanking the gods that his life had been spared. By the time they reached Hori, Kaemwaset, and the dog, the worst of the slide was over. A few rocks and boulders dropped from above, bouncing down the vertical face and raising spurts of dust, but the deafening roar had diminished to a sporadic crack of smashing rocks, and the cloud was thinning over the temple, shredded by the light breeze.

From where they stood, they could not see the columned hall and colonnade court, but they could well imagine how the rear chambers had suffered. The northwest corner of the main court, where they had been standing when the slide began, was covered by dirt and rocks. The wall where Bak had found the shrines was buried. The robbers' excavation had without a doubt been filled in.

An explosive crack sounded from somewhere deep within the temple. Stone grated against stone, a deep and heavy thud set loose rocks to rolling down the slope behind the building, a burst of dust rose above the columned hall. Tracker whimpered. The four men looked at each other, their faces bleak. Another portion of the hall, or possibly the sanctuary, had fallen: a column or two, a few roof slabs.

Bak's eyes darted toward the small figure standing on the hillside trail north of Djeser Djeseru. "Menna hasn't moved from where he stood before the cliff fell. Would not an innocent man have hastened to our aid?" He gave him companions a grim smile. "I'm going after him. I see no further need for you to remain here. No man will rifle the tombs within this temple for a long time."

Bak hurried ahead with Kasaya and Tracker, loping down the ramp the workmen used to haul stones scavenged from the old temple to the new, climbing the opposing ramp onto the terrace of Djeser Djeseru.

Amonked, walking faster than Bak had ever seen him, intercepted them near the white limestone statue of Maatkare Hatshepsut. "May the lord Amon be deluged with offerings! You're safe and well." He clasped Bak's shoulders. "When I saw the cliff face fall . . ." He bit his lip, trying to contain his depth of feeling, and turned to the Medjay. "As for you, young man, standing as you did on the terrace, signaling with that mirror while stones fell around you . . ." He patted Kasaya on the back, shook his head in amazement, patted again. "Words fail me."

Bak was more pleased than he cared to admit with Amonked's unusual show of affection. "Do you know what's happening on the rim of the cliff, sir? Have the men up there caught anyone?"

"I know no more than you do." Amonked cleared his throat, collecting himself. "We were climbing the ramp to Maatkare Hatshepsut's temple when the cliff began to fall. Someone—the lieutenant at the head of the special team of guards Maiherperi sent—shouted a warning." Amonked's smile held only a hint of humor. "You've never seen men run so fast, as if the rocks were falling on us instead of you."

Bak imagined the scene and returned the smile. "When will Senenmut be leaving Djeser Djeseru?"

"I told him you'd placed men on the cliff above, so he wishes to stay, to see the men snared who set off the rock slide. If the truth be told, I suspect he fears returning to the royal house with a threat still hanging over our sovereign's most important project."

"No doubt," Bak said in a wry voice.

Noting the cynicism, another smile touched Amonked's lips. "Did you find the tomb you sought? Or did the slide cut short your search?"

Bak beckoned a water boy, washed the grit from his mouth and spat it out. "We found a tomb, sir, but I've no time to speak of it. We've spotted Lieutenant Menna on the trail north of here. He's come no closer since first we saw him, which makes him look to me like a guilty man. I'm going after him before he has a chance to flee." Refilling the bowl, he drank long and deep, readying himself for the chase.

Amonked eyed the figure on the distant trail and his face

clouded over with concern. "Yes, you must go."

"Kaemwaset can tell you of the tomb." Bak flashed a smile at the approaching priest and turned to the Medjay. "You must remain here, Kasaya. Go to the lieutenant in charge of the men wearing the red armbands and . . ." He raised a hand, silencing the objection he saw on the young man's face. "See that they follow me as quickly as they can, and you come with them. The trail must be blocked so Menna can't turn back this way, and I might need help to snare him."

Bak hastened across the terrace, stopping once when he came upon a foreman carrying a wooden staff about twice the length of his arm. He borrowed the object as a makeshift weapon, a substitute for his baton of office, which was more to his liking than the dagger hanging from his belt. The staff was somewhat thicker than his baton, a little heavier, not as well balanced, and probably not as strong. He offered no complaint. It would suffice.

Leaving the terrace behind, he looked upward to where he had last seen Menna. The officer had not moved. He stood at the far end of a long stretch of trail that traversed the slope below the cliff. From there the path ran almost straight up the incline before turning to the left to climb the cliff, which was much lower and not nearly as steep as at the back of the valley where the temples stood. It was in fact a rough and broken escarpment which gradually tailed off to the east. At the top, the trail followed the rim in a westerly direction to the cliff's highest point behind the two temples and continued on from there.

Why had Menna not moved? Was he waiting for the cliff to collapse above Djeser Djeseru? Was he trying to figure out whether he could safely come into the valley or whether he should retreat? What would Menna do when he saw him climbing the path to meet him?

Bak knew what *he* would do: he would turn around and run as fast as he could back up the trail. Of course, Menna could leave the path where he stood and plunge down the slope to the valley floor, but if he did so, Bak could summon the men toiling in the quarry, who would tear him limb from limb if they learned he was the malign spirit. No, if run he decided to do, he had no choice but to go back the way he had come.

Bak had no option but to follow. The trail split above Djeser Djeseru into two paths. Both ultimately joined another, more frequently used track at two widespread locations, one some distance to the southwest, the other crossing a high ridge to travel in a northwesterly direction. At the north end of the oft-traveled track lay the Great Place, the valley where Maatkare Hatshepsut's father was laid to rest and she was even now having her own tomb dug. At the southern end lay the village where the tomb diggers dwelt. He had no time to go all the way around to either location. Nor could he send royal guards to both. By the time he or they reached their destination, Menna would have arrived and gone.

Trying to look casual, unhurried, he crossed a strip of sand to the foot of the trail and immediately began to climb. Menna made no move to meet him halfway. A clear sign of guilt. As the last of his doubts fled, Bak smiled grimly at himself, at his failure to trust his instincts. After the initial short and fairly steep ascent, the path turned in an easterly direction away from Djeser Djeseru and traversed the hillside in a long, gradual rise to the place where Menna stood.

He strode up the trail, walking easily, as if he had no purpose or goal. Menna was wary, too cautious to descend the path to meet him, but was not yet frightened enough to run. Bak wanted to get as close as possible before the guard officer guessed his purpose and the chase heated up. If he could stand before him face-to-face, so much the better. An unlikely event, he knew.

Halfway along the traverse, he raised his hand and waved, a friendly signal that would ordinarily have brought the recipient toward him. Menna held his ground and did not return the greeting. Bak walked on, using all the patience he could muster to keep himself from breaking into a faster pace.

Again the distance between them shrunk by half. Bak opened his mouth to call out. Abruptly, Menna turned and, taking long, quick strides, began to climb the steeper slope to the escarpment. The words died on Bak's lips and he looked rearward, searching for a reason for the officer's retreat. Kasaya, Amonked, Kaemwaset, and Pashed were standing on the terrace with the lieutenant in charge of the special unit of royal guards. Men wearing red armbands were hurrying toward them from all directions and forming a column, preparing to march. Bak muttered an oath. He had never known an officer to gather his men so quickly. Menna, trained a military man, had guessed their purpose.

Wasting no time on useless anger, pleased the officer had responded so fast, Bak charged up the trail. He was sorely tempted to cut diagonally across the slope, aiming for the spot where the path began its ascent of the escarpment, but experience on the incline above Djeser Djeseru kept him on the trail. Worn reasonably smooth by the passage of many feet, it would be just as fast and far less hazardous.

He soon reached the end of the traverse, the place Menna had remained for so long. As he headed up the much steeper incline, the officer ahead paused and looked back.

"You'll never lay a hand on me!" he shouted.

"Better me than the workmen down there," Bak yelled, pointing at Djeser Djeseru.

Menna's laugh rang loud but hollow, and he swung away to climb on. He could have no illusions about his future should he be snared. If Bak or the royal guards caught him, he would stand before no less a man than the vizier, who would judge him guilty and order impalement or, more likely, burning. If the workmen at Djeser Djeseru caught him, he would be stoned or worse and his torn and broken body thrown to the crocodiles. Whether consumed by reptile or fire, his body would no longer exist and he would be doomed to permanent oblivion, with no hope of an afterlife.

Bak climbed upward at a good steady pace. The heat was intense beneath the cruel sun, quick to sap a man's energy. Sweat poured from him, making the cut on his back sting, as well as several fresh abrasions, souvenirs of the rock slide. His mouth was dry, his stomach empty.

He eyed the man ahead, only a few steps below the point where the trail turned left to rise up the escarpment. For one who claimed to have spent much of his time shuffling scrolls and writing reports, Menna was proving to be both quick and strong. Thanks, Bak assumed, to his many nights in the cemeteries, seeking out old tombs and digging for riches.

Menna turned left and vanished from sight behind a clump of boulders. Bak climbed on, never altering his pace. To wear himself out in one quick burst of energy might cost him the chase—or, maybe later, the battle, if it came to that. He rounded the boulders and looked upward.

Menna, about fifty paces away and not far from the top of the escarpment, stopped to look back. "You've told the men at Djeser Djeseru?"

"That you're the malign spirit?" Bak asked, striding on without a pause.

The guard officer laughed at the appellation, but the sound was brittle, humorless. "Yes."

"I didn't, but they'll learn soon enough."

Menna's laugh turned cynical. "Such a choice bit of news would be impossible to keep quiet."

"The life you led is gone for good, if that's what you're thinking. My presence is much like the first drop of rain in a downpour. If I fail to snare you, others will come." Never slowing his pace, thinking to close the gap between them as much as possible, Bak glanced toward Djeser Djeseru and the unit of guards quickly marching toward the base of the trail. Kasaya, with Tracker on a leash at his heels, hurried along beside the officer leading the column. He felt sure Menna could see them from where he stood. "You've reached the end, Lieutenant."

"My life in Kemet may be over, but I'm a long way from finished. I was a child of western Waset. I know the desert wadis beyond the Great Place like no other man alive."

Bak doubted Menna intended to escape into the desert. He was too much a man of the river and the city. "You were in the garrison this morning. You must've heard that soldiers began searching for Pairi's and Humay's fishing boat at break of day. I'll wager they've found it by now."

"There are other boats, Lieutenant." Menna pivoted and hurried up the trail to the rim of the escarpment, where he disappeared from view.

With a grim smile, Bak hurried after him. The guard officer had given himself away. He thought to escape by water, not lose himself in the sandy wastes.

Bak stopped briefly at the top of the escarpment to get his bearings. He had not traveled this trail since he was a youth, hunting birds and hares in the surrounding wadis, but it had changed very little over the years. The cliff to the west formed a gentle arc, gradually gaining in height all the way to the back of the valley, where it towered above the two temples. Ahead, Menna ran along a trail that eased away from the rim to hug a long and very irregular series of hills atop the ridge separating the valley in which Djeser Djeseru lay from the Great Place.

Below, the royal guards were trotting up the path that traversed the lower slope, spreading out in a line two men abreast, with one of the pair falling back each time the path narrowed. A faint barking carried upward, and Kasaya was looking Bak's way. Bak waved and pointed west, letting the Medjay know where Menna had gone and where he intended to go.

Setting off again, he eyed the landscape ahead. He saw no sign of the guards stationed on top of the cliff above Djeser Djeseru, but he assumed they were there. Menna would either run into their waiting arms or, more likely, he would spot them before he reached them and try to escape, using either the trail that would take him to the Great Place or some ill-defined and seldom used track that would take him into one of the many wadis west of Djeser Djeseru and the Great Place. A desolate, barren region in which he could easily disappear until such time as he could safely work his way back to the river.

Given time, the army would track him down, of course, but . . .

A sudden thought struck Bak. He did not want someone else to snare the malign spirit. He wanted to do it himself.

The realization added wings to his feet and he sped along the trail, his eyes on the man ahead. The short, sharp cheeps of swallows swooping downward to their nests in the cliffs sounded above the rhythmic crunch of his sandals on the trail. Spurts of dust rose each time a foot touched the path, and the dust risen from Menna's flying feet hung in the air, tickling his nose.

The trail veered closer to the rim of the cliff, dropped briefly into the upper end of a wadi that ran off to the right, and went on, sometimes wandering closer to the cliff, sometimes away toward the hill-like projections atop the ridge. Sweat rolled from his body, a stitch formed in his side. The calves of his legs ached and the wooden staff grew heavy in his hand.

The distance between him and Menna shrunk to forty paces, thirty, twenty. The guard officer heard his pounding feet, glanced over his shoulder, and managed an added burst of speed. Bak held his pace; the extra effort required to maintain the distance between them would tax him too much.

The cliff grew higher, the horrendous drop to the valley floor more fearsome. A long hill, more like a ridge, rose to the right. The trail, squeezed closer to the rim of the cliff, rose with it. Bak glimpsed Djeser Djeseru below, pale and insignificant in so large a valley, a series of sharp-edged horizontals in a landscape of sand and stone blunted by time and erosion. The imposing rock face towered above the structure, torn by the elements into towers and crevices and folds and great slabs that appeared to cling by a hair to the parent rock. Its shadows had turned a deep rosy pink, the sunstruck features a multitude of golds and yellows.

A quick glance back gave Bak a glimpse of Kasaya, Tracker and the lieutenant who had come with Senenmut running along the trail atop the cliff, followed closely by a half-dozen royal guards filing out of the trail up the escarpment.

As he neared the top of the incline, he once again began to catch up with Menna. The officer's energy had flagged, his pace had dwindled. Bak gradually closed the distance between them. Less than ten paces apart, close enough to hear Menna's labored gasps, he chased his quarry along a narrow ridge that rose between the cliff to his left and a wadi that opened off to the right. Just beyond, the branch trail angled off toward the Great Place. He saw no waiting guards.

Menna veered onto the path to the right. Bak bounded toward him, covering the gap between them in a half-dozen paces. Flinging the makeshift baton aside, he tackled the officer around the thighs and pulled him down. They rolled in the dirt, with one on top and then the other. Bak tried to get a better hold, failed. His arms were slick with sweat and so were the guard officer's legs. Menna tried to kick free, to strike his opponent in the stomach or high between the legs, but Bak held on tight, restricting movement below the waist.

They rolled off the trail, dislodging a small pile of rocks someone had left alongside for some unknown purpose. The heavy counterpoise at the back of Menna's broad collar snagged on one of the stones. The collar broke and fell away. The officer twisted, grabbed a rock, struck Bak across the side of the head. A glancing blow that made his head ring but failed to knock him senseless. A warning blow, he took it. He let go of his opponent's legs, rolled away, and scrambled to his feet.

Menna stood up more slowly, rock in hand, a calculating

look on his face. Bak backed farther away, as respectful of
the rock as he would have been of a spear. He glanced
around, trying to find the baton he had so thoughtlessly flung
aside. He spotted it six or seven paces from where he stood,
too far. Taking advantage of Bak's distraction, Menna
jumped toward him, rock raised high, poised to smash his
head. Bak leaped aside, spun around and made a fist, and hit
the officer as hard as he could in the lower back. Menna's
spine arched and he groaned, but he stayed on his feet. Retreating a few paces, he dropped the rock and tore his dagger
from its sheath. Legs spread wide, eyes glinting danger-
ously, he practically dared Bak to come and get him.

Bak slipped his own dagger free. They faced each other
about four paces apart, breathing hard, sweat pouring down
their grimy faces and bodies. Bak could tell his opponent
was as tired as he was, but Menna was desperate.

Hearing the sound of running feet, Bak's eyes flitted back
along the trail. The lieutenant and Kasaya, with the leashed
dog running alongside, led a long, straggly line of guards up
the path two hundred or so paces away.

Menna glanced toward the rapidly approaching men, then
leaped at his opponent and struck out with the dagger. Bak
ducked, felt the blade graze his arm and the warmth of blood
oozing out. Menna stepped closer, pressing his advantage,
backing his opponent toward the rim of the cliff. Bak eased
himself sideways, hoping to change the direction of their
struggle and work his way to the baton. He disliked fighting
with the dagger, the closeness of it, the treacherous blade
that could bleed a man to exhaustion or lay waste to an inner
organ. And he feared mightily a fall over the edge of the
cliff.

The guard officer bared his teeth in a mean grin and
moved in for what he clearly expected to be a kill.

Bak leaped at his opponent, striking the hand in which
Menna held his dagger, knocking it out of the way, and
smashed his left fist hard against the officer's chin. Stum-
bling back, shaking his head to clear it, Menna lowered his

shoulders and charged like an angered bull. Bak jumped aside and retreated. His eyes darted toward the baton, no more than a couple paces away. The rim of the cliff equally close. Menna stepped forward and sidled around, trying to get between him and the weapon. Trying to force him over the edge.

Bak threw his dagger. The blade flashed through the air and buried itself deep in Menna's right shoulder.

The officer stopped, raised his free hand to the weapon, felt the moisture leaking out around the haft. He looked down, stared with disbelieving eyes at the dagger, the blood seeping between his fingers, and finally at Bak. His weapon fell from his hand. He dropped to his knees, drew in air, coughed. A trace of red trickled from the corner of his mouth.

Bak walked to him. Kasaya, Tracker, and the lieutenant came running up. A sergeant and a few men were close behind, followed by those strung out along the trail. Menna stared at the men collecting around him. Bak later imagined him looking not at them but at the fate that awaited the malign spirit.

Menna struggled to his feet. Without warning, taking them all by surprise, he pushed Bak roughly aside and lurched toward the rim of the cliff. Before anyone realized his intent, he pitched himself over the edge.

Stunned by the act, Bak hurried to the rim and looked down the face of the cliff. Menna lay about two-thirds of the way down on the steep slope of a tower-like formation that rose above the rear corner of the temple. His body lay twisted and torn, his arms and legs flung wide.

Kasaya and the lieutenant came up beside him and they, too, looked down. The officer's stunned expression changed to one close to relief. "No man could have fallen so far and lived."

Bak nodded. "He knew he was trapped, a man already dead."

A sound of cheering carried on the breeze, softened by distance. Cheering?

"Look at the men, sir." Kasaya pointed downward.

What looked like every man who toiled at Djeser Djeseru stood on the terrace among the statues and column parts, cheering the demise of the man who had, over the past few years, brought into their lives so much injury and death.

Chapter Nineteen

"I don't understand how they could get away with it for so long." Ptahhotep, standing near the paddock wall, shook his head in amazement. "Are the cemetery guards so blind?"

"Menna was their officer," Bak said, looking over the neck of Defender, whose long mane he was combing. "As far as I could tell, they didn't once suspect him. As one of them said: How could they think him guilty of the very crime he was supposed to prevent?"

"They could've at least kept their eyes open." Amonked, standing beside Bak's father, scowled his disapproval. "Their failure to uphold the laws of the land, to satisfy the demands of the lady Maat, is unforgivable."

His porters and carrying chair sat in the dwindling evening light beneath the sycamore tree, awaiting their master's departure. Even with darkness fast approaching, he seemed in no hurry to go on his way.

Bak thought of the men he had talked with before leaving Djeser Djeseru, hunkered around him in the shadow of their hut, crushed by their failure to do their duty and afraid of the consequences. "They must be punished, to be sure, but I'd not be too hard on them, sir. Other than Pashed, who had no time to oversee them properly, they had no one to look to for guidance."

"I suppose far more sepulchers are robbed than we'll ever know—many with the help of a guard or two," Ptahhotep said thoughtfully. "Just think of the temptation. Walking day after day among the tombs, imagining the wealth lying beneath their feet."

Bak caught a handful of mane and began to comb out a knot. Defender whinnied, though his master was sure he was not hurting him. "Not even priests are exempt from temptation. Kaemwaset told me a tale so appalling it would curl our sovereign's ceremonial beard."

Ptahhotep shifted his stance, the better to watch Kasaya spread a thin poultice on Victory's singed rear legs. "Did Pairi and Humay reveal all before . . . ?" He let his voice tail off and looked expectantly at his son and Amonked, who had not yet told him exactly what had happened.

"Before they swallowed the poison?" Bak shook his head. "No, but they said enough to verify what we'd guessed."

"I'd not take my own life like that," Kasaya said, looking up from his task. "I'd try to escape and take an arrow in the back rather than give myself a deadly potion."

Hori, seated on the wall, measured a length of linen against his arm. Using a sharp knife, he cut it off and handed it to the Medjay. "How could they escape?" he asked scornfully. "They were surrounded by royal guards."

Kasaya glared at his friend. "If Menna knew those desert trails, the fishermen did, too. Remember, they played together as children, hunted together as youths."

"*You* remember!" Hori demanded. "Those guards bound their arms with wooden manacles and their ankles with strong leather thongs. Then, instead of staying where they should've on the trail above Djeser Djeseru, they hustled them off to the workmen's village and held them within its walls."

"They snared the two atop the cliff before they could do more damage," Kasaya said, defending the guards more for the sake of argument than because he cared, Bak felt sure. "How were they to know the worst of the lot was running toward them?"

Bak wondered how he would be able to tolerate the pair's

squabbling for another month or so, until Commandant Thuty and the others arrived from Buhen and they would all travel on together to Mennufer. He had not been gone long, but he missed them already: Nebwa, Imsiba, Nofery, his Medjays—everyone. "I know you must return to the city," he said to Amonked, "but before you go, will you share a jar of wine to celebrate the end of the malign spirit?"

As the three men walked to the house, Ptahhotep asked, "What brought the workmen onto the terrace? Did someone tell them you were chasing the malign spirit along the rim of the cliff?"

"Pashed." Bak had to smile. "Like me, as soon as he saw Menna run, he was certain of his guilt. I'd warned him not to reveal the wretched creature's identity, but he couldn't help himself. I can't say I blame him. Would I have been able to hold my silence if I'd stood in his sandals, having watched my work crews suffer injury and death, having seen the most important task of my life being destroyed by a man bent on malicious destruction?"

"Now tell me what you believe they've been doing. And get on with it!" Ptahhotep's smile made a lie of his pretended impatience. "Do you wish Amonked's wife to send servants out in the dead of night, fearing him attacked by ruffians?"

Amonked, seated beside the physician on a low stool beneath the portico, appeared unworried by the possibility. "Menna was a cousin to Pairi and Humay. The fishermen have been robbing tombs since they were children—or so the mayor of western Waset believes—and Menna probably went with them as often as he could." He took a sip of the deep red wine, which smelled of fresh grapes, and smacked his lips in approval. "An uncle who dwelt in one of the local villages used them to crawl through holes too small for a man."

"When the uncle died, they struck out on their own." Bak

dropped onto the earthen floor beside his father. "Thanks to his years of instruction, they knew the types of tombs most likely to contain riches and where best to locate them. They found enough treasure to satisfy them, but as their market was local, they had to break up all objects of worth and melt down the gold. Which decreased their gain considerably."

"Pieces of value would be suspect throughout the land of Kemet," Ptahhotep agreed, "especially when offered by mere fishermen."

Amonked plucked a small salted fish from a bowl beside his feet. Tracker, lying a pace or so away, opened an eye but scorned the contents so temptingly set before him. "They could easily have made an honest living on the river, but chose also to defy the lady Maat. Why they pursued so dangerous a path is beyond me."

Bak, caught with his mouth full, swallowed. "The same could be said of Menna, who'd been schooled to read and write and entered the army at an early age. He had every opportunity to lead an honest and honorable life, but chose instead a quest for riches."

"Perhaps thieving was in their blood," the physician said, looking thoughtful.

"One never knows of course, but Menna, at least, might've turned his back on a life of crime if the lord Set hadn't smiled upon him." Amonked took a sip of wine, added, "He served as scribe to several envoys to various city states at the eastern end of the Great Green Sea, and there he met men who coveted the baubles of the noble and royal personages of Kemet."

"Potential customers," Ptahhotep commented.

Nodding, Bak said, "About six years ago he came back to Waset. He was posted initially in the garrison, serving as one of several scribes in the commandant's office." His tone turned dry, cynical. "Again the lord Set favored him. His first assignment was to organize the older files and take them to the hall of records for storage in the archives. He immediately recognized the possibilities and ingratiated himself with the chief archivist. Within a short time he learned how to search the records and was given free rein to do so."

Ptahhotep picked up a large, cylindrical jar with a tall, thin neck and refilled their drinking bowls. "So he had available to him the same documents Kaemwaset and Hori found."

"Others as well." Amonked released a long, unhappy sigh. "We've no idea how many scrolls he destroyed."

The physician's mouth tightened. "Any man who would do such a thing . . ."

Bak laid a hand on his father's shoulder, quieting him. "Thanks to a document he found a little over four years ago, they located a royal sepulcher, the ultimate goal of every tomb robber in the land of Kemet. This was the final resting place of Nebhepetre Montuhotep's Great Royal Wife Neferu, which is in the valley where Djeser Djeseru is presently being built." He glanced at Hori and Kasaya, approaching the house through the gathering darkness, cutting short the call of a night bird. "The sepulcher had long ago been rifled, its contents stolen or destroyed, but they found a few pieces of jewelry hidden in a cleverly concealed niche. Very valuable pieces. Never before had they entered a royal tomb, and this made them hungry for more royal trinkets."

"The pieces we found in Buhen came from her tomb," Hori said, plopping down beside the dog and rubbing the top of its head vigorously with a knuckle. A low growl warned against such rough treatment and the youth snatched his hand away.

"At that time, the valley was a lonely and empty place. They had it to themselves much of the time." Amonked ate a fish, washed it down with wine. "Thinking Neferu's tomb a good omen, pointing to further riches in the area around her husband's temple, they dug and dug again. They found and rifled several tombs beneath the valley floor and in the surrounding hillsides, but none were royal. According to the men who questioned them, Humay bragged of walking into and out of the sepulchers in the light of day with no one the wiser."

"Suddenly, Senenmut descended upon the valley," Bak said, breaking into a smile. "He claimed it for Maatkare Hat-shepsut and she announced her plan to build her memorial temple there. Surveys were taken, foundation deposits laid. Huts were built and men were not only raising a temple during the day, but were dwelling there at night."

Amonked chuckled. "By that time they'd begun to use the honey jars to smuggle the jewelry more safely out of Kemet. And they'd learned to hold back pieces, thereby increasing the value by keeping the supply lower than the demand."

Eyeing the burned shed at the end of the paddock, Bak thoroughly enjoyed the thought of Menna, Pairi, and Humay standing on the rim of the cliff, looking down upon workmen swarming over the site like ants on an anthill. "Can you imagine how they felt, realizing they'd built up a demand for the stolen jewelry but lost their best source? They must've been furious."

He popped a fish into his mouth, chewed, swallowed. "To make matters worse as far as they were concerned, Menna found a document that mentioned the tombs of six Royal Ornaments, valued women of the harem, located somewhere in the temple of Nebhepetre Montuhotep. Tombs that if found intact would contain priceless items of jewelry. He and his cousins itched to seek them out, to lay hands on their contents, but they had no reason to visit the valley, no excuse to walk the pavement of the ruined temple."

"Once again a whimsical god intervened," Amonked said. "The lord Set, I'll wager."

Bak's good humor faded. "About three years ago Menna learned that the officer in charge of the cemetery guards was to be replaced. As with the chief archivist, he befriended the officer who would make the appointment. He was given the task."

"Is that when they came up with the idea of the malign

spirit?" Kasaya asked, dropping down beside Hori. His hands gave off the tangy smell of the poultice.

"Soon after, yes." Bak took a couple more fish from the bowl, ate them, and took a sip of wine to wash away the salty taste. "If they were to find those tombs, they had to keep the workmen away from the old temple. They could do nothing during the daylight hours, but during the dangerous hours of night, when vicious animals are known to prowl the land and the shades of the dead return . . . Well, what better way than to frighten them?"

"The malign spirit was a brilliant idea," Ptahhotep said. "Utterly heartless, but brilliant."

"You know the rest," Bak said. "The accidents, the injuries, the deaths. We've no way of knowing which of the three did the most damage to man and temple, but Humay admitted they all pretended to be the malign spirit and they all brought about the accidents. He verified my guess that Imen played a lesser role, more a watchman than a participant. Certainly Menna stood at the head, thinking, planning, but all were equally to blame."

"Did Menna rob the tomb the night I was supposed to be guarding it," Kasaya asked, "or could he have taken the bracelets at some other time?"

"We'll never know," Bak said with a shrug. "He was alone in the sepulcher for a short time after Kaemwaset climbed out and before the masons went down to wall off the burial chamber. He could've taken them then, with no one the wiser."

"What of Montu?" Hori asked, waving one of the small fish before Tracker's indifferent nose.

"Humay threw the broken jar into the trash dump at Djeser Djeseru, thinking it would vanish forever. I assume Montu found it among the shards Ani gathered for him. He probably recognized the sketch of the bee—the fishermen's farm was not far from his wife's estate—and thought to catch them pretending to be the malign spirit. Instead, Menna caught him lurking about and slew him."

Ptahhotep flung a bitter look toward the burned structure at the end of the paddock. "Was Menna the man who fired the shed with you and the horses inside?"

"I can't speak with certainty about the fire, but I know for a fact that he was the one who set off the rock slide above the northern retaining wall." Bak untied the knot holding a square of linen to his belt, spread the corners wide, and held it out so all could see. Glittering in the failing light were dozens of beads and amulets, their colors hard to guess with no sun to give them life. With a finger, he separated two from the rest, both tiny malachite images of the Lates fish. "His broad collar broke while we fought. I picked these up after his death."

"Was he on board the fishing boat when his cousins ran down my skiff? When they tried to slay us?"

"He wasn't. It was Pairi's idea, but he and Humay bungled it." Bak recalled that night and scowled. "I suspect I was the target, not you. You were just unfortunate enough to be in the skiff with me."

A long silence ensued, broken by Ptahhotep. "What of the valuables they unearthed through the years? Were any pieces found?"

Bak reknotted the cloth to preserve the contents and laid it aside. "Maiherperi sent men to search the fishermen's farm while we awaited Menna at Djeser Djeseru. They found twenty-three pieces, a few from the tomb of Neferu, the rest from tombs of the nobility. All waiting to be smuggled out of Kemet."

"Beautiful objects," Amonked said. "Superb examples of craftsmanship. A credit to our ancestors' good taste."

"You'll never guess where they hid them." Hori, smiling broadly, his voice bubbling with excitement, was far too eager to answer his own question to await a guess. "In an old, empty beehive set among the occupied hives."

A large moth flew into the flame of a torch planted in the earth far enough away from the portico to keep flying insects at a distance. A quick flare and a soft sputter signaled the creature's demise. Bak heard the gentle plop of hooves in the paddock, while a jackal's howl farther afield roused a dozen or more dogs scattered among the surrounding farms, setting them to barking. Tracker remained mute, though his ears took note of who was who among the canine neighbors. A small fire burned beneath the sycamore, and the soft voices of the men awaiting Amonked carried through the night. The smell of the food they had shared, fish and scorched onions, hung in the air, reminding Bak of the burned shed and the need to rebuild it. The workmen at Djeser Djeseru had volunteered their labor, offering with an eagerness that was touching to make mudbricks and build a proper structure for the man who had risked his life to save theirs.

Hori dropped the small bones of a braised pigeon into a bowl and licked the juice from his fingers. "Now that we've found the princess's tombs . . ."

"They were Royal Ornaments," Bak reminded him with a smile.

The scribe ignored the correction. "Will they be opened so the priests can inspect their contents? Will we be able to see what they contain?"

"Maybe they're empty," Kasaya said. "Maybe they were long ago broken into and their contents rifled."

Amonked reached for another bird. "They're safe, thoroughly covered by the rock slide, and I see no reason to dig them out. I'll recommend to my cousin that they remain as they are."

Bak and his father stood beneath the portico, watching Amonked and his porters walk along the moonlit path beyond the paddock. Hori and Kasaya, walking with them, would leave them at the river's edge to walk on to their parents' homes. As they faded into the darkness, Bak pulled the torch from the ground, laid it down, and flung dirt on the dwindling flame. He was very tired and longed for his sleeping pallet. And he was well satisfied. He had accomplished his task and was free to play. His horses needed exercise. His father's skiff beckoned. Even helping the men rebuild the shed would be enjoyable.

Ptahhotep, gathering together dishes and drinking bowls, said, "No word was spoken of Senenmut, my son. Did he say anything to you? Did he congratulate you?"

Bak laughed. "He left Djeser Djeseru the moment Menna's body fell. By the time I arrived at the temple, he was no doubt at the river, boarding a boat to cross to Waset."

"The swine!"

"Father!" Bak took his parent by the shoulders, smiled. "I had reward enough when I saw the faces of the workmen, when they spoke of the relief they felt, their release from fear."

"Surely Amonked will tell our sovereign that you've earned the gold of honor."

Bak did not reply. Deep in his heart he knew he would never receive a golden fly as long as Maatkare Hatshepsut sat on the throne.